"You look like you're going to a funeral. It's only a kiss, Quinn. They're generally pretty enjoyable."

Goaded, she snapped, "Fine," and lunged forward, plastering her lips against his, and pressing his head back against the sofa. He made an *mhmmf* sound against her mouth, but she could tell by the stretch of his lips that he was smiling. And suddenly she was, too, and noticing that his lips felt okay against hers and that his breath was warm and smoky from the whiskey. It was good whiskey. Her lips opened and her tongue dipped in for a taste.

ONCE TOUCHED

A Silver Creek Novel

LAURA MOORE

BALLANTINE BOOKS • NEW YORK

Once Touched is a work of fiction. Names, characters, places, and incidents are the products of the author's imagination or are used fictitiously. Any resemblance to actual events, locales, or persons, living or dead, is entirely coincidental.

A Ballantine Books Mass Market Original

Published in the United States by Ballantine Books, an imprint of Random House, a division of Penguin Random House LLC, New York.

BALLANTINE and the HOUSE colophon are registered trademarks of Penguin Random House LLC.

ISBN 978-0-345-53702-7
eBook ISBN 978-0-345-53703-4

Cover design: Derek Walls
Cover photograph: George Kerrigan

Printed in the United States of America

randomhousebooks.com

9 8 7 6 5 4 3 2 1

Ballantine mass market edition: December 2015

In memory of JKL,
1917–2014

ONCE TOUCHED

THESE DAYS, WHEN Quinn Knowles needed a pair of ears to listen to her, she sought out long, furry ones in a soft dove gray that stuck out like handlebars on a bike.

People were all right to talk to now and again. But her friends and family were unsuitable at present, for the simple reason that they were part of her problem.

"Okay, so it might not be exactly fair to call love a 'problem.'" Perched on the goat pen's top railing, she leaned forward to scratch Hennie's furry chin. "But it's all a bit much. I can't take two steps without tripping over some blissed-out pair."

Maybelle gave a bleat that sounded suspiciously like a laugh.

"I'm not exaggerating," Quinn said. "The situation is seriously annoying."

In response, the doe stuck her nose in the feeder and withdrew a mouthful of timothy hay. Maybelle had a weakness for timothy.

"I'm willing to give the guests a pass. After all, that's what they're here for." Located on three thousand bucolic acres in Northern California, the setting encouraged relaxation. The amenities and services that her family and Silver Creek's staff provided were designed to pamper the senses. The ranch's restaurant offered delicious food, locally sourced. The cabins, stocked with luxury comforts—cloud-soft beds, combed-cotton bed linens, and bathtubs large enough to accommodate two with lots of wiggle room—created a sensual nest where guests could indulge and, in the true spirit of Marvin Gaye, get it on.

Wilhelmina stepped forward to nibble on Quinn's knee. Because she had a staff meeting to attend later, Quinn moved her leg a tad to the left, avoiding a smear of masticated hay and spit on the front of her jeans, and returned to the topic du jour.

"It'd be one thing if all this love and romance were confined to strangers passing through. But thanks to my family, the love vibe's closing in. And I'm the last one standing."

Both her brothers had fallen, and fallen hard. Ward, her oldest brother, was engaged to be married. Tess's and his wedding was scheduled for January, a mere three months away. Quinn preferred not to think about how fast the date was approaching. She'd attended enough weddings to be able to say with certainty that she was allergic to them.

Reid, her other brother—better and wiser than she was by four years, as he liked to claim—had also succumbed. He and Mia Bodell, their neighbor and one of Quinn's best friends, had announced their engagement last night at the Sunday family dinner. Mia had looked beautiful, radiant with happiness, and Reid couldn't stop grinning. Quinn's mother—equestrian by vocation, hotelier by profession, and matchmaker by some weird and deeply twisted impulse—had wept tears of joy and satisfaction. Her two sons were destined for happily-ever-afters with terrific women.

Of course Quinn was happy for the four of them. But that didn't mean she wanted to join the party. And it was getting old, her running into the lovers with their lips locked and their hands clutching and stroking. Their besotted cooing was driving her up the wall. She'd rather listen to her foster parrot Alfie's loudest shrieks any day.

Even her parents, who should be immune after thirty-plus years of marriage, were afflicted—*infected*—and were behaving like newlyweds.

Whatever was going around her family, Quinn intended to remain immune. The whole point of being a twenty-four-year-old woman in the twenty-first century was that she could be single and totally absorbed in her own thing. Call her selfish, but she had neither the time nor the inclination to deal with guys and their wants and expectations.

And she'd rather be set upon by fire ants than be needy herself.

Albertina ambled over to Gertrude and began mouthing her neck in some communal morning grooming. Gertrude's ears twitched in bliss.

"Don't get me wrong, girls. It's not that I have anything against love. It's just not for me. I can't have a man hanging around and slowing me down when I have so much to accomplish. Mom should understand that."

But Quinn had the sneaking suspicion her mother was at it again—the compulsive matchmaking business. Couldn't the woman leave well enough alone? It was embarrassing. Uncomfortable, too.

There was only one thing to do: figure out how to outwit a mother who was as wily as mothers came.

"You know my mom," she continued. "She's the one who brings you pine branches to chew. Nice lady, right? You'd think she'd be satisfied having two of her offspring happily matched and ready to say 'I do' before the minister. But no. She has to go and hire J—"

"You often talk to your goats, Quinn?" Josh Yates asked.

Speak of the chaps-wearing devil. Quinn teetered but managed to grab the metal bar and right herself before she fell splat onto Hennie. Glancing down, she saw that the animal's almond-shaped eyes were closed.

Dang, she'd gone and talked her favorite goat to sleep.

Luckily Josh hadn't noticed. Even luckier was that he'd arrived a millisecond before she said his name. Which meant somebody in the heavens was looking out for her.

"Oh, hey, Josh. Just a sec." Swinging her legs over the rail, she jumped and landed next to the cowboy who unwittingly was part of her current dilemma. She swiped the dirt off the back of her jeans and caught herself wondering whether she'd remembered to brush her hair when she pulled it back this morning.

And didn't that speak volumes?

She *shouldn't* be worrying about how she looked. Wouldn't be, except that Josh Yates was prettier than she was.

Josh and his cow pony, Waylon, had arrived ten days ago, hired by her parents to help with the fall sale of the cattle and to take up the slack when Ward and Tess's January wedding came around.

His presence was a boon for Quinn as well. It would allow her to take off for a few days and avoid witnessing the steers being hauled away to the market to be sold and processed.

Quinn was happy to work on her family's guest ranch in practically every capacity—she waited tables, led trail rides, herded sheep and cattle, helped train horses, tended dairy goats, and planted the kitchen's vegetable garden. Heck, she even helped out with allergy-inducing wedding events. But she couldn't take part in the slaughter of the cattle. It didn't matter how humanely and painlessly the animals' lives ended. The mere sight of the red and black Angus steers clambering up the ramps and into the trailers was enough to torment her.

That Quinn's family cared enough to hire an extra ranch hand so that she could go off somewhere—in this case, spend a weekend at a wolf sanctuary—and be distracted from her horror and guilt was just one reason she adored them, her exasperating mother included.

Being a fair person, her gratitude necessarily extended to Josh, despite the fact that he was more than a touch unnerving.

It was easy to see why he'd been plucked from the pool of applicants. Josh had grown up on a large Texas cattle ranch and possessed all the necessary experience and wrangling skills; there'd been no breaking-in period. And his easygoing attitude made him a good fit with the guests who took advantage of the miles of trail riding the ranch offered.

It certainly didn't hurt that he had the rugged cowboy look down to a T.

Quinn usually remained unaffected by a guy's appearance. But Josh, with his thick, curly blond hair, caramel brown eyes, squared-off cleft chin, and aw-shucks grin, was why the term *eye candy* had been invented. The rest of him was equally distracting. He was tall, with exactly the right amount of honed muscle. One look, and a woman knew that here was a man willing to work his body hard.

It was this made-to-order aspect to Josh, his rugged good looks and his familiarity with ranch life, that had immediately put Quinn on her guard and made her suspect her mother was trying to extend her run of matchmaking.

Normally this would be enough to put Josh on Quinn's top ten list of people to avoid at all costs. The thing was, she liked him. A part of her secretly acknowledged that if she were to want someone in her life, Josh Yates would be a prime candidate.

And then there was that little voice inside her head telling her that maybe it was time to try again. It was just possible Josh would get the job done where others before had failed.

She'd been on the verge of divulging as much to Hennie and the girls when he'd interrupted her with his comment about talking to her goats.

"Sure I talk to them," she said, plucking a stray blade of half-chewed timothy off the seam of her jeans. "I'll have you know they're seriously underrated as listeners."

"Me, I prefer to share my thoughts with Waylon." Josh's horse was a blue roan paint, possibly even dreamier-looking than his owner.

"Hmm," Quinn said noncommittally. "Well, my gelding Domino is a noble beast, but that can be a problem conversation-wise. I feel petty if I complain to him. Sooner, my Sheltie, is so focused on listening for my next command, he sometimes misses the big picture. As for my cat, Pirate, he's way too critical. There's always the sheep, but they're kind of placid. And really, who wants to talk to a steer?"

Her exaggerated eye roll had Josh laughing. "You've convinced me. Next time I need to share, I'll come over and chat awhile with your goats," he said, and then cursed softly as some of the coffee he was carrying—in not one but two mugs—sloshed over the rims.

"What's with the doubling up of joe?" she asked. "Were you out painting our fair town of Acacia red last night?"

"Well . . ." He drew out the word, as if enjoying the sound of it. From what she'd observed, Josh enjoyed many things. "Figured it was past time I got the lay of the land. Your buddy Jim introduced me to The Drop last night. We shot a couple rounds of pool with two nice ladies, Nancy and . . ." Beneath his cowboy hat, his lips pursed as he searched his memory.

"Maebeth," Quinn supplied. "They work at the luncheonette in town."

"That's right," he said, nodding and smiling again. "They were real welcoming. Invited me down for a stack of pancakes—on the house—as soon as I have a morning off."

"That was friendly of them." She could imagine just how friendly the single women would be toward the new hottie in town, especially now that her brother Reid was very much taken. "So you liked The Drop?"

"Yeah, I did. Fun joint, but"—his voice lowered a shade to a warm rumble—"it would've been even more fun with you there, Quinn. Maybe next time you'll give me a tour of the local scene. Your face is way prettier than Jim's."

"Don't let Jim know. He'll be devastated."

"Here." He extended one of the mugs toward her. A wispy tail of steam floated in the air. "This one's for you. You take it black with sugar, right?"

Unnerved as she was at the prospect of a distractingly good-looking cowboy bringing her coffee and taking the time to indulge in an early morning flirtation, she nonetheless accepted the ceramic mug. Quinn was not the type of woman to turn down caffeine.

"That's right, I do. Thanks," she said lightly as she reminded herself that all the male ranch hands and wranglers at Silver Creek were like brothers and uncles to her. No need to treat Josh any differently.

Together they began walking toward the horse barn. This was Quinn's favorite time of day, when everything was quiet and all about the care of the animals. In the corrals and pastures, she saw the horses' jaws working as they enjoyed their morning hay.

Keeping her tone casual, she continued. "So, you're coffee-ing me up, huh? What's the angle?"

"Waylon's thrown a shoe. Luckily the blacksmith's coming this afternoon. But I was wondering if you'd let me ride Domino this morning. Pete asked me to lead a group."

"You're taking the guests out this morning?" Josh had been here less than two weeks, and Pete Williams, their foreman, was already letting him lead trail rides. In case anyone doubted how well Josh was adapting to his role as ranch hand, here was an embossed seal of approval. The safety of Silver Creek's guests was paramount.

"It's a small group, only six riders. Beginners. Afterward he wants me to ride the fence line."

"And you want me to lend Domino to you?" She shook her head in mock despair. "A pecan pumpkin muffin should really accompany that kind of request, Josh. I mean, you're an okay rider and all, but Domino, he's—"

"Special. A prince." Josh's Texas twang, his dimples, and the cleft in his square chin might be awfully cute, but it was his keen eye in judging horses that was damned near irresistible.

"He's all that and more."

"I know it's a huge favor."

"It sure is," she said, her gaze seeking out her black Appaloosa gelding. He was in the near corral, sniffing the ground for stray bits of hay. "But I guess I'll lend him to you. A really great horse will boost your self-confidence, and I can see yours is a little shaky this morning."

He shot her a sideways glance. "You definitely rattle mine. The girls back home are much easier to ask out."

If he only knew just how challenging she was . . .

No need to go there now, she told herself, and tried

for her breeziest smile as she ignored his comment, saying instead, "It actually works out well, your riding Domino—"

"Since you've got a meeting. Yeah, Pete mentioned y'all would be busy."

She raised her brow. "Checking up, huh?"

His shrug was unabashed. "I figured you'd be happy knowing Domino was enjoying this pretty morning while you're stuck inside talking business and bottom lines. And that might make you more inclined to say yes to a date."

The line was so smoothly delivered, she couldn't help but laugh. "Neatly planned."

Josh tipped his hat in acknowledgment. "Planning's important. I like to get what I want."

Quinn was okay with that—she liked getting what she wanted, too. The question was whether she really wanted to get to know Josh . . . in a more intimate way. Could she bring herself to try to have sex again? Because experiencing yet another colossal failure at intimacy would be beyond mortifying with a man like Josh.

An excellent argument for ignoring his calendar-pinup body, cleft chin, Texas twang, and appreciation for fine horseflesh. But if she continued rejecting every man she met, she'd soon be the oldest virgin in California.

Was it any wonder she talked to goats?

JOSH WAS RIGHT, Quinn thought later. She *was* happy knowing Domino was stretching his legs while hers had remained folded under the long conference table for the duration of the staff meeting. It had been a grim one, with talk of the drought and the need to sell off additional cattle to avoid taxing the land even more. Her father and Pete Williams calculated that an extra seventy head should be included in the upcoming roundup. Quinn knew it was necessary and a smart move when hay and feed prices were climbing ever higher and water growing ever scarcer, but, damn, reality sure could bite.

When her father had raised the issue of bringing more stock to market, she'd offered to cancel her weekend stay at the wolf sanctuary. Everyone around the table had turned her down. Sometimes her family was too understanding.

Across from her, her brothers, Ward and Reid, were talking to Pete about arranging for extra trucks to transport the cattle. She tried not to picture the steers being loaded, their bellowing mixing with the heavy pounding of their hooves on the trucks' flooring.

"Quinn."

She shifted her attention to the end of the table. "Yeah, Dad?"

"I have a favor to ask," he said.

"Sure. What is it?" The meeting had made her acutely aware of every gray hair in his head as well as every line creasing his tanned face, and she was determined to do what she could to help out.

"On your way back from Wolf Peak, I need you to swing by the airport and pick up Ethan Saunders. He's going to be staying here for a while."

"Daniel," her mother said, "are you certain that's a good idea?"

Her father spread his large work-callused hands. "I could hardly say no, Adele. You wouldn't have been able to if Tony had put the request to you."

"Ethan Saunders is coming here? Wow, that name's a blast from the past," Reid said.

"You remember him, Quinn?" Ward asked. "He used to lead you around on Jinx."

Jinx had been her first pony, given to her at age four. She could recall every detail of the little paint—his long mane that she loved to braid, his fondness for peppermints—but the boy who'd walked by their side? "I remember he was tall and had dark hair."

"Everyone was tall compared to you," Reid said.

"Ha. Very funny."

"Ethan was remarkably patient with you, Quinn. In exchange for riding out with us and learning to work the cattle, he'd lead you and Jinx on a circuit around the barns and corrals long after everyone else was ready to drag you off the saddle," her father told her.

"Is this Ethan Saunders related to the Saunderses who live in Washington, D.C., and who were kind enough to send in their RSVP to the wedding promptly?" Tess asked.

"One and the same. Cheryl and Tony used to live on

Cobble Hill Road. Cheryl and Tony married a few years before us. Cheryl was a godsend my first year as a bride, talking me down whenever I convinced myself that I could never live with a man as impossible as Daniel." Her mother turned to her father and winked. He answered with a slow smile.

Watching the exchange, Quinn made a mental note to steer clear of her parents after the meeting or run the risk of catching them canoodling like newlyweds.

Her mother was still talking. "They lived in Acacia until Ethan was fifteen, then Tony got a job with the State Department. They've been in Washington ever since."

"Ethan's a photojournalist. He's worked all over the world," Ward told Tess. "Mr. and Mrs. Saunders often use one of his photographs for their holiday card. His pictures stand out from the run-of-the-mill Christmas trees or white doves with olive branches."

Quinn might not remember what Ethan looked like, but the images he'd captured were unforgettable: the large, pleading eyes of the beggar children in Cairo; the heavy vestments of an Orthodox priest in Turkey; rail-thin boys straddling camels in a race across the desert dunes.

"So what's the problem with Ethan coming here for a stay, Mom?" Quinn asked.

"I just don't know whether this is the place for him. He should stay at—"

"That's the thing. He won't," her father said. "Tony says Ethan refuses. Tony's at his wits' end, darling. I told him Ethan could stay for as long as he needed."

"Which only worries me more. What if—" her mother began.

"We'll do everything we can for him. One of the staff cabins would serve him best. Give him space and privacy."

The deep brackets that framed her mother's pressed lips revealed what she thought of that suggestion. But she must have decided that arguing would be futile. Quinn's dad could be just as stubborn as her mom was persistent.

Shifting his attention back to Quinn, her father continued, "Ethan's insisting on leaving Bethesda by the end of the week. Tony's arranged to get him on a flight to San Francisco on Sunday. I'll give you the flight number and arrival time before you leave. I hope it won't cut into your time at the sanctuary."

"Wait," Reid said. "Bethesda? As in the Walter Reed National Military Medical Center?"

Her father nodded but didn't elaborate.

Quinn opened her mouth to ask what had happened to send the globe-trotting photojournalist to a military hospital, but before she could say anything her mother spoke again.

"You know, Daniel, we could ask Estelle to meet Ethan at the airport."

"We need Estelle to help with the Sunday checkout." Estelle Varga worked the front desk.

"Or I could go—"

"Adele," her dad said.

"Fine. Quinn will pick him up." Her mom looked less than delighted.

Quinn sat straighter in her chair. Well, this was different. Usually her matchmaking-prone mother was all for her spending time with a member of the opposite sex. Logically, she should be doubly eager since the male in question was the child of old friends. But here she was volunteering to drive all the way to the airport on Sunday herself, rather than have Quinn spend time with him. Weird.

But this much was clear: whatever had happened to

Ethan Saunders, both her parents were deeply concerned about him.

And that made Quinn even more curious.

Quinn sat cross-legged on the rocky ground, her binoculars trained on a gray she-wolf that was pacing
inside the eight-foot-high enclosure. It was Una, a wolf
Quinn had adopted several years ago, during her first
trip to Wolf Peak, a sanctuary owned and run by Joel
and Ruth Meyers, former hedge fund managers turned
wolf protectors.

The scars that crisscrossed the wolf's body were no
longer visible, but Quinn remembered them to this day.
Una had just arrived when Quinn came to Wolf Peak as
a college student writing a paper on the differences between dogs and wolves for her animal behavior class.
Introducing her to the wolves in their care, Ruth had
told her about Una.

The she-wolf had been raised in captivity because
some less than bright individuals believed that owning
a wolf was kind of like having a wicked cool dog—
mistake number one of about one hundred that humans
repeatedly made when it came to understanding the nature of these animals.

Una's owner, in addition to having slop for brains,
was a fucking sadist. When Una didn't behave like some
souped-up husky, shaggy pit bull, or whatever canine
he'd envisioned, the guy didn't attempt to place her with
a rescue organization. No, he took her to the woods,
chained her to a tree, beat her, and then shot her, leaving her to bleed out.

Hikers, hearing her howls of pain, had called animal
protection services, which in turn had contacted Joel
and Ruth. They'd arranged to have Una admitted to the
animal hospital and footed the bill for the operations

to remove the bullet, mend her broken bones, and repair her internal injuries. Afterward, they'd arranged to have her transported to Wolf Peak.

The vet did an amazing job fixing her battered body, yet to this day Una was terrified of humans. But because she'd been raised in captivity, to release her into the wild would be to write her death sentence. No pack would accept her, and she wouldn't be able to survive and hunt on her own. Her true nature was forever crippled.

Una's story had cut Quinn to the quick. When she'd discovered that there were ways to sponsor wolves at the sanctuary, she'd chosen Una. Quinn was now responsible for paying for her food and future veterinary care.

"She's looking great," she said quietly. Today was the first time she'd caught sight of the skittish female.

"Mm-hmm." Ruth Meyers's voice was pitched equally low. "Una's found love. She's caught the attention of Griff, the newest pack member. See how he's come to stand over her now that she's lying down? He's guarding her."

"Good for Una." Quinn focused her binoculars on the large male wolf. His coat glinted silver in the sunlight. "Griff looks like a healthy male."

"Not only that, he's a movie star."

"Seriously? What's he doing here?"

"His trainer came down with an aggressive bone cancer. Died within weeks. His widow was hoping to place Griff with another trainer, but no one could take him and she couldn't handle him herself. She called us."

Quinn sighed. The story was too familiar. "I'm glad she knew where to turn."

"Me too. In all likelihood Griff would have ended up being euthanized. Sometimes it seems like there aren't enough shelters for all the creatures in need. Speaking of which, you made any progress?"

"Still saving up. Mendocino County isn't Napa or Sonoma, but even there land doesn't come cheap."

"Have you thought about approaching your family?"

Even though she could feel Ruth's gaze on her, she didn't lower her binoculars. "To help me buy a property, you mean? I couldn't—wouldn't. This is my dream."

"What about just using a piece of the ranch?"

"Not possible. All of Silver Creek is tied up, either as farmland for the ranch or for the guest lodgings and amenities." Which was how it should be, Quinn thought. The ranch was the family's endeavor; the sanctuary would be hers.

"Sorry if I sound pushy, Quinn. I know you'll make the dream of opening an animal refuge a reality."

Quinn smiled. Sometimes Ruth could be pushy. Devoting her life to protecting wolves and educating the public about them wasn't for the meek or timid. "Thanks for the vote of confidence."

"Anytime. So how are your various critters doing?"

"Good." Quinn hugged her crossed knees. "Have I told you about my gelding named Tucker?"

"Don't believe so."

"I spotted him at an equine rescue center near Sacramento. He'd been abused and then abandoned—you know the story. Once I got him healthy, I started working with him on the ground and in the saddle. I've been studying massage therapy and hope to work on him. But he's really shy. Whoever hurt Tucker did a number on him. I don't know if he'll ever get over his fear of people. Especially men."

"So he's with you for life."

"Yeah." Quinn shrugged. She was fine with that. She never fostered or adopted an animal she wasn't prepared to keep forever. "Luckily my friend Mel, who's a wrangler at the ranch, is feeding him his hay while I'm here. Tucker's used to seeing her around the corrals, so the change in routine won't freak him out."

"And what about that other horse of yours?"

"Domino? Oh, he's set for the weekend. One of our new ranch hands took him out for a ride at the beginning of the week. When Josh came back he was grinning from ear to ear. Apparently Domino was one of the sweetest rides he'd ever enjoyed—no surprise there," she added. "I decided to let Josh borrow him again this weekend—they're cutting cattle from the herd for harvesting."

"Sounds like a lucky cowboy."

"Yeah." Her only worry was that Josh might read more into her gesture and think he was going to get even luckier.

"You fostering any new animals?" Ruth asked.

"Only Alfie."

Ruth lowered her binoculars. "What's he, a cat?"

"Nah, that would make life too easy. He's an Amazon blue parrot. Remember me telling you about my friend Lorelei?"

"The one who works at the local shelter?"

"Yeah. She's housesitting and keeping Pirate, Sooner, and Alfie company this weekend. I'm going to owe her big-time."

"Let me guess. Alfie's verbal?"

"To put it mildly. I'm thinking a batch of killer brownies might go a ways toward compensating Lorelei for any hearing loss."

"Ahh, chocolate. The default solution to everything under the sun." Ruth laughed softly and raised the binoculars again, scanning the pack.

"Well, yeah." Before she could launch into a catalog of the ills chocolate could cure, her phone's alarm vibrated. With a frown she pulled it out of her jacket pocket and switched it off. "Drat," she muttered. "I hadn't realized how much time had passed. I've got to hit the road. I'm due at the airport."

She stood and shook out her legs to regain feeling in them after sitting on the cold ground. Ruth rose, too, and tucked both pairs of binoculars into a carrying case.

"Are you picking up a guest?" Ruth asked as they followed the dirt trail back to the sanctuary's center.

"Kind of. The Saunderses are family friends, but we haven't seen Ethan, their son, in years. He's a photojournalist. Apparently he's been in the hospital after being on assignment in Afghanistan."

"The hospital? I hope he wasn't seriously injured."

"No clue. Before I left, I tried to pry more information out of my folks, but they were acting very hush-hush. That he'd been in Afghanistan was all I managed to get out of them." Her parents were being super-cagy. "My guess is either they don't know what happened or they're respecting his privacy. More likely the latter. They're big on confidentiality."

"From what I've heard, that's what makes Silver Creek Ranch such a great place. The VIPs get to enjoy the red-carpet treatment but aren't hounded or harassed. So you're to be your family friend's chauffeur?"

"That's right. It's the least I can do since I got the weekend off. And it'll be nice to have company for the drive home." Quinn lengthened her stride, her curiosity about Ethan Saunders rising to the fore. As someone who'd been around the world photographing everything under the sun, he'd have good stories to tell. And she did enjoy a good story. "I should probably have one of those cardboard signs with his name on it. Ethan and his parents left Acacia almost twenty years ago. I hope I recognize him."

Chapter
THREE

CLAMMY SWEAT COVERED Ethan Saunders's body. It permeated his shirt, making the cotton fabric stick to his heaving chest and gluing his back to the plane's narrow seat. The sling wrapped around his neck to immobilize his right arm and shoulder chafed the skin below his close-cropped head.

He lifted his free arm and swiped his forehead again.

The passenger next to him, who reeked of aftershave and wore a fucking ugly tie that reminded Ethan of the fuzzy blotches that had obscured his vision for days after he finally opened his eyes in Landstuhl, flinched and darted another nervous glance his way. It hadn't taken his neighbor long to decide he wanted to be as far from Ethan as possible. He'd even relinquished territorial rights to the armrest. But there was only so far he could retreat. Hence the nervous glances.

The guy made a comical picture. If Ethan could remember how to laugh, he might have been tempted. Were he a nicer person, he might even reassure the man that he wasn't suffering from some highly contagious tropical disease.

But his kindness had disappeared along with his sense of humor. Besides, he needed all his energy to focus on the metallic latch that fastened his seat's tray. It was the only way to keep the nausea at bay.

The captain's confident drawl came over the PA system to announce the plane would soon be landing. Within minutes the attendants began their march down the twin aisles to verify that seats were upright and trays and possessions stowed. The plane dipped and angled as it began its descent. Fighting the vertigo, Ethan swallowed hard and jammed the back of his head against the seat. Clutching the armrest with his left hand, he squeezed the metal edge until his fingers were as numb as the ones on his right hand.

The wheels of the plane touched the earth with a series of bumps that jarred his body and sent his brain knocking against his skull. He groaned heavily even as relief swept over him.

The hell of the past six hours was over. Only now that he'd survived it did he acknowledge the idiocy of traveling in a damned airplane. Of traveling, period. But he'd needed to get away, far away from Walter Reed, where he'd been transferred after Landstuhl.

His team of doctors, his parents, and even Erin Miller, his New York editor, who'd planned to publish his photographs, had done their best to convince him to remain or at least be transferred to another facility where he could receive therapy and counseling. He'd ignored their arguments and pleas. He refused to be jabbed with one more needle, handed one more plastic cup filled with pastel-colored pills that were 100 percent guaranteed to turn his brain to slush, or subjected to one more test by a doctor who stared at his laptop screen and repeated that he'd need to be *patient*. With the right rehab program Ethan should regain full mobility in his shoulder and arm. With counseling he should get past the horror of the explosion that had ripped through the armored vehicle and sent him flying from the backseat to the rock-strewn ground to land among other bodies.

It was possible the doctors were right, that if he talked and talked he might eventually be able to remember that gruesome tableau without wanting to crawl inside a bottle. Eventually he might accept why he alone had survived the blast, why that wasn't simply some awful, sick joke. It was conceivable that with the right combination of pharmaceuticals, he might succeed in banishing the visions and muting the sounds that assailed him day and night, his own hell on earth.

What they didn't understand was that even if a full recovery was in the cards, he couldn't stay in a hospital room or rehab clinic one more day, wouldn't lie in a bed and receive treatment that should go to soldiers—some of them still teenagers not even old enough to buy a drink—who'd come back from tours of duty with wounds far more grievous than he'd sustained.

He'd shot down the idea of staying at his parents' and receiving outpatient treatment, too. He needed to be in a place where he couldn't see their worried expressions or have to listen to their tentative, anxiety-laden questions. Perhaps because he'd lived in Acacia for a good stretch of his youth, Silver Creek Ranch was the one place where a few positive memories remained—of open land that stretched, reaching out to pine-covered mountains; of horses and cattle.

The signal for the attendants to begin the crosscheck interrupted his thoughts. All around the cabin seatbelts were unfastened as the travelers launched themselves from their seats, intent on seizing their place in the narrow aisles. The man with the fuzzy amoeba tie in the adjacent seat was equally determined. Bowed into a lumpy C shape, he lurched toward the aisle, barreling his way through the two-inch space that separated

Ethan's knees from the seat in front of him. He reached
his destination with a heavy grunt of satisfaction.

There'd been a time when Ethan would have beat
every passenger on board in that particular race. He
was a gold medalist at disembarking from planes and
navigating airports at top speed, his carry-on hefted
over his shoulder, his stride eating up the carpeted cor-
ridors as the promotional posters welcoming him to
whatever city or country he'd landed in passed in a blur.
Now he remained seated as the plane emptied until only
he and the crew standing by the door were left. A minute later, one of the female attendants hurried down the
aisle, sympathy in her eyes.

"Are you all right, sir? If you'd like, we'd be happy to
call for a wheelchair."

"No, thanks." He'd managed to get on the airplane.
He'd damn well walk off it, too. Steeling himself against
the dizziness he knew would come, he grabbed hold of
the seat in front of him and hauled his body up, willing
his legs to unfold. He stood and a fresh river of sweat
snaked down his body. Swallowing his nausea and ignoring the flight attendant's outstretched arm, he stepped
into the aisle.

In the end, Quinn had no trouble recognizing Ethan
Saunders. What was difficult was hiding her shock. He
was so . . . gray. His skin ashen, the sockets of his
sunken dull pewter eyes smudged, his gaze cloaked in
heavy shadows, his short-cropped hair a liberal mix of
salt with the pepper. Even the sweat on his face seemed
gray, as though his body were oozing toxins. Were it not
for the sling holding his folded arm securely about his
middle, she'd have pegged the tall, gaunt man as a
junkie battling the shakes. He walked with the brittle

care of someone three times his age. A few feet behind him, a porter in a red cap pushed a loaded trolley.

"Ethan Saunders?" A part of her hoped she was mistaken. The other, wiser and sadder part knew she wasn't.

He stopped and looked at her, then released the lips he'd been pressing in a thin line. "Yeah." A second passed. "Who are you?"

"I'm Quinn. Quinn Knowles," she added when his expression remained blank.

"The daughter." He made the connection in a low, gravelly voice that sounded as if it hadn't been used in months.

"The one and only."

He looked far from impressed, didn't even bother to give her a once-over, which was interesting since men invariably checked her out and then started grinning like monkeys within seconds of meeting her. Their reaction was off-putting at best, creepy at worst. So Ethan Saunders was either smarter than most of his kind or—

Quinn was presented with the correct explanation when Ethan abruptly lurched to the side and began heaving the contents of his stomach into the base of an artificial ficus tree. He was too sick to notice whether she resembled Miss Universe or Chewbacca.

A few seconds later, Ethan straightened, looking just as gray as before. Because there was no use pretending otherwise, she said, "You're a real mess, aren't you?"

This earned her a grunt. "I'll live."

"I hope so. I like funerals even less than weddings."

His brows snapped together in surprise. Or maybe annoyance. He probably hadn't expected her to joke about death.

Well, it was too late to reform her warped sense of humor. And somehow she sensed he'd appreciate her pity even less.

"Like I said, I'll live."

"Okay, then, we have an almost-three-hour drive ahead of us, so we'd better get a move on. My truck's parked in a nearby lot. I'll go get it and pull up outside in five minutes. There are benches." Turning to the porter, she said, "I'll tip you double if you wait until I return with the car."

The minute they reached the curb, Ethan dragged his wallet from the rear pocket of his jeans, which now hung loosely on his bony frame, and paid off the redcap—with that double tip. He didn't need a baby-sitter, damn it. Alone, he leaned against a metal sign in order not to do a face-plant into the sidewalk. The autumn air felt raw as a slap but good. He'd made it. Now he just had to keep what little remained in his stomach inside it until he reached Silver Creek Ranch, where he hoped to be left in blessed peace until he figured out what to do with the rest of his life.

A dusty red truck pulled up alongside him. The girl jumped out of it. He still couldn't think of Quinn Knowles as anything but a little girl. Of his memories of Silver Creek Ranch, the ones of her as a pigtailed kid stood out.

She'd been kind of cute, with a cowboy hat that was a couple of sizes too big for her. It used to slip forward, covering her face, and he would tip it back up just to see how long it took before it slid down again. Each time he adjusted it, she'd give him a gap-toothed grin. She'd been one happy kid on the back of that shaggy Shetland.

Because his parents had drilled home the fact that he was extremely lucky to be riding out with the Knowleses and learning how to cut cattle from the herd and rope them, he was okay with leading her around—it gave him a chance to study the horses in the corrals and pastures. He'd lift her onto the saddle, guide her pink cow-boy boots into the stirrups, and walk by her pony's side while she chattered to the pony as if he were her best friend. No matter how long they walked, she never wanted to get off that pony. What had she called it again?

He hated that his memory, like his body, kept failing him.

He frowned as he tried to retrieve the name. He'd been able to identify all the horses on the guest ranch—they'd been his gold standard against which every horse he'd ridden since was measured.

No matter how spotty his memory, it was hard to rec-oncile the pipsqueak that she'd been with the Quinn Knowles of today. With her coltish legs, she stood nearly as tall as he. She must be in her twenties . . . so, not a girl. Yet she nevertheless struck him as impossibly young. Not surprising when he felt as old as death.

"All set?" she asked.

"Yeah." He cast a look at the duffel bag and the black cases containing his equipment. Even though he knew he'd never take pictures again, the habits of more than a decade of traveling with his cameras and laptop were impossible to shake. Abruptly he realized his mistake in dismissing the porter. His gear was damned heavy and even his good arm had lost a lot of muscle.

He eyed the rear of the pickup truck, gritted his teeth, and stepped forward, only to freeze as Quinn swooped in. She grabbed the webbed straps of his large canvas duffel bag and hefted it over the back of the truck as if it weighed no more than a pillow.

Then she picked up one of his aluminum-framed cam-era cases.

He put out a hand, intending to issue a sharp warn-ing, a "Careful with that!" only to swallow his words when the box landed as softly as if it contained three dozen Fabergé eggs. The second case was treated with matching care.

He had yet to unclench his jaw when Quinn leaned over the side of the truck. If he hadn't felt like utter crap, if he hadn't lost any interest in sex (a good thing, since he hadn't gotten it up in months anyway), he might have appreciated the tempting wiggle of her ass as she rummaged in the depths of the pickup's cargo area.

If he had, the pleasure would have been short-lived.

She straightened and, turning around, held up a black rubber bucket. "For you," she said, handing it to him. "Compliments of the staff."

She opened the passenger door while he stared at the bucket. "What's this for?"

"In case you feel the need to puke again. I wouldn't want you trashing my truck."

His gaze swept over the interior. The dirt-stained upholstery seemed to be growing dog hair. Various collars, leashes, ropes, receipts, coffee mugs, and candy wrappers were strewn across the seats and floor. At the sight, something strange happened to him. The muscles in his face stretched his mouth into something that felt almost like a grin.

Few things had brought him close to real amusement in a long time.

The emotion lasted only as long as it took him to climb painfully into the truck. He hid a grimace as his shoulder brushed the back of the seat.

No sooner had he settled than she slammed his door shut, ran around to her side, and jumped in behind the wheel like a friggin' gazelle.

The agility she displayed, the complete confidence she had in her body, was bad enough, filling him with envy. But then, without warning, she lunged sideways until her ear was pressed against his chest. Struck by a jolt of shock at the position of her head—a few inches lower and they'd be arrested—and the strange need that pierced him, he registered the splintering pain in his shoulder only distantly.

He sucked in a breath, then spoke through gritted teeth. "What the hell are you doing?"

She didn't reply at first, only plastered herself more firmly against his ribs as she reached across with her arm. Straightening, she waved the seat belt at him before clicking it in place.

"Safety first." With a damnably perky smile she scooted back behind the wheel.

He glared through the windshield, torn as to which angered him more: that he missed the pressure of her streaky blond head with its thick and somewhat snarled ponytail against his chest, or that she obviously viewed him as too pathetically weak to manage something as basic as buckling a seat belt.

The first only exposed his sad-sack needs. Forget sex. It seemed like an eternity since he'd been close enough to feel the warmth of a woman's body or to catch her scent.

Quinn smelled of sunshine and pine needles.

The fragrance was implausibly sweet after the stale, antiseptic odors of the hospital or the rank stench of men's bodies living in close quarters in a desert clime, the funk of the latrines, the acrid stench of gun and rocket blasts, or the reek of blood, fear, and death permeating the air. It pissed him off that with one careless gesture she'd made him think about all those things, when remembering what had happened in Afghanistan was what he'd come to California to avoid. He didn't want to reflect, remember, need, or feel, goddamn it.

Still staring through the windshield, he spoke through a clenched jaw. "I'm injured. I'm not an invalid, and I'm not a fucking baby. Got it?"

He heard the hiss of indrawn breath as his words struck. He was pretty sure he'd wiped that chipper smile off her face.

Good. He didn't want to be on the receiving end of any more of her sly wit or effortless charm. And while the Ethan Saunders of old would have gone out of his way to straighten out any SOB who spoke that way to a woman who'd merely, if misguidedly, been trying to assist him, that version of himself had disappeared months ago. The sooner she and everyone who came into contact with him understood that fact, the better.

What a jerk. Quinn was still fuming when she pulled onto the highway.

She wasn't simply taken aback by Ethan's snarky comment; she was embarrassed, too. After all, she'd only been trying to help. The guy had a sling strapped around his middle, and it was obvious from the way he used his left arm it wasn't his dominant side.

Along with chagrin, resentment crept into the mix. Guys generally liked her—at least until they tried to sleep with her. It seemed that Ethan Saunders was the notable exception. Maybe he preferred hard-ass witches. Or maybe he liked women who sat around docilely and batted their fake eyelashes at him while he barked out orders. And why in God's name was she even thinking about what kind of woman Ethan Saunders liked?

She glanced to her right. His expression was as stony as Mount Rushmore, but a lot grimmer. And to think she'd been looking forward to his company on the drive back home. Suddenly Acacia seemed far away.

Annoyed with both herself and him, she picked up her iPod from where it was wedged between an empty coffee cup and a crumpled ball of M&M's wrappers, her favorite road candy—she liked to suck the colored coating off and then bite into the chocolate—and scrolled through her playlists. An impish impulse had her selecting the one she'd made for her mom for Valentine's Day, because what better way to show her love than compile a playlist of the most treacly stuff on earth? The gift had been perfect. Her mom had adored it. And she would bet her bottom dollar that Ethan was going to hate it.

The Bee Gees' "How Deep Is Your Love" came on in surround sound. Her truck might have over a hundred thousand miles on it and the suspension might be shot to hell, but the sound system rocked.

When a groan reached her, she bit the inside of her cheek to hide a smile and oh so casually turned up the volume.

Her brand of vengeance was sweet but unfortunately short-lived. A quick glance to her right revealed the tendons in his neck standing out in relief. His left hand gripped the bucket as if it were a lifeline. The sight killed her desire for petty revenge faster than air escaping a popped balloon.

She let her foot up on the accelerator and then flicked on the indicator, intending to ease into the breakdown lane.

His fierce growl put a stop to that. "Don't you dare pull over, or I swear I'll ditch this bucket and hurl all over your precious truck."

But she'd learned her lesson. Sympathy didn't work with this man. "Try it, buster, and you'll be the one ditched. At the speed you walk, I'd estimate you'd make it to the ranch in about a month." Ticked off as she was by his earlier rebuff, a part of her couldn't believe she was talking this way to someone who couldn't even arm-wrestle. But it seemed that, as medicine, rudeness went down a lot better than kindness.

Infuriated, he glared at her.

That was fine with her. She'd take his death stare over his emptying his guts any day.

"Who'd have thought you'd grow up to be a royal pain in the butt?" he asked.

"Who'd have thought you'd grow up to be a Neanderthal?" she countered. Giving him her sweetest smile, she began humming along to Neil Diamond's "Song Sung Blue."

WHEN QUINN OPENED her front door four hours later, she was greeted by a series of barks and leaps from Sooner, a figure-eight pass between her legs by Pirate, and eardrum-splitting squawks from Alfie, who was doubtless doing somersaults from one perch to the next in his oversized cage in the study.

Her friend Lorelei was the only sentient being under the roof who chose not to greet her acrobatically. She remained curled up in an armchair, reading. One of Sooner's more ambitious leaps and spins must have entered her field of vision, for she looked up from her book. With a smile of greeting, she removed two bright orange earplugs. "You're back."

"Yeah. Brilliant idea," she said with a nod at the foam plugs. Brushing past Sooner's wriggling black-and-white body, she sank onto the drop-cloth-covered sofa with a groan of relief and patted the cushion next to her, so Sooner would know he had permission to join her.

Her cat didn't need permission. Pirate jumped up and then took a stroll along the back of the sofa, brushing his body against Quinn's head. From the study, Alfie began barking.

She grinned. "Boy, it's good to be home. Got any more earplugs?"

Lorelei laughed. "No, but I can't recommend them enough. They make all the difference. Francesco got them for me after our first takeout dinner here. He brought over these great burritos from this new Mexican place on Route 101, just south of Ukiah. The guac was to die for. He's such a sweetie," she said happily.

Francesco and Lorelei had been dating for almost a year now, and from what Quinn could tell, Francesco wasn't just a sweetie; he also had intelligence and good taste. He was crazy about Lorelei.

"Yeah, you could do worse," she said. "Like fall for the guy I just had to spend three-plus hours with. Luckily, he slept most of the drive." The second Ethan had fallen asleep, his closely cropped head resting against the window and the tightness in his jaw relaxing somewhat, Quinn had eased up on the gas to smooth out the ride. Judging from the dark circles beneath his eyes, she had a feeling he hadn't slept in a while.

"This is the guy you were picking up at the airport? The family friend?"

"His parents are friends. The jury's out on Ethan." She blew out a breath. "It's possible he's a prince."

"From your tone I'd guess he was more toad than prince."

"Mm-hmm. A prehistoric toad. Still . . ." She sighed and stroked Sooner's head, which was resting on her thigh. He was gazing at her with fixed devotion—a balm after the hostility Ethan had displayed. "To be fair, it's hard to tell what he's like. He's pretty beat up. I imagine he's none too happy about his limitations. What I can't figure out is why he's chosen to come here. I parked as close as I could to the cabin he's staying in, and even then he looked ready to pass out by the time he reached the cabin door. And he's big—whip thin but tall. Hard to lug." *Impossible to lug,* she added silently, since she'd have been terrified of hurting his arm. "Luckily I'd called my dad as soon as we reached Acacia, so I didn't have to drag Ethan up the path. He and Mom were waiting at the cabin to help get him inside and settled."

Her parents had managed to hide their dismay, but Quinn knew them, knew what signs to look for before they were quickly erased. Even had they known theoretically what shape Ethan was in, the reality had clearly taken them aback.

It was strange, but despite their rocky start and Ethan's less than charming attitude, she'd been reluctant to leave him. There was a part of her that felt possessive toward him, as if it were her responsibility to make his snapping, snarling self better. What was even odder was that when it became clear that there were at least one too many bodies in the cabin Mom had had readied and Quinn had offered a casual "See y'all later," she'd felt the weight of Ethan's dark gaze as she crossed the cabin to the door.

She'd been tempted to turn around, thinking, hoping, that his expression might hold something other than irritation or hostility.

She shook off the memory, telling herself not to be foolish. She was good with animals, not surly, injured men.

"So my beasts behaved?" she asked Lorelei as she shifted her hand to scratch Sooner behind his velvety ears.

"Oh, they were great. And once I got these babies," Lorelei said, tossing the earplugs in the palm of her hand, "I could even hang with Alfie without rupturing my eardrums. You definitely want to invest in a pair."

"What's that? I can't hear you." With a grin Quinn cupped a hand to her ear. The parrot's high-pitched yaps had segued into the blast of a truck horn. His previous owner must have put his cage next to an open window on a busy street because Alfie could mimic the rat-a-tat percussion of jackhammers, the rumble and grind of garbage trucks, and the wail of ambulance sirens, an entire catalogue of obnoxious sounds.

Lorelei laughed. Raising her voice, she said, "Let's go put a smile on that crazy bird's beak. Otherwise he'll start tossing peanut shells. How does he throw them so far, anyway?"

"What can I tell you? He's a major blue-fronted Amazon talent."

"That's for sure. His wind-up is no joke."

"FYI, I owe you a batch of my killer brownies for this weekend of pet-sitting. I'll bring them by the shelter."

"That'd be great. Marsha needs some cheering up. Budget cuts," she said by way of explanation.

"They're that bad?"

"Yeah. We were operating on a shoestring before. It's dental floss now." The grimace on Lorelei's face had nothing to do with Alfie's piercing squawk as they neared the study.

"I'll make it a double batch, then."

Quinn stepped inside the room. Spying her, Alfie flung his electric green-and-yellow body at the bars of the cage, his wings flapping madly. "Quinn, Quinn, Quinn!"

She walked up to the cage and, inserting her fingers, scratched Alfie along the side of his neck, gently ruffling his short feathers. He stretched his neck farther and began whistling softly.

"Jeesh, you really have a way with males, don't you?" Lorelei said.

Unbidden, the image of Ethan's scowling face sprang to mind. She certainly hadn't wowed him. "I specialize in the four-legged and winged variety."

"That so? What about a certain cowboy named Josh? He sounds a lot like Alfie with his 'Quinn this' and 'Quinn that.' We crossed paths yesterday when I went to say hi to the goats—Mel and Adele spoiled them with tons of treats, by the way. I bet Josh would let you run your fingers just about anywhere you want." Lorelei grinned.

If only the idea of running her fingers anywhere near Josh filled her with a smidgeon of excitement. Now that she'd had a couple of days to clear her head from the dizzying effect of Josh's stunning looks and smooth charm, her ambivalence was back in full force. She kept her gaze fixed on the patch of royal blue just above Alfie's curved beak. "Not sure I'm interested."

"Why in the world not? He's certainly interested in you. Actually, he seems perfect for you."

Quinn shrugged. "Maybe that's the problem. He's *too* perfect." She hoped that was the reason for her indifference. Unfortunately, her present attitude toward Josh was the same resounding *meh* she'd had toward the other guys she'd dated or attempted to get physical with.

"So a guy who's perfect for you—who loves horses, knows ranches, and seems to like and be liked by just about everyone—is flawed, huh? Go figure. Quinn, sweetie, has anyone ever told you that you're hard to please?"

Oh yeah, but not so gently or affectionately.

It was one thing for her to be disappointed in herself and her inability to dredge up any kind of enthusiasm, quite another for men to look at her and find her lacking. Or worse. There'd been a whole bunch of words that had followed each of her disastrous attempts at sex. The words of choice had been *unresponsive* and *stiff,* as well as the favorite: *frigid.* Unlike the guys whose egos she'd bruised, Quinn knew female frigidity had been busted as a sexual myth, so she'd been kind of able to shake that one off.

Fucking tease was the term that really hurt, muttered furiously as her rejected sex partner yanked on his jeans and kept his gaze averted. The label didn't simply make her out as weird or abnormal in her responses. It cast her as cruel and manipulative, as if she enjoyed leading a man on only to refuse to put out at the crucial sticking point.

Quinn didn't believe she was naturally a mean person. But clearly something happened to her whenever she tried to be intimate with someone. After her last failure, she'd come to the conclusion that she'd rather skip the whole sex thing—even if a "perfect" guy was interested—than face that accusation again.

What with Alfie's antics—he'd spread his beautiful wings and was flapping them against the bars in a plea to be sprung from his cage—Lorelei hadn't noticed Quinn's silence. "Well, I think you're going to have to resign yourself to being pursued by that smooth-talking Texan with the same energy Sooner devotes to running down your flock of sheep."

Forewarned was forearmed. And Quinn was pretty sure she had more brains than the average sheep.

Ethan was glad Quinn had left the cabin. It meant he no longer had to make his screaming muscles hold his shoulders back.

"Ethan, son, it's good to see you, but for God's sake, sit down," Daniel Knowles instructed with more than a hint of exasperation in his voice.

Grateful that Daniel hadn't tacked on the all-too-obvious "Before you fall down," Ethan dropped onto the loveseat, which was positioned at a forty-five-degree angle to a wood-burning cast iron stove. In the corner of the room stood a double bed with a frame constructed of gnarled tree limbs. He fixed his gaze on the patchwork quilt covering the mattress until its squares of blue stopped swimming and the room stopped tilting. Now, if only Daniel and Adele would follow their daughter out the door, he could release the groan of agony bottled inside him.

Instead he forced himself to be polite, his payment for being allowed to escape the fear in his own parents' eyes. "It's good to see you, too. Neither of you has aged a day."

"We haven't been living in a war zone," Daniel replied.

"What happened, Ethan?" Adele asked.

A world of shit, too horrific to describe in this rustic cabin that, after the cement block he'd bunked in, seemed as luxurious as a penthouse suite in the Four Seasons. "An IED exploded as our Humvee passed. The impact banged up my shoulder and arm. My head took a hard knock."

Adele's choked sound of dismay reminded him of his mother's. He didn't glance up to check whether she, too, had tears slipping down her face, as his mother did whenever one of the doctors came in to evaluate him.

"A bang and a knock," Daniel echoed dryly.

His shoulder hurt too much to shrug. "I'm alive." Unlike the others who'd been riding in the vehicle, or that child who couldn't have been more than eight years old, damn it. Blocking the horrifying memory, he looked up at Adele. Yup, her eyes were awash in tears. "Thanks for taking me in."

Adele's expression grew warm as a soft smile lifted her cheeks. He thought he remembered that look and how it would settle over her face when one of her kids ran up to her with some story to share. Even then he'd understood that she was a beautiful woman.

"Of course, Ethan," she said. "You should stay and recuperate for as long—"

"I want to earn my keep while I'm here."

Adele's eyes widened in surprise. They were a softer blue than Quinn's, which had bright shards of light emanating from the irises.

"What kind of work were you envisioning?" she asked, as if he hadn't been about to topple over three minutes ago.

"I'll wash dishes if that's what you need, but I'd like to be outside if possible. I've been staring at walls too long." Staring as he remembered the blood and the pain and the death, and growing sick with guilt. He longed for the sweet blankness of hard labor, the glimpse of the fir-covered mountains breaking the horizon, and the scent of crisp, clean air when he inhaled—all so different, so not *there*.

"Uh, Ethan, I think you should take a couple of days of R&R before we put you to work. In the meantime we'll see where we can best use an extra pair of hands," Daniel said, keeping his gaze fixed on his face, rather than on the sling immobilizing his arm.

Ethan wasn't fooled. "I can do the work." He had to.

"Of course you can. Now, the refrigerator and the cupboard are stocked, but if you're hungry for anything else, just ring the kitchen—I left a list of numbers on the counter by the sink. Just tell them who you are. The kitchen staff will be more than happy to bring you food. Our phone numbers are there, in case you need us." The brisk cheer in Adele's voice couldn't quite mask the worry there.

Ethan had traveled the world, photographing the jungles of Borneo, the Sahara desert, the slums and palaces of the great capitals, but now this generous woman wasn't sure he could manage on his own in a simple twenty-by-thirty-foot cabin.

He hated that she might be right.

"I'll be fine," he said, more harshly than her well-meaning kindness deserved. And even if he weren't okay, he'd rot in hell before imposing on the Knowleses any further.

Chapter
FIVE

As LORELEI PREDICTED, Josh wasted little time hunting her down. She'd only just finished grooming Tucker, her rescue gelding, the next morning when she heard him call out, "Hey, Quinn, brought something for you."

She glanced over her shoulder. He was standing about five yards away—his time at Silver Creek Ranch more than long enough for him to know that Tucker didn't tolerate men too close. Meeting her gaze, he smiled and held a paper bag aloft. The movement caused his faded denim jacket to rise, exposing a tan corduroy shirt and a megasized Texas star belt buckle.

"I got a pecan pumpkin muffin for you. Maebeth and Nancy say hi."

She leaned closer to Tucker and stroked his chestnut neck to communicate her calm, hoping the gelding would do no more than twitch his ears and shift his weight from side to side.

"That's really nice of you, Josh. Uh, you know I was only kidding about your needing to ply me with muffins, right?"

"Domino was such a treat, I figure you deserve one, too. And besides, now that I've been down to the luncheonette for breakfast, I'm kinda hooked. Especially since Maebeth has started slipping me a few extra pieces of bacon."

"I'm sure she appreciates your appetite."

He smiled as if he knew just how much Maebeth appreciated a man like him. "Want me to hold on to this until you've finished with Tucker?" He jiggled the bag and then cursed when he realized what he'd done. "Damn!"

Already nervous, Tucker had shied at the bag's strange rustling, jumping sideways as though his hooves had become springs. The lead rope slipped through Quinn's hand. She followed it as smoothly as she could to prevent him from spooking more.

"Easy, Tucker," she said, moving with him as he skipped sideways. Her hand closed about the rope, offering a light resistance, while she continued to use her voice to soothe and reassure.

It took several more sidesteps before her horse calmed, for his head to drop and his body to relax a bit—his flight instinct was still strong. With a cluck she led him back to the spot where she'd been grooming him.

Raising her voice a little, she spoke to Josh. "Just stand there quietly, okay? I'm going to brush him lightly on this side before I release him. I want him to see you're not a threat."

"Got it." He made sure to keep his voice low.

A few minutes later she unsnapped the lead rope from the halter and stepped away from Tucker as he whirled on his hind legs and took off at a pounding gallop, not slowing until he was on the other side of the paddock. Gathering her grooming tools, she placed them in the carryall before ducking between the fence's railings.

"Real sorry about that, Quinn. I was sure I was far enough away. That rescue of yours would shy at his own shadow, wouldn't he?"

"He's come a long way. But his fear factor skyrockets

when someone does anything out of the ordinary. Some moron did a real number on him."

"Yeah, Jim mentioned that to me. Here, take this," he said, plucking the carryall from her fingers and passing her the paper bag. "I might eat it otherwise."

She took the bag and opened it. "It does smell awfully tempting." Retrieving the muffin, she eyed it, and bit deep. "Mmm," she said and swallowed. "They do an epic job baking at the luncheonette. Thanks."

"Hope it goes some way toward forgiving me for spooking your horse."

From the corner of her eye she caught him looking at her. She swept the back of her hand over her mouth in case she'd left a trail of brown sugar and pecans, telling herself that, no, that wasn't vanity. It was good manners. Her mom would be proud.

"What's that look for?" she asked when he continued to regard her. Had she left a streak on her cheek?

"I was just wonderin' about you."

She swallowed. It wasn't enough that he'd brought her a muffin, now he had to tell her he was *thinking* about her? Despite the alarm bells ringing in her head, she couldn't help but feel a little flattered. And wasn't that messed up? "Why were you wondering about me?"

"The rescue thing," he said.

Her brow furrowed beneath the sweatband of her Stetson. "What about it?"

"Well," he began as they walked toward the corral where Domino and Josh's horse, Waylon, were dozing near the water trough, "I've been hearing about all the different animals you've rescued and such. You strike me as a sunny kind of person. You've got so many healthy and happy animals here to enjoy." The sweep of his arm encompassed the barns and corrals. "Isn't it kind of depressing to see so many who've been hurt or treated so badly?"

She shrugged uncomfortably, not liking to have to ex-

plain such a fundamental part of her character and a
touch annoyed that Josh apparently believed that just
because she lived in a beautiful place among healthy
and well-cared-for animals, she wouldn't be interested
in helping ones in need. That it might be too much of a
downer. "It's something I've been doing a long time. If
I can heal them and find homes for them where they'll
be loved the way they deserve, that's worth dealing with
the ugliness of their condition."

"I noticed your family treats the stock differently.
The roundup and loading this past weekend had a
real . . . well . . ." He paused, searching for the word.
"*Easy* feel to it. It was interesting."

"The roundup and loading is straight-up Temple
Grandin."

"Come again?"

"Temple Grandin. She's an animal scientist. She's got
amazing insights when it comes to animals. I had my
family and Pete attend one of her seminars on ways to
reduce stress for livestock heading for slaughter. Her
ideas make you rethink your notions about animals and
how they see the world. I have some of her books—"

She stopped. She had a tendency to get nerdy fast
when she talked about Temple Grandin, Buck Branna-
man, Monty Roberts, or Jane Goodall, her personal
superheroes.

Josh rubbed his cheek. "Yeah, well, I'm not much of
a reader. I'm much better at doing, practicing until I get
it just right. Know what I mean?"

Though he hadn't taken a step toward her, somehow
his body seemed nearer.

She swallowed. Yup, she had a pretty good idea just
how determined and active a learner he'd be. Enthusiastic, too. No dragging his heels for this cowboy.

"Maybe you could tell me more about this Church
person—"

"Temple," she corrected with a smile.

"Right, Temple." Twin dimples appeared when he smiled back. "We could go to The Drop together some night this week. How about it, Quinn? You free on Friday?"

"I . . . uh . . ." Shooting the breeze and munching muffins with Josh while they were on the job was fine and dandy. A date at the Drop would change things. He might start thinking she was interested in more. Her heart began thudding in panic. "Sorry, this Friday I'm waiting tables at the restaurant."

"Okay. Then how about the Friday after that?"

Her brain froze. Unable to come up with a viable excuse, she scanned the barn area looking for an escape. Spotting her brother Reid talking to Jim, she mustered a cheery casualness. "Sure. Sounds good. But hey, you know what? We should have Reid and Mia come with us. Reid's been to Temple Grandin's clinics, so he can tell you about her, too. And I need to catch up with Mia and make sure she isn't spoiling Reid too much."

Something flickered in Josh's expression. Astonishment, probably. She doubted women did anything but jump at his invitations. And she bet she was the first one to suggest a double date. To his credit, he recovered quickly. "That'd be fun, too."

"Great." Never let it be said that she was as easily corralled as one of their long-wooled Lincoln sheep.

"Hey, Reid," she called out, waving to catch her brother's attention. "Are you and Mia up for a night at The Drop Friday after next?"

Reid walked over to them. "Yeah, why not? We haven't been down to The Drop in a while, and Bruno's doing better. Mia won't worry too much about leaving him on his own for an evening."

"Who's Bruno?" Josh asked.

"Mia's dog. He was poisoned. It was touch and go for a while, but he pulled through like a champ," Reid said.

"So we're all set then," Quinn said brightly, then added as if the thought had just occurred to her, "Maybe we can even round up a bunch of the guys so we can fill the place with cowboy boots. What do you think, Josh?"

"I'll be sure to ask around." His enthusiasm seemed a little forced.

Reid cocked his head, doubtless wondering why she was acting like her social calendar was the most important thing on her mind at seven in the morning. Then he shifted his attention to Josh. "Pete was looking for you. He's over at the sheep pen with Ward. They're trimming hooves this morning and could use an extra hand."

"I'll get right over there. Don't know much about handling sheep, though."

"You'll get the hang of it pretty quick," Reid promised.

"See ya around, Quinn," Josh said before heading off toward the sheep barn, the smallest of the three weathered barns.

Reid pinned her with a gaze that was laser bright. "What was all that about?"

"He wants to go to The Drop."

"On a group date?"

"No." She grinned. "That was my idea. I'm going to get Ward and Tess to come, too. Like I always say, the more Knowleses and soon-to-be Knowleses, the merrier."

Reid laughed. "Poor dude. Bet he didn't see that one coming." His expression turned serious. "You let me know if he starts sniffing around in earnest."

She snorted. "Don't be such a big brother. I can take care of myself."

"Perhaps, but Josh strikes me as a smoother operator than the guys who usually hang around you."

He was. Funnily enough, it didn't make Josh any less likeable. And because she was feeling the effects of

Josh's potent appeal, she found herself once more wondering whether she shouldn't just go for it and get the whole sex business over with, because boy, the Texan certainly had the walking, talking, six-foot-tall stud muffin thing going on. "I thought you liked him."

"I did. Until about three minutes ago." His tone was only half joking. "Hope he doesn't start acting stupid. Dad won't be any too pleased if he catches Josh making goo-goo eyes at you instead of working. He wants to speak with you, by the way."

"Dad? About what?"

Reid shrugged. "No clue. He's up at the main lodge."

Her feet were already moving. He fell into step beside her, the two of them following the gravel road that led up to the main lodge, where the public rooms—the lounge, the bar, the restaurant, and the conference rooms—were located, as well as the offices used by her family and the lodge's staff.

"Don't you have the trail ride to lead this morning?" Quinn asked. She had checked the schedule. Their foreman, Pete, had put her in the afternoon slot. She'd lucked out—Pete told her the riders were advanced. She was itching for a good run on Domino.

"Jim's taking it for me," Reid answered. "Mia and I are meeting with Tess and Phil to figure out an advertising strategy for the wine auction we're going to hold."

Phil Onofrie was in charge of reservations and marketing. He and Tess, who did the events planning and handled all the social media stuff for the guest ranch, made a formidable team.

"An auction?" she asked.

"Yeah, Mia and her assistants, Johnny and Leo, pulled off a minor miracle—saving what they could of the wine."

"I still can't believe that Mia's psychotic cousin tried to sabotage her by emptying all the fermenting tanks and wine barrels in the cellar. I hope he rots in jail."

"You're not alone, sis. I was worried Jay had destroyed it all, that the juice fermenting in the tanks would be unsalvageable. But my girl's a fighter." Reid's voice rang with pride. "Mia did a barrel test over the weekend. The young wine shows real promise."

"Awesome. She did say that the harvest had been excellent."

"Yeah. Of course, now that she's tasted what's been saved, it only magnifies the winery's loss. I figure the best way to get people talking about the wine and raise Mia's profile as an up-and-coming vintner is to auction it as a future."

"Clever you."

"I hope so," Reid said. "I want to make it a splashy affair and get Jeff and Roo to cook up a pre-auction dinner to dazzle the guests and get them in the mood to bid high."

"This auction sounds like it's going to be seriously swank, which means Phil, Ward, and Tess will be seriously stoked," she predicted.

"More important is getting the bidders stoked. If we can raise a decent amount at the auction and have a good harvest next year, we might just make it. So fill me in," he said, switching topics. "How was the trip to the sanctuary?"

"Amazing. Una's looking great. And she has a buddy, a retired movie star." She explained about Griff, the newest pack member at Wolf Peak.

"And Ethan, how was he?"

"Grayer than the wolves. You'd have thought he'd been in prison."

"I expect where he's been is another form of hell."

"Well, he's in paradise now."

"Maybe, maybe not. Ethan's definition of paradise might be quite different from ours, kid. And after what he's seen in Afghanistan, he might not be in a frame of mind to recognize its existence."

She glanced at her brother. For all his laid-back mellowness, he could be surprisingly perceptive.

They'd reached the main lodge. The large planters in front of it were filled with gold and maroon mums in anticipation of Thanksgiving. The ranch was booked for the holiday, and then things would taper off until Christmas and New Year's.

Reid opened the door and held it for Quinn. She stepped inside the spacious foyer with its honey, wood, and cream tones and felt the familiar sense of pride wash over her at what her parents had accomplished in opening up the ranch to paying guests. The decision had initially been a monetary one, the revenue allowing her parents to continue to raise their horses, cattle, and sheep carefully and responsibly, which didn't come cheaply. But her parents' talents—her father's business savvy and her mother's genius at creating environments that delighted the senses—had made Silver Creek Ranch successful beyond their expectations. If the dry weather continued, her parents' foresight in welcoming paying guests might be what saved the entire operation.

Quinn and Reid waved to Natalie, who was working the front desk and had a phone pressed to her ear. She mouthed "Hi!" back. From the dining room came the clink of silverware as the guests tucked into one of Jeff's hearty breakfasts or spread jam or clover honey on Roo's steaming popovers and buttermilk biscuits. As they opened the door that led to the business offices, Quinn made a mental note to nab a few popovers. The muffin Josh had given her had been tasty, but nothing compared to Roo's baking.

In the carpeted hallway, she and Reid parted ways, Reid heading toward the meeting room, she continuing down to her father's office.

He was on the phone, so she took up her favorite position, perched on the corner of his enormous desk, and ran her fingers over one of the clay sculptures she'd made for him when she was a kid. From the length of the ears, she must have been trying for a rabbit. The misshapen terra-cotta blob sat on her dad's desk in pride of place as if it were a Frederic Remington.

It was clear he was trying to wrap up the conversation. "For sure . . . Yup . . . You bet. I'll talk to Adele and see if there's something we can do. . . . I know you do, Joe. I'll call as soon as I can." With a goodbye, he hung up and blew out a long breath.

"Joe who?" she asked.

"Trullo." His leather chair creaked as he shifted in it. "He's offering us his property."

"And?"

"The price he's asking is steep. On the plus side, it abuts our land to the south—"

"But it's also closer to Route 128." Route 128 wasn't a super-busy road, but there was still traffic.

"Exactly. The property doesn't have the same level of privacy we enjoy here, which is a minus. But it's still a good parcel of land. And I don't particularly like the idea of not knowing who might buy it and what they might decide to do with it. Guess I'm kind of on the fence."

"Mom'll be sure to have an opinion."

"Count on it." Her dad smiled.

Maybe this was why she'd yet to enter into a relationship with a man. Quinn couldn't imagine one that would be as strong and as vital as her parents' partnership. Even when they disagreed over something, their love for each other shone through.

"Reid said you wanted to speak to me. What's up?"

"How was Ethan on the trip back from the airport?"

Her fingers had moved from the sculpture to trace the whorled grain of the desk. They stilled. "You saw him."

"Yeah." His reply came with a sigh.

"Did you and Mom find out how he injured his arm?"

"It's his shoulder," her dad corrected. "There was a roadside explosion—"

"My God." She felt suddenly ill.

"That was pretty much our reaction. He also admitted he got knocked in the head, which I'm assuming means a concussion at the least. He refused to say more about what happened."

"It must have been bad. Really bad."

"Yes. No wonder Tony and Cheryl were beside themselves." He glanced at her. "Ethan wants to earn his keep."

"What? Are you kidding me? What can he possibly do, Dad? Listen, I don't want this to get back to Mom because she's already convinced she knows everything, but I actually agree with her. Silver Creek may not be the place for him right now. He should be in rehab and doing serious PT." How ironic that only minutes ago she'd told Reid that Ethan had come to paradise. Now she was arguing that they should boot him out of it.

Her father's chair creaked again as he leaned back. "As a matter of fact, your mom and I already discussed this. She's come around to my way of thinking." His voice suggested he was pleased. Winning Adele Knowles over was an achievement, even for him. "Quinn, the man needs to be of use while he recovers, doing something with visible results, not squeezing balls or lifting weights. Isn't that an essential part of your philosophy, that animals and humans alike are at their best and happiest when they're useful?" He paused to pin her with his steady gaze, and she tried not to squirm like a little kid. "Isn't seeing a horse shut up in a box stall all day long, with no room to run or graze, no chance to socialize with the herd, a heartbreaking sight? How many dogs have you fostered that spent their days cooped up in a tiny room, basement, or crate and were only given a fifteen-minute walk as exercise?"

"Too many," she admitted.

"Same with Ethan. He's already spent two weeks stuck in a hospital room. Let's give him the chance to recover his strength and peace of mind his way. So how about it, Quinn? You ready to take him on?"

"Wait. Me? What am I supposed to do with him? Why not have Pete assign him some task?"

"Your mother thinks he should start with you. She's worried he might try to work too hard too soon under Pete with all the other ranch hands around."

Men and their lame-brained macho competitions. "Yeah, he probably would hurt himself," she conceded. "But seriously, Dad, what can I ask him to do when he looks barely strong enough to lift a toothbrush?"

"Come up with some light tasks until he's built up enough strength to work for Pete."

She must have looked as unhappy as Sooner when she pulled out the washtub for bath time, for her father asked, "Can I count on you, sweetheart?"

Puffing out her cheeks, she blew the air out noisily. "Of course you can. It's only that we didn't hit it off so well."

Her father looked amused at her admission. "Really? You've always been able to get men to follow you around like puppy dogs. Well, consider helping Ethan recover your repayment for all those times he led you around on Jinx. He helped make you the horsewoman you are."

"Laying it on a bit thick, aren't you?"

Unrepentant, he grinned. "I told Ethan to rest up for a couple of days. That should give you time to come up with some jobs that need doing."

"It'll call for some seriously creative thinking. I can't

even set him to weeding the vegetable garden. The weeds would humiliate him."

Her father was still chuckling when she slid off his desk. "Quinn, honey, don't mention what happened to Ethan to anyone. It's his story to tell."

"Of course." She could keep secrets better than he knew.

"And don't make it obvious that you're going easy on him. I can't imagine he'd take it well."

"Oh, I already figured that one out for myself—the man's as proud and stubborn as they come."

"Then you'll be well matched, won't you, Quinn?"

"Ha, Dad. You're a hoot and a half. A comic of epic proportions. The stories they will tell of your wit."

"Enough," he said with a grin. With a wave of his hand he dismissed her. "Go on. If memory serves you have a salary to earn."

It took several minutes before Ethan answered her loud rap on his cabin door.

"Hi," she said. Her glance swept over him. He was still dressed in the same clothes he'd worn yesterday, and the left side of his face was creased. His hollow cheeks were covered in heavy stubble and, like the hair on his head, gray was mixed in with the dark brown.

In a word, he looked like crap. And if he'd managed to sleep, it hadn't left him rested. Or improved his mood or eased his pain.

When it was clear he didn't intend to return her greeting, she said, "You've been assigned to me."

"What? Why?"

"Because you're lucky?"

He snorted.

So maybe he was strong enough to use a toothbrush, she thought as she caught a hint of mint on his breath.

He had good teeth, white and strong. And his lips were nice. Not too thin, but not too fat. For some reason thinking about his mouth distracted her, so she lowered her gaze to the sling cradling his arm.

"Can you use it at all?" she asked, careful to keep her voice casual.

"The sling's coming off."

"And you didn't answer my question," she said mildly.

The brackets framing his mouth deepened. "Don't worry about me."

"I wouldn't dream of it. When you're ready to work later this week, report to the goat pen at six A.M. It's past the sheep barn." The imp in her had her adding, "You'll know you're at the right place when you see six of the cutest does ever. Oh, and here, catch." She tossed a paper bag filled with one of Roo's biscuits *and* a popover, thinking she'd probably go to heaven for that generous act alone.

He caught it against his chest with his good arm. Not sloppy in the reflex department, she noted.

He scowled. "What's this?"

"Room service. Oh, okay, it's a peace offering."

When his scowl deepened she said, "Look, don't get bent out of shape. I'm just sorry about the drive from the airport."

"What the hell do you have to apologize for? I'm the one who acted like a prick."

Her eyebrows rose. "True." It was nice that he didn't hold a grudge.

"You do, however, have piss-poor taste in music."

And she'd go to her grave before admitting that Morris Albert's "Feelings" wasn't her all-time fave.

"Better get used to it. My goats are especially fond of the Captain and Tennille." Then Quinn left him to brood in his cabin before she could discover anything else she liked about him.

Chapter

SIX

THE SKY WAS the color of slate when Ethan walked past the corrals. Shadows of men moved with quiet efficiency among the horses; the animals had their muzzles to the ground as they sniffed for hay. They paid no heed to his presence. The men glanced his way, their gazes probing beneath the brims of their cowboy hats. Then, presumably identifying him, they ignored him as well, returning to their chores.

These were men who knew how to leave a body alone. He appreciated that even as he tried not to resent them for the ease of their movements.

It had taken him curse-filled minutes to peel off the jeans and shirt he'd slept in, if sleeping was what you'd call the nightmare-ridden hours he'd endured. The shower had washed away the cold sweat covering him. But he couldn't do anything about the new film that had coated him while he dressed.

A mordant smile lifted the corners of his mouth as he imagined Quinn's reaction were he to show up at her goat pen naked as the new day. He was sure the sight of his sorry hide would rob her of any sassy quips or the teasing laughter he sometimes heard in her voice . . . leaving only pity.

He passed the sheep barn. Its double doors were open, framing a gold rectangle of light. A disjointed chorus of *baa*s emanated from deep inside. He'd have paused to look at whatever was going on, but he didn't want to be late; in fact, he intended to be the opposite.

If Quinn was surprised to see him when Daniel Knowles had suggested he take a couple of days off before reporting for duty, she didn't show it. She merely paused in the midst of filling the raised feeder for the congregated goats that were bumping each other and stretching their necks to grab at bits of hay, and said, "Couldn't wait to get cracking, huh?"

"Something like that."

"Hold on a sec. I'll be right with you."

She probably hadn't meant the suggestion literally, but he leaned against the metal railing of the goat pen on legs that felt like rubber. He'd walked a little over a quarter of a mile, the longest distance since he'd left Afghanistan on a stretcher.

Finished filling the feeder, she went to the gate and opened it. "Come on in," she said, and then led him to the side entrance of a small barn. They entered a room with a concrete floor, a stainless steel sink and counters lining the wall to their right. At the end of the counter there was a large, plastic-lined garbage bin with smaller tubs arranged next to it. On the opposite wall stood an industrial-sized refrigerator. Between them was a large storage cupboard. The air inside the room smelled of soap, which made sense, since the place was as immaculate as a surgery room but a whole lot nicer to be inside.

She was looking at him. "So you ditched the sling, huh?"

"Yup." He'd gotten damned good at one-word responses.

"Wiggle your fingers."

He had a sudden memory of one of the soldiers at

Walter Reed who'd lost his right hand. The poor bastard was probably still there, learning how to live with a prosthetic. Slowly he forced digits as stiff as concrete to move.

"Not bad," was the verdict. "Though I'm not sure you're ready to play any piano concertos."

He glanced at Quinn. Her light teasing aside, he could imagine how it must irk a beautiful young woman like her to be stuck with a wreck like him. Because now that nausea wasn't blanketing his vision, Quinn's loveliness was startlingly clear: her glowing skin, her searing blue eyes lit by diamond chips, her wide cheekbones, and her soft, full lips that looked as if she'd just been thoroughly and expertly kissed.

When Ethan was a kid, his teacher at Acacia Elementary used to have the class play a game. It was called something like "What Doesn't Belong Here?" He, standing beside this perfect woman in her perfect, spotless world, was the oddball.

But one thing he knew about Adele and Daniel Knowles: their kindness and generosity were deep-seated and totally genuine. Quinn must have inherited it, for all she said next was, "Go wash up and we'll set to work. Oh, and use the soap in the pump bottle. It's antibacterial."

While he washed his hands, he tracked her movements as she crisscrossed the room, pulling out neatly folded washcloths and a stack of metal pails from the cupboard next to the refrigerator. Setting them on the counter, she filled one of the buckets with feed pellets from the large bin.

When he stepped away from the sink to dry his hands, she took his place, turning on the water and filling another bucket before squirting some of the antibacterial soap into it. Picking up the two buckets, she hooked her fingers around the stack of still-empty pails and lifted them, too. "Grab the washcloths and follow me."

He looked at all the stuff she was carrying. "I can at least carry the empty pails for you, damn it."

With a roll of her eyes, she thrust them toward him so he could grasp the handles in his good hand. "There. Now that your male ego is satisfied, can we get a move on? Coco gets witchy if she's kept waiting."

The clanking of metal marked their progress outside. The noise had one of the goats removing her nose from the feeder. Looking at Quinn, she bleated imperiously.

"Yes, Coco, you'll go first."

He watched Quinn set the bucket of water on the ground next to a wooden platform roughly the size of a cot with an odd-looking headboard at its end.

"You can set the pails down here." She pointed to a spot in the middle of the platform while she walked over to the headboard and poured some pellets into a trough that he hadn't noticed before.

The imperious bleat came again.

"I hear you, Coco. You could try to be a little more polite, you know."

She brushed past him and the air turned fresh. He inhaled, and her scent—it reminded him of a spring garden—entered his bloodstream. Something inside him tightened and became an ache different from all the others. This one sweet and beguiling.

The sky had lightened. He could see her tall, leggy form as she moved among her goats, continuing her cheerful chatter as they bumped her affectionately with their shoulders and gummed her down vest.

Wrapping her hand about the goat's leather collar, she snapped a lead line on it and led her back to the platform.

"So this here's Coco, my most demanding Toggenburg." Dropping a kiss on the bony ridge above the goat's eye, she continued, "Coco, this is Ethan. He's going to get to know you today. Up, Coco." She gestured, and the animal leapt onto the platform and made a beeline for the trough, her neck fitting into the vee of the headboard, which Ethan now understood served as a kind of yoke.

Quinn sat on a low bench and got to work, talking as she picked up one of the washcloths and dunked it into the bucket of soapy water. "Before you begin milking, you have to wash the udder and teats first," she said, swabbing them with gentle efficiency. "The only good thing about this drought is that the girls aren't playing in the mud. Frankly, I'd do a jig to see them caked in it from nose to tail. There, all done." She set the cloth and bucket aside. "Now, watch carefully. As I said, Coco's a bit of a diva. She gives a lot of milk but doesn't tolerate fumblers. On the upside, if you can milk Coco, the rest of my girls will be a breeze. I'll—"

"Wait. You intend to have me milk your goats?"

"Yup. It's your new job. Consider yourself enrolled in Milking 101. See this? This here is a teat." She brushed the distended teat with her index finger. "You ever handled one before?" The ghost of a grin lifted the corner of her mouth.

Damn, he liked her sense of humor. Clearly the moment had come for a little tit for tat. "I've had experience with something similar, but I've never been especially interested in milking any of them." He paused as if considering. "Suckling, definitely."

There was enough light to catch the fiery blush that stole over her cheeks. She cleared her throat and coughed. "Excuse me. Must have swallowed some hay." She made a show of coughing again. "Right. Good. Now, where was I? Oh, yeah. You'll need to bring your A-game with Coco. Take a seat."

He looked around. "Where?"

"Here." She patted the space next to her. "You need to see what I'm doing."

He shrugged inwardly. What the hell? He could give it a try. He sat, and she scooted an inch or two closer to the goat's side.

"Watch and learn." Quinn made a circle with her index finger and thumb. She brought it to the base of the teat until the back of her hand rested against the engorged udder. "You begin by pushing up against the udder like this and feeling for the milk. When you do, you're going to close your thumb and index finger and draw the milk down, the rest of your hand squeezing as you do." As she uttered the words, a stream of milk shot from beneath her closed fingers and landed on the wood.

"Don't you need a pail?"

"First I have to check that the milk is clear, with no dark lumps. Now that I've seen it's fine, you can place the pail a few inches in front of her hind legs."

He grabbed one of the metal pails and positioned it as instructed.

"Okay, I'm going to demonstrate again. Then I'll start milking for real."

As he watched her hand moving up and down, drawing milk from the udder, he wondered whether she had any idea how erotic the act was—not her milking a goat per se, but her hand grasping and tugging on warm flesh and coaxing forth a jet of liquid. It was earthy and unabashedly sensual.

Then her other hand joined in, working the second teat. Quinn pumped rhythmically, the milk hitting the pail in a steady stream. "Once you've started milking, you'll notice that the bag—a.k.a. the udder—empties. When it's less full, you can press higher. See?"

"Yeah," he said, and then, figuring she wanted him to look, he leaned in. A mistake, as once again he was distracted by her nearness. He told himself to concentrate on the goat and not the girl, on the rich tang of warm milk rather than the lighter, floral scent emanating from Quinn. It was damned hard.

And, Christ, she really must be unaware, or at least totally unaffected and uninterested, because she began chattering away, telling him all about her goats and the cheesemonger who used their milk to make cheese for the ranch's restaurant, selling any extra that remained at the farmer's market in town. Meanwhile, Ethan watched her long, supple fingers and wondered what they'd feel like against his skin. . . .

"Okay, now put your hands over mine so you can get a better sense of what I'm doing."

He bit back the instinctive *No. Hell, no* that sprang to his lips. He'd been to Afghanistan. Surely he could manage to milk a goat. Surely he could handle touching Quinn Knowles. "Right," he muttered.

She stilled her hands. He placed his larger ones lightly over them.

For a second she was silent. Then she said, "Here we go."

Was there a slight breathlessness to her voice? he wondered. But then her hands began moving, her fingers opening and squeezing as she worked the teat, his own following, learning, feeling the softness of her skin and the strength in her fingers. Warm milk streamed into the pail, the sound growing deeper as the pail filled.

"Pay attention to the rhythm," she instructed.

Oh God, the rhythm. And no, it wasn't a slow thrust and grind but that didn't make it any the less carnal. He frowned, trying to concentrate. *Up, open, down, squeeze,* he recited silently.

"Got it?"

Jesus. "Yeah, I think so." His voice was rough.

"Good." Without warning, she slipped her hands

from beneath his and sat back, crossing her arms about her middle.

He knew a moment of panic as he tried to remember Quinn's motions, tried to feel for the milk in the udder that was waiting to be released. Then a minor miracle occurred. A stream of milk spurted into the pail, followed by another—nowhere near as strong or evenly paced as when Quinn had worked the teats, but still.

Ethan made himself maintain the tempo and smooth it out, even as his arm and shoulder began to throb from moving these few inches. Within minutes both his shoulders, biceps, and forearms felt as heavy as if he'd been chopping wood for hours. He set his jaw and continued, reaching ever higher as the goat's udder softened.

After what seemed like an eternity she said, "You can ease up now. She's at empty."

He lowered his hands and bit back a groan.

"Pretty decent job for your first time."

Who would have predicted her words would make him feel like he'd just been awarded a Pulitzer?

She reached up to pat Coco's shaggy flank. "Coco obviously thought so, too, since she didn't kick you in the gut. You up to milking Gertrude? She's a real sweetie."

God help him. This was harder than any of the PT exercises he'd been given. "Yeah." He surreptitiously clenched and relaxed his right hand to keep the muscles from stiffening any further.

"Good. Then I can—"

"Morning, Quinn. Brought you coffee." It was a man's voice, laced with a Texas accent.

Beside him Quinn started. "Oh! Hi, Josh."

Ethan looked up and encountered an assessing gaze. He had a hunch this Josh guy had been measuring the inches—of which there were none—that separated Quinn and Ethan.

"Hey there," he said with a dip of his cowboy hat.

"Hey," Ethan replied.

The word still hung in the air as Quinn scrambled off the bench. She strode over to where Josh stood by the pen and plucked the coffee mug from his hands, speaking in a rush. "Not necessary to bring me coffee, but since you did, it'd be criminal to let it go to waste." She took a few quick gulps while he and Josh continued to eye each other, and then said, "Ethan, this is Josh Yates, one of our new ranch hands. Josh, this is Ethan—"

"You're the photographer the guys are talking about. I have some buddies in Afghanistan. Marines. Camp Leatherneck. You been there?"

Guessing what was coming, Ethan tensed. "No. I was embedded with a unit in Kandahar, to the east. Camp Nathan Smith."

"Right. Is it as effed-up over there as they say?"

"Yeah. Pretty much."

"I thought so. I considered enlisting." He gave a shrug.

Ethan couldn't blame him for his decision. It wasn't as if he'd signed up to fight, either. And it wasn't Josh's fault that so many others had died. That's where Ethan knew he and Josh differed.

"Bet you saw some bad shit, huh?"

Christ, did people really expect an answer to that question? What did they want, a list detailing the horror, the blood, the carnage, the total mind-fucking wrongness of some of the things he'd witnessed? Experienced?

Apparently unfazed by his silence, Josh asked, "Who were you photographing?"

"Army grunts. Just your average Joes." A number of them younger than Josh.

"Oh, yeah, sure. So, did they finish their tour of duty and return home for some well-deserved R&R?"

What he wouldn't give to make that so, rather than have to live with the fact that Archie Donovan, Aaron Smith, and Casey Logar had died mere feet from him. If they hadn't had the bad luck to be assigned to escort him into Kandahar, they might be alive. Instead they died for a fucking photo shoot.

They weren't the only casualties that haunted him. From deep inside a familiar pain clawed at him. But then Quinn spoke. Though he couldn't make sense of what she was saying, he clung to the sound of her voice. Gradually the pain loosened its hold.

". . . I have some needy goats to milk and a pen to clean before I lead the morning trail ride."

Goats. Milk. Pen. The words brought him back from that dusty road in the hell that was Afghanistan. He blinked, weak with relief. If she'd been anyone else but the disarmingly beautiful Quinn Knowles, daughter of his parents' close friends, he might have kissed her out of gratitude.

Luckily she didn't seem to have noticed anything off about him as he relived the harrowing pain or his slack-jawed relief at being freed from those memories. Her attention was on Josh.

No big surprise that the wrangler was equally focused on her. A woman like Quinn would have men lined up from here to South America hoping to date her.

"Oh, yeah. About that trail ride," Josh said. "I'm your backup."

A frown of confusion crossed Quinn's face. "I thought Pete assigned Jim—"

"Nope. Jim's off to the dentist with a real bad toothache. I volunteered to take his place. Have to admit, I'll be jealous of you on Domino. Any chance you want to swap and ride Waylon?"

"Thanks, but no. Domino's feelings would be hurt."

"Had to give it a shot." Turning to him, Josh said,

"You seen her Appaloosa? A real beaut. Rides like the wind. And how about these goats? She takes real good care of them. Talks to 'em, too." He chuckled.

Ethan got the message loud and clear. Josh brought Quinn coffee. He'd ridden her horse. He'd witnessed Quinn in a conversation with her beloved goats. Next on the cowboy's to-do list: get Quinn somewhere private.

"Nothing wrong with talking to goats. They're more interesting than many humans I've encountered," he answered with a cool stare, even as he reminded himself that Quinn had two older brothers and a father who were more than capable of taking Josh out of the picture if need be. Besides, Quinn didn't seem to mind Josh's attention, though right now she'd ducked her head and was staring in apparent fascination at a tiny hoofprint in the dirt.

To his credit, Josh met his stare with a level gaze. Of course, it was likely the cowboy recognized that Ethan wasn't exactly a threat. Josh could have him flat on his ass before he could even land a punch anywhere near Josh's pretty mug. And in terms of competing for Quinn's attention, well, that was a non-issue on so many levels, never mind that she was the first woman to make him feel and notice things—good things—in months.

Josh returned his attention to Quinn. "Since you're so busy this morning, you want me to groom Domino for you?"

Ah, so Josh didn't know Quinn quite as well as he should.

Ethan remembered the way she'd been with that pony of hers. The brushes had been bigger than her hands but that hadn't stopped her from doing her level best to make that shaggy pinto coat shine. He doubted she would have outgrown the need to spend special time with her horses, connecting with them as she brushed their coats, inspected their hooves, and checked for any soreness in their bodies.

The bright smile that she pinned on her face came as a surprise, except when he realized that it was a shade *too* bright, as if she was eager to be rid of Josh. "That would be so great, Josh. Thanks!"

"Anytime, Quinn." Along with a slow smile, Josh's voice had dropped, going all husky. The guy was slick. "I'll catch you in a few, then." With a nod to Ethan he said, "Good to meet you."

"Yeah. Likewise." No reason to hold it against the Texan for asking about Afghanistan. It was natural. Plenty of people sounded off on topics about which they knew jack.

And so what if the guy was making the moves on Quinn? Who was he to judge, or denounce Josh as a little too practiced with his moves, or wonder whether he was right for Quinn?

The guy probably thought he was perfect for her, but Ethan had looked at people through lenses for many years. He knew Josh wasn't seeing Quinn clearly. Because for all her easy banter, for all that Quinn appeared to be struck by the cowboy's good looks and charm, she also seemed slightly uncomfortable around him. Why, he didn't know.

Best to stay out of it. He could easily imagine Quinn setting him straight. She wouldn't mince words telling him to keep his nose out of her business. He of all people should respect that. Besides, why go looking for problems when he could hardly deal with his own?

LIFE AT SILVER Creek Ranch was something Quinn generally navigated with ease. She didn't mind the long hours or shifting gears as she moved from one job to the next, one minute shoveling manure into the wheelbarrow and rolling it to the pile, the next minute tidying herself up and flipping on the charm switch to lead ranch guests on a two-hour ride or heading over to the main lodge and helping the waitstaff when the ranch's restaurant was short of servers.

But suddenly her world seemed complicated, doubly so. *Men,* she thought with a sigh.

She didn't know which male troubled her more, Ethan or Josh. And she didn't like having either one invade her thoughts while she stood in front of Major's long brown nose and eyeballed his rider's spanking new cowboy boots peeking through the stirrups.

The boots belonged to a guest named Sharon, half of a couple, and she was as new to riding as her boots. But she and her husband, Paul, seemed to love each other, so clearly she had smarts and experience that Quinn sorely lacked.

"How do those stirrups feel, Sharon? You want to be

able to keep your legs long and your heels down when Major starts to move."

"I guess they feel good." Sharon managed a smile.

"You look great on him, hon," Paul said, who was far more comfortable in the saddle than his wife, even though he'd confessed it had been nearly a decade since he was last astride a horse.

"That's 'cause he's standing still. All bets are off once he starts going."

"No worries, Sharon. Major and I will take care of you," Quinn assured her with an easy smile. "You, Paul, Mellie and Leonard, and Katherine and Stephen will be riding with me. Domino and I are going to take you on some of our favorite trails."

"And the others get to go with Josh?" Katherine asked, her pout matching her tone.

"That's right. He'll be taking the more experienced riders this morning." And the less flirtatious ones, too. It was sheer good luck that Katherine wouldn't have been able to keep up with the faster-paced ride, because the overt come-hither glances she'd been casting Josh's way had quickly gone into *Houston, we have a problem* territory. Had Katherine bothered to look over at Stephen, she'd have beheld a supremely pissed-off spouse.

Even if Katherine had been an intermediate rider— and from the way she slouched in the saddle and held her reins, it was clear she was anything but—Quinn didn't want her and Stephen anywhere near Josh. The other guests didn't deserve to be treated to a marital blow-up on their trail ride.

Domino had been standing patiently while Quinn checked stirrups and cinches and adjusted the riders' hands on their reins, urging them to relax their death grip. Each contact made her remember another pair, this one surprisingly sensitive and strong. Even now she could recall the warm weight and steady pressure of Ethan's hands covering hers as she taught him to milk.

Quinn was the first to admit she had a tendency to act impulsively. Her suggestion that Ethan place his hands over hers was a perfect example. In her own defense, she'd believed that, given the stiffness in his injured shoulder and arm, hands-on learning would be the best way to teach him. He'd caught on amazingly quickly— but not before the heat from his body transferred to hers. Not before her body started listening to his, communicating on some level she wasn't used to.

Even now she was feeling odd and unsettled.

Grasping Domino's reins in her left hand, she raised her leg, placed the toe of her boot in the stirrup, and swung herself up into the saddle, finding the other stirrup with her right foot. Settling her weight in the cantle, she leaned forward and ran her hand up the crest of Domino's neck, saying hello to her gelding.

He looked good. Josh had brushed him until his inky black coat gleamed and the white spots on his haunches stood out like giant snowflakes. Even his black ears, which had swiveled at the familiar caress, were at their glossiest.

For that alone she should be able to shake off her annoyance with Josh, irrational though it was. It wasn't his fault he'd been unaware that Ethan had been injured in Afghanistan, especially since Ethan had discarded his sling. And though he was noticeably thin and haggard, the morning light had softened his drawn expression and the shadows in his eyes.

Nor could she blame Josh for behaving like an armchair general. If he had friends who'd been deployed in Afghanistan, he'd probably heard just enough to think he knew something about what it was like for the men risking their lives. But while she didn't know all the details of what had happened to Ethan, she instinctively understood that he'd chosen Silver Creek Ranch as a refuge from those questions. Unfortunately, the Texan hadn't picked up on the fact that a little discretion was in order.

For whatever reason, perhaps because he was caught up in the excitement of discussing the war, Josh hadn't noticed how still Ethan became when asked about the soldiers with whom he'd been stationed and where they were now. No, *still* wasn't the right word. He'd become frozen, locked in his memories.

Josh hadn't noticed the change, but she had. She'd looked into Ethan's face and known that whatever he was feeling right then, it was infinitely worse than the pain that had had him bent in half and puking his guts into the base of the airport's potted plant.

Determined to divert Josh's attention, she'd begun rattling off her morning list of chores, praying he'd get the hint and leave, or at the very least stop talking about Afghanistan until Ethan could escape from wherever he was trapped.

It had worked. She'd babbled on, listing everything she could think of until, from the corner of her eye, she saw Ethan relax, inch by inch. And Josh had abandoned his Q&A to offer to groom Domino for her. She'd accepted. She'd have agreed to a lot of things if it meant giving Ethan a chance to wrest free of his demons.

In a perfect world, she'd have figured out a way to be rid of both men: Ethan, who was hurting and withdrawn yet whose touch left her flustered and hyperaware of things she usually never noticed, like the dark crescent his lashes made against his cheeks, the intelligence that pierced the shadows of his gray eyes, the light brown hair sprinkling his forearms, the intensity of his focus as he'd taken over the milking, his large hands working the teats.

And then there was Josh, so handsome and comfortable with himself, who seemed intent on pursuing her with a happy and steady cheer that was making her feel like a seesaw. One minute she wanted to resist him, the next she found herself tempted to yield.

Quinn knew most women would be dancing on air to have a man like Josh paying so much attention to them. They would be counting the hours until next Friday night in the hopes he might pay even closer attention, like on the dance floor, or on one of the sofas tucked away in a corner of the bar.

But other women didn't have her miserable track record to haunt them.

The prospect of another screw-up, this time with someone she saw every day, filled her with the dread one might feel walking into an exam unprepared. It didn't matter that she would be with Mia, Reid, Tess, Ward, and anyone else she could drag to the bar.

With a hard tug on her battered brown Stetson, she lowered the brim over her brow, shielding her expression. She had a hunch Josh would be tickled pink to know how worried she was about a simple date.

"You set over there?" she called to him. His group being bigger, he'd only just mounted Waylon.

"Ready to roll," he answered with that disarming grin that made her want to fuss with her hair and maybe dab on some lip gloss, even as she contemplated galloping straight for the hills.

As she urged Domino forward, leading the group out of the corral, she wondered whether Ethan had ever smiled as easily or as often. And how would she feel if he ever smiled at her?

Ethan leaned against the pillar that supported the extended overhang of the horse barn and watched Quinn and Josh ready the group of riders. He wasn't sure why he'd stopped at the corrals, since he was bone tired after having helped Quinn milk two more of her goats before she'd told him that milking class was over for the day.

Her horse Domino was a superb animal, as sleek and muscled as that pinto pony of hers had been shaggy and round. He saw her mount lightly and then reach forward and caress her gelding's black mane.

A memory flashed in his brain. It was of Quinn's bright blond pigtails flopping on either side of her pony's brown and white neck as she laid her torso against it and combed his mane with her chubby fingers. It did something inside him to recall that uncomplicated gesture of love and to see it alive and well today. After the hatred and fear he'd seen in too many faces and the despair he'd witnessed in too many places, the simple happiness Quinn displayed around animals was like stepping into the light after the suffocating gunmetal grays and dusty camo colors of Afghanistan, where innocence and joy died too quickly.

So there was the answer as to why he was standing in the shadows of the horse barn: Quinn. She drew him. The sweet animal-crazy kid he remembered had grown into a startlingly beautiful woman who was fascinatingly different. How could there not be a magnetic pull?

Yet he would have to ignore the attraction. While he might harbor a few middling reservations about Josh and whether the Texan was good enough for Quinn, Ethan had no illusions about himself.

He'd never be the right man for her.

First off, he was too old for her. Yet even if there hadn't been ten years' difference between them, there were all the life experiences that set them apart, making a gap a gulf. Second, too much darkness clung to him. He'd be shade in her sun-kissed world. And finally, though he loved the beauty of Silver Creek, he didn't belong here. He wasn't sure he belonged anywhere—

Absorbed in his thoughts, Ethan hadn't heard the footsteps until they were almost upon him. The realization was freaky. In Afghanistan he and the troops had twitched at the rustling of leaves, the unexpected cry of a bird. The soldiers would reach for their weapons while he prayed he survived the ambush.

"Morning, Ethan. You're up early." Daniel Knowles's glance took in the cream and gray hairs stuck to Ethan's shirt. "Quinn put you to work already?" There was a touch of concern in his voice.

"It was my idea," Ethan told him.

"So how did it go? She's a hell of a taskmaster," said a guy with shaggy blond hair and blue eyes that were almost identical to Quinn's.

"She had me milk a few of her goats. An interesting experience. You're Reid, right?"

"Yeah." He thrust out his hand. "It's been a long time. Good to see you, Ethan."

"We're glad you're here," said the third man. "I'm Ward, in case you don't remember."

"Sure I do," Ethan replied. Ward was the one who most closely resembled Daniel, with dark hair and a broader frame. "No matter how hard I tried, I could never beat your time when it came to roping a steer."

The senior Knowles laughed. "Unfortunately for the rest of our egos, Ward's only gotten faster."

"Hope you'll come out and ride with us when you're ready," Ward said.

"Thanks." Due to the shrapnel that had been buried in his shoulder by the IED blast, there was no way he'd be able to ride like his usual self, or even like the lucky kid who'd learned to gallop over these rolling hills. He'd have to get a lot stronger if he wanted to climb into a saddle and stay there once his mount moved forward.

And he wanted it. Wanted to feel the powerful flow of a horse beneath him again. Which meant he would have to do significantly more than milk goats to regain his strength and mobility. He remembered the soldiers' workouts. Endless push-ups, sit-ups, squat jumps. The floor of his cabin was a hell of a lot nicer than any spot on the army base. He had no excuse.

"So she introduced you to the goats," Reid said. "Don't let them or Quinn drive you crazy. Believe me, they can."

Ward nodded in agreement. "Quinn's like a force of nature. She leaves most of us reeling."

"But we're rooting for you," Reid told him. "Right, Dad?"

Daniel smiled. "We are indeed."

What would her brothers and father think if they knew that, far from driving him nuts, there was something about Quinn that helped beat back the madness, the darkness in his soul?

If they cared as much about her as he suspected, their laid-back geniality would vanish. They'd do whatever was necessary to keep him the hell away from her and her herd of goats.

And they certainly wouldn't be rooting for him.

As the specter of her group date with Josh loomed larger, Quinn found herself increasingly enjoying the time spent in Ethan's company. His prickly monosyllabic reserve was the perfect antidote to her pre-date jitters. And as her dread increased, his complete disinterest in her as a woman was like chocolate buttercream frosting on a perfectly baked cake.

Every morning he arrived punctually at the goat pen to help feed and then milk the does while she supervised and carried the pails full of milk into the storeroom's refrigerator for George Alston, cheesemonger extraordinaire, to pick up later.

The routine lasted until the fourth day, when he announced, with the steel-jawed determination she'd come to recognize, his intention to start mucking out the pen for her. Naturally, they'd argued.

"I want to work, damn it. You've got to give me more to do."

"You don't need to do more. Why don't you rest?" Sure, he was moving better now, not in that frighteningly stiff way he'd carried himself at the airport when she'd first seen him, but that didn't mean he was ready to take on more.

He looked at her as if she had the wits of a slug. So very refreshing. "I rested in the hospital. You want me to sit around on my ass from nine A.M. on?"

"Of course not. But that doesn't mean you need to shovel goat droppings. Why don't you take some photographs?"

The second she uttered the suggestion, his expression closed tighter than a sealed vault.

"I'm finished with photography."

Clearly this was dangerous territory. She ventured into the minefield nonetheless. "But why? You're really good—"

"Leave it alone, Quinn."

She was learning Ethan-speak. What he actually meant was leave *him* alone, and that was something she wasn't going to do—until she looked and saw the depth of pain in his eyes. "Fine. Go ahead and pick up the droppings in the pen if that makes you happy. It'll give Hennie extra time to trail after you like Mary's little lamb."

His glower made her feel better about having caved to his demands. She much preferred it to the shuttered look he'd worn earlier or the bleak light in his eyes.

And if he was going to shovel shit, at least her goats' leavings were a lighter load than horse or cow manure. She didn't want him straining his injury.

And Hennie *was* overjoyed. The doe had taken an instant shine to Ethan. After Ethan finished milking her, she stuck like a shadow as he led the other goats from the feeder to the milking stand. When he bent over to position the pail and began working, she'd sidle up and begin nibbling on his collar. Never once did he push her nose away. It was cute as anything.

Ethan was also the first person outside of her family to be able to distinguish the goats.

When she mentioned this to him, he looked at her for a long moment, long enough that she succumbed to temptation and bit into the pear and cinnamon muffin she'd filched from Roo—the one she'd given Ethan having disappeared within seconds.

"Yeah, well, I generally make an effort to remember a female's name once I've put my hands on her teats."

She coughed her muffin halfway across the pen. Maybelle beat the other girls to it, scarfing down the crumbs.

When she recovered, she swiped the back of her hand across her lips to wipe away any stray muck, and noticed that the corner of his mouth was tilted up. "That's real big of you," she said tartly. "No wonder Hennie's smitten. She's probably got you confused with Romeo—the buck she and the girls visited a couple weeks ago."

There, she thought. That would show him she wasn't thrown by the idea of his fondling other women's breasts. And please God, don't let him guess that she still remembered the weight and warmth of his hands over hers.

And what would it have felt like if Ethan had slid those hands up her body until he reached her breasts, caressing them and then teasing her nipples with his long fingers?

With a convulsive jerk, she pulled herself up short. Where had that thought come from? The reason she liked hanging out with Ethan was because he *wasn't* interested in her. Never once in the time they'd spent together had he acted as if he was mentally undressing her or figuring out the quickest way to get her to a place where he could do so literally.

"Very funny. Listen, I need you to assign me some more jobs."

She had trouble switching gears, still embarrassingly stuck on the hands-fondling-breasts fantasy starring a guy who exuded indifference the way others did Old

Spice. And wasn't that proof that she was the only creature in this pen thinking about sex? Except perhaps
Gertrude, who was a little slutty.

"Seriously? You've already taken over the goats' care.
I know this is a working ranch, but it's also a *resort*—
you know, a place where people relax."

"I don't do relaxed."

No kidding. He specialized in intense and brooding.

She scrambled to come up with something else that
would allow him to exercise but not overtax his shoulder. "Can you groom a horse? I can help pick out the
hooves—or you can manage yourself," she tacked on
quickly when Ethan's lips thinned to a flat, irritated
line. "Frank and Mel, two of our hands, went to visit
family now so they could be back here for Thanksgiving, so we're understaffed. And Dad, Ward, and Reid
are spending the morning stacking a new load of hay
that's come in, so I'm sure our foreman, Pete, would
appreciate your help."

Her dad would be fine with the suggestion. Ethan
could use his good arm to brush off the horses if need
be, and honestly, she couldn't think of any other tasks
to give him. She doubted he'd be too thrilled at the prospect of picking squashes and kale or spreading compost
around the rows. Besides, working the garden was
solitary—the last thing Ethan needed. He should be in
the company of men. And animals. Along with dogs,
horses were some of the best medicine in the world.

"When you're finished mucking out the pen, come on
over to the corrals. I'll introduce you to the herd. Oh,
and can you do me a favor?" she added casually.

"Yeah."

"Keep Sooner here with you. I'm going to be grooming Tucker, and I don't want him getting nervous." It
wasn't an outright lie, just a taffy-like stretch of the
truth. Her rescue gelding did get nervous, but it was

men who made his eyes roll back and his hind leg kick out in fear, not dogs. And her Sheltie was well trained. She could have asked him for a down/stay at fifty paces during the entire time she worked with Tucker. But the germ of an idea had sprouted.

In response, Ethan eyed Sooner, who was sitting with his head cocked now that she'd spoken his name. Then he looked back at her.

She held her breath, waiting for Ethan to call her out on her BS request. But he merely shrugged with his good shoulder. "Suit yourself."

She intended to, especially as her idea had taken root and she was beginning to see its potential. It could be perfect. Epic. Not to brag, but she had a genius for these things.

"Stay," she told Sooner. Then, flashing Ethan a bright smile, she said, "When you're done here, just tell him to find me."

The sheltie was like a mini Lassie. Or maybe he was just another male who'd fallen under Quinn's spell. Either way, after Ethan had finished shoveling the goats' pen and kicking around a scuffed-up soccer ball for a few minutes with Hennie—the real reason the nanny goat liked him—all he had to do was open the gate and say, "Find Quinn," and the dog rose from his alert crouch and shot off like a bullet toward the horse barn.

Ethan followed more slowly.

The fiery chestnut with the white blaze must be the one Quinn called Tucker. She was bending over his rear right leg, carefully picking out his hoof. Though the horse's ears twitched back and forth, his raised hoof remained cradled in her hand.

Ethan stood some distance away, figuring she'd deal with him when she was finished tending to the horse.

Around him the ranch hands were crisscrossing the open space between the barns and the corrals. As usual, he sensed that they did a quick scan, identified him, and left him alone. No reason they should interrupt their morning's work.

"Hey, Ethan. What's up? You escaped the goat pen?"

Ethan nodded but kept his gaze trained on Quinn and the chestnut. They were a far more interesting sight than Josh. "I'm finished, is all."

"Hmm." Josh came to stand beside him. "She's something, isn't she?"

The horse was a gelding, so Josh had to be referring to Quinn. But there could have been a whole crowd of cheerleaders, a throng of glamorous models, and even a herd of cowgirls and Ethan would have assumed he was talking about Quinn. He'd spent several days now waiting for the radiance of her beauty to dim. She was captivating when cranky and undercaffeinated; she was breathtaking at thirty feet away, wielding a hoof pick. The amazing thing about her was that she didn't even make an effort to enhance her allure. She just was.

"Yeah," he replied. No point in saying otherwise. "That's a nice horse. Looks like he's got thoroughbred in him."

"He's a rescue. Apparently he was in real bad shape when Quinn got him. Still spooks at his own shadow."

Ethan could relate.

"So, you into her?"

Ethan shot him a look. "Into her?"

"Yeah. Into her," Josh repeated.

"I babysat her."

The corner of Josh's mouth twitched. "Bet she was something."

"She was four."

"She ain't four now."

For some reason Ethan's fingers had curled into a fist. "Doesn't matter," he said flatly.

"Well, yeah, it does. Because I do like you. The thing is, I like Quinn a whole lot better. I've asked her out, you know. We're going to the local bar Friday night. Word has it that Quinn is very choosy. I'm going to do everything I can to get her to choose me."

"Have a great time."

Josh's smile was slow but didn't stop until it had stretched wide across his face. "I plan to," he said. With a laugh he slapped Ethan's injured shoulder, nearly sending him to his knees. "You and I should grab a beer sometime. Not Friday, though."

Ethan was saved from unlocking his jaw and attempting an articulate reply by Quinn. Finished cleaning out the hoof, she lowered it to the ground, straightened, and gave his rump a pat before moving to stand by his head. Ethan watched her say something as she unsnapped the lead rope attached to the gelding's halter. Releasing him, she stepped back and the horse sprang into motion, a fiery streak tearing across the corral. Midway he bucked, flashing his copper belly and the matching white stockings on his hind legs.

The grin on Quinn's face slipped a fraction when she turned and found the two of them observing her. Bizarrely, that made Ethan happier; Josh didn't rank as high as her horse.

Her dog, Sooner, had been waiting with the patience of Job by one of the corral posts. At a signal from Quinn, he bounded forward, his body quivering, ready to obey his mistress's next command.

"Morning, Josh. Is Pete around?"

"Yeah, he's in the barn. Wheeler's got a cut on his shoulder."

"Bad?"

"No. It won't need stitching. He should be done cleaning it by now. You want me to get him?"

"No, thanks. I'm going to volunteer Ethan's services. Find Pete, Sooner."

The three of them—Josh seemed loath to let Quinn out of his sight—followed the dog toward the horse barn with its sloping roof.

As they neared it, two wranglers came out, carrying lead ropes. Quinn stopped to say hello and then introduced Ethan to them.

He shook their hands and learned that Jim and Rick had worked at Silver Creek for five and seven years, respectively. Unsurprising. The Knowleses were the sort of people to foster loyalty.

"You mind grabbing Chester and Rush's tack, Josh?" Rick asked.

"Sure thing. I'll be there in a few."

"Sounds good. Good to meet you, Ethan."

"Likewise."

With friendly nods the two wranglers continued on their way to the pasture to bring in the horses that would be used on the trail ride that morning.

"So you know horses, Ethan?" Josh asked.

"Some."

"Huh," Josh said.

"That chestnut looks like he's got some Thoroughbred in him."

"Who? Tucker? Yeah, I'd say so, too," Quinn replied.

"Josh told me he's a rescue."

"Yes."

"Good for you."

Her cheekbones became even more pronounced when she smiled in real pleasure. Ethan realized he'd become pretty good at gauging her happiness.

"From what the guys tell me, Quinn's got a whole

menagerie of rescued animals. The one I want to see is the parrot. I hear he's incredible," Josh said.

"He is. No doubt about that," Quinn said with a laugh.

"I've never seen a parrot before. Maybe after we come back from The Drop you can introduce me to him," Josh suggested.

"Um, Alfie goes to sleep pretty early," she answered.

And there it was: a slight tightening in her expression that dimmed the wattage of her smile. Had Josh even noticed?

"Hey, Ethan," Quinn said abruptly. "You should come to The Drop. A bunch of us are going."

Apparently Quinn's ideas about date night at the local bar were distinctly different from Josh's. The look on the Texan's face confirmed he was less than happy about Quinn's spur-of-the-moment invite. He'd lost that *you can't help but love me* grin he'd been flashing her way. Ethan wondered how she would react were she to know that Josh had gone out of his way to stake his claim.

Not your problem, he reminded himself. "No thanks. I prefer drinking alone."

Josh's grin reasserted itself. Quinn's smile dimmed. And Ethan told himself that he was a fool for caring about either one.

THE DROP WAS full of people Quinn knew and many that she loved. The bar—a reconstructed old barn—was her and her brothers' local hangout, their favorite after-hours escape from the demands of being accommodating hosts for nearly 365 days out of the year. The Drop was owned by Nell and Beau Donovan. The couple had bought the barn about five years ago and renovated it, decorating the beamed and whitewashed interior with faded chesterfields, wingback armchairs, tree stump coffee tables, and a long zinc bar that Beau's family had delivered all the way from New Orleans. Nell and Beau ran the place with an unhurried efficiency as attractive as Beau's Louisiana accent. In addition to the comfy chairs and sofas and funky tables, the space was large enough to hold a pool table at one end and a dance floor at the other. Since it was Friday, the place was crowded. People were kicking back and relaxing, racking up the pool balls, twisting to Fats Domino, or leaning against the zinc countertop, sampling the new Harvest IPA that Beau had on tap this week. Everyone looked like they were having a fine time.

Quinn had never been more twitchily claustrophobic. That's what came from feeling like some sort of trophy a certain eager and too charming Texan wanted to bag. At a table with Mia and Tess, she sat hunched over her beer, trying to make herself invisible.

"You could just dance with him, you know," Mia observed.

She scowled at the burl of the tabletop. "Right. You know where dancing leads."

"To a lovely dark corner?" Tess said.

Quinn's tension ratcheted up a notch. "Not helpful, Tess. Don't you have a wedding to go plan?"

"Afraid not. Mine's all set to be absolutely beautiful, and Mia and Reid want to wait until after next year's harvest—"

"And I already know where I want to have the ceremony. On the terrace that Reid built for me," Mia interjected.

"So we've got plenty of time to work out the remaining details for Mia's special day. Although I've already found a dress I think you'll love," Tess said, her expression becoming animated. "It's made of vintage lace."

Quinn groaned. The noise reminded her of the one Ethan had made when she inflicted the Bee Gees and Neil Diamond on him during the drive from the airport. In hindsight she realized how unusually cruel she'd been. But at least she'd relented and put him out of his misery before subjecting him to Neil Sedaka's "Breaking Up Is Hard to Do." Tess could go on about wedding dresses forever.

"No wedding dress talk, please," she begged.

Tess leaned back in her chair and folded her arms across her black scoop-necked sweater. "Then how about you explain why you're hanging with us—not that we don't love you—instead of letting Josh dance with you? He keeps glancing over, by the way, so I'd say your minutes are numbered."

Quinn slumped deeper in her chair. "I thought Mae-beth was doing her best to distract him."

"She is," Tess said.

"She should try harder," Quinn muttered.

"Her heart might not be in it unless he's a Leo," Mia said.

"What?" Quinn straightened in surprise.

"I think she must have consulted an astrologist who read her chart. Apparently she's destined for a Leo," Mia said.

"No," Quinn said.

"Yes indeed. That's why Maebeth knew it would never work out between Reid and her. Remind me to thank your mom for giving birth to him in May," Mia said.

"If I had to guess, I'd say another reason Maebeth might be holding off on giving Josh a full blast of her charm is that it's pretty clear he came here with you tonight," Tess said.

"We came as a group. This is not a *date* date," Quinn insisted.

Mia took a sip of wine—she'd ordered a glass of her own pinot noir, which was understandable since the Bodell Family Winery produced really good stuff. Even Quinn, a rank wine ignoramus, could taste its superiority. "Gee, Quinn, I never expected you to react this way to Josh being interested in you. What don't you like about him? He gets along with everyone at the ranch—your mom can't say enough good things about him."

Tess nodded in agreement. "That's right. She was tell-ing me just the other day how well he handled the fe-male guest who came a-knocking on his cabin door the other night. He marched her right back to the lodge be-fore her husband could even miss her."

The guest's name was Sally. She'd been even more de-termined than Katherine, the woman who'd wanted to ride with Josh on the trail and maybe take some "private lessons," too.

Tess wasn't finished singing Josh's praises. "He's quick-witted, cute, and likes horses as much as you. What's stopping you from seeing whether you guys hit it off?"

Only about six cringe-worthy attempts at sex, that's what, Quinn retorted silently. Looking at her friends' expectant faces, she wondered whether maybe Tess and Mia had joined forces with her mother in her quest to pair off every person on the planet. She tamped down the thought. That road led to true paranoia. "I do like Josh. I just find him a little overwhelming, that's all." Actually, what she found overwhelming was what Josh represented: a man who was interested in her sexually.

Mia patted her forearm. "I can sympathize. Josh is kind of like Reid that way. They both can turn a woman's brain to mush with just a smile. But at least in your case it's a level playing field. Josh might have met his match in the looks department."

Quinn gave her friend a hard look. "Don't start that again. I thought you'd kicked the habit of selling yourself short, Mia. Don't you know Reid goes all goofy when you walk into a room?"

Mia's smile lit up their corner of the bar. "He does kind of, doesn't he?"

Quinn resisted the urge to shake her head in despair. "Yeah, kinda. But with Josh and me, it's not a question of a level playing field, it's one of leagues. It's obvious Josh plays in the majors." Whereas she hadn't even made it out of the peewee league when it came to sexual experience. It was hard to think of a metaphor for striking out when one had a vagina. Refusing to take the plunge? Blocked? Just another example of how ill-equipped she was . . .

"Now who's selling herself short?" Tess asked.

"Huh?" For a second she was scared Tess had read her thoughts. "Oh, you mean about Josh? Believe me, I'm not." She glanced about the bar, and when her gaze landed on the man in question, she lowered it quickly, pretending a rapt absorption in the condensation forming on her beer. "I wish Ethan had come along," she said abruptly. "He's spending too much time by himself."

"Ethan Saunders? I imagine he's flat-out exhausted from all the work he's been doing. Ward says he's pushing himself pretty hard," Tess said.

"My point exactly. He should be unwinding. Having some fun with the guys. Holing up with his demons can't be good."

"Have you been able to get him to talk about Afghanistan at all?" Mia asked.

She shook her head. "He's awfully good at shutting a person down," she said, recalling the look he'd given her when she'd asked why he refused to continue with his photography.

"I can see how that might be," Mia said. "We have to respect that."

Mia would definitely empathize with Ethan's hurt. She had a lot of pain she'd kept bottled up inside her. She'd lost her mother really young, never knew her father, and then had grown up with her cousin Jay, the sociopath who'd sabotaged their family winery and attempted to kill her dog, Bruno. Thank God things were better for Mia now. Not perfect, given how much wine had been lost, but at least Mia had Reid's love and support as well as all the Knowleses'.

But Afghanistan . . . the war took "bad" to a whole new realm, one where Quinn was totally out of her depths. She sighed. "The thing is, it's hard to question a guy about a crazy war in the Middle East at six A.M. when he's milking one of your nanny goats. I need to find something to get him more involved. He's too isolated."

"He does have that solitary loner quality to him, doesn't he? But Ward really likes him."

"Reid does, too."

"I was thinking he needs a dog," Quinn said.

"A dog?" Tess said blankly.

"It worked for Mia, didn't it?"

"True. Bruno came into my life and made it a million times better."

"As I recall, another male had already begun working his magic on you," Tess said with a wicked grin that had Mia blushing.

Quinn pretended not to notice. "I was originally considering loaning Alfie to Ethan—"

The chorus was instantaneous: "Alfie?" with Tess adding, "Quinn, you've got to be kidding."

She shrugged. "You can't deny he has a certain charm, and he's definitely attention-grabbing. But I may have abused Ethan's ears enough when I forced him to listen to the playlist I made for Mom. Besides, Alfie's cage would take up too much space in his cabin. So a dog it is." As she spoke, the idea of finding a dog for Ethan grew ever more urgent. She could easily picture some rescued canine curled up on the sofa beside him. She bet he wouldn't even be aware of it when his hand moved to stroke its fur. "Because really, is there any better therapy than unconditional canine love—at least until Ethan's strong enough to get on a horse?"

Her friends exchanged smiles. "No, Quinn, there isn't," they said in unison.

"And you have been talking about getting another herding dog for Sooner to teach his tricks to," Tess added.

"Ethan definitely strikes me as a working-dog kind of guy," Mia said.

"Yes, and yes again. Wow," Quinn said marveling. "Who'd've thought a girl from Queens, New York, and a wine geek would make such awesome soon-to-be sisters-in-law?"

"Kindly remember that thought the next time you try to convince me to lope on Brocco and I refuse," Tess replied.

"Come on, Tess, I'm only trying to correct a gross error of judgment. You're going to love his lope. It's as easy as sitting in a rocking chair. And I have a feeling Mia's itching to see what Glory can do in a higher gear."

"Quinn," Mia said, leaning forward to pat her hand, "this is what we vintners call wishful thinking."

"It's what the rest of the world calls it, too," Tess added dryly.

"To be clear, there will be no loping until after the auction for our wine. I'll need all my energy—and limbs—for that," Mia said.

"Come on, I've seen the way you both watch Ward and Reid when they ride out."

"Sorry to disillusion you, Quinn, but what we're actually thinking about is how they're going to look when they ride back. All sweaty."

"And a little dirty," Mia said, making Tess laugh.

"And in need of a long, hot shower—"

"And maybe some other things."

"Amen to that."

The two clinked their glasses in camaraderie.

"You are so shallow," Quinn said.

"Mmm." Tess nodded. "And happy."

"Oh!" Mia straightened in her chair.

From the sudden sparkle in Mia's eyes, Quinn didn't have to work her brain too hard to guess who was approaching their table.

Tess tucked a lock of her dark hair behind her ears. Another tell.

Quinn glanced over her shoulder to welcome her brothers, and her tension, momentarily relieved by her friends' conversation, returned. Josh was with them. A little wildly, she scanned the bar's interior for Maebeth, thinking to call the woman over and give her a talking-to about the folly of pinning her romantic hopes on an astrology chart. This town was too small for that kind of nonsense. The number of available men born under the sign of Leo might be a big fat donut hole.

The woman was nowhere in sight. And wasn't that perverse, because Maebeth knew how to make herself *seen*.

"Hey, Quinn, feel like a dance?"

She really wanted to say no. But now she had four pairs of eyes and ears trained on her. To refuse to dance would only lead to questions. And Ray Charles was singing. Everyone would know something was wrong if she didn't get up and dance.

At least she could set the stage for an early departure. "I'm not very good," she warned as they made their way to the dance floor.

"That's okay. I am."

The Texan hadn't been exaggerating. He had the moves. Within seconds of stepping on the dance floor, Josh had her twirling, dipping, and spinning before reeling her back to the hard wall of his chest with the same confidence he showed in everything else, and drawing her close as he settled his large hand against the small of her back. Just as panic set in and she began to recall the hurt and angry faces of every other guy she'd attempted to get physical with—a collage of disappointment—he would release her with an easy fling of his arm so she twirled like a top.

The second time he whirled her back into his arms, he

grinned down at her. "What do you mean, you're not good at this?"

"This is all you, I promise."

"Need a partner to make the dance fun. Dang, you look pretty tonight. And you smell nice, too. I like your perfume." He dipped his head.

Freaked, she blurted, "Do you know that ambergris, a time-honored ingredient in perfume, is made from the fatty excretion of a sperm whale? And that musk comes from the anal glands of civets?"

Josh's brows drew together in confusion. "Come again?"

"I'm not wearing any." When he still looked baffled, she clarified. "Perfume."

"Oh, yeah. Right. I guess a woman who looks like you doesn't need it. You clean up good, Quinn."

It was true, she had taken a shower. Between the dust from the trail ride she'd led in the morning and then the lanolin coating her from neck to toe after grappling with the Lincoln sheep so Mel could deworm them, Quinn had looked a little like Pigpen in the *Peanuts* comic strip, with her own personal dirt cloud. But to guard against encouraging Josh into thinking this was anything more than a group outing, she'd gone out of her way to dress as she did around the livestock. Along with her jeans and boots she wore a long-sleeved Henley. Once a deep eggplant purple, it was now after many washings a soft lavender.

"Uh, thanks. So where'd you learn to dance?" she asked in the hope of steering the conversation away from how she looked or smelled.

"There were a couple of honky-tonks in the town closest to the ranch. The ladies sure loved to dance. So I learned."

Deftly he spun her and then, with a mischievous grin,

dipped her low over his arm, holding her there as the last notes of the song ended.

His face was inches away. "Feeling a little dizzy here, Josh," she said breathlessly.

"Dizzy looks good on you, Quinn." Slowly he pulled her back up, this time letting her feel every inch of his hard body, and grinning even more widely as the onlookers clapped their hands.

"Thanks for the dance." She took a wide step back so she could breathe. "It's, um, getting late and I have a ton of stuff lined up tomorrow."

"Yeah, me too," he said. "Mind if I bum a ride back to the ranch? I don't think Jim's ready to leave yet."

Yup, Josh surely had the moves.

Chapter
TEN

BEING A SEXUAL failure and secret virgin was an exhausting business, Quinn decided as she drove Josh back to the ranch. She spent a good portion of the three-mile trip pretending that everything was hunky-dory, that it was okay that Josh had his arm casually slung across the back of her seat. After all, he wasn't doing anything; it wasn't his fault that while he was talking about how great a foreman Pete was and how much he liked the other wranglers and interacting with the ranch guests—except the ladies who came on too strong—she was holding a mental debate about whether it would be too obvious if she parked the truck close to Josh's cabin so she wouldn't have to deal with him asking to come inside her house.

Josh was a chatterbox compared to the last man who'd ridden in her truck, she thought with a certain nostalgia for Ethan's taciturn presence. There'd been no need to worry about deflecting a pass from him.

She wondered what kind of woman would rouse Ethan's interest. A sophisticated globe-trotter like him? A journalist? Or would he go for a temperamental artist? Maybe he was already involved with someone. Her brows drew together in a frown as she pulled into the staff parking area and turned off the ignition. While she'd been obsessing about the possible women in Ethan's life, the rest of her had obviously come to a decision: best to park here rather than at her place. Now all she needed to do was make a quick exit and she could go home, where she wouldn't have to think about men and have her brain reduced to a gloopy mess.

She hopped out of the truck, aware that her heart was beating faster than normal. Determined not to betray her nervousness, she adopted a brisk tone. "Well, that was really nice." She shoved her hands deep in her pockets and walked with her arms locked by her sides.

Josh ambled beside her with that easy, rolling gait. "Yeah, it was."

When they got to the row of cabins reserved for the staff, she noticed that most were dark. But the windows in Ethan's glowed bright. She wondered what he was up to at this hour of the night.

Josh came to a stop and so she did, too, because it would've looked weird otherwise.

She glanced about, up and down, looking everywhere but at his broad chest or, heaven forbid, his face with his wide, slanting cheekbones and firm lips. He really was almost ridiculously attractive.

She swallowed. "I, uh, I'm going to head off now." She even took her balled hand out of her pocket to point up the path in case he didn't know where she lived. Could she be any dorkier?

The corner of his mouth twitched. "Okay."

Somehow he'd moved closer, taken one of those smooth steps he'd exhibited on the dance floor. "Mind if I kiss you, Quinn?"

A thousand excuses sprang to mind. Was she that chicken? "Uh, I guess not."

His lips parted in a smile, and then his head was descending, tilting on a slight angle as it did. She waited, frozen, for his lips to touch hers.

Josh's kiss was like so much else about him. Practiced and confident, it held the promise of a good time. His lips remained firm, not all of a sudden feeling too wet or mushy or creepily suction-cup-like—and yes, she'd experienced all of those distressing transformations. They moved over hers in an unhurried exploration, sampling and learning.

She should respond and kiss him back, she knew that.

An unexpected thump had her jumping backward out of the loose circle of Josh's arms. The noise was followed by another one, a loud bang. She turned her head to locate the source and identify the sounds. The thump had come from chair legs hitting the narrow porch belonging to Ethan's cabin. The slam of the screen door as Ethan went inside had caused the sharp bang.

Ethan must have been sitting in the darkened space between the door and the window, his chair tipped back so that it rested against the cabin's rough timber siding. Had he watched Josh kiss her? The idea made her strangely queasy.

Josh seemed unfazed by the interruption. He reached up, skimming his fingers along her cheek as he carefully tucked a strand of her hair behind her ear. "You're real pretty, Quinn. I've been thinking about kissing you since I came here."

"Josh, I'm not sure I'm ready to—"

"Hey, I didn't say that to pressure you. I just like you, Quinn." He touched her cheek again. "Do you like me?"

"Well, yeah." It was the truth. Josh was a nice guy. And the kiss he'd given her hadn't been bad, she reminded herself. It was really possible he possessed the necessary skill to make her relaxed enough to eventually consider sex. And that was a good thing. Because it was clearly past time she got over her hang-up, did the deed, and joined the rest of the world. "Yeah, I like you," she repeated, trying her damnedest to sound assured.

"Okay, then." Slowly he brushed the pad of his thumb over her bottom lip. "We'll see how things go."

She could only smile weakly, all too aware of just how terribly things could go.

Quinn was roused from sleep by a loud hammering on her front door. She squinted blearily at her bedside clock. It was two-thirty. In Quinn's experience, with the exception of lambing, calving, and foaling season, nothing good ever happened at two-thirty A.M.

The knocking had roused her animals. Sooner began barking, and Pirate leapt off the bed as if it were on fire. Swinging her legs over the edge of the mattress, she hurried toward the door, her bare feet slapping the cold wood floor. She yanked it open to find Ethan outside.

"Quiet, Sooner," she said distractedly, her eyes never leaving Ethan. "What is it? What's wrong?"

"Your horse—"

Her heart lurched. "Domino?"

He shook his head. "Not the Appaloosa. The chestnut. Tucker. He's acting strange. I think he's sick."

Sick. The word was like the firing of the starter's gun. She sprinted back to her bedroom, scooped her jeans off the floor, pulled on some socks, and plucked a sweater from a chair and dragged it over her T-shirt, already running out of her room and toward the mudroom next to the kitchen. There she shoved her feet into a pair of boots. In the kitchen she grabbed her cellphone. Jamming it into her pocket, she ran back to where Ethan stood and blew past him, Sooner on her heels.

*   *   *

The moon was bright enough to confirm what Ethan had said. Tucker stood in the pasture near the fence. Normally he carried his head high, alert to every noise and movement. But when Quinn ran up to the fence line with Ethan, who'd caught up, he didn't even raise his head. His muzzle inches from the ground, he pawed the dirt with his right foreleg.

Then the gelding sank to his knees. That's when she saw his heaving flank. It was covered with dirt.

"Oh, no!" Quickly she ducked between the rails to reach him. Grabbing his halter, she tugged it and clucked loudly.

Though Tucker pinned his ears, he didn't shy, rear, or even swing his head and bare his teeth. She'd have preferred any of those reactions to the horse's obvious determination to lie down.

"Come *on,* Tucker. Up, up," she repeated, tugging on the halter until he finally rose to a stand. "Thank God," she said, exhaling in relief.

"What's wrong with him?"

"I'm pretty sure it's colic. I've got to walk him to keep him from rolling. Can you get me a lead rope? They're—"

"I know." And he was off, running. She spared a thought for what the flat-out sprints were doing to his shoulder, but then Tucker dropped his head to the ground once more, and her worry for her gelding eclipsed all else.

She'd gotten Tucker to the gate when Ethan ran back with the lead rope bunched in his left hand. Instead of swinging his right arm, he held it locked against his side. While he may have taken on more and more jobs around the horses over the past few days, he was far from pain-free. She was going to owe him big-time for tonight.

"Thanks," she said as he passed her the lead line. She snapped it on Tucker's halter while Ethan opened the gate. When she and Tucker walked through the opening, the horse didn't so much as flinch at the strange man standing close enough to touch him.

At any other moment Quinn would have been grinning from ear to ear. Right now his lack of response filled her with fear. She glanced over her shoulder.

Now that they were nearer the barns there was more light, thanks to the floodlights attached to their exteriors, and she was able to see the gelding more clearly. The dirt sticking to his side was thick, clumpy. A bad sign. How many times had he been down, trying to relieve the pain in his gut by rolling?

"I need to call the vet." Even as she spoke, she shoved her hand in her front pocket for her cell and began scrolling for the number. Every member of her family—Pete Williams, too—had Gary Cooney, the best large-animal vet in the area, programmed in their address books. Anxiety made her clumsy. She bobbled the phone. Her cry of dismay as it slipped from her hand turned into a gasp of surprise when Ethan caught it.

"Here." Straightening, he pressed the phone into her hand. "Give me the rope. I'll walk him while you telephone."

"Tucker won't let you—"

"Call the vet, Quinn. I'll take him." He took the rope from her and stepped up to the gelding.

For a second she opened her mouth to argue, but then snapped it shut. Though Tucker's gait was sluggish, his hooves practically scraping the crushed gravel, he nonetheless followed Ethan's lead, the two circling the open space in front of the barns.

Gary Cooney answered on the third ring. "Cooney," he said, sounding remarkably alert for someone answering the phone at close to three in the morning.

"Gary? It's Quinn Knowles. It's my horse Tucker, the rescue. I think he's got colic. I don't know when it started—sometime after the six P.M. feeding, I guess. It looks like he's already rolled. And he's still trying to. I'm worried. Can you come out?"

Over the line, Cooney exhaled heavily. "Unfortunately, I'm covering for a colleague who's on vacation. I'm on my way to a farm west of Willits. A prize bull escaped and ended up entangled in a neighbor's barbed wire fence. I'm almost there now, but I can't predict how long I'll be."

"Tucker's in a bad way, Gary."

"You're walking him?"

"Yes."

"Good, but let him rest, too, unless he tries to roll again. No food, no drink—"

"Banamine?"

"No medications, either. Nothing until I can examine him. I'd have you take him to the hospital now, but my assistants would essentially be doing the same as you— walking him—and the strange environment might only add to his stress and agitation. I'll be there just as soon as I can."

"Okay." She pressed the off button and hung her head. "Damn," she whispered.

"He can't get here?"

"No. Not yet. There's an injured bull near Willits."

"So?"

"So I have to keep him on his feet. I don't know what's caused the colic, but it's possible that by rolling he's made his condition worse. Rolling can end up twisting the small intestine. And that can be fatal." She swallowed. She couldn't dwell on that. What Tucker needed was for her to follow Cooney's instructions, and when he arrived he would save her horse. Pocketing her phone, she went over to Ethan. She stretched out her hand, ready to take the lead from him. "You don't have to stay—"

"Screw that," he said bluntly. "I'm not going to leave you alone for who knows how long until the vet shows."

She looked at him. He was still thin. He was still hurting. His cheeks were covered in a three A.M. stubble. But it struck her that Ethan was a handsome man.

His weren't the features of a cover model—Ethan's face was more ascetic, with sharper planes. And though his deep-socketed eyes were still shrouded by whatever had happened to him in Afghanistan, they radiated keen intelligence. For some reason his sharp features and enigmatic gaze reminded her of the wolves at Wolf Peak: beautiful and mysterious.

When he cocked an eyebrow and said, "So, we should walk him, right?" she shook herself mentally, abruptly aware that she'd been staring at him. Linking him to the wolves in her mind was as foolish as it was romantic. Quinn could only imagine how hard Ethan would laugh if he had the slightest notion of her thoughts. For her part, she decided to blame them on worry. It could do a number on a normally sane mind.

"Thanks for sticking around." She fell into step beside him.

"No reason to thank me. I owe your family. I could walk Tucker into December and I'd still be in your debt."

That didn't sit well. "You don't owe us anything. We're friends. Besides, you're already earning your keep. And in my book, alerting me that something was wrong with Tucker puts me in *your* debt. How'd you find him?"

Ethan shrugged his left shoulder. "I was walking around down here. I do that sometimes. I happened to notice that Tucker wasn't sleeping like the other horses in the pasture. He wasn't even resting near them, and usually he likes to stand near his buddies, especially that big fellow—"

"Harper," Quinn supplied.

"Yeah, and that bay, who's their sidekick."

"Bristol. He and Harper have been Tucker's pasture buddies since he was cleared by Cooney—the ranch's vet—and allowed to mingle with the herd." She reached out to stroke the chestnut's neck. It was too warm for her liking. Fever?

"The vet will come, Quinn," he said quietly.

"I know." She pushed back the fear for her horse.

Ethan began talking again. "Anyway, something about him caught my attention. He wasn't behaving normally. He's often restless, but then he settles down with his head near Bristol's withers, right?"

"Yeah. You've noticed a lot about him." It didn't come as a great surprise. The man was observant. After all, he'd been able to identify each of her goats in a couple of days' time. She imagined he probably looked at things as if he were holding his camera and focusing his lens on them, seeing details others missed. "But why were you down at the pastures? I, uh, saw you go into your cabin after Josh and I . . ." Her voice trailed away.

"Kissed?" His tone was dry.

"Yeah. Sorry if we, um, disturbed you."

"Why would I be disturbed? Who you kiss is your own business."

Her cheeks went hot in the cool night. "Well, yeah . . ."

"I was out here because I couldn't sleep. That's all. It had nothing to do with you or Josh. I simply miscalculated."

"Miscalculated?"

"I should have had two more shots of whiskey."

It took her a second to understand. "That's what you take to sleep? Whiskey?"

"That's right. I'd rather chug Jack Daniel's over popping pills any day or night." He brought Tucker to a halt. "Do you know what you're doing?"

His words rang in the sudden stillness. "What I'm doing? What do you mean?"

"With Josh," he said with a trace of impatience.

"Oh."

"Do you know what you're doing with him?"

No. "Sure I do."

A long moment passed. Then he shrugged. "To each his own."

"What's that supposed to mean?" she asked.

"Nothing."

"Josh is nice."

"Can't argue with that."

"He's a really good dancer."

His mouth flattened. "Essential, for sure."

"And he knows how to kiss. Exceptionally well." She was sure of it, never mind that his kiss hadn't done a whole lot for her. At least it hadn't sent her running for the hills. "So as far as I can see, there's no downside to my spending time with him."

"Like I said, to each his own."

She narrowed her eyes and would have pressed him to explain exactly what he meant by the obnoxious comment, but at that moment Tucker lowered his nose to the ground and folded his knees. "Oh God, he's going down. Pull on his lead. I'll poke him in the ribs. We can't let him roll."

He'd lied to her.

A full day's work helping the ranch hands, followed by the exercise routine he'd devised in his cabin and topped off with a nightcap consisting of three shots of whiskey, should have been amply sufficient for the job of knocking him out for the count. A tried-and-true recipe, the combination of physical exhaustion and the anesthetizing properties of the alcohol let him pass at least a few hours in a dead-to-the-world sprawl on his bed. But seeing Josh wrap his arms about Quinn, cover her mouth with his, and then kiss her lingeringly had messed with Ethan's head. When he retreated to his cabin, the room had shrunk two sizes.

He'd remained inside until he couldn't take it anymore—and until he was sure they were gone. Escaping his cabin, he went out to breathe in deep draughts of the cold night air in the hopes it would quash the need to drive his fist into something that looked an awful lot like Josh's face. Deciding to walk off his anger, he headed toward the barns. All was quiet and shuttered for the night.

It was peaceful there, so he lingered by the pastures, following the dark line of fence until he reached a clump of horses sleeping together. Resting his forearms against the top rail, he stared into the night. By then his eyes had grown accustomed to the darkness and he noticed something was amiss with one of the horses. It was the chestnut that Quinn had adopted. The gelding kept lowering his head, but not in a natural way, more stiffly, and then shifting his weight from side to side. He'd never seen a horse do that repeatedly, fixedly.

For a fraction of a second he hesitated to go to Quinn's. What if the kiss had been a prelude? Damned if he wanted to interrupt any more scenes between her and Josh. But then he recalled the way Quinn's face lit up when she talked about Tucker. He turned on his boot heels and hustled up the road to her house.

That's when he was treated to his second torture of the night: Quinn answering the door clad in a gray T-shirt that had THE MIGHTY QUINN emblazoned across the front. The shirt's hem barely reached the top of her thighs, which left a whole lot of not just mighty but naked Quinn to admire.

She liked hot-pink panties. They played peek-a-boo with him as she ran back to her bedroom to change. He was pretty sure that image of Quinn with her long slim legs pumping and her panties flashing was forever burned into his retinas.

Other parts of him caught fire, too.

As he tamped down the unwanted flames that licked him, he kept his gaze fixed in the direction of her bedroom, half expecting a heavy-lidded and smug-looking Josh to stroll out from there. But only Quinn emerged. Dressed now, she tore past him, Sooner a furry streak at her heels.

If Quinn hadn't been so distracted by Tucker's colic, he was sure she'd have caught that he was lying through his teeth when he said that witnessing her and Josh's kiss hadn't caused tonight's bout of insomnia. She'd have certainly called bullshit when he blurted that tired line, *To each his own.*

Except in Quinn's case it wasn't some trite truism—or shouldn't be.

She should be with someone who understood her and appreciated how exceptional, how simply and unfailingly wonderful she was.

But it wasn't his place to tell her that she was amazing and that Josh had more flash than substance, so he dodged her question. And then Tucker scared the shit out of them both by trying to drop to his knees in the middle of the crushed-stone courtyard.

Luckily, between his tugging on the lead and Quinn's jabbing him in the ribs, they got him moving again. For once Ethan didn't relish the silence, because it would allow Quinn to worry about how much pain Tucker was in.

"You cold?" he asked to distract her.

"No." Her teeth clicked together, her body blatantly contradicting her words.

So Quinn Knowles wasn't good at being taken care of. Funny, that.

"Here." He passed her the lead and shrugged out of his jean jacket. "Put this on. You're shivering. The last thing you need is to catch a chill."

She must have been freezing, for she accepted it with a wan smile, shoving her arms into the sleeves as she walked. "With no rain, it's easy to forget it's November—almost Thanksgiving. You'll be here for the holiday?"

"Yeah." Then, remembering he wanted her to talk, which meant he would have to as well, he said, "Why?"

The shoulders of his jacket flapped a bit when she shrugged. "I simply wondered whether you'd be traveling back east to see your parents or maybe a close friend."

"No. I need to keep some distance from my family. They're okay now that I'm here. Less worried." Another reason he owed the Knowleses. "But going back east involves . . . expectations." Expectations that would inevitably lead to disappointments. Along with the messages from his parents wanting updates on how he was doing, he'd received a half dozen emails and texts from Erin Miller, his editor, asking about the photographs he'd taken in Afghanistan. She had a writer lined up for the introduction who was eager to work with him. But as he'd already told Erin, his agent, Roger Snowe, and his parents, the pictures weren't going to see the light of day, contract be damned.

Realizing the silence had gone on too long, he cleared his throat and said, "So what about you? You have plans for Thanksgiving? I remember your parents would pull out all the stops for the holiday."

If she was surprised that he'd suddenly turned into a chatterbox, she didn't show it.

"Yeah. They love that stuff. I guess I do, too, but not when it comes to Thanksgiving. Knowing that forty-six million turkeys will meet their bloody demise isn't cause for celebration in my opinion."

"So, no fighting over the drumstick for you. Vegetarian?" he guessed.

"Yup." The set of her chin told him she was prepared for a snide comment.

"Makes sense."

"It does? Well, yeah, of course it does," she amended hurriedly. "Not many people see it that way, though. The cattle rancher's daughter, and all that." She gave another shrug. "Anyway, the whole feasting-on-big-dead-birds thing isn't for me. And there's no friend you're going to leave brokenhearted by your absence?"

He looked at her and cocked an eyebrow. "Brokenhearted? Are you asking me if I have a girlfriend?"

"You mean am I being intrusive? Only fair, isn't it, after your sage comments about Josh? So, yes or no?"

His lips twitched but he suppressed his smile. "No girlfriend. Had one. Dara and I called it quits before I left for Afghanistan. We decided it was for the best." And though he'd liked Dara a lot, he was relieved he didn't have to deal with her expectations any more than anyone else's. "Last time I heard from her she'd started dating a Spanish artist she represents."

"Represents?"

"Dara owns the Brendel Gallery in New York City, where I've had some shows."

She looked like she was about to ask him another question, but just then the rumble of a car engine reached them. Quinn checked her watch. "That must be Gary Cooney. Thank God."

* * *

The vet examined Tucker from head to tail, checking his gums, probing his belly, listening for gut noises, taking his temperature, and then finally performing a rectal exam. Standing on either side, Ethan and Quinn had held the gelding steady throughout. It was no challenge at all.

Tucker's lack of resistance, lack of response in general, alarmed Quinn. She'd have actually welcomed a display of his normal skittishness.

Stepping back, Cooney removed the surgical gloves and cleaned his hands and arms off with antiseptic wipes.

"I felt a torsion in the small intestine, Quinn. I'm sorry, but he's going to need surgery."

She stroked the side of Tucker's face. "I was worried that might be the case."

"Colic surgery is not an inexpensive procedure. To give you a rough estimate, you're looking at a final bill of around ten thousand dollars. Maybe more," Cooney said. "The success rate for surgery is higher than it used to be, but there can always be problems, and I've only been able to feel a part of the intestine. When I open Tucker up, I may discover he's in far worse shape than I anticipated. In which case you'll have to consider putting him down. Then, too, there are the possible post-operative complications, the long convalescence—"

Quinn cut him off. "I understand what you're saying, Gary, and how serious colic can be. I know what's involved, the costs as well as the risks. But I still want you to perform the surgery." She had enough money in her savings account.

Cooney nodded. "That's what I thought you'd say. I'd be irresponsible if I didn't give you the complete picture. Okay, then. Let's get him to the clinic. I'll have my staff at the ready so we can start as soon as possible. Will you be able to load him?"

"He's too sick to flip out. The van's in the tractor shed."

She turned to Ethan, but before she even opened her mouth, he said, "I'll help you take him to the clinic. Do you want to bring Sooner, too?"

In all of this, her dog had been crouched at the perimeter of the circle they'd been walking, waiting for Quinn to finish. And Ethan had the wits to think of him. Something clogged her throat, making speech impossible. With a nod, she turned and ran to the shed.

FIVE HOURS LATER, Quinn turned the empty horse van into the private road that led to Silver Creek Ranch. Ever since Gary Cooney pronounced the words *torsion, small intestine,* and *surgery,* she had been functioning on automatic. She was used to animals in pain, their bodies bloodied and broken from being hit by a car, beaten by a human, or caught in the relentless jaws of a hunter's trap. Seeing Tucker suffering was different. Perhaps it was because when she'd adopted him, she vowed to keep him safe. Yet there he was, in agony once again, and it was possible that nothing might save him this time.

But now the surgery was over. The incision Gary Cooney had made along Tucker's abdomen was stitched, and the vet was guardedly optimistic about the gelding's chances for a recovery. With the attendants monitoring him for the next twenty-four hours, there was nothing else to do but climb into the van with Ethan and head back to the ranch. And now that she'd reached their destination, the adrenaline that had been pumping through her system fizzled, leaving her drained. She gripped the steering wheel tightly, certain that otherwise she would slide right off the seat to land in a heap by the pedals.

Ethan had already propped her up too many times. Propped her up and kept her from losing it completely. Were she to teeter on the edge again, as she had when they were walking Tucker together or later as she watched the clock's hands for hours in the clinic's waiting room, she knew he'd be there, murmuring something or laying his hand on her arm, the pressure light but somehow, like the rumble of his voice, instantly calming.

Her gaze slid to the right and took in the angles of his profile, his aquiline nose, the sharp slash of his cheekbones, the jut of his jaw. Why hadn't she seen it before? she wondered, irritated at herself. She supposed she'd been so taken aback by the grayness of his pallor and the toll inflicted by his injuries that she had missed what now struck her as obvious. Ethan Saunders was as strong as the planes of his face.

She wasn't dumb or naive. She recognized that what he'd lived through in Afghanistan must have been bad. Terrible.

But in seeing him more clearly now, she realized that the flesh wounds alone wouldn't be reason for him to turn his back on his normal life or to put away his camera. There must be a deeper trauma he'd suffered, a hurt so devastating it had made him seek refuge at Silver Creek. She now suspected that he wasn't convalescing so much as exiling himself.

She needed to discover what else had happened to him. Maybe there was a way to help him.

"Ethan?"

He'd been looking down at his knee, next to where Sooner's black muzzle rested—the dog was sitting in the space by Ethan's boots. At the sound of her voice, both males turned their heads. Only one spoke. "Yeah?"

Ethan's gaze held hers for a second, and then it sharpened. "What's wrong? Are you okay?"

"About as okay as I can be. Why?"

"You look funny."

Right. No empty flattery with Ethan. "I was only going to say— *Damn*," she muttered under her breath, unable to finish her sentence. They'd reached the main lodge, and she saw her family hurrying through its carved double doors. Someone must have been keeping watch.

She braked, and they quickly surrounded the trailer. Accompanying her parents and brothers were Mia, Tess, and Roo Rodgers, the ranch's pastry chef. As she opened her door and slid to the ground, she caught Roo's Australian accent among the other voices as the questions came thick and fast: *What happened? What did Cooney say? Will Tucker be all right? Why didn't you call? What can we do?*

Despite her exhaustion, Quinn smiled. Her family could be as annoying as the best of them, but they were always there for her, ready to show how much they cared when she needed it. And she didn't need to walk into the lodge's enormous kitchen to know that Roo would have been engaged in some serious baking this morning or that Jeff would have whipped up some sort of veggie dish or frittata to ensure she had enough protein. They'd be plying her with comfort food for the next week.

She glanced around. No guests were wandering around, so she let out a piercing whistle. Her mother frowned but, like the rest of them, fell silent. Quinn knew to take advantage of the moment.

"We have Ethan to thank. He's the one who found Tucker. We were lucky enough to get him walking and call Cooney before the intestinal tissue started to die. Even so, he'd rolled—"

"So it was colic?" Ward asked.

"Yeah. Sorry I didn't text. I was . . ." *Too panicked to type,* she thought.

"Busy praying?" Mia supplied sympathetically.

"Pretty much." She shared a small sad smile with Mia, who understood. She'd been through a very similar hell when her dog, Bruno, had been near death.

"What did Cooney find, sweetheart?" her dad asked.

"During his initial exam here, he found a small intestinal torsion. Unfortunately, there's more. Once he was able to open Tucker up, he discovered an impaction in the large colon. Tucker had ingested a fair amount of sand. He couldn't pass it."

"Sand? But we put the hay on mats or use a feeder."

Reid spoke up. "That's true, Dad, but I've seen Tucker nudge his hay around when he eats. A lot ends up on the ground. He and Gomez both do that."

"That's what Cooney thought might have caused it," Quinn said. "Thanks to the drought, the ground has turned into a giant sandlot. So from here on out we have to keep Gomez and Tucker from playing with their hay."

"We'd better tell Pete to keep an eye on all the horses at feeding time, just to be safe," her mother said.

"Cooney suggested that for the ones who insist on eating their hay on the ground, we should supplement their feed with psyllium."

"I'll let Pete know. Damn, I hate this drought," Ward said.

"It's even worse south of us," her dad observed. Shifting his attention to Ethan, he said, "So our thanks are in order?"

She watched Ethan scan the faces encircling them.

"I simply found Tucker, that's all." His tone was as guarded as his expression.

"Ethan did way more than that, Dad," she contradicted. "Not everyone would have realized there was something off with Tucker—not with only the moon-light to go by. And he helped me walk him."

"Tucker let you near him?" Reid asked.

"The horse was sick."

Obstinate man, Quinn thought. From the quick duck of Reid's dark blond head, she guessed he was amused by Ethan's refusal to take any credit for saving Tucker. Her parents were less circumspect. They were beaming at him. Naturally enough, they all remembered how Tucker had been when he first arrived at Silver Creek. He only allowed Ward to approach because her brother had a bucket from which he dribbled precious grain on the ground. Since then Tucker hadn't let men approach him, even the ones he saw every day.

"And Ethan also helped me load him in the van." *Plus he kept me calm in the waiting room—as calm as I could be. And he instinctively knew that having Sooner there to stroke would soothe me,* she added silently. But her family and Roo didn't need to know how far Ethan's helpfulness had extended beyond getting Tucker to Gary Cooney's clinic, because then their expressions would become speculative, and a barrage of questions would ensue. Questions that would involve her. Questions she wasn't ready to answer.

"So what's Cooney's prognosis?"

Despite her fatigue, Quinn smiled at Ward. He was a bit of a control freak, her brother, always wanting to have the facts laid out so he could act accordingly. The trait would have been supremely annoying except it made him really good at running the guest ranch.

"Guardedly optimistic," she replied. "Cooney was able to extract the sand from the colon and cut out the twisted portion of the intestine. Tucker was still under the effects of the anesthesia when he came out and talked to us. He wants Tucker to stay at the clinic for five days, maybe more. Then he'll come home to several weeks of stall rest. Cooney didn't sugarcoat the gravity of his condition or pretend he's out of the woods, but I figure Tucker's a survivor." She was counting on it.

"And he's receiving the best of care," her mom said.

"I'll talk to Pete about a stall for Tucker. I don't know how well he's going to handle being confined for that long," Ward said.

"He might do better if he could have his buddies Harper and Bristol next to him," Ethan said.

She was becoming familiar with the lump that would choke her whenever Ethan showed this part of himself. It was a big, messy clump of emotion. Sweet but scary. She swallowed hard.

Ward nodded. "Good idea."

"Excellent one," her dad said.

"So Gary will keep us updated, right, Quinn?" Reid said.

Her mother answered before she could open her mouth. Quinn was grateful, because now that the adrenaline had left her system, she was beginning to feel like crap. "Of course he will. He's a terrific vet and he knows how much Quinn cares about Tucker. I'm more worried about you, Quinn. You look terrible, darling."

And to think some people claimed Adele Knowles was the soul of tact. "I'm fine, Mom."

"Well, how about a cuppa, then? And Jeff and I made a special brekkie for you," Roo said.

Quinn's stomach rumbled loudly.

"That's a yes, then." Roo winked.

"And I'd love to take a photo of those maple walnut muffins for the website before they vanish. They look amazing," Tess said.

"Of course they are. I made 'em, didn't I?" Roo said.

Their colorful pastry chef was nothing if not confident of her talents. Deservedly so.

"Let's all go in," her mom suggested.

"I might be coaxed into eating a muffin or two," her dad said. "Come join us, Ethan."

"Yes, Ethan, you must be starved," her mom chimed in. Her parents hadn't become hoteliers for nothing.

"Thank you, but I'll take a pass. The goats need milking." With a nod to the assembled group, he walked away.

She watched him head down the gravel road that led to the barns and corrals and beyond them the goat pen.

"I always liked that about Ethan. You give him a job and he sees it's done," her dad said.

"That's true. Not many teenagers would have walked Quinn around on Jinx. He did it unfailingly and without complaining," her mother said, slipping her arm around Daniel's waist. "Still, I'd have preferred to have him come and eat with us."

She watched her dad press a kiss to her mom's forehead. "Next time, sweetheart."

Quinn wasn't so sure. Ethan was determined to maintain his self-imposed exile. Good thing she was as dogged as they came.

Ethan had saved Hennie for last so that when he was done milking her, he could reward her by kicking around a ball. She was getting damned good at blocking. Though most of the soldiers at Camp Nathan Smith preferred football or vicious, elbow-swinging games of basketball during their downtime, he'd played some soccer with them, too. Ethan was pretty sure the soldiers would have dug having a goat for a goalie. He could imagine the raunchy comments that would fly as fast as the ball over the rocky patch of ground that served as a playing field. Aaron had been an amazing player; his moves left everyone literally standing in the dust.

Unbidden, the image of the last time he'd seen Aaron rose before him. Ethan squeezed his eyes shut.

"Hey, Ethan."

He opened his eyes but kept his head lowered. Josh's heavy drawl was the only ID required. "Hey."

"Hanging with the nannies, huh? Which one is that again?"

"Hennie," he replied.

"Damn, but you're getting good at that milking."

He didn't pause in the tempo he'd established, and for a moment the *swish swish* of the milk hitting the pail was the only sound. "You here for a reason, Josh? Or are you hoping to get some tips on your technique?"

Josh laughed. "Don't want to ruin your day, man, but my technique yields way sweeter results than milk in a bucket. So, word has it you and Quinn had quite the night."

Ethan had wondered how long it would take Josh to get to the point. "Her horse got sick."

"Yeah. Colic, huh? That can be real bad."

His fist pressed against Hennie's udder. She wasn't at empty yet, damn it. He couldn't get up and walk away and leave the doe with milk in her bag. That would hurt. "Yeah. The vet had to operate."

Josh whistled. "Must've cost a pretty penny."

Ethan remembered the figure Cooney quoted to Quinn. He didn't share it with Josh. "I guess."

A silence fell between them, and Ethan began to hope that was the end of the conversation. He was doomed to disappointment.

"Not sure I'd have opted for surgery myself."

Ethan glanced over his shoulder. Josh looked serious. "You'd have put him down?" he asked, in case Josh didn't understand that was the only other option Quinn faced.

"Yeah. If it had been Domino or even one of the trail horses, I could see the point. But Tucker's a rescue. And given the way he shies at everything under the sun, he won't ever be able to be ridden by a guest, and I'd lay odds he'll never work cattle. Quinn would have a hell of a time selling him, so it's not like she'd ever recoup the money spent on the operation. On top of that, colic surgery doesn't always succeed. Tucker could die next week of complications, or he could come down with colic again four months from now. Then all that money would have gone to waste."

What Josh was saying was reasonable. Pragmatic. A number of ranchers might come to the same conclusion. Spending the kind of money Tucker's operation cost when his chances of making a full recovery were by no means guaranteed wasn't something everyone would deem wise. That Tucker didn't earn his keep the way the trail or cutting horses on the ranch did made the decision even more problematic.

Ethan thought about Quinn, about how scared she'd been for the horse, and how her voice had shook when she'd spoken to Cooney and reiterated her determination to save the gelding if it was at all possible. He remembered wanting to wrap his arms about her, pull her close, and press his lips to the corners of her eyes, blotting the tears that threatened.

And when the operation was over and Cooney came out of the operating room to discuss the surgery, he remembered the trembling that seized her, and how he'd wanted to kiss her. Really kiss her because she was brave and generous, the most beautiful woman he'd seen in a long time.

He realized the sound of spurting milk had ceased. Hennie was done. Thank fuck. He straightened and lifted the bucket off the platform, taking care not to slosh its contents, and then stepped back. Hennie nimbly leapt to the ground, butting him affectionately before trotting off to rejoin the other does.

For a second he simply looked at Josh who, from the tip of his cowboy hat to the toes of his stitched boots, radiated supreme self-confidence. Was he ever troubled by a moment's doubt? Did he ever question his assumptions about the world? Ethan wanted nothing more than to send Josh on his merry way so he could share his views with anyone who would stop to listen—Quinn included. But she seemed to like Josh, and certainly appreciated his kisses. Ethan's mood soured at the thought.

"Let me give you a piece of advice, Josh. If you want any chance with Quinn, never breathe a word of the choice you'd have made for Tucker."

QUINN DIDN'T BELIEVE in ruminating. They had several hundred head of cattle for that. And the day had started on a great note: she'd called the veterinary clinic and was told that Tucker's temperature was in the normal range, he was drinking, and he had even nibbled a bit of alfalfa. Just as great, Cooney had given her the green light for an afternoon visit. Quinn knew the gelding's situation could change on a dime, but so far things were looking good for her horse. Reason enough to pay it forward and create some good karma by adopting an animal in need.

And by acting quickly, she would catch Ethan before he'd had a chance to retreat into his shell like a two-legged hermit crab.

Since she planned to go to the shelter alone, she borrowed her brother Ward's Jeep, stowing a large crate in the cargo area and placing a plate of brownies piled almost as high as the pyramids of Güímar in Spain on the passenger seat. Marsha and Lorelei, who ran the shelter on a shoestring budget, deserved nothing but the seriously decadent best when it came to chocolate indulgence.

She stopped in town on the way. A cup of joe was in

order, and the baristas at Spillin' the Beans knew exactly how she liked hers: a triple-shot espresso with two sugars because everything in life should be strong and sweet. She'd downed half of it by the time she reached the end of the block and entered the general store, which also housed the post office, the branch bank, and the luncheonette—one-stop shopping at its funkiest and finest—to pick up her mail and extend Maebeth and Nancy their invitation to celebrate Thanksgiving at the ranch.

Her mom had been delighted with the idea. "How nice," she said when Quinn had floated it after they finished the breakfast Jeff and Roo cooked. "I hope Nancy and Maebeth haven't already made plans, but if they have, invite them to come by for pie and coffee, Quinn. We'll be at the table for some time."

"Will do. And you're including Ethan in the head count, right?"

Her mother had looked at her strangely. "Of course."

"I'm only asking because he and I got to talking about Thanksgiving while we were walking Tucker. He said he had no plans." She kept her voice casual.

"Certainly we want him with us. I only wish we could have Cheryl and Tony join us, too. They're so worried about Ethan. We're all hoping he'll agree to come to Ward and Tess's wedding so that they can see him then and try to get a sense of his plans for the future." She sighed. "I'm afraid it'll take some heavy-duty convincing to get him to New York for the wedding, though. And I'll ask Josh—"

"To the wedding?" Quinn squawked, sounding like Alfie when she vacuumed near his cage.

"Oh!" Her mother's face brightened. "Would you like that, darling? I'm so glad you and he have become friends."

She thought fast. "You know, Mom, I'm not sure that

would be fair. Jim isn't on the guest list, is he? And he's worked for us for four years. And we'll need dependable ranch hands here to make sure everything's running smoothly while we're away. Otherwise Dad would worry."

"True. But we definitely need to invite Josh to Thanksgiving dinner. He was so sweet the other day, talking with Pete about his favorite side dishes. Apparently Josh's mother makes a macaroni and cheese with poblano peppers. This is the first year he won't be home with his family. I was thinking you might make the poblano macaroni and cheese for him, Quinn."

Aha, at last the matchmaking moves were coming out into the open. Unlike her brothers, she knew the trick to dealing with Adele Knowles: play dumb.

She pinned a smile on her lips. "Sure, Mom. I guess I can boil up some noodles and melt some cheese, drop in some peppers, and voilà."

Her mother barely managed to suppress a shudder. "I know he'll appreciate it. Josh is such a dear." Her voice rang with happy conviction.

"He is. Absolutely. The ranch guests have all taken a shine to him. Got to go, Mom. Alfie's been neglected." Seizing the excuse, she had beaten a hasty retreat before her mother could begin singing Josh's praises. When Adele liked someone, she didn't just hit a couple of notes; she offered up bonus tracks.

Soon Quinn would have to think about Josh, whether his kiss bore repeating, and if she wanted to venture further into new, *virgin* territory with him. She was certain she'd told Ethan the truth when she'd pronounced Josh a good kisser. Better still, he was a decent guy and likeable, which meant she probably should give it a shot and see whether they set off any sparks.

Heck, she'd be pleased if she could manage a little fizz.

But when she tried to picture Josh and her together, memories rose up of failures with other guys she'd also believed good and kind. The fear that history would repeat itself ballooned in her mind. The thought of seeing that look come into his eyes and for his smile to harden into a sneer . . . well, it would just suck. Plain and simple. Obviously she needed to stick a pin in her apprehension and watch it deflate to laughable proportions, but that was easier said than done. Until she managed it, she intended to keep a low profile. When that failed, as it was bound to at Thanksgiving, she wanted Josh to have plenty of distractions.

Who better than Nancy and Maebeth?

Stepping inside the building, she spotted the two of them working behind the counter. The luncheonette's tables were full, with only a couple of the round stools empty, but that didn't prevent either from glancing at the door and flashing a smile of welcome.

A few customers looked up, too, and on her way to the mailboxes she waved to a couple of familiar ones as she passed the cork bulletin board with its multihued fliers offering used tricycles, brass headboards, and guitars for sale as well as announcements for tai chi lessons and reading groups. Quinn had her own mailbox, separate from the rest of her family, because of the number of animal magazines and rescue newsletters she received. Today was no exception, but she didn't bother to look at any of them, just shoved the elastic-bound roll under her arm and made her way over to the lunch counter.

Nancy and Maebeth were a few years older than she, but Quinn considered them friends and shared a sense of solidarity since they all worked in the service industry. The two women could have easily gotten jobs at Silver Creek, but they liked being the epicenter of town gossip. And they loved their regulars, who left with their bellies full and their faces wreathed in smiles put there by Maebeth's and Nancy's easygoing chatter.

"Hey, Quinn," Maebeth said as she cut a slice of pecan-sprinkled coffeecake and slid it onto a white china plate. "Heard you had some trouble with one of your horses."

"Tucker's holding his own. Cooney's letting me visit later today."

"Good to hear." She placed the coffeecake in front of a customer who was poring over the sports pages and then gestured at the glaze-topped cake. "Want me to cut you a piece? It's fresh from the oven."

"No thanks, I'm still eating my way through the goodies Roo baked yesterday to cheer me up."

Nancy came over with a toasted bagel. With deft movements she smeared it with cream cheese and then added smoked salmon, chives, and two slices of lemon. "Lucky you. I love her desserts. I still remember this hazelnut cake she made last winter. To. Die. For."

"Come join us at Silver Creek for Thanksgiving, and I'll put in a request for the hazelnut cake."

They both paused to flash her smiles.

Nancy spoke first. "That's real nice of you, Quinn. But I'm celebrating with my folks. They like to make a big deal of it. Dean sits on my pop's lap and helps carve the turkey, and this year Kayla's helping Mom bake the apple pie."

"Can't miss that. But if your feast is on the early side, you and the kids could come around afterward. If you don't have room for more dessert, we do takeaway."

Nancy laughed. "Your mom probably has super-nice containers."

"Could you doubt it? We usually congregate at my folks' house around five o'clock, after we've tended to the animals. It also gives Roo and Jeff a chance to finish up at the restaurant and join us."

"Thanks. I'll see how pooped the kids are." Nancy picked up the bagel-and-lox plate and brought it over to a man who was sitting at the other end of the counter and was brave enough to tackle the crossword puzzle with a ballpoint pen.

"And how about you, Maebeth?"

"Honestly? I'd love to join you. I hadn't gotten around to making plans yet. My folks are away on a cruise and my brother's having Thanksgiving with his in-laws. They're up in Madeline, kind of a haul. Some friends were talking about ordering Chinese and eating a few Peking ducks and watching a marathon of *Friday the 13th* movies, but I really love turkey and stuffing, ya know?"

Dear Lord, chowing down on sliced duck *and* watching slasher movies? Wasn't that overkill? "It'll be awesome if you come, Maebeth. Mom will be really pleased—you know how much she likes parties."

"What can I bring?"

"Oh, you don't have to—" Quinn began, but then inspiration struck. "Actually, you know what? Josh was talking about this side dish he loves. It's a macaroni and cheese made with poblano peppers."

"Yum, sounds delish."

"Could you make that?"

Maebeth frowned. "Wouldn't you rather make it?"

"Oh, no." Quinn shook her head firmly. "You're a way better cook than I am. Why don't you talk to Josh and get the recipe from him?" Mission accomplished, she checked her watch. "Listen, I gotta skedaddle. I need to see some gals about a dog. Catch you two later."

Karma, the fates, the Almighty, or possibly a combination of all three were definitely smiling on her this morning, Quinn decided forty minutes later as she stood in the exercise run of the animal shelter looking at an Australian shepherd that had been dropped off two days ago.

The Aussie was a blue merle with bicolored eyes, one blue and the other brown. His name was Bowie. Quinn threw the ball again, watching him tear across the enclosure, jump, and catch it in midair. He was fast, almost as fast as Sooner.

"He's good with Frisbees, too," Marsha said, brushing her hands against her jeans. Lorelei was still working on her brownie.

Bowie ran back, dropped the tennis ball at her feet, and wagged his hindquarters.

With a smile she picked up the ball and threw it even farther. One advantage to having brothers was that she had a good throwing arm. They'd been so proud when she started pitching on the high school softball team. "What's Bowie's story?"

"He's three, right, Marsha?" Lorelei popped the last of her brownie in her mouth and licked her lips. "That brownie was amazing, by the way, Quinn."

"If you and Francesco and Marsha drop by on Thanksgiving, I'll make a couple of batches for dessert."

"And there goes ten pounds straight to my ass," Marsha lamented.

Quinn snorted. "Nonsense. You'll burn it off running around with rascals like Bowie here. So he's three, socialized, and likes balls and Frisbees. Why in the world hasn't someone adopted him?"

Marsha made a face. "We thought we had a couple lined up to take him. The husband loved him, but when he brought his wife to meet Bowie yesterday after work, it all fell to pieces. She was freaked out by his eyes." Marsha rolled hers. "Sometimes this job makes it really hard to respect the human species. The thing about

Bowie is that we can't place him just anywhere. Look at him. He needs exercise and lots of it. You can throw that ball for an hour and he's still raring to go."

A good example of the breed. "How'd he end up here?" she asked.

"A kid in his twenties dropped him off. Just got a job as a sales rep for a fastener manufacturer and he'll have to travel two weeks out of every month. The job's located in Michigan."

"No family member would take him?"

"He'd only had Bowie for a few months or so. Right, Marsha?" Lorelei said.

Marsha nodded. "The original owner enlisted in the army. And since the dog ended up with this kid, I'm guessing the soldier's family wasn't able to care for him, either. We have to place him with someone who understands his needs and who'll do right by him, Quinn. But no pressure," she said with a laugh.

Some things were meant to be, Quinn thought.

Bowie was back. He dropped the ball again, wagged his rump mightily, backed up, and then waited, quivering with anticipation, as his blue and brown gaze bounced between Quinn and the dirt-and-saliva-covered ball.

She picked it up and looked at his open smile. Good teeth, she noted. "He's obviously healthy. Any sign of aggression?"

"Healthy and up to date on his vaccinations," Nancy confirmed. "And he's good with the other dogs. Bowie does want the ball, but he doesn't take it out on another dog when he comes in second."

That was important. She had Sooner to consider. Friendly competition was fine; bloody, fur-flying fights were not.

She tucked the ball behind her back.

Bowie whimpered.

"Bowie," she said, and brought her free hand to her eyes. "Look."

The dog tracked her hand. Gazing up at her, he cocked his gray and white head expectantly.

"Sit, Bowie," she said, and gave him the hand signal, folding her extended arm.

The dog dropped his haunches on the ground.

"Good boy." So far, so good. One or both of his owners had cared enough to give him some training, and he seemed to have accepted it happily. She held her hand out, her palm facing him. "Wait." She backed up several paces. Tucking the ball inside her shirt, she squatted down and opened her arms wide. "Come, Bowie."

He bounded toward her.

She dug her fingers in his fur. His coat was good, but he needed a bath and a brushing. Any dog in his situation would. After patting him, she rewarded him with a long throw of the ball. "I'm going to the clinic to visit Tucker. I'll likely stay an hour, maybe a little more."

"Perfect. It'll give me time to bathe Bowie and get the stink out," Lorelei said. "I need to do something to burn off the second brownie."

"You've only had one."

"The second one's been calling my name these past ten minutes."

Quinn laughed. Then she turned to watch her next adoptee. Marsha had him pegged. The dog was tireless. He ran straight to her, dropped the ball, and gave her a doggy grin. Then, perhaps worried she hadn't noticed the wonderful gift he'd brought, he lowered his nose and gave the ball a push so it rolled to the toes of her boots.

This time she lobbed it high. As the ball arced in the air, he raced back to the other side of the pen and leapt to catch it, all doggy grace and joy. She smiled. "You'll do, Bowie. You'll do nicely."

EYES CLOSED, AN ice pack strapped to his shoulder, Ethan sprawled in his chair. Every now and again he contemplated getting up and fetching his bottle of whiskey to further numb the pain. Even with the ice pack, his shoulder hurt like the blazes—as if he'd been stabbed with a red-hot poker. But he remained where he was because, one, he was too tired to get up, and two, he refused to hit the booze before six o'clock. Besides, the abused shoulder was his fault. When Pete, the ranch's foreman, had asked if he wanted to help clear some overgrown trails, he'd jumped at the chance to work someplace where he wouldn't have to listen to Josh.

Six hours of clearing brush and sawing limbs made him think there must be better ways to ignore the Texan's mad desire to share.

With a low curse, he let his head fall back against the wing of the chair. What had compelled him to open his mouth and offer Josh advice about Quinn yesterday morning? It was a classic case of no good deed going unpunished. Now the cowboy acted as if Ethan were some kind of sage or, worse, his best bud, talking until Ethan thought his head would fucking explode.

Whacking at brush and hauling fallen limbs seemed

the perfect escape until Ethan realized that the work left him *too* alone, unable to block thoughts that inevitably circled back to Quinn and the real reason he regretted ever uttering a syllable to Josh. It wasn't because Ethan had become Josh's go-to guy when he needed to share—which was always—but because he'd consciously decided to encourage Josh to pursue Quinn even though the Texan didn't understand or fully appreciate her.

And didn't that make him a pompous ass? Who was he to judge what Quinn needed or wanted in a relationship? Maybe she'd been telling the truth and was happy to be with Josh, who seemed to love life—and had a hell of a good time living it—from the moment he woke up until he closed his eyes at night.

Even if she was looking for someone who recognized that she was far more than the pretty package she inhabited, that didn't make him a potential candidate to replace Josh. He wasn't ordinarily stupid, so why did he keep forgetting that?

Probably because he liked her a little too damn much.

If he knew what was good for him, he'd be out clearing trails for the rest of the week.

The knock on the door had him frowning. Christ, had Josh decided it would be fun to hang out? At least the solution to this problem was blessedly simple, involving no effort except to slump deeper in his chair.

The knock sounded again, and Ethan scowled. Josh might appear to be an easygoing Texan, but he was tenacious as a New England lobster.

He let the ice pack fall to the chair cushion as he stood and crossed the room to the door. He yanked it open with a snarl of "What?" but then had to suck in a breath because more and more often the sight of Quinn tied his insides into a Gordian knot. She was dressed in what he'd come to realize was her preferred wardrobe:

jeans that hugged her long legs, colorfully stitched cowboy boots, and a sweater that was on the wrong side of ratty so that it wouldn't matter if a goat nibbled its hem or a horse smeared hay on the shoulder. Her long hair was down, its honeyed ends brushing the swells of her breasts.

"And hello to you, too," Quinn replied, and he almost felt grateful that she'd spoken before he began thinking about what those breasts would look like covered by his hands rather than that decrepit sweater.

"What do you want?"

Seemingly unfazed by his hostile tone, she said, "I brought someone to meet you. This is Bowie."

He looked down and into one bright blue and one dark brown eye framed by a white and speckled gray head, folded ears, and a black leathery nose. "That's a dog."

"Gosh, I am so proud of you." An impish grin teased her lips.

He drew his brows together. A smile would only encourage her.

"Yes, this is a dog. I thought you might like a cabinmate."

His frown became genuine. He folded his arms across his chest. "Why would I want one?"

"To sleep."

Talking to Quinn was always interesting. "A dog will help me sleep?"

"I guarantee bunking and working with Bowie and helping train him as a sheepdog will be a better sleep aid than chugging Jack Daniel's every night. It's possible Bowie might even improve that nasty disposition of yours."

"Thanks, I'm doing just fine."

"Of course you are. But you'd also be doing me a

favor," she said. The tentative note that entered her voice told him how unused she was to asking for them.

He set his teeth. "I'm not in a charitable mood."

"Say it ain't so," she said. "Listen, he's a rescue—"

"I don't care what he is. Go ask Josh to help you with him. Believe me, he's itching to do you a favor so you can be all grateful."

"Fine. Be a jerk—you're so excellent at it. Bowie used to belong to a guy who enrolled in the army. He apparently gave Bowie to a friend, but then the guy couldn't keep him. I thought that might matter to you." Her gaze flicked over him coolly. "I should have known better."

She had the dog on a leash. He'd been sitting by her side with his muzzle lifted as if listening. Animals paid close attention when Quinn was around.

Giving the leash a quick tug, she said, "Let's go, Bowie." Without sparing Ethan a second glance, she walked quickly away, the dog trotting by her side, leaving him feeling like something far worse than a jerk.

Even after Ethan's knocking grew insistent, she took her sweet time answering. Letting him stew in his remorse, he supposed.

The door opened, and a Wagnerian caterwaul greeted him. The nearer, more immediate barking of the two dogs was a soothing lullaby compared to the wailing of sirens and percussive rat-a-tat-tat that came from God knows where.

"What the hell?"

She didn't deign to respond, merely turned on her heel and walked past the large, cloth-draped sofa, where a black and white one-eyed cat crouched like a mountain lion and welcomed him with a death glare.

As she passed the dogs, Quinn made a short chopping motion with her hand and Sooner quieted. Bowie, however, continued barking, perhaps rattled by the racket coming from the next room.

Quinn disappeared into it.

He followed her. Perhaps her taste in movies was as lousy as the music she favored and she liked her apocalyptic flicks cranked to the max. But as he crossed the threshold, the noise, still at an earsplitting level, changed to manic shrieks of "Quinn! Quinn! Quinn!"

The source was just as outrageous. A parrot was doing flips worthy of an Olympic gymnast and catching himself with his beak and talons on the suspended swings and the metal bars of a cage that stood nearly as tall as Ethan. Flashes of color whizzed through the air as it flipped—bright green, yellow, red, and blue.

He guessed the bird was from the Amazon, by way of hell. Fiendishly clever, it hadn't stopped its screaming call as it somersaulted and dove kamikaze-style, quieting only when Quinn stepped up to the cage and stuck her fingers inside. It scrambled close to press its head against them. Obligingly she scratched the area behind its beady eye, where blue feathers met green and yellow ones.

"This is Alfie."

"Not Beelzebub?"

Her lips twitched. That she had even a tiny smile for him was nothing short of miraculous considering what an ass he'd been minutes ago.

"He's loud when he's excited or when his schedule is changed. This is his free time, when he gets to go out of his cage and hang out. Sooner and Pirate are accustomed to him flying about, but I'm worried Bowie might get overwhelmed."

Fair enough. He could imagine the parrot getting major kicks out of strafing innocent sheepdogs. "Okay, what do you want me to do with the dog?" Even as he spoke, a part of him wondered if Quinn didn't have him as spellbound as the animals in her care.

"If you really don't want him in the cabin with you, would you mind taking him for a walk so he can get used to the scents? And he likes to play ball." While she spoke she opened the cage. The parrot flapped its wings in quick succession and then hopped onto Quinn's outstretched arm, scrambling up its length until it was perched on her shoulder. "I know I'm asking a lot from you—"

"Knock it off, Quinn," he said irritably. "Enough of this 'I'm beholden' crap."

Her blue eyes flashed, reminding him of a summer storm. "Forgive me. I just spent an hour and a half at the clinic with Tucker, so I *am* feeling kind of beholden to you for saving him. So you'll have to deal with the fact that I'm grateful you were there and did the right thing. But I understand that doing two kind acts in as many days is probably dangerous for a wannabe misanthrope like yourself."

He scowled. He didn't know how Quinn managed it, but she had a way of making him feel like Superman one moment and then about as bighearted as a dung beetle the next. The woman had serious talent.

"And I would have asked my parents to dog-sit Bowie, but they're meeting with a neighbor about some land he wants to sell."

"How did Tucker look?"

Quinn's shrug made the parrot squawk and then resettle himself even closer to Quinn's slender neck. Then he began raking the strands of her hair with his beak. Ethan recalled the morning he'd learned to milk the goats, how he'd grazed the silky strands with the back of his hand and caught the sweet scent of flowers when he inhaled. No wonder the damned bird was besotted, Ethan thought.

"How'd Tucker look? Almost as exhausted as when I first rescued him. And he's lost too much weight—it's crazy how a serious illness can do that to a body."

Was she including humans as well as animals in that statement? he wondered as self-consciousness pierced him. He could hardly blame her. He barely recognized himself when he looked in a mirror.

"And the stent bandage wrapped around his belly is freaky, but the main thing is he's still alive." She smiled. "He ate a little alfalfa with me and let me run a soft brush over him."

"Good." He nodded. If he'd had any sense, he would have forced his feet to carry him out to the living room and coax some soldier's dog into walking with him. Instead he opened his big mouth. "Why didn't you ask Josh to help you?"

From the flush on her cheeks, he guessed she was surprised by the question. Suddenly she became preoccupied with scratching Alfie's breast until he cooed in ecstasy. As the throated avian purr continued and the silence between the humans stretched, Ethan wondered if she intended to ignore the question.

"It's, well . . . I'm not sure Josh and Bowie would suit."

He made some noncommittal grunt, forcing his mouth to move and preventing a smile from settling on his lips. "Not convinced I'll suit him any better," he said, adding gruffly, "Don't make the mistake of thinking this is going to become a regular thing. I don't want to be involved in your pet projects." *I don't want to be involved, period.* But somehow he already knew that Bowie was going to be sleeping on the floor by his bed tonight. "So where's the leash?"

"There's a bunch of 'em hanging on the hook in the mudroom just off the kitchen. Balls are in a basket underneath."

* * *

All things considered, that hadn't gone too badly, Quinn thought. It would have been folly to expect Ethan to willingly, gladly accept the idea of fostering Bowie. He was too intent on shutting the world out.

But she was counting on Bowie to nudge him in the right direction. It happened, and not just in the movies. A prickly antisocial or painfully shy person acquired a dog and a transformation occurred. Sometimes the joy that came paw in hand from the nonjudgmental love of a dog crept over a person slowly, and sometimes it swept in on a warm cascade. Whichever way it came about, she couldn't believe Ethan would remain unaffected. Bowie was too great a dog.

The house was quiet, Alfie back in his cage and happily practicing whirring noises while he chewed a carrot. He loved it when she used the food processor to chop onions and cilantro for her guacamole and salsa. There was enough guac for two. And, refusing to analyze why, she'd prepared a couple of extra butternut squash quesadillas. She could eat them tomorrow if Ethan behaved true to form and refused to be social for more than thirty seconds.

She laid the tortillas on a silicone carving board and began spooning beans, goat cheese, Monterey Jack, diced squash, and guacamole onto half of the tortilla, folding the other half over the filling, until she had a row of neat semicircles. She wasn't much of a cook—no need to be when she counted professional chefs among her friends—but she did have a few recipes down. This was one of them.

First she'd gotten a dog, and now she was fixing extra food in case Ethan was hungry.

Why didn't you ask Josh?

Of all the people in her world whom she would have

expected to press her—repeatedly—about Josh, Quinn would have thought Ethan to be the very last. He'd asked a good question, though. It ranked right up there with why she spent yesterday and today consciously avoiding Josh and suggesting to Maebeth that she cook one of his favorite dishes. Wasn't Josh what she ought to be looking for in a guy? They shared the same interests, he understood ranching, he was nice, he was attractive, and he hadn't made her go cold with dread or embarrassment when he put his tongue in her mouth.

And yet . . .

It occurred to Quinn that her character might be far more twisted than she'd acknowledged. Perhaps in addition to her sexual hang-ups, she yearned for the unobtainable. If so, then she'd really hit the jackpot with her fascination with Ethan. It was equally possible she suffered from self-delusion, believing she could sneak past his prickly-as-barbed-wire demeanor to find the man he'd been before he went on assignment in Afghanistan.

But even if she found the Ethan of old, what made her think that he might be remotely interested in her or that he would be the man for her?

AT THE ARMY base, once the guys had warmed up to Ethan, they often talked about wives and girlfriends, pulling out creased photographs or clicking on laptops to show pictures or videos of smiling faces and puckered lips blowing kisses. The gamut ranged from demure angels posing in flowered sundresses to decidedly more earthy sisters in thongs and pasties performing seriously acrobatic pole-dancing routines.

Along with the women were other images of those that had been left behind to await the soldiers' return: pythons, ferrets, horses, cats, parakeets, turtles, and iguanas, but most of all, dogs. He'd seen cherished pics of dogs of every shape, age, and variety, from nine-month-old pit bulls to grizzled Chihuahuas.

They were loved, those animals, and missed as deeply, if differently, as the girlfriends and family members were.

Ethan's thoughts turned to Bowie's owner. Had he been deployed to Afghanistan? If so, where had he been based and what kind of action had he seen? Did he have photographs of Bowie that he scrolled through as he lay on his bunk, the images momentarily transporting him to a place far away from rocket blasts and sniper bullets?

How long would it take for the soldier to hear that Bowie had been placed in a shelter? One thing Ethan already knew: the news would add worry to the omnipresent fear and exhaustion that weighed heavily, like a sweat-drenched blanket, on every soldier deployed.

He'd walked Bowie around the ranch's outbuildings, letting him sniff and pee on posts or tufts of dried grass that held some special canine significance. Then he took him to an open area, not too hard to find on a ranch the size of Silver Creek, and began tossing the ball.

The dog caught his every throw. Ignoring his shoulder, he launched the ball ever farther and higher until the growing darkness made it impossible to distinguish the gray speckled fur.

"Sorry, boy," he said when the dog trotted up to him, dropped into a crouch, and, with a nudge of his snout, rolled the ball toward his boots. "You've got the moves, all right, but the fun has to end. My arm's gonna fall off if I keep this up." Bending over, he snapped the leash onto Bowie's collar.

They walked back to Quinn's house. The light over the front door was illuminated and the small house looked neat and cozy. Appearances could be deceiving. Bracing himself for a blast of parrot-induced mayhem, he knocked and heard Quinn call, "Come in."

This time when he stepped inside he caught the cultured tones of David Attenborough explaining how the giraffe enjoyed grazing on the leaves of the acacia tree.

Sir David's voice faded and the camera zoomed in on a giraffe stretching for a dainty morsel. Then Quinn spoke. "There's beer in the fridge. I left a bowl of food for Bowie on the counter. If you're hungry, help yourself to some quesadillas. And there's chips and salsa. The food's under the metal mesh domes. Pirate likes to raid."

He waited to see whether she'd shift her gaze away from the giraffe that was delicately and deliberately denuding the branches of the spiky acacia. When he noticed that Sooner and her one-eyed cat were seated on either side of her like furry animal bookends and that their attention, too, was glued to the TV, he gave a mental shrug. A beer might not be so bad. A quesadilla would save him the hassle of scrounging for food.

He left Bowie in the kitchen chowing down on a bowl of kibble. He assumed it was the caviar of dog foods. The dog had taken one sniff and then plunged into the mix.

His two fingers wrapped around the cold neck of a beer. An earthenware plate piled with golden-brown quesadillas and a couple of spoonfuls of salsa balanced in his other hand, he rejoined Quinn. An elephant was on the screen now, plucking high-hanging berries from a tree with surgical precision. It must be an "animals eating" segment of the program.

Ethan sank into a club chair with a grunt of pain. Luckily his grunt coincided with the crash of a tree toppled by an African bull elephant. Nonetheless, he glanced over at Quinn, relaxing when he saw that her gaze was still riveted on the screen.

"The walk go okay?" she asked.

"Yeah. He's a good dog." He bit into the quesadilla. It was damn good. Three more bites and it was gone. He picked up another one and dipped the pointy end into the salsa.

"Aussies are smart. Highly trainable. I think I'll start him on the basics of herding in a couple of weeks once he's had a chance to acclimate and has met a few sheep."

"Mmm." He took a sip of his beer to wash down his last bite of butternut and black beans. Antelope were thundering across the savannah. Over the TV, he heard the click of toenails on wood. Bowie came straight to his chair and lay down by his feet.

Ethan tried hard not to be pleased. "You know David Bowie doesn't really have bicolored eyes, don't you? He got punched in the eye when he was a teen. A fight over a girl."

"That so?"

At least she didn't ask who David Bowie was.

"I'm pretty sure there are ways to post a message saying you've got Bowie here at Silver Creek that the army will forward."

She nodded at the screen. "It's why I adopted him, to make it as easy as possible for Bowie's owner to reunite with him once he returns home. If that can't happen, I'll do my part to give Bowie a great life."

He chugged the beer, despite the fact that his throat had closed with emotion. Quinn often did the unexpected; he should never be surprised by the size of her heart.

"So the shoulder's paining you?"

Caught off guard, he said, "Yeah. A bit," and then cursed silently.

"Perfect."

He paused with the bottle halfway to his lips. "Excuse me?"

She stood. "Finish your food. I'll be back in a couple of secs. Just have to get my table."

What was she up to now?

The table was a massage table that she unfolded with the efficiency of a vacuum cleaner salesman. He wasn't buying.

"Forget it, Quinn," he said flatly.

"I'm going to start calling you Dr. No," she said, whipping out a white sheet. With a snap of her wrists, it billowed like a sail before settling over the table. "Don't you know that you're supposed to jump at the chance when a woman offers you a massage?"

Every atom in his body screamed, *Hell yes*. Thankfully he still had a few functioning brain cells left. "Sorry, not interested."

Amazingly, she didn't look surprised or even skeptical, which meant he must have become an exceptional liar in the past thirty seconds. No, what she looked was determined. Ethan was beginning to recognize that when she thrust her jaw out just so, it was a sign that Quinn Knowles had the bit between her teeth.

"I've been learning equine massage. It's something I was already planning on doing with Tucker. Now I really want to. I'm hoping it will help him relax and handle being confined to a stall better. But I need more practice. I can use you."

"I'm not a horse."

"But you're an ass a lot of the time, so that qualifies, doesn't it?" She must have caught the ghost of a smile on his face. "Come on. I dare you," she said.

He exhaled wearily. "Do you ever give up?"

"Nope. Wanna know a secret? Ward and Reid live in terror of me."

He believed it. "Will you stop talking if I say yes?"

"Guys," she said, shaking her head. "There is nothing wrong with conversation, you know. There are days when getting more than five words out of Ward is a major achievement."

No wonder he liked Ward. "Yes or no?"

"Fine." She exhaled loudly. "You take off your shirt and I'll hit the mute button."

Oh, Christ. The shirt. If he reneged now, she would know immediately that it was because he didn't want to show her what his shoulder looked like. He had his pride.

Feeling as if his molars might crumble to pieces, he

unbuttoned the heavy flannel shirt. Shrugging it off, he tossed it onto the chair he'd vacated and kept his gaze fixed on the weave of the rug.

His hearing suddenly extra acute, he caught the sound of her breath whooshing out—in horror? Pity?—and then there was silence, a charged silence. He regretted his demand that she stop talking. If she'd been talking, then she wouldn't be absorbing the sight of his wounds.

"Should I lie on my front or back?" he asked gruffly.

She made a strangled noise, then coughed. "Could you, um, please lie facedown?" Her voice was now stiff with formality. At any other time he'd have glanced at her face to read it. He refused to do so now. Were he to see naked pity there, he'd never be able to forget it.

He did as instructed. The cotton sheet she'd draped over the table was rough as cement against his skin.

Squeezing his eyes shut, he prepared for the worst.

The sight of Ethan's naked torso hit her like a hard punch, leaving her breathless and reeling. He was broad-chested, his nipples a dark tan against his pale skin. Brown hair sprinkled the space between, covering the taut swell of his pecs. A thicker line of hair formed a path, starting at the flat of his stomach, just above his navel, and continuing down. Her gaze reached the top of his low-slung jeans and skittered back up.

Oh God, he was beautiful. Not in a beefcake hunk or overpumped, steroid-fueled bodybuilder way. There was no flash, no excess. He was simply bone, sinew, and lean muscle.

She'd seen men's chests before, had touched a number of them. Six, to be exact. But not even Mark Adams's naked torso—he was the last man she'd attempted to have sex with—had made her react like this, not even when she'd been rubbing it with her own.

What had she done? Why had she given in to impulse once again? This compulsion to fix things was a weakness of hers. A habit that might be okay when it came to rescuing orphaned baby bunnies and donating her time and energy at shelters and sanctuaries but verged on dangerous when it involved a man who made her heart beat crazily.

But maybe you don't only want to fix him. Maybe you've been looking for an excuse to touch him, a nagging voice suggested.

The idea was startling in its novelty and pretty darn terrifying.

She looked again and this time couldn't seem to resist the pull he exerted on her. But all too aware of what happened to the cat that was curious, she approached the narrow table with a tentative step. She took in the taut skin stretched over his back, the still-red scars snaking over his right shoulder, a road map of pain. She could see the tension radiating off him. What had made her think she could do this, offer relief to his suffering?

But backing down wasn't an option.

Opening her palms, she touched him.

If she used her body weight to press and knead, she reasoned, he wouldn't feel the trembling of her hands or guess that the tremors coursed through her entire body. If she focused on the pressure points and worked the knots constricting his muscles, holding and waiting for them to loosen and relax, then she wouldn't be tempted to caress the taut skin or stroke the puckered lines that covered his right shoulder in the hopes that she might absorb the hurt.

She told herself to forget that the body beneath her hands was Ethan's. She made herself close her eyes to the breadth of his shoulders, to the lean proportions of his back, to the awful scars, evidence of the agony suffered by this man she was coming to admire so much. It was simply her hands listening to a nameless person's body. Listening, gauging, probing, kneading.

Grunts and short *mmnf*s punctuated the quiet as she located trigger points and worked at the knots in his muscles. When they began to ease, his breathing deepened. Every now and again he released a low groan that coursed through her like an electric charge.

Her breasts grew heavy, her nipples tingly, as if they were missing or anticipating something. His touch. Knowing that the small of his back would be as tense as the area of his neck and shoulder blades, she began walking her hands down his spine. With each shift of her open palms over hard muscles and ridiculously soft skin, sparks ignited low in her belly, making her ache. Making her hot.

Hot, when she'd been labeled cold so many times.

She reached the waistband of his jeans, and for the first time in her life, her fingers itched to continue on, sneak beneath the denim and touch the firm globes of his butt.

And do what? Jump a guy who'd shown no interest in her? She couldn't manage sex with guys who were *willing*. What was she thinking, to try what would surely be a pathetic and clumsy sexual pass at Ethan?

She was out of her depth—way, way out. Drawing a shaky breath, she forced her hands to travel back up his spine and over his shoulders in a brisk sweeping gesture before stepping away from the table. "There, all done," she said in a chipper tone that sounded all wrong.

He rolled off the table so quickly it might have been glass shards he was lying on rather than a combed cotton sheet. Keeping his back to her, he grabbed his shirt and shoved his arms into the sleeves with rough efficiency.

With the body she'd worked on—so beautiful, so pain-ridden—hidden from view, she wrapped her hands tight about her middle. The feelings roiling inside her weren't so easily contained, however.

"How do you feel?" she asked, unable to stop herself.

Ethan answered in a low, jagged growl, like a trapped animal looking to escape. "How do you think I feel?"

That was just it. Quinn didn't know. From the rigidity of his muscles when she first touched him, she'd have hoped the short session would have helped him feel better. But of course that wasn't what she really wanted to know. She wanted to hear him say he'd felt that electric awareness, that sense of connection, that blast of excitement, the heat of which lingered.

The thrill must have been wholly one-sided.

Bowie saved her from having to mumble some inanity about restoring elasticity to the fasciae. Now that Ethan was upright, he went over to him, wriggling his hindquarters with happiness.

The dog got a glimmer of a smile from him even if she didn't. Since broaching the topic of what Ethan thought of her was impossible, she returned to her campaign to convince him to care for Bowie.

"He likes being with you," she said. "You must remind him of his previous owner."

He tipped his head to look at her. The angle made the slash of his cheekbones and the thin blade of his nose even more pronounced. *Oh, crap,* she thought with despair; she was getting hung up on his looks, too. How humbling. No more would she be able to smile with a secret superiority at women who went as gooey as a bag of sun-warmed caramels over a handsome man. It was true that Josh could make her thoughts fuzzy, but then again he was *trying* to charm her. He *wanted* to kiss her. Ethan was just being his difficult self.

"All right, I'll take him with me until he's used to that crazy-ass parrot. No longer," he warned.

She nodded tightly. It didn't make her necessarily

happier that she suddenly understood why Josh could never have the same effect on her as Ethan did. Josh might charm, but he couldn't make her feel so intensely that one minute she was gnashing her teeth at his stubbornness, the next moved to tears by a glimpse of the anguish lodged inside him. Not once had he said or done anything to make her heart swell to bursting.

But at least she now had the answer to the morning's question of what to do. There would be no further "experimentations" with Josh. The weight that slid off Quinn's shoulders as she made the decision told her it was the right one.

Tomorrow she'd find Josh and let him know that they could be friends but no more than that. What she would do about Ethan and her growing attraction to him . . . well, she had no clue, since Ethan seemed unmoved by her charms.

Chapter
FIFTEEN

THE COLD MORNING air made the tips of Quinn's ears tingle. She should have grabbed a jacket and scarf, but a five o'clock call from George Reich, the manager of the guest ranch's restaurant, asking her to fill in for one of their waitresses, Liz, who'd come down with a nasty cold, made her top of choice—a hooded sweater—a nonstarter. Instead she'd had to rummage in her closet in search of an ironed white shirt.

She'd have had better luck finding a four-leaf clover or a unicorn. At last she remembered the load of whites in her dryer, but then lost another fifteen minutes ironing the wrinkles out of a fitted button-down. When the shirt was finally up to Silver Creek Ranch's sartorial standards, she'd whipped it on, brushed and braided her still-damp hair, and bolted out of the house, the braid thumping the space between her shoulder blades as she hurried up the path to Josh's cabin.

By her estimate, she had just enough time before she had to report for waitressing duty to let Josh know she wasn't interested in pursuing things further with him—and boy, she hoped that when the words came out of her mouth they wouldn't sound quite so lame.

But all words, brilliant or cringeworthy, flew out of her

head when he opened the door to his cabin. He was dressed, but his denim shirt clung to his torso. From the vee of skin where it was unbuttoned at the neck, she caught the scent of soap. Hurriedly, she looked up. His lashes were still wet, clumped together in thick, dark spikes, and his chocolate brown eyes shone with happy surprise.

"Hey, Quinn."

"Um, hey, Josh." She swallowed. Determined to sound less rattled, she tried again. "I, um, wanted to see you because, um—*mmphh*—"

The rest of her sentence was locked away, sealed by Josh's lips. The kiss seemed to go on forever, and when at last he released her and stepped back she could only stare stupidly at him.

"Yeah, I've been wanting to see you, too, Quinn. I've been thinking about you, hoping I'd catch you soon, and here you are." He gave her a lopsided grin. "I'm real glad you came by. The bummer is I've gotta go. Pete wants me to take some advanced riders out. Folks named the Dorseys and the Watts."

"Oh yeah. They've been coming here forever. They're friends—they live in the same neighborhood in L.A."

"Pete told me one of them's a movie director." He pronounced "movie director" with the same awe a six-year-old said "Santa Claus."

"Yeah. Campbell Watt. He directs action films. His wife, Patricia, works in TV. Josh, I wanted to talk about us. I like you—"

His face blocked out her thoughts once again as he swooped in for another kiss, this one mercifully briefer than the last. But when he raised his head and whispered, "Damn, Quinn," his voice had a husky rasp. "I sure do like the way you taste. Sweet and salty at the same time."

"Peanuts."

At his blank look, she explained, "I was in a rush and

grabbed a handful of peanuts as I went out the door." She hadn't expected to be sharing them.

"Best nuts I've ever had." He grinned and traced a finger down her cheek. But then something must have caught his eye, for he abruptly looked up and past her. "Awesome dog, Ethan," he called. "Where'd he come from?"

She spun around. Even from this distance the fierce disapproval in Ethan's glare reached her, answering the question she hadn't yet formulated. Yes, he'd seen her and Josh kissing. Again. She went cold and then blushed fiery hot with embarrassment as without a word—not a "Good morning, Quinn" or even a "Hey, this dog snores like a truck driver"—he turned and stalked off in the direction of the barns, Bowie's silky coat rippling as he trotted alongside.

"So I'll catch you later, okay, Quinn?" Josh was already moving past her.

"No, wait." She caught his shirtsleeve. Determined to get the words out before he hurried off, lured by the glitz of showbiz people, she spoke in a rush. "It's about us, Josh. I'm sorry, but it's not going to work." She paused, casting about for something more intelligent and original to say than *It's not you, it's me,* since she'd already uttered that tired phrase to a half dozen or so guys, but her brain came up empty.

Josh must've thought she'd finished. "Oh."

For a second his face looked blank. She steeled herself, ready for his disappointment, perhaps even an argument. What she wasn't prepared for was his casual shrug and even more careless response.

"Well, okay, if that's what you want. Listen, I really gotta run. The horses should be spotless for the VIPs. See you around." With a quick smile he was off, jogging toward the barns.

She stared at his retreating figure in astonishment. Well,

this was a first in the chronicles of her disasters with men. What had just happened? Josh had been the one to kiss her in the first place, right? He'd been the one to say he wanted to see how things went between them. Shouldn't he have shown a smidgen of disappointment at hearing that she didn't want to go out with him?

It was perverse, she knew, to be miffed that he'd taken the news so well. She should be doing cartwheels that his ego wasn't bruised, that he hadn't vented or, worse, decided she needed persuading.

At least it was done. Now all she had to do was clear the air with Ethan, and suddenly that struck her as a much more daunting task. Even if she had the time to run after him and explain, what would she say precisely? That she hadn't actually been kissing Josh but trying to break things off with him? How would she broach the topic? She couldn't think of a single opening that wouldn't result in a garbled mess of awkwardness and embarrassment. And how vain of her to think that he'd care what she said.

But there was no time to run after Ethan. She'd used up all her spare minutes with Josh. She had to go up to the lodge and serve the hungry guests.

Why did her relations with the opposite sex often feel like for every step forward, she took two steps back? Was it any wonder that she avoided anything deeper than casual friendships, let alone sexual relationships, when she was lousy at every aspect of them?

Ethan had learned from his time in Afghanistan that few things cut a situation down to essentials like military jargon. His present state definitely qualified as FUBAR—fucked up beyond all recognition.

Last night Quinn, with just five strokes down the length of his back, had given him his first hard-on in months. When a guy hadn't achieved an erection in that long a time it was kind of a big deal. A big fucking deal.

But Quinn's gift tortured, filling him with conflicting impulses. As he felt his cock thicken and swell, pressing against the fly of his jeans, a part of him wanted to throw his head back and shout in triumph. And had the woman who'd performed this minor miracle been anyone but Quinn Knowles, he would have done his damnedest to get her naked, beneath him, and wet for him before seeing to it that he gave her as much pleasure as one body could give another. But it was Quinn whose touch was magic, and he'd declared her off-limits. Sweet-talking her into letting him put his hard-on to work was out of the question. She deserved better than to have someone as damaged and messed up as him inside her. Yes, he might bring her pleasure; it was guaranteed he would ultimately bring her pain.

Yet he wanted her, ached to bury himself so deep he couldn't tell where he ended and she began. That sweet, slick warmth sheathing him the closest to heaven that he would ever come.

Almost any guy on the face of the earth would rejoice at recovering the ability to use his penis for anything besides putting out campfires. Not him. For him it raised some difficult and uncomfortable truths that were as impossible to ignore as the wood he'd sported inside his jeans.

He didn't like that Quinn was able to make him feel things no one else could. He'd gotten so good at shutting himself off. Damned if he wanted her to wield that kind of power over him.

There was another, deeper explanation why he wasn't doing backflips and yelling hallelujah now that his cock was rising to the occasion. He didn't deserve an erection. A person didn't have to be Sigmund Fucking Freud to recognize that it was a symbol of life, the promise of a future, the tool of *creation*—and why should he get one when he'd deprived others of ever experiencing anything again?

That should have made his penis go as soft and wrinkled as a three-day-old balloon, but no. He'd remained hard and aching for her.

If that weren't enough to make him curse the capricious fates, this morning he'd taken the dog Quinn had maneuvered him into pet-sitting out for a morning pee and nearly bowled into her and Josh. From the kiss she was giving him, Ethan bet she'd given *him* a boner, too.

Unlike the first time he'd caught them in a lip-lock, the dawn's light allowed him to see everything all too clearly. An hour later he was still choking on the wave of jealousy that had swamped him.

Damn it, if he'd been the one kissing her, his hand wouldn't have rested limply on her shoulder. He'd have had his fingers twined deep in her long braid, holding her still so his mouth could devour hers with long, deep kisses, feeding the pent-up hunger consuming him.

There'd be no daylight between their bodies. He'd have Quinn up against the cabin's wood siding, his chest plastered against the soft mounds of her breasts, his free hand cupping her sweetly rounded ass, his cock probing the welcoming cradle of her thighs. His need for her would be hot enough to melt the layers of denim separating them. Then there she'd be, open and wet for him. With one hard thrust he'd be inside her.

He could spin enough fantasies around her to last a year of nights. They all boiled down to this: he wanted to know her taste, to memorize the feel of her every curve, of her every scented hollow, and fill himself with it.

And he couldn't have any of her.

Given the way his luck was running, it came as no surprise that the first person he spotted after leaving the goats milked and fed would be good old Josh. But there was no opportunity to compound his jealousy with colossal stupidity by going over and trying to rearrange the Texan's pretty face. Since Josh was astride his horse, Waylon, a roan that shone like blue steel, Ethan wouldn't have been able to reach it in any case. Four other riders were with him. From their relaxed but alert postures, he guessed they were advanced and about to enjoy a good, hard ride.

When a second wave of jealousy hit him, he shook his head in disgust. Damn it all, what was happening? Why was everything making him *want*?

Daniel Knowles came out of the horse barn and approached the group of riders. From the laughter and banter, Ethan guessed they must be regular guests at the ranch. Daniel stepped back, allowing the riders to fall in line behind Josh as they moved out. Spying Ethan, he gave a wave and began walking toward him.

Just then, a voice addressed him. "Good morning, Ethan."

He turned and was greeted by Adele Knowles's warm smile. Her eyes were so similar to Quinn's that it was hard to meet them.

"So this is the new dog?"

"Yeah, this is Bowie."

Adele extended her hand so Bowie could sniff it. "Pretty boy. I saw Quinn up at the lodge. She's still serving a few guests who came down late to breakfast. She was worried about Bowie making things difficult for you around the horses. I'd be happy to take him for you—"

His fingers tightened around the leash. "He'll be fine with me. I'm taking him to clear brush. He can fetch sticks."

"That's very good of you." Adele's voice rang with approval.

It wasn't good of him. He was simply a perverse bastard. Quinn had foisted Bowie on him. Now he didn't want to give him up.

"Quinn said she talked to you about Thanksgiving the other day. We have such wonderful memories of the holiday with your parents when you were young. Do you remember them?"

He nodded. His favorite part of the day had been the long trail ride. Everyone saddled up—even Quinn, with a lead rope attached to her pony. After the ride there'd been a feast delicious and big enough to send them all into a semi-comatose state, perfect for watching the game on TV. Good times.

"Yes, I do."

"I'm so pleased you'll be joining us."

Had he said that to Quinn? He'd been out of his mind to agree to such a thing. Those Thanksgivings represented tradition. Laughter and warmth. Sharing. "Thanks, Adele, but I'm not really into social events these days."

The look she gave him made him feel about two feet tall. "I spoke with Cheryl today. I told her you'd be with us. It made her so happy. She's been terribly worried about you. Please do this for her. And for us."

Two mothers ganging up on a body were impossible odds to beat. "Of course."

She beamed infectiously. As annoyed as he was at being blatantly managed, he felt the corners of his mouth twitch. Quinn had learned her tricks from a master.

He wouldn't have thought it possible, but Adele's smile became even brighter when Daniel joined them.

After another round of human and canine introductions, Daniel said, "I didn't realize Quinn was planning on getting another dog. She's got her hands full with that bird. And now Tucker's sick."

"Love can change a person's plans," Adele said.

He offered Daniel the non-turtledove-and-sparkly-rainbow answer. "Bowie's owner is in the military. She adopted him so he wouldn't leave the area. It'll make it easier to reunite them."

"Quinn's good when it comes to thinking about others," Daniel said.

"Yes. Where she runs into difficulties is figuring out what she herself needs," Adele said.

A hell of a conversation to be having with Quinn's parents. He wondered how fast Adele's smile would cool and how swiftly Daniel would boot him off the ranch if they knew that last night he'd been like some pimply adolescent with a rocket in his pocket for their only daughter, and a hair's breadth from showing her what *he* needed.

As for Quinn, he didn't see that she had any problem getting what she wanted and needed. As far as he could tell, she had everyone wrapped around her finger, and Josh right where she wanted him.

"Guess what, darling. Ethan's joining us for Thanksgiving."

"You'd best get some riding in before then, son. I heard Pete's got you clearing the trails?"

"Yeah."

"Your shoulder's doing okay?"

"It's still attached." Though he was loath to admit it, the massage Quinn had given him hadn't only worked a miracle on his lower half. This morning he could shift and rotate his shoulder without coloring the air blue with his curses.

He hated thinking how much Josh was enjoying those talented hands.

"That's good. How about you take a break at around three o'clock and join me for a ride? I'm checking the water level in the ponds and tanks—the drought's making that more important than ever. And there's some land for sale that I want to look at, too. Adele and I have been talking with the owner about buying it. But I always say a person sees things differently from the back of a horse."

"You sure you want the company?" Quinn was an impossible craving, a forbidden indulgence. He accepted that. But getting back in the saddle was something he could consider doing. He was fit enough now. Between the barn chores and the push-ups and planks he'd been doing in his cabin, a fair amount of his strength had returned. A ride on the trails crossing the ranch's rolling hills would allow him to shake off his fixation with Quinn, leaving nothing but the horse moving beneath him, the cool air rushing against his face, the wash of browns and greens coloring the distant mountains.

"Why not? You don't jabber." A twinkle entered Daniel's eyes. "To tell you the truth, the real bonus is that if I lend you my gelding, I'll have an excuse to take Bilbao out. Ward gets to have way too much fun with him."

This was a classic Knowles gesture of generosity, making it seem as if they were the ones receiving the kindness. Bilbao was a flashy three-year-old, but anyone who knew horses would give his eyeteeth to spend an afternoon on Kane's back.

"Glad to help out," he said.

"We'll have to put Ethan on the payroll, Daniel."

"Not necessary," Ethan began, but Daniel spoke over him.

"Someone with your abilities would be a great addition to the ranch. But I expect you'll soon be back to wandering the world and sharing what you've seen with the rest of us."

No, those days were over. His body might have begun healing, but he knew instinctively that no matter where he aimed his camera lens, all he would see through the viewfinder would be the faces of the soldiers who'd lost their lives.

Chapter
SIXTEEN

IT WAS THANKSGIVING Day and Quinn was not in a charitable mood. She was thankful, to be sure. Tucker had come home, his chestnut midsection bisected by a belly bandage that replaced the stent bandage he'd worn during his stay at the clinic to promote drainage and prevent infection, a common post-op danger. Not all vets would have gone to the trouble of inserting a stent, but Gary Cooney was the kind of vet who always went the extra mile for an animal, regardless of whether it was an expensive show horse or an old goat past breeding age. Thanks to his exceptional care, Tucker was doing as well as she could hope for a high-strung horse recovering from major abdominal surgery.

For years now Thanksgiving had been relegated to her least favorite holiday. Even Valentine's Day was better because at least she got to laugh at the gag gifts she and her brothers exchanged. Reid usually came up with some doozies, like ridiculously girly underwear. But there was nothing funny about Thanksgiving. Couldn't people find a way to give thanks without gorging themselves on gruesomely killed turkeys and geese?

To be honest, this year her sour mood wasn't due exclusively to the holiday. It was also linked to Ethan and

Josh. Since the morning she'd called it quits with Josh, she'd begun to feel like she was back in the fifth grade and contagious with the grossest case of cooties ever. Ethan certainly acted that way. He basically pulled a disappearing act whenever she approached, only deigning to exchange a few terse words when others were around or when he was handing Bowie over for playtime with Sooner and Pete's cattle dogs.

His attitude stung. She'd thought they were becoming friends. She supposed she must have freaked him out when she gave him a massage. Had it been obvious that she liked the feel of his body beneath her hands far too much, more than she'd ever enjoyed touching a man? If so, he couldn't make it any clearer that the attraction was one-sided.

And Josh? Well, the weirdness continued there, too. He hadn't bothered to talk to her once since their last conversation. Not that he'd really been around to see, let alone talk to. Where once it had seemed that Josh was everywhere she went, these days a Bigfoot sighting was more common.

If there was a glimmer of brightness in the holiday, it was the outing on horseback. The hour-plus trail ride was the only part of the day she truly enjoyed. All available staff was invited. She refused to let the fact that this year the ride included Josh and Ethan dim her enjoyment at being out for a pleasure ride with her family and friends.

It was certainly not the moment to ask one man what the hell was wrong with him or quiz the other as to why he was so darned happy to have no future anything with her.

Not that she'd have succeeded. Ethan, on board Kane, was trotting at the front of the group of sixteen riders with Pete, Ward, and Tess. Only the presence of her mom riding by Ethan's side would have been a stronger deterrent. She felt self-conscious enough without having her family witness Ethan giving her the ice-cold shoulder.

Opting to ride along with Mel and Frank, a married couple who'd worked as ranch hands for years now, and just behind Jim and Josh, she at least solved the mystery of where Josh had been hieing off to. Anyone within earshot learned it. Not even the pounding of the horses' hooves, the jangle of bits, or the creak of leather could muffle the enthusiasm in Josh's voice.

"Those pancakes at the luncheonette? The finest, Jim. And they serve 'em right up until closing."

"They do? Since when?" Jim asked.

"Well, let's put it this way. They do for me." Josh made it sound like he'd obtained a standing reservation at the French Laundry. "And the day before yesterday? Apple cider donuts. Maebeth packed a box for me. I brought it back for Campbell and Patricia as a going-away present. Know what? They've invited me to visit the set of Campbell's next movie. Sweet, huh, Jimbo?"

She couldn't help but glance back. Jim looked appropriately envious, but since he was one of the kindest guys around, he said, "For sure, dude. And it sounds like you're getting treated like royalty by Maebeth."

Expecting Josh to answer with his signature cocky grin, she was surprised when his face flamed beneath the brim of his hat. And his expression? He looked . . . *sheepish*, though she'd never seen a sheep's face turn bright red.

"Yeah, Maebeth's been real nice to me. She's coming today, you know."

Quinn missed Jim's reply, for up ahead Ward and Pete had reined to a halt. The group of riders was in one of the meadows, this one roughly a hundred acres in size and presently empty of Angus cattle or Lincoln sheep to prevent overgrazing.

It must be time for the races.

The riders formed a loose circle around Ward. He was already speaking, and as she caught his words, she realized that he'd been explaining the origin of the races to Ethan, which had begun when she was twelve and riding Bandit, a sweetheart of a paint horse who'd taught her so much. Thirty years old this year, he was still just as bighearted and dependable, his job now to carry guests on trail rides.

"Since we're mostly wrangling cattle or leading trail rides, we don't often have the chance to test our horses against each other. Dad came up with the idea of holding a friendly competition once Quinn was big enough to have a fighting chance and not cry too much when we creamed her."

Not waiting to see whether Ethan smirked in response to Ward's comment, she said, "Rewriting history much, big brother? I seem to remember you sulking like a baby the first time Bandit and I beat you by two lengths."

"It was by a nose, brat."

"Still feeling the sting, huh?"

With a shake of his head, he returned his attention to Ethan. "Excuse the interruption. My kid sister has so few chances to tout her accomplishments." Ignoring her loud snort, Ward continued. "So Dad's picked this spot and is going to draw names at random for each heat. The race is straightforward. It starts over there by that outcrop." He pointed to a rock formation a few hundred yards in the distance. "The finish line will be here. We've delegated Tess and Mia to officiate. Tess will start the riders off and Mia will call the winners at this end."

It was a nice way to include the two in the event, Quinn thought, since her future sisters-in-law still persisted in their vow to never break out of a trot. She wondered why her dad and Ward hadn't found something for Ethan to do as well. He could run the stopwatch. Usually it was passed around randomly.

Shielded by the brim of her hat, she let her gaze travel over him. He must have done a bit of riding in the years since he'd left Acacia because he was handling Kane with ease. The large chestnut was tossing his head in excitement. All the horses were pumped up this afternoon, frisky and chomping at the bit. They knew this wasn't a typical workday outing.

She'd been surprised to see him on Kane. Her dad was funny about certain things. One, he was super-obsessed about his tractors. Two, he considered Kane, who'd been foaled on the ranch, *his* baby. Even she had trouble wheedling a ride on him. But Ethan had taken him out twice now. When she'd remarked on the fact, her dad had merely smiled and said, "Ethan does a real good job on him."

Something was up, and it annoyed the heck out of her that she'd been left in the dark.

Unlike most of the men, Ethan was hatless and he'd shaved this morning—it was Thanksgiving after all. The dramatic lines of his face were on full display: the slash of his cheekbones, the dark ledge of his brows above his flint-gray eyes, the blade of his nose, the jut of his chin, the thin lips that looked too severe to smile, his cropped salt-and-pepper hair. Taken individually, they were just parts of his face. Together they formed a stark, uncompromising beauty.

As if he'd felt the weight of her gaze, Ethan turned his head. And she forgot how to breathe. When had he become the handsomest man she knew? On the heels of that terrifying thought, she realized that his mouth remained pressed in a stern line. No tiny upward hook at the corners of his mouth, no crinkle of crow's-feet by his eyes telegraphed his quiet amusement. She'd grown used to seeing the tug of a reluctant smile and a flash of something irresistible illuminate his gray eyes and soften his stoic demeanor.

Afraid of what he might see in her expression, a longing that left her confused and invited scores of remembered inadequacies, she looked away quickly, focusing on her father, who withdrew two small squares of paper from his breast pocket. Unfolding them, he said, "Looks like we'll be starting this year's races with some serious flash. Adele, you're up against Josh. Now remember, honey, he's just a rookie."

Her mom was astride Forester, her dark bay gelding. As she gathered up her reins, she asked, "Shall I go easy on you, Josh?"

"Heck, no. Where would the fun be in that?" Josh replied.

Whoops and laughter erupted, everyone quickly getting into the spirit of the races. With wide grins on their faces, the two contestants trotted off with Tess, who was riding her favorite horse, Brocco.

Quinn had seen enough of Waylon in action to know that he was a fine horse, with some serious go in him. He topped Forester by a couple of hands, and he was only six years to Forester's twelve.

No matter. Adele and Forester smoked the Texan duo.

Quinn could tell by the almost comical expression on Josh's face when Waylon crossed the finish line a generous length behind Forester that he hadn't been expecting a woman old enough to be his mother to leave him in the dust.

Perhaps he should have checked out whose name was on the plaques and trophies in the glass case in the tack room. Adele Evers had been a champion rider and barrel racer.

Though everyone else at Silver Creek knew exactly what class of competitor she was, they all clapped loudly, and Quinn yelled, "Way to go, Mom!" after she had circled back and was trotting toward them.

"Oh, that was fun! Forester does love to run. And since I have to head back to the house to get the turkey in the oven, I thought I'd give him a chance." She leaned down and patted him on his arched neck. "No hard feelings, Josh?"

He swept off his hat in a gallant gesture. "No, ma'am. But I'd like to challenge you to a rematch real soon."

Her mother laughed. "Any day you choose." With a wave, she urged Forester into an easy lope and headed back to the ranch.

Ward and Reid's were the next names in the draw. Some serious trash talk was immediately exchanged. She could even hear them as they headed to where Tess was waiting to start the race.

Her brothers thundered toward them neck and neck. Then Reid leaned just a little more forward over his gelding, and Sirrus, his nose stretched forward, inched past Ward's black gelding.

"And it's Reid and Sirrus for the win!" Mia called, not even attempting to hide her elation.

When her brothers rejoined them, Ward was subjected to a round of good-natured ribbing.

Holding his gloved hand up, he said, "No offense, Mia, but maybe you should stick to judging wines."

Formerly shy Mia merely wrinkled her nose. "Or maybe you should just gallop faster next time, Ward."

"Ooh, burn," Quinn said gleefully.

Reid guided Sirrus over to Mia. Wrapping an arm around her, he leaned in for a kiss.

Ward made an exasperated noise. "Right, do we need any clearer evidence that the judge's vision is flawed? Look at that ugly mug she's kissing." He shook his head in mock despair.

"Over at the vineyard that's what we call sour grapes,

dude," Reid replied. "Why don't you go keep Tess company so she can soothe your wounded pride?"

Quinn was still grinning when her father spoke. "Time for the next draw. In this heat we have Quinn up against Ethan."

"What? But Dad, he can't—" She swallowed her objection at the stone-cold look Ethan shot her.

"Ethan can't what, Quinn?" her dad asked.

"Nothing," she muttered. If Ethan was fool enough to risk re-injuring his shoulder racing, that was his business. And no, she would not be foolishly offering any more massages.

Calls of encouragement as well as a few razzing comments from Reid followed them as they loped toward Tess. Ward rode on the other side of Ethan, her brother having decided to stay with his fiancée for the remainder of the races.

Quinn looked straight between Domino's black ears, worried that if she let her gaze stray to Ethan she'd get distracted by the way his long thigh muscles hugged the saddle and how tall he sat, following Kane's rolling gait with surprising ease. It occurred to her that he might be an even better rider than she'd thought. Still, even Reid had to work to beat her. A win was certain.

It would have been difficult for Quinn to escape developing a competitive nature when she had two older brothers and worked most of her day among physically active men. It was an adrenaline rush to pit her athleticism against theirs, hold her own, and sometimes even blow them away. And being the daughter of a former champion brought out the compulsion to give every race her all.

The problem was that with their present audience, she couldn't protect Ethan by sandbagging, even if she'd wanted to. Everyone, even Josh, knew how fast Domino was. But she wasn't inclined to throw the race in any case. A good trouncing was what Ethan deserved for once more being as friendly as winter in Siberia.

They pulled up next to Tess, and Quinn had Domino execute a turn on the haunches, just to remind Ethan what real riders could do. "Prepare to eat my dust, buddy."

He raised a brow. "Don't believe that's Kane's plan."

"That's the ticket, Ethan. Don't let Quinn psych you out. She's the queen of trash talk."

"Losing is such a bummer, isn't it, Ward? Of course I can only speak theoretically, unlike you."

"Make sure you beat her by a country mile, Ethan."

Tess cleared her throat. "Ahem. If the riders are ready?" She was obviously taking her role as race official very seriously.

Ethan had already gathered up his reins and was sitting deep in the saddle. She bared her teeth in a mocking smile. "Yeah, let's get this party started."

"All right, then." Tess paused for a beat. "On your mark, ready, set . . . go!"

With Tess Casari's shout of "Go!" still ringing in the air, Ethan closed his legs, bringing his heels to Kane's barrel, and opened his fingers around the reins. Kane was a superb animal, and that was all the signal he needed to leap forward. Within seconds they were at a full gallop, tearing over the open field.

She'd had an even better start; he expected no less from her. She was two heartbeats ahead of him, with Kane's nose at her leather-covered knee, and Ethan's eyes right at her shapely ass, those taut cheeks encircled by a pair of dark brown leather chaps, drawing his gaze like a bull's-eye. He couldn't hang back here. The sight was too hypnotic.

Dragging his gaze from Quinn's rear, he fixed it where

it belonged. The finish line was ahead, two hundred yards away.

Damn, but he'd missed this exhilarating, hell-bent-for-leather kind of riding, of feeling a good horse's awesome power thundering beneath him. He'd missed the challenge of staying balanced over his mount's neck so that he was helping it, not hindering it. Ethan's hands followed the dip and rise of Kane's copper neck. Below, the horse's dark red forelegs stretched long as he ate up the ground.

He didn't know Kane well, so it was difficult to gauge how much was left in his tank and if it was sufficient to beat Quinn's Domino.

Could he do it?

Pride and the rush of pitting himself against this woman who was driving him crazy demanded he try. He leaned even lower over Kane's neck, so the ends of the gelding's long mane whipped the front of his shirt. Clearly loving the race and bred for speed and endurance, Kane responded, surging forward until he was neck and neck with Domino. He sensed as much as saw Quinn's sideways glance and hoped to hell astonishment was stamped on her face.

Less than a hundred yards to go. It was up to Kane now and how much he wanted the win. Ethan's sole job was to make sure he encouraged Kane to go for it and didn't do anything to get in his way. Hunkering low, he brought his hands even farther up the bobbing neck beneath him. The gelding's ears swiveled back and, as if turbocharged, his hooves drummed even faster. Ethan grinned into the wind as the chestnut pulled away from Domino and tore across the finish line.

Daniel was still crowing when the assembled riders pulled into the open area between the corrals and the horse barn and began dismounting and then tending to their mounts.

"If you can believe it, I enjoyed watching Kane run that race almost as much as if I'd beaten Quinn myself. You did a good job with him, Ethan."

"Thanks. I appreciate the loan. He's a great horse, Daniel." Unknotting the cinch, he pulled off the saddle, only now feeling the twinge in his shoulder. He glanced over at Quinn. It was highly doubtful she'd give him another massage—even if he were masochistic enough to ask for one—since she'd barely looked at him since offering a terse "Congratulations" after they'd slowed to a jog to circle back to the group. Betraying herself, she added, "Helluva run for a greenhorn," with a cold, slashing glance meant to leave him looking like a Christmas ribbon.

Yeah, she was good and pissed at having lost to him.

Ignoring the voice that whispered that he'd be behaving the same way if Kane hadn't made that last-second surge, he focused on enjoying the moment, which included reveling in Quinn's ire.

"Mind sharing where you've been honing your racing skills?"

"Several months before Afghanistan I was on assignment in Dubai. Met a man who bred Arabians. Aziz heard I liked horses, so he invited me to ride with some of his exercisers in exchange for photographing them. We'd go to the Warqa Desert. They gave me some tips. Before that, I spent some time with gauchos in Argentina. Played some polo in Chile—"

"Wait, don't tell me," she interrupted. "And before that you went foxhunting in Ireland."

He inclined his head, making sure not to smile. She already looked angry enough to spit nails. "Irish fox-hunters are crazy bastards, every last one of them. They breed terrific horses, though."

Narrowing her eyes until they were sharp slivers of blue, she shook her head. "If I'd known you've been spending the years riding all over the world, I might have put some effort into the race."

"Bull," he said without heat. "You wanted that win as bad as I."

Her lips tightened, but she had the grace not to bother to lie.

"Who knows," he added, "maybe someday you'll have enough experience to beat me."

QUINN HADN'T THOUGHT the day could get worse. She was still feeling as if Ethan, her dad, and perhaps her entire family had pulled a fast one on her. Had they all known Ethan rode whenever he had a moment to spare? And if he'd hung out with gauchos on the pampas, then he might even rope as well as she.

Did he have to be any more attractive?

And because she had to make some effort with her appearance before the Thanksgiving meal, she'd been forced to cut short her time with Tucker, Sooner, and Bowie and placate Alfie with some grapes and sliced bananas before stripping off her clothes and jumping in the shower. Knowing it would please her mother, she pulled on a burgundy knit pencil skirt that ended mid-calf, paired it with a gathered embroidered blouse, and tugged on her favorite boots. Deciding that everyone was going to razz her for having lost to Ethan, she took the extra time to dry and brush her hair and apply gloss to her lips; she should look good when she faked a smile.

It was funny how things worked. If she hadn't spent those minutes primping to boost her confidence, maybe she would have arrived at her parents' house with it intact. Instead that few minutes' delay put her on a collision course with Josh and Maebeth and blasted any self-assurance she possessed to smithereens.

Since it was a little past five o'clock, they must have thought everyone was already inside. Or else they were so lust-addled they simply couldn't keep their hands or mouths off each other.

She'd stumbled upon lots of lovers around the grounds of Silver Creek. But never when she was carrying a platter full of brownies.

"Oh, crap!" she cried as the dish slipped from her nerveless fingers, dropped on the toes of her boots, and then bounced onto the path, her brownies getting a nasty coating of gravel.

Maebeth's face was a magenta hue—doubtless an exact match to Quinn's—as with one hand she shoved her dress to a basically respectable midthigh length and with the other grabbed at the scooped collar where Josh had shoved it aside to reach her breast.

Josh was marginally more presentable. Quinn thanked God Maebeth hadn't gotten to work on his belt buckle. But the snap buttons on his shirt made a distinct *click click* as Josh refastened them and then jammed his shirttails inside his black jeans.

Quinn stood there feeling like a fool until she finally realized she couldn't leave two dozen brownies lying in the dirt. She knelt down and blindly rearranged them on the chipped platter—damn, she'd liked that piece. She had just dropped the last smushed square onto the messy pile when the door of Maebeth's Charger opened and then slammed.

Maebeth held a large Pyrex dish covered in tinfoil. "I better take this inside so it can go in the oven," she said with a strained brightness.

"I'll be right there, Mae honey. Just need to speak to Quinn about something."

Wow. "Mae honey" and public makeout sessions. Josh hadn't let even a spore of moss settle on him.

No, really, we don't need to say anything to each other. But Quinn's protest remained a silent one, her tongue turned to lead in her mouth.

The rest of her was just as useless. She stood with her platter of ruined brownies—a minor tragedy right there—feeling like a complete dolt for not having a single witty or breezy or even cutting remark to offer in order to demonstrate how totally unfazed she was by this situation. Could she be any more lame?

The sound of Josh clearing his throat interrupted her thoughts. "Quinn, I know you must be feelin' a little weird at seeing me and Maebeth together."

Understatement of the century. "No, I'm happy for you." And a part of her was, truly. "It's kind of *quick*, you know?" As in lightning fast.

"I guess it would seem so to others. But the crazy thing about Mae and me is, well, we just clicked. She's so terrific."

"She's great."

"Yeah." He grinned. "Plus, we really get each other." He looked at her, and his expression sobered somewhat. "You and me, well, something was missing, right?"

She gave a tight nod.

"It's not that I don't think you're really sweet, Quinn, 'cause I do. It's just I knew we really didn't feel the same way about things—important stuff. And, well . . ."

At his hesitation her nerves went on high alert. "And what?" she prompted even as she dreaded his answer.

"I could tell that something was off when we kissed, like you were holding back or that maybe you weren't into it . . ."

A whirring began in her head, a defensive mechanism to block out the hurt of his words. She'd heard a variation of them too many times before. They all boiled down to the same message: something was wrong with her. Luckily she and Josh hadn't gotten naked together, or his choice of words might have been crueler. *Holding back* would have turned into *cold, not into it* transformed to *cock tease*.

The trees bordering her parents' grounds became a fluid blur of brown and blackish green. She was grateful for the failing light, though she doubted Josh would bother to note her expression. "I hope things work out for you and Maebeth, Josh. Really I do. I, um, need to go inside and see whether Mom needs help with the feast."

Sometimes having a reputation as a brownie junkie came in handy. Her mother took her terse explanation of tripping over a stone and dropping the platter without a lengthy cross-examination. It helped, too, that the house was full and that her mom, Tess, and Mia were rushing about the kitchen, putting the final touches on the dishes. Every burner on the stove was occupied. Bowls upon bowls of food crowded the marble countertops. In the center of it all were the two turkeys, roasted to a golden brown and resting on matching platters.

Quinn averted her gaze.

"Don't worry about the brownies, Quinn. We'll make do with the pies and Roo's hazelnut cake. One can't eat brownies every day," her mother said, transferring bright green string beans from a pan into a serving dish and then sprinkling chopped parsley over them.

"Mom, brownies are the staple of champions."

Her mother replied with a skeptical "Hmm" before adding, "I heard Ethan did a superb job on Kane."

"Harsh, Mom. Really harsh," she muttered.

She heard Tess choke back a laugh. Mia became suddenly absorbed in the challenge of arranging steaming rolls just so in the breadbasket.

Her mother merely smiled. "Darling, can you tell everyone it's time to come to the table? And then if you can give us a hand with the dishes? And do cheer up, darling. I've got you seated next to Josh."

Oh, no. No way in hell . . .

She had just switched her name card with Maebeth's and, with grim determination, was circling the glass- and china-laden dining table to put her folded cream-colored card next to that of Francesco, Lorelei's boyfriend, when Ethan's voice had her jumping the proverbial mile.

"Care to explain why you're messing with the name cards?"

She glanced over to where he stood with his good shoulder propped against the doorjamb. He'd dressed up, too, in a crisp white shirt and dark brown jeans. He looked ridiculously good, and that only depressed her more.

As if he intended to wait there until he got an answer, he crossed his arms and cocked his head. His gray eyes were unwavering.

Imagining what words he would choose to describe her deficiencies and instinctively knowing that they would cut even more deeply than Josh's, she scowled. "I haven't seen my friend Lorelei in days and she and Francesco don't know as many people here as Maebeth does, so I switched places with her. No biggie."

If possible, his gaze became even more intent. "You were next to Josh. Won't he be disappointed?" he drawled.

It came as no surprise that he knew where she'd been seated. If he'd been at the house for any length of time, her mom would have put him to work carrying stuff like the warming trays that were ready and waiting on the sideboard. Ethan was the sort who noticed and paid attention to the tiniest of details. It's what made his photographs so good, so striking and memorable. Right now she'd have preferred if he had the acuity of a brick.

"Believe me, Josh won't miss me. I'm eminently replaceable. And since you've memorized the seating plan, you'll realize that my switching places puts me farther away from you. I'm all about spreading happiness today." Aware that her voice was woefully short on humor, she brushed past him to summon the others to the table.

The meal was delicious. That was the near-unanimous and very vocal assessment. But Quinn honestly could have been sharing a flake of hay with Tucker for all she'd been able to taste. For the most part she simply stared at her plate, willing the pile of food to evaporate, since there was no way she could swallow it down. Even though she didn't particularly enjoy looking at mounds of butternut squash, farro pilaf, and green beans—she'd passed on the poblano-spiked mac and cheese, shock of all shocks—it was better than letting her glance drift down the table to where Josh and Maebeth were rubbing elbows . . . and likely other body parts beneath the cloth-covered table.

It shouldn't hurt. The rational part of her understood that. But somehow the fact that she'd been the one to break off her and Josh's nascent relationship no longer carried weight. What mattered was that five chairs down and across from her were Josh and Maebeth, already happily hot and heavy, and here she was, unable to exchange the most basic of kisses without alerting Josh to the fact that sex freaked the bejesus out of her.

Comparisons were odious. Generally she tried to resist them, but right now she couldn't shake the compulsion to ask why she couldn't manage to enjoy an act that everyone else seemed to have no problem with.

So while she might not be eating her farro, she was gorging on self-pity with a side of disgust.

The conversation around the table was as abundant as the food and flowed as easily as the wine Mia and Reid had selected. With sixteen people it was easy to zero in on snippets. Tess was telling Ethan about some of the more colorful characters in her old neighborhood in Queens, New York. Frank and Mel were talking to Jim and Mia and Reid about the best fertilizers for Mia's grapes. And on her right were Lorelei and Francesco, who worked as a general contractor; they were discussing the local economy with her dad and Ward and Marsha.

"I took Ethan to look at a property that's for sale next to ours. Joe Trullo's place. With the ongoing drought, I'm still of two minds as to whether it's a sound investment."

"Has he lowered his asking price?" Ward asked.

"Nope, which means it's unlikely it'll sell anytime soon. But I've told Joe I'd like the chance to match any offer he receives. We've been friends and neighbors long enough that he's agreed—though he's not particularly happy I haven't snatched the parcel up."

"Hard to believe anyone is going to want farmland when water's as scarce as hen's teeth," Ward said.

"The drought's making it hard for the entire county," Francesco observed. "I'm lucky to be getting steady work. I have a number of jobs—but they're in Sonoma and Napa. Second homes for San Fran folks. Money's still flowing there, even if the water's down to a trickle."

"Good for you, Francesco," Ward said.

Her dad nodded in agreement. "Shows word is getting around about the quality of your work. That's how Adele and I built up our business in the beginning. Here's to another successful year for you." He raised his wineglass.

"I'll second that!" Lorelei said with a smile, and leaned in so her shoulder bumped Francesco's lightly.

"How are things on your end, Marsha? Are you getting as many animals as before?" her dad asked. "I know it was real bad a few years back."

"No, the numbers aren't quite as high—thank goodness. Of course any homeless or abused creature is heartbreaking and we still have far too many come through our shelter's doors. I only wish that the work Lorelei and I do in finding forever homes for them could impress the bureaucrats wielding their budget axes. I've been told we may have to close." As if to wash away the bitter taste left by her announcement, she took a long sip from her wineglass.

Quinn couldn't even manage that. She was numb with shock. What would happen to all the lost and abandoned animals in the area?

Mia was seated a few seats away but must have overheard Marsha's comment. "My God, Marsha, that's terrible news. There's got to be some way to save the shelter."

Dredging up a smile, Marsha made a noncommittal noise. Quinn figured her friend was doing her best not to spoil the holiday mood.

"What will you and Lorelei do if the shelter closes?" her dad asked.

Marsha shrugged. "We'll be all right. I'm single, I can relocate if necessary. And I know Cat Lundquist over at the animal emergency hospital would love to have Lorelei back on staff." Before taking the job as Marsha's second in command, Lorelei had worked as a vet tech for Dr. Lundquist.

"Cat's great, but it wouldn't be the same as what we do at the shelter," Lorelei said. "Those animals really need us."

"Yeah, they do. Ours is a no-kill shelter. It's fairly obvious that if the remaining shelters start to become overcrowded, more animals will be euthanized."

"We'll just have to bust our butts even more for the

animals who come to us," Lorelei said. "And figure out a way to appease those numbers-obsessed bureaucrats."

Damn it, Quinn thought. Here she was feeling sorry for herself when her friends might end up losing their jobs. And how many animals would be left to die in the woods or dumped by the side of the highway if there was no local shelter?

"What about private donations? Would they be enough to prevent your closing?" she asked.

"That would depend on the amount we received. At the very least it might buy us time to figure out a way to convince the agency to let us continue our work."

She did some quick math, calculating Tucker's vet bills and making sure she left herself a cushion to absorb any future costs for her animals. "I've been saving up some money. I have around forty thousand I can donate to the shelter. Consider it yours. Happy Thanksgiving."

She must have spoken at one of those odd moments when there was a sudden lull in the conversation, people chewing a last bite of turkey and cranberry sauce or buttering a cheddar and chive biscuit, for her offer sounded amplified, though she hadn't raised her voice.

Then everyone seemed to speak at once, lauding her generosity but also showing theirs by adding to her contribution.

Okay, she thought. While she might be a muddle-headed screw-up when it came to men, at least she knew how to open her heart and soul to animals. This was what she was good at. The rest—the guys, the sex . . . well, she needed to shut the door on all of that again. It was that simple.

THE THANKSGIVING MEAL had gone well into early evening, with Nancy arriving with her two young kids in time to sample Roo Rodgers's desserts and weave new stories into the conversation. The chatter and laughter flowed for more than an hour after the last piece of apple pie and hazelnut cake had been consumed and every cup of coffee and mint tea drained.

Through it all, Ethan had watched Quinn. Watched and tried to figure out what the hell was wrong with her.

He waited some more, until he knew Alfie's special time to spread his wings and squawk like a banshee would be over. Bowie was growing used to the bird, but Ethan wanted to ask his questions without the parrot's unique brand of racket filling every corner of the house. It would be too easy for Quinn to ignore him then.

Bowie knew the way to Quinn's. He was panting eagerly by the time they reached her door. Ethan had him sit while he knocked. He took her shout of "What?" as invitation.

She was still in her skirt and top, sitting on the sofa with her legs curled under her. Sooner and Pirate were in their habitual spots, flanking her. From the extended roar he heard when he entered the house, he didn't have to glance at the TV to know that tonight's viewing was dedicated to the big cats. She'd probably chosen it to make Pirate happy.

Because that's what she did. She made others happy.

It was why he'd known something was off, really off, when she'd spouted those lines about being replaceable and spreading happiness by moving farther away from him. There'd been a brittle self-mockery to them that had taken him aback. He was the one who had the market cornered on negativity. Yet as the meal progressed and he continued his scrutiny, he realized something more disturbing. She was hiding a deep sadness.

Even when she made that magnificent, outsized, impulsive, and beautiful gesture to Marsha and Lorelei, offering them a generous donation to help keep the animal shelter open, a shadow had still obscured the radiance that was Quinn Knowles.

He found he seriously disliked the idea of her being sad.

A quick folding of his arm had Bowie dropping onto his haunches. The dog was whip smart when it came to hand signals. Ethan couldn't wait to see whether he was as fast a learner and as obedient when it came to sheep work.

Unsnapping the leash, he released Bowie from his sit and the dog trotted to the sofa, collapsing beneath Quinn's folded legs.

He studied her for a second. Yeah, whatever had been bothering her was still there. She was staring just a shade too fixedly at the cheetahs chasing down an antelope. Not quite believable when she averted her gaze from a roast turkey.

"You going to tell me what the hell's wrong with you?"

She flicked him a disdainful look. "I'm assuming

you're talking about the money I gave to the shelter? FYI, I can do whatever I want with my earnings. And don't feel you need to stay."

He dropped down into the big overstuffed chair. "Bowie likes the evening visit."

"I wasn't talking about Bowie. He's welcome." She returned her attention to the screen.

He sank deeper in the chair and propped his booted feet on the coffee table. "Of course you can do what you want with your money. I wasn't talking about that." He paused, momentarily distracted when the cameraman zoomed in on the distinctive markings in a litter of black leopard cubs. "But what were you saving the money for, anyway?"

"Excuse me?"

"When you offered Marsha the money, you said you'd been saving it. What for?"

She gave him a sideways glance before making a study of her lap. Apparently spotting a piece of lint, she picked at the burgundy fabric with her slim fingers. "Someday I want to open an animal sanctuary. Not just for dogs and cats, but for larger animals. There's nothing like that in this area for animals that, for whatever reason— age, infirmity, trauma from severe abuse—aren't being adopted. I was saving to buy some land. But Marsha and Lorelei are doing important work and their efforts need to be supported."

"You're pretty remarkable, you know."

"Of course I am."

He continued as if he hadn't heard her voice dripping with sarcasm. "Do you have any idea how few people in this messed-up, self-absorbed, and self-important world shelve their own desires in order to help others?"

"Stop right there," she said sharply. "There are plenty of good people doing great things for others. I'm fortunate that I have the means to be generous, but it doesn't make me better or in any way remarkable. For all you know I'm overcompensating."

"There you go again, spouting BS. What's with this 'overcompensating' and 'I'm replaceable' crap? Did Josh say something to you? Did the idiot spout off about Tucker?"

"What?" She frowned. "No, he's never mentioned anything about Tucker." She paused as if struck by that, then returned to her brooding fixation with the animal program.

"So what did he do?" he persisted. For some reason he really wanted to make Josh's face a little less pretty.

"He didn't do *anything*. We just ended things."

He sat up. "Wait. You're not telling me he broke up with you."

She gave him a look, which he was damned if he could decipher. "No. I'm the one who called it quits. It's old news, anyway. I told him days ago, the morning after I brought Bowie home," she added. "But Josh was all for it. If I broke his heart even the teensiest bit, believe me, he's over it."

She'd been breaking up with Josh on the porch that morning? Friendliest breakup he'd ever seen, but then Quinn didn't exactly follow convention. He chose not to dwell on the surge of satisfaction that rose inside him at knowing Josh wouldn't be putting his hands on her again. "Well, that explains why he was all cozy with the bleached blonde today."

"The bleached blonde has a name. It's Maebeth. And she's nice. And she's really, really into him."

"So why are you down in the dumps? Are you annoyed that he's not heartbroken?"

"What is it with you? First you don't talk to me for days, now you want to cross-examine me?"

"I was preoccupied." *With you,* he added silently. *A persistent condition.* "Sue me."

"I would, but I don't have money for a lawyer," she replied with mordant humor. "Here's an idea. You could leave. That would be an excellent solution."

"I'd rather have a beer. Want one?"

"So kind of you to ask. Since you refuse to leave me in peace, I might as well drink."

Without further ado, he went into the kitchen and grabbed two longnecks from the refrigerator. He rummaged around in her cutlery and utensil drawers until he found a bottle opener and popped the caps. Spying a bottle of whiskey sitting on the counter next to a neat row of shot glasses, he placed two over the bottle of Jack Daniel's and returned to the living room.

Sooner had abandoned his place to lie on the rug. Bowie, too, had moved, and now lay beside the smaller dog.

Ethan dropped down on the empty cushion next to Quinn. The weight of his body caused hers to tilt toward him, their shoulders bumping. She righted herself and scowled afresh. "That's Sooner's place. And that's my whiskey."

She certainly was tetchy tonight.

"He abdicated. Here," he said, and passed her a beer. "I figure whatever's bugging you may require more than an IPA." Placing the bottle of whiskey on the coffee table, he set up the shot glasses and filled one to the brim and the second half full. He slid that one toward her. "Cheers."

"Didn't your mother teach you about equality?"

"For all I know you're going to get sloppy on even this minute amount of whiskey. I hate tears. As I recall, you used to bawl awfully loudly."

"I was, like, four years old." Shooting him a lethal look, she reached forward, plucked the bottle from the table, opened it, and filled the shot glass to the brim. "My house. My whiskey. My shot glass. My inebriation." Picking up the glass, she tossed its contents back, and set it back down with a sharp rap.

"Impressive," he said dryly. "Now, will you please tell me what the hell is wrong?"

She flopped back against the sofa, and Pirate jumped off in a feline huff. She eyed Ethan balefully as if he were somehow to blame for that, too.

"Fine. All righty, then. You want to know why I'm mad? I'm good and bloody sick of guys making me feel like a freak. I'm trying my best to get this whole sex thing over with and either get past the 'God, this is awkward and excruciatingly unpleasant' aspect and accept that's how it's going to be for me or decide to call it quits forever. I'm trying to settle the issue here, damn it, but it doesn't help to have guys talk about how they can tell I'm not 'into it.' Well, duh."

His ears were ringing. He shook his head, hoping for clarity. "Did you just tell me you're a virgin?"

"Don't worry. It's not communicable."

He couldn't even smile. "And you were going to embark on this fucking experiment of yours with Josh?"

"He seemed like a perfectly viable candidate."

"Jesus H. Christ," he muttered, and downed his own whiskey, wishing it were a double. "The guy has all the subtlety of a Texas longhorn."

She reached forward to grab her beer and said something that sounded like, "We can't all be timberwolves."

"What?"

"Nothing." She sank back against the sofa. "And there was nothing wrong with Josh. He was a perfectly good kisser. I'm sure of it. The problem's with me. It's always been."

"Always? Just how many candidates have you auditioned for this job?" What a surreal conversation. She was a virgin at what, twenty-four? A part of him wanted to run screaming for the door. The other part, well, he didn't care to examine too closely how weirdly possessive her being untouched made him feel.

"You're not nearly as funny as you think you are. I don't know." She shrugged uncomfortably. "Six, I guess—Josh was unlucky number seven. I've been trying to do the deed since freshman year in college. At least with Josh I realized pretty quickly that it wasn't going to work out. We didn't have to get naked or anything."

Thank God. He realized that his heart was pounding, hammering at the walls of his chest. The whiskey had done nothing to subdue it. He poured himself another shot and drank it, feeling the burn all the way down to his gut.

The mega-amped drumming of his heart continued unabated. It wasn't the only thing going haywire. The air in Quinn's living room had become charged. Electric. It made his skin prickly, made his muscles twitch and tighten. Did she have any idea of what this conversation was doing to him?

She'd shifted and was sitting kitty-corner now, her folded legs angled on the cushion between them. She had the beer bottle between her hands and her fingers were busy shredding the label into soggy confetti.

His gaze traveled up, taking in the gentle swell of her breasts. Christ, he could chug the entire bottle of Jack Daniel's and it wouldn't dull his wanting her. She had her hair up now, had done one of those things women did, twisting it and somehow looping it around so that the ends poked through a honey-blond donut. He imagined loosening the mass with his fingers and having its silken weight cascade over the backs of his hands as he cradled her head and brought his mouth to hers.

Had he telegraphed his thoughts? Was that why she swallowed convulsively? Was that why her pulse was jumping at the base of her neck, its tempo as crazy as his own? He wanted to press his lips there and then let them travel over her body and discover other pulse points.

The tension in him redoubled.

But she was a virgin and, from the sound of it, a spooked one. He could only imagine what had happened to make her think there was anything wrong with her sexually. What he knew was that there were a lot of assholes in the world and that when their sexuality was threatened or when it became obvious that they'd failed to arouse their partner, they were quick to find fault elsewhere. Now he had seven assholes he wanted to punch.

"I doubt very much that you were the problem, Quinn, or in any way to blame."

Instead of replying she tipped her beer to her lips. "I'm afraid I can't agree. I'm kind of messed up. I know I look normal, but when the clothes come off and the touching starts, well, I just go kind of numb. Sometimes I get scared, but mostly I'm numb."

Had Galahad been sent on a quest involving Quinn Knowles, he would have failed. Ethan was sure of it. In a desperate attempt to block out the image of Quinn naked and where on her delectable body he'd like to touch her first, he pinched the bridge of his nose—hard—and almost missed her whispered confession.

"But I felt something when I touched you."

Slowly he lowered his hand. "Did you now? Interesting. I felt something, too."

"You did? What—what—" she repeated, and then paused as if gathering her courage. "So what did you feel?"

"Hard," he said, deciding bluntness would be the most effective tool with her. "No small feat, since I haven't had an erection in months."

"Oh." A wealth of emotions stole across her face: embarrassment, excitement, pride . . . Humor won out. "I guess you're not the only one who's been numb. So, are you cured?"

He shrugged. "Who knows? I may be as sexually dysfunctional as you."

"So we could be flops together?"

"Misery loves company."

She snorted. "You seem awfully calm about your, um, condition. I thought men got all weird about that or began popping Viagra like they were Pez."

He might have replied that he didn't give a shit about a lot of things anymore, his ability to achieve an erection included. Instead he said, "It simplified things."

He took advantage of her silence as she considered this by saying in a bored voice, "I suppose we could see if our sorry states could be improved. One friend helping another out."

"So we'd become fuck buddies?"

The intentional vulgarity was an act of phony bravado, he knew. He grimaced nonetheless. "Is that what you kids call it nowadays?"

"And what term would you use, Gramps?"

He raised a single brow in challenge. "How about plain old 'lovers,' brat?"

"Oh." The silence stretched between them, and he wished he knew what she was thinking. "But it would just be sex, right? Because, you know, I'm not looking for a relationship. I don't have time for neediness—"

As if he did.

"—and you men seem endlessly needy."

"I'll do my best to keep any whining and clinginess in check," he said dryly. "As for the rest, I'm not looking for a relationship, either, so relax."

"Good to hear." She took another slug of beer and lowered the bottle. Her gaze raked him. "And how *up* for this *Masters of Sex* experiment are you? Semi? Quarterly?"

"Ha. Very funny. Let's just say you might have your work cut out for you." He had a hunch that having her focus on his rather significant problem might make her forget her own. "By the way, do you have any condoms?"

"I'm a virgin, not a moron. Of course I do. I keep a supply in my medicine cabinet and change it monthly."

He tilted his head, intrigued. "Worried they'll expire?"

"Nope. Worried my mother will poke around in it—the statistics on medicine cabinet snooping are outrageous—and ask questions if, one, I don't have any and, two, they sit unused. I also keep some in the bedside table since she's a canny one."

"You're exaggerating wildly."

"Only a little." She brought the beer to her lips and finished it off. "Mom's going to be so disappointed about Josh. She was trying to set me up with him, you know."

Adele poking around in her daughter's stuff? Wanting Quinn and Josh to date? Both ideas were ludicrous. He eyed her shot glass, her half-empty beer. "How drunk are you?"

"Not even buzzed. I may be a flop at sex but I can drink with the best of them."

Damned if he was going to let the sex be lousy. Then a stark and uncomfortable realization struck Ethan. He'd never attempted to seduce a woman before. Never had to. A look, a stroke of a finger, a simple "Come home with me tonight" had always been sufficient to get what he wanted.

Trust everything to be different with Quinn. Why was he doing this again? Oh, yeah, because he thought he might die if he didn't touch her soon.

He stretched his legs out long and then patted the tops of his thighs. "Why don't you come here, Quinn?"

She looked at him as if he'd just sprouted a second and even uglier head. Christ, how ham-handed had those guys been with her? Were they the doofus surprise-in-the-popcorn-box types?

"You scared?" he asked quietly.

"Absolutely freakin' terrified."

He nodded. "You look it. You realize we're not going to do anything you don't like or want or that doesn't feel good."

She gave a tiny and wholly unconvincing nod in turn.

"You don't need to be scared with me, Quinn. I lived with terror for six months. I saw brave men battle it every waking hour. It sucks and has no place between lovers. Can you trust me and let it go?"

WHAT HAD SHE done? She had no clear idea how she and Ethan had gotten here, with him inviting her onto his lap as the first step to possible fornication. She'd needed to vent, big-time. That fact she willingly acknowledged as well as this next one: that for once she'd needed to spill her frustration and anger into human ears rather than fuzzy gray ones.

But she hadn't expected it to come to this. Surely this was the most unusual run-up to sex ever, she thought, eyeing his lap and the brown denim stretched over his lean thighs and the not negligible bulge just inches below his belt buckle.

Was he telling the truth?

He had to be. No man would willingly admit to sexual impotence. And she'd given him an erection? The notion filled her with a thrilling sense of power.

"Quinn?"

She dragged her eyes up. His mouth was crooked in a small smile. "I have a face, too, you know. Come here," he said, his voice easy, almost a sleepy rumble.

She knew what he was doing, recognized the technique. She used it herself on animals wracked with fear. He was slowing everything down, his movements, his speech—she bet even his heart rate was dropping to lessen the chances of startling her. Something like gratitude unfroze her muscles enough for her to smile a little.

And she did trust him, had ever since the night they'd spent with Tucker. Even at his most irascible and prickly she knew Ethan would try to help her with her problem. And he wasn't being prickly now. He was being kind of amazing.

And she'd made him hard?

With her eyes locked on his, she inched toward him and tentatively put her hand on his thigh. His muscles beneath the denim were as unyielding as cement.

"Um, the sofa might be more comfortable," she said breathlessly.

"You wound me. Here." He placed his hands on either side of her waist and, as if she weighed no more than she had at age four, lifted her and settled her across his lap. She tried not to squirm, but she was very aware of how many of their body parts were touching and brushing. And those thighs, they weren't merely rockhard. They were warm. And she was absorbing his heat. She shifted again and her shoulder pressed against the wall of his chest. A memory flashed bright and vivid of his naked torso. Her heart began galloping and there was nothing, absolutely nothing she could do to rein it in.

Fighting panic, she looked up. This close, Ethan's eyes glittered like chips of mica ringed with black. She'd never noticed how thick his dark lashes were, either. She pulled back, wanting him to look *familiar*.

"Hi," he said.

"Hi." The word came out a weak whisper. "You know, this is incredibly awkward."

"I know."

He did?

"We might be completely incompatible."

She hadn't expected that, had never heard a guy say anything but, *Babe, I'm gonna make this so good for you* . . . or some equally unnerving variation.

"Yeah." She bobbed her head manically.

"We're going to have to take this step by step. I think you should kiss me and see whether you like it." He paused. "And I'll let you know my verdict. We can take it from there."

Oh. So he might call it off if she was a lousy kisser, huh? The other guys hadn't seemed to think she kissed badly. She could do this, she was sure of it. Frowning, she leaned forward, only to pull up short when she saw that his eyelids were crinkled with mirth. "What?"

"You look like you're going to a funeral. It's only a kiss, Quinn. They're generally pretty enjoyable."

Goaded, she snapped, "Fine," and lunged forward, plastering her lips against his, and pressing his head back against the sofa. He made an *mhmmf* sound against her mouth, but she could tell by the stretch of his lips that he was smiling. And suddenly she was, too, and noticing that his lips felt okay against hers and that his breath was warm and smoky from the whiskey. It was good whiskey. Her lips opened and her tongue dipped in for a taste.

One kiss became two. Two turned into three. Then his tongue joined hers in an easy tangling mixed with slow sweeps and she lost count. She wasn't even sure she knew her name anymore. Her world had narrowed to wet heat and pulsing sensation.

He certainly knew what he was doing in the kissing department. He'd let her take the lead, answering her thrusts and glides, then slowly introduced his own moves, probing and drawing her tongue deeper, nibbling on her lower lip as he switched the angle of his mouth, kissing her just a little harder, as if every taste fueled his hunger. His mouth roamed, too, traveling over her face and kissing the arch of her brows, the shell of her ear, the nerve-sprinkled path down the column of her neck to where her pulse hammered, and then returning to her parted lips to catch her gasp of surprised pleasure.

"Do you like me kissing you, Quinn?"

Oh, yes. "It's all right."

"Mmm." He kissed her again, slowly, deeply and then raised his mouth to whisper. "Obviously I have to work on my technique."

Her lids grew heavy at the idea of him kissing any better.

She felt the brush of his nose as he dropped a beguilingly light kiss on the corner of her mouth. "Do you want me to touch you, Quinn?"

"I, um . . ." She swallowed hard. "Yes, I guess so."

He nuzzled the side of her temple where her hairline began. Who knew that was such a sensitive spot? Had no one ever kissed her there or did Ethan have some special power over her? And why was he still only kissing her?

She unglued her tongue to ask, "Do you want to—touch me?"

"I might."

She was torn between laughing and elbowing him. But either reaction was preferable to the ones she usually had: either a blank numbness that resembled a winter whiteout or a growing unease that made her skin crawl like an army of ants on the march.

"Lift your arms for me," he said, interrupting her thoughts.

"What? Why?" she asked panicky.

"Because I enjoy seeing what I'm touching."

She could do this. She'd been naked with Mark and Randall and Tim and she'd liked them a lot less than

Ethan. Her arms nevertheless were as heavy as thirty-pound weights as she raised them.

He moved far more quickly. The blouse veiled her for a moment. Then it was off and she fought not to hunch her shoulders.

His hoarse curse had her looking up.

"Damn," he repeated. "It's possible I've been around goats too much lately, but your breasts are lovely."

She snorted with sudden, helpless mirth and felt a spurt of gratitude that he'd dispelled her anxiety—even temporarily. "Maybelle's got a fine pair of teats, I'll have you know."

"That may well be." His smile was wry. "I guess I prefer ones that aren't hairy."

Her laughter caught and became a soft gasp as he placed his hands over her. She felt the heat of his palms through the lace of her bra and her nipples grew pebble-hard and aching. Her gaze flew to his.

His gray eyes glittered mesmerizingly. "You're perfect, Quinn," he breathed, sounding as stunned as she felt. Then his mouth captured hers and he kissed her as if it had been years since he'd last tasted her.

Urgently his mouth devoured as his hands caressed, stroked, and kneaded. She should have been recoiling, but she was caught in the currents of pleasure swirling through her and pooling deep and low. An insistent, demanding pleasure, it made her arch into him.

He'd already unclasped the catch of her bra, dragging the lace over her breasts and the straps off her shoulders and down her arms until they slipped free. His hands returned to her, cupping the undersides of her breasts and lifting them so he could suckle, drawing one nipple and then the other into his mouth, laving their sensitive tips with his tongue until she cried out helplessly, pressing closer.

She hadn't realized that one of Ethan's hands had quit

her breast until she felt his fingers skimming up the length of her bare thigh. She jumped and then somehow, rather than creating more distance, his hand was there, touching her through her panties, rubbing the silky fabric against her cleft as her center clenched and pulsed.

"You're wet," he whispered roughly and pressed a kiss against the inside of her breast.

"I—" She whimpered and instinctively tightened her thighs, closing them about his strong fingers. "Yes."

"That's good, Quinn. Really good." His voice was a rich rumble.

She didn't know about that but then coherent thought fled as he slipped beneath the elastic to find her slick flesh. He stroked, gliding, probing, and circling, setting her nerves afire, enticing her hips to follow his fingers in a dance that left her dizzy. Everything inside her spiraled in faster and tighter circles, its nexus where Ethan's fingers caressed. And when his mouth latched on to her nipple and raked it with his teeth, she spun off as pleasure burst wildly inside her. She came with a broken cry.

Boneless, she collapsed against him, wracked by tremors even as his fingers quieted, cupping her soothingly. His other hand stroked her hair, which had somehow come loose from its bun. "Has anyone ever given you an orgasm, Quinn?"

In answer she rubbed her forehead back and forth against his chest. "They tried to," she whispered.

She felt the warmth of his breath against her hair as he kissed the top of her head, the tightening of his biceps as he drew her to him even more snugly, possessively. Then, in a move as disconcerting for its fluidity as for its lack of warning, Ethan rose to his feet, lifting her with him. Wordlessly he strode toward her bedroom.

A short distance, it was long enough for her fears to come crashing in, breaking through the sensual daze created by his kisses and the shattering release he'd given her.

It made her remember that this was more than a high-octane make-out session. This was more than being brought to climax with an ease that was actually kind of disturbing—why had Ethan succeeded and no one else? This was about her losing her virginity, having another person *inside* her.

This was about no longer being herself.

Okay, she'd achieved an orgasm in his arms—the man must have magic in his fingers—but that didn't mean she could do *this*. And somehow, because she'd managed the one, it made her imminent failure that much worse. It would become a true disaster rather than an awkward flop. And no longer would she be able to label herself sexless, which would leave seriously hung up—screwed up—the only remaining designation.

And Ethan would know.

The cotton quilt felt cool against her shoulder blades and the middle of her back as he laid her down in the middle of her bed. His hands went to the waistband of her skirt and she shivered as his fingers brushed her stomach.

His gaze burned. So did his words. "Quinn, I want to see all of you and touch you everywhere. Will you let me?"

The temptation to babble an excuse as to why this— him and her naked together—was a supremely, colossally bad idea was nearly irresistible. But she would not be a coward. Not with him.

Her tight nod made the muscles in her neck ache.

The skirt and her panties came off awfully quickly, in one long sweep down her legs and past her bare toes.

And then she was buck naked and he was hunkered by the edge of her bed, taking her in with those eyes that missed nothing. She realized she hadn't even managed to unbutton his shirt while they'd been on the sofa. *Lame, Quinn, really lame.*

He was nodding and for a second she thought he was confirming her assessment. Then he said, "You're as beautiful as I thought."

"What?" she said, momentarily distracted. "Wait. You mean you've thought about me? Naked?"

"Of course. You're stunning, Quinn. Effortlessly sensual."

Effortlessly sensual, huh? It boggled the mind.

As he spoke, his fingers had gone to work on his shirt, undoing the buttons. He didn't bother with them all, simply opened the shirt wide enough to pull it overhead and toss it next to a chair. She had a moment to note the flex of muscles over his ribs, the breadth of his shoulders, but then he stood and his hands went to his belt buckle. Her mouth went dry when, with the same alarming efficiency, he unfastened it and unsnapped his jeans, shucking them off along with his boots and socks. He stood before her, narrow-hipped and muscle-thighed, the entire package encased in black knit boxers.

Package. The word blared in her brain. Surely she could have picked a better word. Or maybe not. For all she tried to wrench it away, her gaze remained fixed on the very prominent area where the black fabric was stretched.

Sucking in a shallow breath, she wondered what he'd do if she hyperventilated.

And why the hell didn't he sense her growing panic, damn it? And why did her body grow hot and tight all over again when, with the same calm efficiency he'd displayed in stripping her clothes and his own, he shoved the waistband down his hips and thighs and stepped out of them.

Her mouth went as dry as Southern California.

She'd seen some penises in her life. A couple had been comical-looking, one kind of scary and angry-looking, another frankly underwhelming. Ethan's was none of those. Jutting out from a patch of dark brown hair, it looked impressive. Capable. Seriously functional.

"You certainly don't seem to be suffering from any problem at the moment," she accused. *Unlike you,* a nasty voice reminded her.

"What can I say?" He shrugged as if his very large erection was no biggie. "Many women would be pleased they had this effect on a man."

"I'm not 'many women.'"

His lips twitched but he didn't laugh, probably knowing he'd be risking castration if he did. "Remember how I said I wasn't going to do anything you didn't want? That holds true whether we're dressed or naked, whether I'm standing here or moving inside of you."

Oh God, did he have to speak in such a way that she was forced to rise to the occasion and be *reasonable*?

"Fine. Let's just do it and get it over with."

He cracked a smile. "Your enthusiasm overwhelms me."

"Little nervous here, okay?"

"I'd never have guessed." He put a knee on the mattress and then, supporting himself on his arms, he stretched over her, his body kissing hers in a skin-grazing brush. The hair covering his legs tickled hers and the silkier strands on his chest teased her breasts. For all his leanness, he seemed very solid—muscle, sinew, and long bones—above her. Another part of him was unquestionably so. His penis prodded, demanding attention, demanding entrance.

What disturbed her most was that she *felt* it all. She

was hyperaware of everything about Ethan when normally her senses shut down as if she'd been dropped in liquid nitrogen and flash frozen.

Ethan made her hot. Hot and twitchy with awareness and something she was very, very afraid was desire. Wanting Ethan made her even more vulnerable.

"Touch me, Quinn," he whispered.

She drew a shuddering breath and placed her hands against his ribs, a safe, neutral, unsexy spot. She guessed wrong.

Against her flattened palms, his skin was fire-warmed satin. Her hands rose and fell with each heavy breath he took, and she felt the crazy pounding beat of his heart enter her bloodstream and call to hers.

In answer, her hands slid over taut skin. Reaching his chest, her fingers traced the flat discs of his nipples, circling them again as they puckered for her. A shuddered breath escaped from his lips.

The sound was irresistible. It drove her. She reached up to palm his shoulders, her left hand smoothing the ridges of his scar and then, in a long, deliberate sweep, followed the length of his back to cup the taut globes of his buttocks. His shudder was replaced by a groan, helpless and rough.

Her gaze locked with his. She couldn't have looked away even if she'd wanted to, not when his eyes were blazing bright. Yet he hadn't dropped his weight on top of her, hadn't begun grinding against the apex of her thighs, hadn't moved a muscle, even though it was clear he wanted to. His restraint, his control said so much, spoke to her as loudly as his need.

She could trust him.

Could she trust herself, find the courage to let him in, not knowing how that would alter her?

Her gaze shifted to his mouth and she remembered the searing pleasure of it. If there was a man who could make her forget her fears, however irrational yet now ingrained, this man holding himself in such fierce check was the one.

She spoke in a whisper. "The condoms are in the drawer on your right."

A smile she'd never seen before lit his face. It was achingly tender and proud.

"That's my Quinn." His lips moved as he lowered his head to capture hers, claiming them in a lingering kiss that had her fingers curling into his muscled butt. Releasing her, he stretched an arm and grabbed the nightstand's drawer pull.

She heard him rummage inside the drawer. The crinkly scrape of foil was amplified, portentous. It sounded like a big effing deal.

He shifted back, aligning his body and settling over her, letting her feel his solid weight.

She was right. It—everything about Ethan and what he and she were doing—was a big effing deal. But she was too distracted by what he was doing to succumb to full-blown panic—yet. He was busy, kissing her everywhere—her mouth, her breasts, the hollow of her belly button, the cradle of her hips—with a hunger that summoned the sizzling heat inside her. His hands streaked over her, making her gasp and writhe. If his touch made her hot before, now it ignited an inferno of flames that licked and stoked. And that feeling, of being wound tighter and tighter, of reaching for something extraordinary, unforgettable, and sublime, began again. And she was too consumed by it to ask why Ethan alone could kindle it. All she knew was that he was rocketing her to a world of pure sensation.

His mouth blazed a trail across her hips. Inches below, his hands caressed her thighs. Urging them apart, his fingers brushed her curls.

Her breath caught and then came out in a gasp as his

fingers parted her and stroked her clitoris in aching passes and glides. Delving deeper, rubbing harder. Each foray left her moaning softly as her hips followed the dance of his fingers. Only dimly did she register the rip of foil, the movement of his free hand smoothing the condom over his erection.

His muscled thighs nudged hers wider. And then she felt the blunt head of his penis press against her. With sudden clarity she remembered how big he was. . . .

"Quinn."

"What?" she gasped. A boulder had somehow lodged in her windpipe.

"Don't tense up on me. I don't want to hurt—"

Fear, wet and chilling, doused her. "But it's going to." She pulled away from his weight, from the blunt tip of his erection, pressing deeper into the mattress.

His hands clasped her hips, holding her gently but blocking her retreat. "Yeah, it will," he said quietly. "But it'll hurt less if you relax. Just lie back, and—"

"Wait, don't tell me. Think of England?"

His breath huffed out in a soft laugh. "I'd rather you thought of me and how much I want to please you."

Under the circumstances, she shouldn't have found his crooked smile so charming. Especially when her own lips felt like they'd been pumped full of novocaine.

"Quinn, sweetheart." The endearment came out a rough whisper. "I want to come inside you now. I want it more than I've wanted anything in a long time. Will you let me?"

His request, so simple and unvarnished, made her heart ache and melted the last of her defenses. Slowly her muscles relaxed.

Trust—it came down to trust.

Drawing a deep breath, she looked up at his face. His expression was intent yet somehow more open than she'd ever seen it. Slowly she nodded, then raised her legs, wrapping them about his hips. Opening herself to him.

"Ah, Quinn, you humble me," he whispered before he claimed her mouth in another fervent kiss. Taking her hands, he linked their fingers. "Now keep your eyes on mine," he commanded softly.

As her gaze locked with his glittering gray one, she felt him press against her core, aligning himself. Her breath hitched.

"Easy, there." His voice was quiet for all its intensity. "It's me with you, and I'm going to try my damnedest to make this painless and maybe even pleasurable for you."

No false promises with Ethan.

"Okay."

"Hold on tight, sweetheart."

With a powerful thrust he entered her and changed her world forever.

Seconds passed with racing hearts and sawing breaths. Sheathed deep within her, Ethan held himself still. Quinn knew he was trying to give her time to accommodate him and accustom herself to the intrusion.

"Quinn? Are you okay?"

He was referring to the pain, of course. It had come in a searing flash when he entered her, sharp enough to cause her to flinch and close her fingers about his, gripping hard. But the pain had been quickly eclipsed by a new and staggering sensation. Of being so *filled*, stretched and so very, very taken.

He felt even bigger than he'd looked. Thick and hot, and he was *pulsing* inside her. It was as if Quinn could feel his life force beating inside her. The throbbing cadence rocked her womb and touched her heart. She squirmed, trying to adjust to his presence; she felt his weight press down on her, his large body covering and surrounding hers.

My God, is there any part of me he isn't touching? she thought, feeling panic set in.

"Quinn?"

"I'm not sure about this." Her voice sounded small, shrill. She was slipping ever closer to outright panic.

"Well, as long as the jury's still out—"

"Oh my God, are you actually amused by this?" She was on the verge of kicking his shin, elbowing his ribs, hell, doing her best to buck him off, when he nuzzled the sensitive spot behind her ear and sparked a shimmering warmth inside her.

"I'm not laughing, sweetheart. That's happiness you hear," he said, his voice a soft rumble that caressed. "You feel incredible, Quinn. So let's see whether we can't improve things for you." He withdrew a fraction and then flexed his hips, pushing into her at a slightly different—upward—angle this time, touching a thousand nerve endings and inviting them to dance.

A confused "Oh!" escaped her.

He moved again, now lengthening his stroke a fraction before he rocked his hips into hers.

She shivered and felt her muscles clamp tight around him.

He took up a steady rhythm. The stroke was smooth, purposeful, yet she sensed that he was holding himself in check. She was helpless to ignore the thrill of his body's leashed power.

"Better?" he whispered.

Oh, yes, much better, she thought. She arched, welcoming his slide home, meeting his hips in a delicious grind that left him groaning. Moving his mouth to the side of her neck, he scored her sensitive flesh with his teeth and then licked it with a slow lap of his tongue.

He'd freed her hands to caress her breasts, fondling them and teasing her nipples with light pinches and tugs, sending sparks shooting through her. Spurred by the sensations rocking her, her own hands skimmed over muscle and bone with increasing greed, eliciting fevered exclamations and whispers of encouragement as his hips pumped, taking her ever higher.

She found the rhythm. Began to meet his thrusts with her own, exchanged breathless moans with his. They ground and kissed in an erotic dance of tangled limbs and arched backs and clasped hands.

Thoughts fragmented as she strained against him, reaching for more. And he gave it to her. Latching onto her breast, he drew her nipple into the warm cavern of his mouth as his fingers found her clit, plucking and stroking. Overcome, she sobbed, clutching him, tears escaping down her cheeks. And then everything splintered as his hips pumped even harder, sending her flying toward a heart-stoppingly crazy moment of beauty, one made impossibly perfect when his harsh cry joined hers.

Chapter
TWENTY

FOR LONG SECONDS Ethan simply dragged air into his overtaxed lungs. Not only were his lungs overtaxed, his brain was fried, and his muscles were as weak as pulled taffy. Not surprising, since he'd never worked so hard at sex in his life. But the result, Quinn's cry of pleasure as her body tensed and trembled under his, was the sweetest reward. Perhaps that's why he felt so strangely at peace when ordinarily he might be wondering what it meant to have just experienced the most stunning climax of his life.

When slowly he began to process what had just happened in Quinn's bed, he wasn't even particularly worried by how thoroughly she'd reduced him to a quivering, sated mass. Jesus, it felt good.

But he was worried about her. Shadows blanketed the room, making everything softer. Except Quinn's eyes. They shone too brightly. And she was blinking too rapidly. Beneath his lips Ethan tasted the damp salty tracks that crossed the slope of her cheekbones. Heard her breath hitch in a failed attempt to stifle a hiccup of emotion.

That she, a virgin, had come for him a second time was extraordinary, especially when he considered how she'd been callously twisted into so many self-doubting knots by other men. But he wasn't sure if the pleasure she'd found in his arms outweighed the enormity of her initiation. He could only imagine what she was feeling.

He tried to remember what he'd felt when he lost his virginity. Chest-thumping exultation, mostly. But he'd been a callow youth of sixteen, his partner a senior in the D.C. high school he'd transferred to when his dad got a position at the State Department. Sarah Rafferty had been far more experienced, so there'd been no comparing of notes with her. He remembered only being full of gratitude that she'd deigned to allow him beyond third base—because that's how he'd thought of sex back then. Thank God Quinn was getting a somewhat more mature version of that idiotic sixteen-year-old kid.

"You all right?" he asked.

"Of course."

Yeah, and I'm Robert Capa, he thought, the comparison between him and one of the best war photojournalists ever just as unbelievable.

He needed to give her a chance to regroup and find the Quinn she knew, the one who was spunky and brave. It would entail allowing her to ignore the part of herself he'd laid bare tonight: a woman who was as effortlessly sensual as she was generous.

Planting a kiss at the corner of her mouth, he stroked the side of her face and eased out of her as gently as he could. At her involuntary wince, his gut clenched.

"Don't move," he said. "I'll be back in a sec."

Rolling off the bed, he strode to the bathroom, removed the condom and dropped it in the wastebasket under the sink. Turning on the hot water, he ran a washcloth under it until it had thoroughly absorbed the heat. He wrung it out and carried it back to the bedroom.

She'd drawn the covers up and lay with the heels of her hands pressed against her eyes, and kept them there even when he sat on the mattress. His tug on the sheet covering her had her lowering them.

Her eyes were huge. "What—"

"Shh, let me do this for you." He placed the damp cloth between her thighs before she could clamp them together.

She was silent as he wiped her down gently and then cleaned the insides of her thighs.

Her exhale was shaky when he removed the cloth and set it aside. "Thank you," she whispered.

"You're welcome." Even as he spoke he was aware that the chest-thumping primordial thrill that had coursed through him at sixteen was back—in spades. Knowing he was the first to have touched Quinn and shown her pleasure was as heady and potent as any whiskey he'd ever tasted. And, damn, he wanted those firsts with her to continue. Indefinitely.

There was only one problem. Quinn didn't merely have to process the fact that she'd made love for the first time; she had to deal with the aftermath. The difficult stuff. Questions like, *What did I just do? What did it mean?*

Rigor mortis was stealing over her. Any stiffer and she'd crack from post-coital stress. It was time to get Quinn used to the idea of having a naked male— namely, him—in her bed.

If Quinn guessed at his thoughts, she'd probably un-stiffen those limbs real quickly so that she could brain him. Time to offer up a distraction, he decided. She'd do better if he talked rather than followed his own desires, which involved wrapping an arm about her middle and hauling her close to him so he could stroke and pet her at will.

Casually he stretched out on the bed beside her. Cradling his head in his hands, he stared up at the ceiling and breathed slowly, deeply. Any more chill and he'd be asleep. As sensitive as she was, she'd pick up on that.

"It could have been a fluke," he said, not glancing away from his study of the rough-hewn beam-and-plaster ceiling.

"A fluke?"

He heard the slide of hair against the pillow as she turned her head. From his peripheral vision, he saw she'd shifted onto her shoulder, her head propped on her fist. The sheet half covered her breasts. A major gravity fail that the sheet hadn't dropped like Newton's apple.

"Yeah." His biceps bunched as he shrugged. "A fluke."

"How so?"

"The sex was pretty spectacular, Quinn. That's unusual on the first go-round between partners." He let that sink in and then added, "Perhaps you didn't know that."

"It certainly wasn't what I expected."

"How so?"

"Well, I didn't expect it to be so much, to have it feel so vital." Her voice was careful, as if she were finding her way through a jumble of thoughts and emotions.

He couldn't *not* touch her. He rolled to face her. Her lower lip was caught between her teeth. He wanted his own there, biting down on that sweet ripeness, tugging a moan loose from her. He smoothed a hand over her silken shoulder and brushed his lips against hers, letting his tongue caress the spot her teeth had worried.

Seconds passed while they let their mouths speak with clinging lips and exchanged breaths. He felt her body soften and her skin grow warm in response. When one of her hands moved to his chest, palming it, he smiled against her mouth and murmured, "I think we should make sure this isn't just a one-time aberration, don't you?"

She pulled away from him, her expression astonished. "You're not actually serious about the fluke thing?"

"You might not react this time. I might not."

"You're kidding, right?"

He fought a grin.

She must have caught sight of it, for the hand on his chest poked hard. "Not funny."

He caught her lips again and coaxed a smiling kiss from her. "Okay, I'm betting things will go okay, but practice does make perfect, Quinn."

"That might be all good and well in theory, but . . ." Her voice trailed off, and she ducked her chin.

"But what?" he asked huskily.

She lifted her head and her eyes were huge enough for him to lose himself in their beauty. "There's a little matter of soreness. Now I know what all the novice riders mean when they say they're saddle sore."

Something inside him squeezed tight. She was lovely, funny, and honest. A person could learn a lot from Quinn Knowles. "Then I'll just have to be a little creative, won't I?" He gave her a slow smile. "In that spirit, why don't you lie back for a spell?"

TUCKED AWAY IN Tucker's stall, Quinn currycombed her gelding and let her thoughts roam. No one was there to catch her dreamy smile. Tucker was busy butting a yellow rubber ball the size of a cantaloupe. Ethan had hung it in the corner of his stall while she'd been feeding Tucker his ration of hay. Not only had her horse not freaked out at Ethan's presence but he'd further surprised Quinn by taking an active interest in the installation. As soon as Ethan had finished attaching the nylon rope, the horse had walked up and slammed the ball with the side of his head, sending it swinging in a wide arc. By the time he'd chomped his way through his flakes of hay, he'd become quite proficient at batting the ball, stopping it with his muzzle, and then sending it flying in the opposite direction.

Who knew her gelding had ambitions to be a tetherball champion?

Ethan, apparently. His quiet discernment was one in an ever-growing list of reasons why she'd fallen so hard and fast.

A week had passed since he turned the most rotten Thanksgiving ever into a night of wonder, revealing aspects of herself Quinn had nearly lost hope of discovering. That night had been followed by others no less staggering. Hours filled with whispers, entreaties, delirious laughter, and low, drawn-out groans as their sweat-slick bodies moved against each other.

More quickly than Quinn would have believed possible, she had become one of *them,* one of those people she stumbled across regularly at the ranch. Blissed out and in love.

As a Californian, she recognized the tectonic shift that had occurred. Ethan had shaken things—beliefs, feelings, her very heart and soul—forever altering the landscape inside her.

It was possible that if she'd chosen another man to give herself to, the effect would not have been so dramatic.

How to describe what happened when he made love to her? So difficult when the experience changed every time. Sometimes it felt like he'd catapulted her into the stars: dizzyingly bright and awesome. Floating back to the earth, to the circle of his arms and to the slow, deliberate kisses he pressed to her flushed skin, she willingly abandoned that spectacular diamond-bright world, exchanging it for one where she was cocooned in warm, burnished gold.

Sometimes the pleasure was like a giant wave. With each pump of his hips, the swell grew, magnificent and relentless, so powerful that she feared it might break her into a million scattered pieces. But then she would feel Ethan shuddering—quaking—as he poured himself into her and she knew that she wasn't alone. The knowledge made her cry out with joy as the wave broke inside her.

Then there were raw and even raunchy couplings with climaxes hitting her like sudden explosions, making her legs and toes stiffen and her fingers curl into his sweat-slicked flesh, her voice helpless and harsh as she called his name, stunned by the near violent beauty of their mating.

There was only one constant to what she and Ethan shared. Each time the act struck Quinn as more profound.

While the lovemaking was beyond anything Quinn had imagined—and she had a pretty vivid imagination—it was the other things she saw in Ethan that made her heart melt. For instance in those drifting moments before sleep claimed them, he invariably wrapped an arm about her middle and hauled her into the warm curve of his body.

For twenty-four years she'd slept alone. Who'd have thought she would enjoy spooning? Crave feeling their bodies pressed together as their breathing found the same rhythm? Again, the answer was Ethan. Apparently he could read her as well as he could Tucker.

The flick of Tucker's tail brought her back to the confines of the stall, fourteen feet square. While she'd been lost in her musings, she'd exchanged her currycomb for a soft brush. She moved from his withers to his belly, brushing the red coat that had been covered by his bandage, now removed. The incision running along his abdomen looked good. The risk of infection now past, it would heal in a neat straight line, so different from the jagged scars marking Ethan's shoulder. A lasting testimony to the violence he'd experienced.

Would he ever tell her about that day? Really tell her, rather than offering the carefully edited and scrubbed version of how an IED exploded near the armored vehicle he was riding in—horrifying enough though that one was?

From the first she'd wanted to help Ethan heal both physically and emotionally. Now it had become imperative. Because he held her heart, hers ached with the pain she glimpsed in his.

Eleven creatures in the animal world were known to mate for life. While she didn't necessarily identify with *Schistosoma mansoni* worms—parasitic and ugly to boot—she'd always thought the monogamous bonds of swans, wolves, gibbons, bald eagles, and, of course, turtledoves were extraordinary. Magical. The same held true whenever she read about a man and a woman who'd found each other in high school, married at eighteen, and then, after seventy years of marriage, passed within hours of each other.

Now she recognized why those stories never failed to move her and caused her throat to tighten, thick with emotion. It was because she belonged to that group of beings who had one mate, one love for life. Her heart had found hers.

But those stories and articles, poignant examples of lasting and true love, were rare for a reason. While she might know that her heart now belonged to Ethan, she couldn't demand or expect him to feel the same, that she was the *one*. . . .

And unless he was able to heal and banish the pain festering inside him, Quinn feared there would be no real chance for the two of them.

It used to be that Tucker would signal the approach of a human even better than Sooner. No more. He didn't toss his head or pin his ears when Ethan approached the stall and said, "Hi there. Came to see how you were getting along."

Tucker answered first by sending the tethered ball careening into the stall's boards with a satisfying *thwack*.

"As you can see, we're having a smashing time."

"So he still likes it?" Ethan asked from the half-open sliding stall door.

"Oh, yeah. Once Gary Cooney clears him to return to the pasture I'm going to have to string a ball from one of the oak tree's branches so he can keep his skills sharp. Maybe he can get Harper and Bristol to play."

Tucker once again hammered the ball at the stall wall.

"Something tells me he may be in a different league from those two."

Harper and Bristol were knuckleheads. Sweet and mellow as could be, though. Along with Brocco, Tess's favorite horse, they were a beginner rider's dream.

"Could be," she agreed. "So how was Domino?"

Ethan had borrowed her gelding to ride out with Ward and Reid to check on the cattle.

"Smooth. Incredibly responsive. You did an amazing job training him."

She was pleased he liked her horse. After the Thanksgiving Day ride, her family had begun lending Ethan their mounts on an almost daily basis. By now he'd ridden not only Kane but also Rio, Sirrus, and Forester. Serious competition for Domino. She'd held off offering Ethan her horse so as not to raise any suspicion among her family that anything had changed between her and Ethan.

"Domino was a dream to bring along." She picked up the carryall and placed the soft brush back in its spot next to the other brushes. "Our yearling Rush is like that. You've seen him, right? The dark chestnut colt?"

"The one who wants to race every horse that enters the pasture."

"Yeah, he's got the moves. Plus Rush remembers everything. And speaking of quick learners, are you ready to teach Bowie 'come bye' and 'away to me'? Sooner loves showing off his skills."

"You've got the time?"

Seriously? She was in terrible danger of wanting to spend every hour of the day with him. She liked being with him out of bed as much as in it. Today he was dressed in faded jeans and a dark blue flannel shirt. Stuck to it were a few stray white hairs, evidence that he'd been brushing against the spotted white blanket that covered Domino's flank and descended nearly to his gaskin.

The navy blue of his shirt made Ethan's eyes seem darker. She loved how changeable they were. Loved even more how they held her own gaze with a magnetic intensity when he was deep inside her, holding himself still so she could feel his erection pulse as her core muscles quivered and contracted around his thickness. Heat would blaze in them as he started to thrust with long, sure strokes . . .

He took the carryall from her. "Let's go."

With a goodbye pat to Tucker, she stepped through the narrow aperture. Ethan slid the stall door shut and grabbed her hand in his. Hand holding. That was part of her life now. A warmth as delicious and heady as mulled cider filled her.

He set a fast pace. Luckily she had long legs, so she didn't have to trot to keep up. It was midafternoon, a lull in the day before the feeding and watering and sweeping up commenced. The chill in the air guaranteed that the hands would be taking a coffee break in the staff room adjacent to Pete's office. It being midweek, there wasn't even too much tack to clean and inspect for damage, either. Between now and Christmas and New Year's it would be the weekends when they'd be running at full capacity. Then there'd be a blessedly slow period in January, with mostly repeat guests visiting, those who already knew how tranquil Silver Creek Ranch was in the still of the winter.

She was grateful for the lack of activity; no one was around to see her so obviously attached to Ethan. So far she and Ethan had managed to keep their new status on the down-low and she wanted to keep it that way for as long as possible.

Their steps rang in quick crunches of dirt and stone on the road that led to the cluster of staff cabins and then a quarter of a mile farther to her family's houses.

"We can practice with Bowie in the backyard, where there'll be fewer distractions," she began, only to have Ethan surprise her with a tug as he veered abruptly, heading up the gravel path to his cabin. "You remember we left Bowie at my house, right?" she reminded him as they jogged up the narrow porch.

"I know." He jammed his key in the lock and pushed the door open. "Didn't want to haggle with Alfie and Pirate over you. Or have Sooner give me the look."

"What look?"

"The one he levels when I'm about to kiss you."

"Oh." A delicious shiver rippled through her.

"Yeah." Pulling her inside the warmth of his cabin, he spun her around so her back was pressed against the planked wall. Her breath caught and he stole it, plastering his mouth over hers. Like the roaring velocity of a Formula One, their kiss went from hot to incendiary in two seconds flat.

When they broke apart, gasping for air, he muttered hoarsely, "Damn, I want you."

Heat sizzled inside her. Still unused to being struck by this lightning flash of need, she shifted restlessly.

"It's the middle of the day," she noted in a rare attempt to be the voice of reason.

"Doesn't matter what time it is. All I have to do is see you, Quinn." His teeth raked the side of her neck as his hands set to work, tugging at buttons, opening zippers, finding flesh in quick, needy strokes.

"I don't know what you're talking about," she replied weakly, her body turning fluid as he cupped her breasts, squeezing them as he ground his hips against hers.

"Yeah, I know it's crazy. You're not *that* beautiful. But damned if I can do anything about it." Like a plumb line he dropped to his knees and yanked off her boots, sending them flying backward, then grabbed the waistband of her jeans and peeled them down her legs. Hooking his fingers around the elastic waistband of her panties, he slowly dragged them down, revealing the triangle of curls between her thighs.

He touched her. A testing rub of his index finger that ended in a rough whisper of "Jesus," when he found her wet for him. "I have to taste you."

He parted her and brought his mouth to her clitoris and kissed it, lavishing it with strokes of his tongue.

Her fingers raked his hair, then clenched, grabbing strands as the pressure built and built. A deft flick over the straining nub had her exploding with pleasure, sparks shooting through her.

He rose, one hand gripping her hip, steadying her so she wouldn't collapse in a boneless heap. The other dug into his pocket, pulled out a foil packet, and tore it open with a flash of white teeth.

On fire, she grabbed the condom from him and then zeroed in on his jeans, yanking at the buttons and shoving his jeans and boxers down.

He sprang free, and a second wave of need hit her. With shaking hands she rolled the condom over his rock-hard length, his heat penetrating the latex.

His erection was a glorious thing, and she wanted it inside her. Desperately. A whispered "Please" tumbled from her lips.

His grip on her hips as he lifted her was a little rough, a lot delicious, and supremely exciting. She knew what to do now, how to wrap her legs around his hips and guide him inside. Knew to drag air into her lungs when she felt the blunt head of his penis breach her, because when he pushed inside to the hilt, he would make her

forget everything but moving to the rhythm of their
bodies.

The things she'd learned. The very best kind of tutor,
Ethan had given her an education of the senses, sharing
his knowledge with brilliance. Inspired, she eagerly absorbed his lessons in passion, soon growing confident
enough to offer her own so that together they experienced
something as wondrous and ever-changing as the cosmos.

Today she reveled in his unbridled passion: the strength
of his arms as he held her pinned against the wall's
grooved planks. The pump of his hips, fierce and perfect in the arc of pleasure it followed, unerringly finding
the spot that made her gasp, shudder, moan. His restless
mouth that devoured as if maddened for the taste of her.
His hoarsely whispered words that made her clench and
writhe against him.

She was so close.

Ever watchful and attuned, he knew her body, sensed
it quickening in their race to promised ecstasy. His large
hands cupped her rear, squeezing and drawing her down
as impossibly he drove ever higher with a grinding
shimmy of his hips that had her clutching at him, whim-
pering as the pleasure pierced almost painfully sharp.

The hot wind of his breath teased the shell of her ear.
"Come for me, Quinn. I want to feel it."

Her body obliged his command; the orgasm swept
through her.

The aftershocks continued, Quinn's inner muscles milking him even after Ethan had come, too, with a final
powerful thrust of his pelvis and a low groan that
sounded as if it were ripped from deep inside.

Her eyelids were too heavy to open, even when she
heard a soft thud as his forehead hit the wall next to
where hers rested. She could only smile weakly at the

rapid rise and fall of his chest while he struggled to calm his heart. She loved what they did to each other.

Minutes passed—she thought—as they drifted along in some altered state. *Definitely a Marvin Gaye moment,* she mused dreamily.

He moved, shuffling backward with her still wrapped around him and his jeans halfway down his legs, a feat almost as impressive as the blistering hot sex against the wall he'd given her. When the backs of his calves bumped the bed's wood frame, he dropped down, bringing her with him so that she landed sprawled across his chest. The most amazing thing of all? He was still inside her and his hands were still covering her butt.

She liked that. A lot. Who'd have known? A week ago the mere thought would have sent her screaming in a flat-out run to the door.

"You okay?" he asked, his hands tightening again. He lifted his head to kiss the hollow below her clavicle and then make the journey up the side of her neck.

She shivered as her nerves danced. "Yeah. What was all that about?"

"You mean just now?" he asked.

"Yeah."

A pause and then he met her gaze. His gray eyes were cloudy, dazed from passion. "Honestly? I'm not sure. I just really wanted you."

Inside her socks her toes curled. *Good,* she thought. She wasn't alone in her wonder at the intensity of what they shared. *Keep it light,* she told herself. "Well, it's good to be wanted."

His mouth quirked in a funny and ridiculously boyish smile. "And I think I'd been fantasizing about taking you against the wall of my cabin for so long, well, I just had to make it a reality. The real thing's pretty good with you, Quinn."

And she fell just a little deeper.

ETHAN WAS MAKING a serious effort not to think. He'd gotten good at it—avoiding reflection—and lying here, with his arms full of Quinn, with his brain pleasure-fogged from sex, blocking any kind of introspection should have been as easy as rolling off a log.

And yet his thoughts persisted, traveling in increasingly narrow circles, zeroing in on a central theme. Permanence. And Quinn.

Good sex was nothing to sneeze at. Great sex, the kind that was a pleasure so acute the sweat poured off you and lightning danced up your spine as you came and came, emptying yourself in a hot rush, and when it was over you were so wrung out that your muscles were like putty and deep down in the marrow of your bones you felt a happiness as extraordinary as a four-leaf clover—well, a man would be a rank fool to turn his back on anything that rare.

Ethan didn't consider himself a fool.

And yet he was amazed to have found that kind of physical ecstasy here, at Silver Creek Ranch and with Quinn Knowles, who for all these years had lived in his memory as a pigtailed kid barely taller than two stacked hay bales.

He no longer had anything close to resembling a life plan, so why not stick around the ranch and see where things went between them? He was pretty sure he could convince Quinn that he wouldn't be needy—no matter how much in fact he did need to lose himself inside her, and hear the sweet catch to her voice and see the light shining in her blue eyes as he made love to her.

His cellphone sounded, a reminder of everything in his previous life. He tightened his hand around Quinn's waist.

"Who's that?" she asked, reasonably enough given the unusual ring tone. That's what he got for playing with his phone apps during an airport layover.

"My editor. Erin Miller."

"Grim ring tone." Quinn's chin was propped on his chest. As she spoke her chin dug in, prodding him—exactly what Erin intended to do as well.

He managed an even, casual tone. "That's Wagner's 'Ride of the Valkyries.' It suits her." He made no move to grab the phone from where it lay on the floor.

"So, a force to be reckoned with?"

He gave a noncommittal, "Mmm." Erin came from a family of writers and journalists. She was tenacious as hell when a project caught her interest. His had.

"So what does she want?"

"My photographs. Erin wants to publish them. She's having a hard time accepting the word *no*."

Quinn's chin moved a couple of inches sideways. It wasn't hard to guess where her gaze had shifted: to the corner where his camera equipment was stowed. He hadn't gone near the black and metal boxes, hadn't unlocked them, hadn't picked up his cameras to cradle them in his hands or dust them off and painstakingly wipe the lenses clean in a ritual as careful and loving as a mother bathing her infant. The memory cards, the rolls of 35 mm film he used for his ancient Leica—the first camera he'd ever owned, bought for him by his parents when he graduated from high school and which traveled with him everywhere—sat equally neglected. Only one of his cameras was missing. The Nikon. He'd had it with him on the way into Kandahar. It was gone, destroyed in the explosion. At least that was a fitting loss, unlike the loss of human lives. Nothing he could do would ever make up for those deaths.

He realized that Quinn's gaze had been fixed on the equipment cases for far too long. Tension invaded his body, chasing away the post-coital mellowness. Damn it all, he'd come to Silver Creek to forget his photography and shut out everything that had happened in Afghanistan.

"I'm not surprised your editor wants your pictures. Why don't you talk to her?"

"Because we've said everything that needs saying. There's nothing she can add that will change things or make me change my mind. I told my agent to return the advance we negotiated, with interest. She hasn't lost out," he said flatly, so that Quinn would understand that was the end of it.

She ignored the message. "Not monetarily, perhaps, but she's lost out on sharing your work and what you saw in Afghanistan with the world. You must have taken a ton of photographs. What will you do with them all?"

His molars hurt. Consciously he unclenched his jaw. "Nothing."

"Nothing? Ethan, you're a gifted photographer. Your work has appeared in magazines. You've been documenting an important period in American history—"

If there was a being even more tenacious than Erin, it was the woman lying on top of him. Talking would do no good, either with Erin or with Quinn. To make them understand why he couldn't look at those images would involve telling them what had really happened that afternoon with its horror, pain, and death . . . all of which would have been avoided if not for him.

Talking was like probing the wound with a hot poker. And his scars hadn't healed. He didn't expect they ever would, but he'd learned to leave them alone, just as he left his camera equipment and all the images stored on memory cards and film locked tight and stowed away in the corner of his cabin.

Instead of answering he dug his fingers into her thick hair and tugged, drawing her down until her lips met his. His tongue teased the curved seam of her lips.

She pulled back a fraction to look at him. "Is this by any chance an attempt to distract me?"

Damn straight. But this wasn't simply about redirecting Quinn's attention. He wanted to recapture that sense of rightness that her touch alone could provide. He'd come to crave it.

"I'd like to do a lot more than distract you, sweetheart," he said with a grin, capturing her lips again. This time he deepened the kiss until their breaths turned ragged and their hands roamed, impatient and greedy, and her body softened, melting into his. Damn, but he loved how she responded with such open and immediate generosity.

The honesty of her response had him relaxing. Giving her a final kiss, he whispered, "I think we could make both of us forget our own names in a few short minutes, but I figure you and Sooner want to show off your herding commands to me and Bowie while there's still light. Later, though, after Alfie is tucked away for the night, I intend to test my hunch to the max."

Seeing the blush that stole over her cheeks, his grin widened.

"Well, it just so happens I've been thinking that Alfie might benefit from an earlier bedtime." She sat up and stretched, and he took a moment to look his fill at the creamy globes that rose enticingly when she arched. "So, you ready to learn from a master? Because Sooner puts all other herding dogs to shame."

She was perfect. In bed and out of it.

Permanence had never been especially important to him. He'd lived as a nomad with a camera on the hunt for that perfect shot. In such a life, women came and went. Just as he did.

The loss of his photography was an unrelieved ache, but Ethan knew that were he to raise his camera and look through the viewfinder, all he would see would be the ghosts of men who'd become his buddies. The pain would slice straight to his heart.

The closest he came to a sense of wholeness was when he was with Quinn. He'd never expected to feel anything like it, and he was damned if he was going to lose that, too.

Permanence was looking awfully good.

Quinn let it slide, or pretended to at least. She'd seen the way Ethan had withdrawn when she asked about Erin Miller. He wouldn't answer his editor's calls, refused even to contemplate returning to his photography.

As Quinn dressed and dragged her fingers through her hair to comb out her tangled locks, her gaze strayed again and again to the cases containing his camera equipment. Those boxes held such promise. And so much pain.

It scared her that Ethan was still hurting from his time in Afghanistan because she knew the strength in him. His inability to speak about what happened there only underscored how harrowing it had been. If he couldn't handle discussing it, what made her think she'd be able to hear about it? The cocoon that protected her and protected so many who had no loved ones, friends, or family serving and risking their lives would be revealed for the wispy, flimsy thing it was.

A part of Quinn wished she could continue the pretense and act as if she weren't aware that Ethan was still hurting, still haunted. She could see herself ignoring his wounds as determinedly as he did and the two of them falling into an easy routine in this beautiful and peaceful setting, so far removed from the horrors he'd experienced. She sensed Ethan might even be hoping that she'd begun to spin dreams of a future with him so as to provide him with one more excuse to remain here rather than deal with his past.

But while Quinn had grown up protected, she wasn't naive. If Ethan didn't address his problems, then staying here at Silver Creek—trying to have a real and lasting relationship with her—would only work for the short term. Even loving him as she did, she knew it would be a Band-Aid where open-heart surgery was required.

That was the trouble with loving. His pain had become hers. And whatever she and Ethan had could never thrive, might not even survive unless she did everything she could to heal him.

The question was how to convince Ethan to confront the demons that haunted him, knowing that even if she succeeded—and that was a stretch—he might never forgive her interference.

The sky was streaked with orange, rose, and gray when Quinn called a halt to the training session. She and Sooner had begun it by demonstrating to Ethan how to signal Bowie to "come bye"—circle in a clockwise direction—and then move "away to me," where he'd proceed in a counterclockwise direction. It took a few attempts, but then something clicked between man and dog. When Bowie switched directions three times in a row while trotting around the wooden picnic table in Quinn's backyard, she knew it was the optimal time to stop and end the day's training on a high note.

"We'll be able to have Bowie working the young sheep by the end of the week," she predicted to Ethan.

"Really?" he said. His tone reminded Quinn of the day Ward had been handed the keys to their dad's car.

"Yeah. You know, I hadn't expected Bowie to catch on so fast." With a grin, she teased, "Trying to show Sooner and me up, are you?"

Ethan's arm snaked about her middle, pulling her close. "It's in my interest to get these moves down quickly so we can go back inside and work on some others."

"What could we possibly do inside that we can't do here?" she asked innocently.

"How quickly the girl forgets. I guess a refresher course is in order." His arm tightened, drawing her flush against him. His first kiss tickled the corner of her mouth. His second nibbled on her lower lip, and when, with a soft moan of invitation, she opened her mouth, he entered with a bold sweep that had her toes curling in her cowboy boots, her hands fisting around his neck, and her body arching into his lean length.

His taste and scent flooding her, she rose on tiptoes, pressing even closer as her mouth opened wider beneath his . . . only to jump back with all the elegance of a startled stork when a woman's voice called, "Hey, Quinn, are you out here? Oh, sorry!"

Though Quinn's muscles kind of worked, her vocal cords were paralyzed. At least it was Tess who'd surprised them. Had her brothers or, heaven forbid, her mother, come upon her and Ethan necking, Quinn would never hear the end of it.

Tess broke the short silence. "I didn't mean to barge in and interrupt," she said in a voice that held more than a trace of amusement. "I only came by to remind you of tomorrow's dress fitting."

"Right! Looking forward to it," she said brightly, which only made Tess grin, since Quinn never expressed enthusiasm for anything wedding related. "Mia's coming?"

When Mia and Reid announced their engagement, Tess had immediately asked Mia to be a bridesmaid along with Quinn and Anna Vecchio, Tess's oldest friend. That kind of spontaneous generosity and kindness was why Tess was going to be a wonderful wife and a really great sister-in-law.

But it'd be nice if she'd stop looking so outrageously entertained right now at having caught Quinn and Ethan making out.

"Absolutely. She's leaving Bruno in Reid's care. We'll be going in your dad's car—"

"Naturally." Her dad had a thing about cars and tractors. He liked them *big*.

"Ward's driving us so that we can drink as much champagne at lunch as we want. Departure's at nine o'clock. I'm pretty sure we'll have time to get some Christmas shopping in before lunch. Anna's reserved a table for us at Paradiso and has planned the menu. She and Paradiso's chef go way back."

"A good thing we have the fitting beforehand."

"I know. We'll still have waists and functioning brains."

"I promise I'll be ready at nine sharp." She sounded as chirpy as a cheerleader, but Tess's joy was infectious. And she was glad to have a chance to pick up some presents. The bridal shop was in Union Square and the restaurant was in Pacific Heights near Fillmore Street. Between those two neighborhoods they would pass a number of stores where she could pick up fun things for her family and not break her new and much-reduced budget. Perhaps she'd get super lucky and find something for Ethan, too. The question was what to give the man who already had her heart, even if he didn't know it.

"Good." Tess gave her one last twinkling-eyed look and then took pity on her, switching her attention to Ethan, who'd been all cool-guy silent since her arrival. "I hope you'll consider coming to the wedding, Ethan—it's in New York. Ward and I want close family friends celebrating with us."

At her side Ethan shifted his weight the way Tucker did when he was about to bolt. "Thanks, but with all the Knowleses away, I'm thinking Pete will need an extra hand."

Quinn recognized a golden opportunity when she saw one. Her mom had told her how anxious his parents were. Remembering what Ethan had looked like when he first arrived, she could well imagine how relieved they would be to see him now. And she'd lay money on the odds of Erin Miller being in New York City as well . . .

Pretending she hadn't caught his reluctance to attend Tess and Ward's wedding, she said to Ethan, "No need to worry about Pete and the guys. Josh will be taking up the slack."

"And the goats? Josh doesn't know Hennie from Maybelle."

Man, he was grasping at straws, but that didn't stop her heart from swelling at hearing that her nannies had made his list of things worthy of his care. "Mel will milk the does. And I have Lorelei and Francesco lined up to dog-, cat-, and parrot-sit."

She met his squint with a bland smile.

"And I'm sure Quinn would love to have a date to the wedding," Tess said brightly.

Yeah, Tess was going to fit right in with her family,

each member generous as all get-out but still capable of annoying the pants off her.

"I think I can handle going solo—" she began, only to fall silent, distracted by the weight of Ethan's arm landing chummily across her shoulder.

"Well, I do like to help Quinn with any problem," he said, a rumble in his voice now.

He'd picked a fine time to show off his sense of humor. Before Quinn could demonstrate her appreciation by doing something subtle, like poking him in the ribs with her elbow, Tess spoke.

"So you'll come?" At Ethan's nod, she beamed. "That's great. Everyone will be so pleased to see your name in the yes column."

And that included her, Quinn thought, though she wasn't going to admit just how happy she was at his decision to attend Ward and Tess's New York wedding. The thrill was selfish. With Ethan there, she'd have someone to laugh with because he got her offbeat sense of humor. On the dance floor she'd be able to step into the circle of his arms and feel his strength and the heady arousal that would steal through her veins as they moved together under the chandeliers' lights. And when their gazes met she'd see the glittering light in his gray eyes and know that he, too, was counting the minutes until they could steal away and continue their dance skin to skin.

She wanted that. Even more, she wanted Ethan to face his past, and in New York he wouldn't be able to turn his back on it so easily. But in forcing him to confront his demons, Quinn realized she might be risking losing him forever.

Chapter
TWENTY-THREE

THE NIGHTMARE GRIPPED Ethan with claws curled long and sharp as a bear's, digging deep until it felt as if he were being rent into bloody strips. He fought it, but the images, the sounds, even the smells, an unholy perfume of gunmetal, oil, and sweat, continued in a relentless onslaught.

He was in the Humvee, behind the passenger seat. Casey Logar was driving, Archie Donovan riding shotgun. Aaron Smith sat behind Casey, sucking hard on a wad of chaw, his dark jaw thrusting and cheek muscles jumping under the dome of his helmet. Rocks, kicked up by the tires' treads, pinged the vehicle's undercarriage in an angry staccato that punctuated the tense hum reverberating inside.

Ethan stared out the dusty window, studiously ignoring the disgruntled vibes emanating from Casey. And that was when he saw it: the red rubber bounce of a child's ball, the pumping of thin arms and legs that matched the determination stamped on a little boy's face as he chased it, a tableau that was the picture of innocence.

But Ethan knew what was to come. For this was more than a nightmare. It was his past, relived in horrifying clarity. He remembered the strange prickle at the back of his neck, the way his gut clenched at the sight of that bright, perversely cheerful flash of red—a harbinger of a deeper-hued one spilling from bodies and mixing with the dun-colored earth. When he heard the panicked shout of an adult yelling at the child, he suddenly knew with awful certainty . . .

His own agonized scream ripped from his throat. He jackknifed up shuddering, gasping as he drew cool air into his burning lungs.

For a second he didn't know where he was, only that it was night and the air was scented with pine and lavender and that he was alive while four others were gone forever. Three good guys, brave soldiers, sons, brothers, husbands . . . beloved. And a little boy, whose simple game ended in mayhem and death.

Oh God. God-fucking-damn it, why? he whispered silently. His breath still coming in raw pants, he bowed his head while tears that stung like acid fell from his eyes.

Disoriented though he was, he recognized the hand that touched his heaving shoulder, the voice, quiet for all its alarm that asked, "Ethan? Are you all right?"

He flinched. "I'm fine." He forced the words out. "I had a bad dream."

"Maybe if you talked about it—"

Tension chilled the sweat on his body until it felt as if he were encased in ice. "Back off, Quinn. You don't understand."

"I could if you'd let me."

The guilt he carried bubbled to the surface, thick and toxic. "Not interested."

Pretending not to hear her soft gasp at his cutting words, he swung his legs over the side of the bed and reached for his jeans, shoving his feet into them and yanking them up. His flannel shirt was draped over the arm of her chair. He remembered Quinn unbuttoning it mere hours ago and kissing her way down his stomach, making his muscles jump and his blood pump thick and urgent. They'd made slow, sweet love. With a silent curse, he scooped the shirt up and shrugged into it, not bothering with the buttons.

"Where are you going?"

Her voice was guarded. In that moment he despised himself for having hurt her. But he didn't turn around. "I need some air. Go back to sleep."

The night sky was vast and terrifyingly beautiful. The distant stars sparkled like shards of glass, the space between them obsidian black. Ethan stared up at the cold splendor, his eyes stinging, his right hand clenched around the long neck of a whiskey bottle.

The liquor he'd grabbed from the kitchen cabinet on his way out hadn't done its job. Instead he sucked in the winter night, half of him wishing it would offer some kind of anesthetic, the other half, infected with lingering guilt, wishing it would cut even deeper until he bled out. As he deserved.

Why had he survived when Casey, Archie, and Aaron's last breaths had been among rubble and twisted burning metal?

He had to tell Quinn what happened back there in Afghanistan, even though he knew it would change everything between them. The sharp flash of regret stabbed him as he thought of how he'd hurt her just minutes ago, treating her badly when she'd given him only honesty and generosity, and how he would hurt her—disappoint her when she saw him for the man he truly was.

Shifting his weight, he rose to his feet and entered the house. Sooner and Bowie looked up from their oval dog beds and then, seeing it was only him, lowered their heads onto their front paws and slipped back into slumber. Silently he pushed open the bedroom door.

Even in the dark he could make out the spill of her long hair over the white of the pillow, the points of her shoulders and hip. Between them, the rigid set of her spine betrayed her wakefulness.

He sat down on the edge of the bed, and when she remained silent and still, refusing to roll over, he knew he deserved no less. He ached to reach out and gather her in his arms, to coax the sweetness out of her until she responded caress for caress, then to lose himself in the haven of her body, the only place where his soul was soothed.

Instead he began talking. Although his eyes were trained on the line of gray that marked the edge of the woven rug on the wooden floor, his mind saw faces, sharp-eyed and wary, as ready to react to any attack as their muscle-honed bodies beneath their fatigues.

"In Camp Nathan Smith I was embedded with a unit of soldiers. They were regular army, not special ops, Marines, elite fighters—many of them just kids, really—who came from all across America, podunk towns and big depressed cities. Some of them came from a family with a tradition of service. For others, the military was the only chance at advancement they'd get. I hung out with the men; played dumb-ass video games and vicious games of ultimate Frisbee and touch football; ate the crappy food in the mess with them and listened to them bitch about it; accompanied them on patrols; watched them pump iron, train, and clean and inspect their weapons. Through it all I took pictures. While I worked, we often talked. Sometimes they told funny stories. At others they sat around shooting the shit with their buddies. Then there were moments when things would turn on a dime and the talk would be about home, families, loved ones, and the war, the fucking ugly elephant in the room. These soldiers, they started out as subjects for my documentary, but over the course of the months I was with them, some also became my friends.

"The first time I had the dream—nightmare—was at the hospital after I refused the sedatives and sleep meds they were pumping into my system. I had a few bad nights when I first got here at Silver Creek, then it went away for a few blessed weeks. I don't know what made it come back—"

He could guess at the trigger, however. His editor's repeated calls and voice messages, Erin's persistence more than a match for his stubborn refusal. Her determination to have him complete his project burrowed like a chigger, going deep until it reached the memories he'd tried to bury.

With his elbows digging into the muscles above his knees, he clasped his hands together until his fingers hurt. This was the hard part. "The dream I have is of that last day. I was wrapping up my project, had taken hundreds of pictures. But one of the things that happens when you're photographing people and talking to them is that new topics to record inevitably spring up. I couldn't stop myself from thinking about one of the questions all the guys kept coming back to when they spoke about the war and their role in it.

"Every one of them wondered what the army would be leaving behind when the U.S. ended combat operations and the Afghan forces took over. Were the effort and risk worth it if Afghanistan descended into even greater chaos and violence? So I got this idea to finish my project with portraits of some of the professors and students from the University of Kandahar. I wanted to show the people back home the faces of the individuals who'd be carrying on the effort to promote education in this hellish pocket of misery, show them that there was something in this part of the world besides rocket launchers, bombs, grenades, hatred, and fear. My grand idea ended up costing four lives, three of them men I'd come to think of as friends."

His chest hurt when he inhaled and he faltered, hanging his head. Continuing, saying the words, reliving those terrible minutes was too damned hard.

Suddenly there was a warmth against his back. He closed his eyes at the well of emotion that rose up inside him as Quinn wrapped her arms about his middle and pressed her cheek against his shoulder.

"Please tell me what happened."

He kept his eyes closed, concentrating on the warm press of her body. "I'd contacted the university and explained my wish to finish the project with the faces of Afghan students and academics. After I'd provided my credentials to him, the vice chancellor, Omar Hasan, was delighted to have me come to the campus. He was even open to my photographing female students. As we were setting up a time and date, Hasan suddenly got excited. If I could arrange to come the following day at two o'clock, there was going to be an award ceremony for students who'd distinguished themselves in the civil engineering department. Afterward he'd personally give me a tour of the campus. I told him I'd check with the major at the camp to see whether he could provide an escort into the city but that I'd get back to him if there was a problem.

"Major Burrell assigned a detail to me. Corporal Aaron Smith, Specialist Casey Logar, and Specialist Archie Donovan. Good guys. Real good guys. He also said I could have the services of an interpreter, Ahmad Zadran, in case I wanted to interview anyone—by that point everyone at the base knew my technique. I liked to talk to my subjects whenever I could. The major said

he'd arrange to have Zadran come to the base and that
he'd instruct Corporal Smith to plan our departure at
thirteen hundred hours."

It was time to quit being a weak-assed shit, Ethan
thought. Enough with the stalling and filling in the picture with as many details as he could remember, all to
avoid talking about that fateful decision, that deathly
ride.

He forced the words out. "One o'clock the next day,
the four of us—Aaron, Casey, Archie, and I—are waiting beside the Humvee for Zadran to arrive. Only he's a
no-show. Five minutes pass, then ten minutes. I've got
my camera bag stowed in the back—and every minute
now feels like an hour. At fifteen past I turn to Smith,
the senior officer, and say, 'Let's leave without him,
Corporal. The vice chancellor at the university spoke
decent English. He can provide any translating I need.'

"Casey Logan speaks up. 'Corporal, sir. I submit we
wait for the translator the major assigned our detail.'

"I knew Casey was up for a promotion, a big fucking
deal for him, and that he probably figured following
protocol was the way to go in the run-up to his review.
Maybe he was already envisioning what the rank of corporal would feel like. Me, I only cared about getting to
the university and not insulting the administrator who'd
invited me there by showing up late, so I reply with,
'Come on, Corporal Smith, the translator's not going to
show, and it's nearly thirteen hundred thirty. If we delay
any longer, I'm going to be late. Damned if I want to be
the disrespectful American who interrupts a university
ceremony.'

"What the hell was I doing second-guessing any of
these soldiers, throwing my weight around? I knew the
men had all gotten into my project, were excited to be
part of it, and I used that to sway Smith. We got into
the Humvee, and just before Casey started the engine,

he looked back and shot me a pissed-off look. I remember thinking I wished I'd had my camera out and captured that scowl to razz him with it when we returned to camp.

"It was a little over a ten-mile ride into Kandahar. The GPS put the university at a quarter of a mile farther, which meant we'd be cutting it close. Casey was driving, like I said, and though he still radiated his disapproval, he was driving at a good speed, aware I'd be cutting it close. I was staring out the window. The immediate environs of the camp were desolate. Then we drove past a small orchard. Pomegranate trees." He paused. "You know the myth of Persephone?"

"Yes," she said quietly. "Because Hades tricked her into eating the pomegranate, she was forced to remain with him in the underworld for part of the year."

"Yeah. So there I was cruising past this orchard and thinking that pomegranates, like poppies, were the perfect symbol for this place because few other places I'd visited made me think of hell and death as much. And wasn't that fucking prescient?" His laugh was hollow.

He felt her head move and knew that she was pressing a kiss into his shoulder. Ironically, the spot was centimeters away from his scar. His narrative—his confession—was making his wound ache as if his flesh and ligaments were freshly torn and bloody.

Whoever said time heals all wounds hadn't been to war.

He couldn't stop now, though.

"We were driving by a cluster of houses, set back a little ways from the road. We'd just rolled past, back to a landscape of gravel and dusty earth, when I saw it: a red rubber ball about the size of soccer ball bouncing on the hard ground, its path leading directly into the road. Ten feet behind the ball, a little boy was running to catch it.

"The men saw it, too. Casey reacted as anyone would, easing his foot off the gas. But then we heard the shout, and it wasn't just a 'Stay the fuck away from the road, kid, a car's coming!' kind of yell but a scream of sheer terror because the little boy was running fast, getting too close to the ball . . . to the road.

"The four of us realized in that instant what the scream meant. No time to react—for Casey to throw the wheel, slam on the brakes, or do anything. There wasn't even time to pray.

"The IED blast sent the truck into the air like some giant had kicked it. I remember flying even farther, then hitting the ground and feeling as if my body had been ripped in two. From where I lay I could see twisted hunks of metal through the choking smoke. I could make out bodies, blood staining the camo a dark red and seeping into the dirt underneath them. The others didn't move, and already I knew that I was alive and they weren't. I must've passed out. When I came to, there were two medics hovering over me—Hasan had called the base when we didn't show and the major had sent out a search party for us.

"That's the nightmare that torments me in my sleep, but when I wake up it's worse. Because then I know that if not for me, those other men might still be alive. Did I mention that Casey Logar wasn't just up for promotion? He was also engaged, his fiancée seven months pregnant."

Quinn choked back her tears. If she'd thought she loved Ethan before, that emotion seemed paltry now that she'd heard his story, knew what he'd suffered and the guilt he carried. Such a heavy load. Her heart ached for him, and she wished somehow he could see himself through her eyes rather than his own damning ones.

When she lifted her cheek from where it rested against his shoulder blade she felt him stiffen as if preparing himself for a blow or the condemnation he doubtless expected to see in her gaze.

Her hands slipped under his flannel shirt and with her flattened palms she urged him to turn toward her. A touch of gray spilled through the window, illuminating his face. She was grateful for the faint but growing light. His expression was stern. Guarded. When a man revealed so much pain, how could he not wish to protect himself while he was at his most vulnerable?

She hoped her words might do the same as the creeping dawn and chase the darkness from his soul.

"I love you, Ethan." Her voice was quiet and clear. Sensing that anything else she said in an effort to absolve him of his supposed crimes would be met with fierce resistance, she acted, covering his mouth with hers, laying her palms against his chest, her right one absorbing the heavy thud of his heart.

In a flash, the kiss turned fierce, tongues tangling and lips clinging with desperate hunger and need.

His hands moved like quicksilver over her, touching all the secret places he alone had discovered and knew would leave her gasping as desire rocked her. Before he could wreak total havoc, she twisted, pushing him down on the rumpled sheet. Straddling his hips, she pinned him.

Beneath her, the heated steel of his erection burned. She sank lower, riding it, as she kissed her way down the taut column of his neck to the hollow located at the base of his throat. Scooting back, she continued her erotic journey, laving the dark discs of his nipples, the stark ridges of his abdomen while her fingers busied themselves, tugging at his zipper and then shoving his jeans down. Freed, he sprang into her waiting hands. Pulsed as her lips touched his bulbous head.

"Quinn, oh God—" His words ended on a groan of agonized pleasure as her tongue licked him in a slow sweep.

Opening her mouth, she took him deep. She'd come to love this, the taste of him, an extraordinary and unique blend of salt and tangy spice, the essence of the male animal. She loved the urgency she was able to rouse in him as she alternately lapped and sucked, his fingers curling in her hair, his tendons standing ropelike against the strong column of his neck, his hips bucking under her as his control slipped. The pleasure stark on his face as she quickened her pace and her hands joined in caressing him, pumping and squeezing.

She knew he was close, and heat pulsed urgently inside her. When his fingers stayed her, she looked up, questioning.

"I need you to take me inside and feel you come with me. It's how I find peace."

The unvarnished honesty of his request had her blinking back fresh tears.

Quick work was made of the condom. Rising onto her knees, she positioned him at the entrance to her core and sank down, taking him inch by inch, reveling in the sensation of him filling her. Their eyes locked as he gripped her hips and began to move, his thrusts as tight and controlled as a great engine gathering steam. She followed him, answering his thrusts with a rolling grind of her hips as their gasps and whispers filled the air. Together they traveled to a magic place far from the shadows that hovered.

STANDING IN A bridal shop in front of one of those nasty three-way mirrors, dressed in a floor-length satin gown while a woman with a mouthful of very sharp pins knelt inches away from her butt, wasn't exactly Quinn's idea of a rockin' good time. Thank God for great soon-to-be sisters-in-law, crisp champagne, and a bridesmaid's dress that even Quinn had to admit was stunning—not that Tess, Italian beauty and event planner extraordinaire, would ever choose anything ugly.

Mia, who was also wearing her bridesmaid's dress, was grinning. "Wow. Just wow. Tess, you have some kind of crazy talent. Not every woman could find bridesmaids' dresses that, A, are this gorgeous, and B, can make the three of us look equally fantastic. Don't you agree, Anna?"

Anna Vecchio, not to be left out of all the San Francisco fun, had arranged to have her fitting done simultaneously in New York. She twirled in the rectangular screen of Tess's iPad, showing off her dress, her dark hair flowing out behind her. "It's beautiful. And we do look amazing. I love the rosy gold color on the two of you. *Brava, cara,*" she said and then launched into rapid-fire Italian that had Tess laughing and swiping at her eyes.

"Translation, please," Quinn said.

Tess gave a little hiccup and swiped at her eyes. "Anna was just saying that she knew there'd been a reason why she let me leave New York. The reward was seeing me happier and more beautiful than she had ever imagined. And that's all because of you and your family, Quinn," she said.

"Aw," Quinn said, and risked the seamstress's wrath by going over and hugging Tess. "You're not so bad yourself, city girl."

"I also told Tess that it was totally worth losing her if it meant my restaurant's cellar would be stocked with the finest California pinot noir," Anna said.

"The jury's still out on how the few barrels we saved will mature, but thanks for the vote of confidence," Mia said.

Quinn plucked two more glasses of champagne off the silver tray, passed them to her friends, and then took one herself. Directing her attention to Anna, still framed in the iPad screen, she asked, "Anna, is your glass full?" At Anna's nod she continued. "Then I propose a toast to Tess, who's not only the anti-bridezilla but is also the rare and generous woman in having chosen gorgeous dresses for her bridesmaids rather than cringe-inducing horrors—not that you sell those here," she said with an extra-bright smile for the store's manager. "To the future Tess Casari Knowles."

Glasses were clinked and then drained, and then Quinn and Mia stood docilely while the two seamstresses made their final pinnings.

"So I guess this fitting means we'll have to keep on the straight and narrow for the remainder of the holiday season," Quinn said after she'd changed back into her own skirt and silk blouse. "Too bad. Roo makes the most amazing Christmas log."

Mia gave a pained look and glanced at her bridesmaid's dress, now back on its hanger. "Do you think I should ask to have the waist let out a little?"

From behind the heavy silver curtain of the changing room, Tess said, "Don't you dare, Mia! You looked amazing in that dress. And, Quinn, you haven't experienced real temptation until you get a whiff of my mother's panettone. I could eat one every day all December long."

Then she stepped out from behind the curtain and Quinn and Mia both gave an "Oh!" followed by "How absolutely lovely!" and "Ward won't know what hit him."

Anna said, "Come closer," and then gave a happy cry. *"Bellissima!"*

No translation needed for that or for the radiant smile on Tess's face.

The lace trumpet gown with its off the shoulder sleeves caressed Tess's knockout curves. The gown was a creamy white, the perfect foil for Tess's olive skin tone, dark eyes, and long brown hair. She looked elegant and beautiful and wonderfully romantic.

"It's the closest I could come to the dress my mother wore for her wedding," Tess said. "As you can see, Mia, I don't have an inch to spare, either. What I do have, however, is a formula—a regimen, if you will—designed to keep the pounds off during the holiday season."

"Do share," Anna said, leaning forward.

"It's simple. For every slice of chocolate log or, in my case, enormous wedge of panettone, engage in two hours of sex."

Quinn had just taken a sip of champagne. She spewed it out—luckily nowhere near Tess and her glorious dress. She patted herself dry while around her the others snorted in laughter.

"Seriously, I tried it this fall when I made a huge batch of penne with a sauce of tomato, cream, and five cheeses. It worked like a charm." Tess grinned.

"Love that recipe of your mother's. The most delicious calorie bomb in existence," Anna said. "And you didn't have to wear your crisis pants all week?"

"They remained in the closet."

"A miracle diet." Anna clapped. "Fantastic! I'll put it to the test with Lucas tonight. We're going out to a friend of mine's pop-up restaurant tonight. His desserts are divinely decadent."

"Report back next week," Tess told Anna.

"But make sure you keep the results between us. If news of Tess's miracle regimen gets out, Reid is going to be hand-feeding me cake," Mia said. Biting her lower lip, she blushed.

"I don't see anything wrong with that picture," Anna said. "Do you, Tess?"

Tess laughed. "Can't say I do. What else is winter for? Come to think of it, I may let Ward in on my secret routine when we get home."

"Hello!" Quinn waved her hands. "Could you please remember that two of these men happen to be my brothers?"

For a woman dressed in a lace wedding gown, Tess's expression could only be described as wicked. "Don't tell me you and Ethan aren't up to the prescribed minutes, because I won't believe you. Not after what I interrupted yesterday afternoon."

Before Quinn could begin to formulate a pithy response, Mia gave a very uncharacteristic whoop. "Yes! I've been wondering when the pair of you would be caught out in the open."

"Only a matter of time," Tess said.

"Well, hallelujah." Mia grinned at Quinn's baleful look. "What? Of course we knew it would happen. You gave Ethan a *dog*, Quinn."

"And who is this Ethan?" Anna interrupted.

"He's a photojournalist. Very handsome, very intense. You'll love him, Anna. He's coming to the wedding."

"He is?" Mia asked.

"Mm-hmm." Tess nodded. "Didn't want Quinn to be all by her lonesome."

"You know, Tess, you're slipping a little as perfect sister-in-law-to-be."

Tess gave an eloquent shrug. "Mia, you want the job?"

"Nope. I'd rather hear all about this much-awaited development. Ethan's a really good man, Quinn."

Mia and Tess didn't know the half of how good a man he was. A lump formed in her throat as she remembered the raw pain in Ethan's voice while he recounted what had happened on that dusty road to Kandahar. "Yeah, he is."

Something of what she was feeling must have shown on her face, for Tess said, "It's the real thing, huh?"

Quinn gave a small nod.

"I saw that same expression staring back at me in the mirror when I got together with Ward. A little terrified and a lot soul-deep happy. I never felt a tenth of that when I was with David."

"David was too busy giving you emotional whiplash," Anna said. "A selfish man to the end—even when he dressed it up as concern for you."

Tess's first husband, David, had died from a brain tumor. But instead of telling Tess about his illness, he'd decided to keep Tess in the dark and even did his best to push her away emotionally by being deliberately cruel so she wouldn't mourn his death. A frigging lousy way to treat anyone, let alone a loved one. It was more than simply lousy. It was cowardly.

It made Quinn appreciate Ethan's courage in opening up all the more. It would have been easy for him to continue stonewalling her. Instead he'd revealed something he believed to be truly awful about himself.

"Maybe you're right, Anna," Tess conceded. "But perhaps because of what David put me through, I can love Ward all the more and appreciate how good and strong he is and what a wonderful husband and father he'll be." Looking at Quinn, she smiled. "I'm glad you and Ethan are together."

"Yes, we're really happy for you," Mia said, nodding.

"I'm looking forward to meeting Ethan when he comes to New York," Anna said. "I'm only sad that I didn't get to loan you my nonna's lucky scarf—I'd have been three for three."

Anna had inherited a very nice silk scarf from her grandmother and firmly believed that it was lucky. Tess and Mia had bought into the lore, and now it was talked about as if it were a talisman that brought true love.

"Tess, I'm sorry," Anna continued. "But I have to go back to the restaurant."

"Of course! Say hi to Rupert for me. And call me tomorrow and tell me how every dish was."

"*Prometto.*"

Tess smiled. "I only wish you were coming with us."

"We'll have our time in New York. All of you come prepared to eat, drink, and dance yourselves silly— almost as fun as marathon sex." Blowing a kiss in their direction, Anna signed off with a jaunty "*Ciao, care mie.*"

After thanking Dominique, the bridal shop's manager, and the in-house seamstresses for giving them a perfect morning and double-checking that the dresses would be shipped to the Waldorf-Astoria in New York, where Tess and Ward and Quinn's family had booked rooms for the wedding, Tess slipped behind the silver curtains and reemerged dressed in a navy pencil skirt and a white fitted silk blouse and the high-heel pumps she favored. An artfully knotted bright silk scarf completed the outfit. She looked nearly as glamorous as she had in her wedding dress.

"The city girl is back," Quinn noted.

Tess laughed. "I never thought I'd admit this, but I've gotten used to the soft ground and the comfort of my cowboy boots. Still, it's fun dressing up and going out on the town with you both, isn't it? And I'm using today to get used to wearing heels on sidewalks again, so be prepared to cover a lot of ground, ladies."

With a cheery wave to Dominique and a last round of thanks, they stepped outside. Pedestrians were bundled in wool coats and lightweight puffers, their bags bumping against their legs as they hurried along Grant Avenue. The outsides of the stores were decorated with lots of evergreens, gold and silver, and winter-wonderland-themed windows. The holiday season was in full swing in Union Square.

"I do love this season." Tess smiled brightly. "Ready to hit the stores? We're going to go full tilt and work up an appetite so we can do justice to the lunch Anna's treating us to."

"We'll do our best to keep up, right, Mia?" Quinn said as they walked past the hardy souls drinking their coffee and curled over their cellphones and tablets in the outside seating areas of the cafés.

"We'd be lousy bridesmaids if we didn't," Mia replied. "I hope I find something for your dad, Quinn. He makes shopping for my uncle Thomas easy. Luckily, I was inspired when it came to finding a present for Thomas and his girlfriend, Pascale."

"What did you get them?" Tess asked.

"I commissioned Madlon Glenn to paint a watercolor of our winery."

"Madlon Glenn. Wait, that's the guest who helped you organize the artists' retreat at the ranch, wasn't it, Tess?" Quinn asked.

"Yes. She's so talented."

"I think Thomas and Pascale will love the scene I bought," Mia said. "I had it framed and it looks so beautiful."

"That's a brilliant gift, Mia. Maybe I should contact Madlon. She might have a view of the ranch that I could give to Adele and Daniel. Hey—" Tess exclaimed suddenly. "Here's another idea. What if I ask Ethan to take a picture—"

Quinn shook her head. "I don't think Ethan intends to take photographs anymore."

"Not ever?" Tess's surprise showed on her face. "What a shame."

"I know." Quinn couldn't say more. It was Ethan's story to share. Nor could she tell Tess or Mia how much she hoped to change Ethan's mind about his work—if only she could figure out how.

Luckily Tess didn't press her. "Well, I haven't reached out to Madlon in several weeks. Maybe she has a painting she's willing to part with."

"Unfortunately, I'm still clueless about what to give Daniel," Mia said. "Any suggestions, Quinn?"

"Yeah." She made a noise of sympathy. "He's a tough one. All Dad really wants is a new, bigger, and shinier tractor. He told Mom he *needs* one," she said with a laugh.

"Sorry, no can do. All my money has to go either back into the vineyard or toward the auction and tasting night we're holding in the spring."

"I hear you." Quinn had her own reasons for saving and rebuilding her nest egg. Her dream of opening an animal sanctuary hadn't disappeared when she donated most of her money to Marsha and Lorelei's shelter. It had merely been delayed.

There was an upscale liquor store in the middle of the block. Naturally Mia's feet slowed to a stop as they came abreast of it. Tess and Quinn waited as their friend drank in the window display with its cleverly stacked wooden wine crates and bottles propped at an angle so passersby could easily read the labels.

From the intensity of Mia's gaze, Quinn knew she was imagining a crate of her own wine displayed so prominently in a San Francisco shop.

"But you know, Mia, next to a tractor, what Dad loves is a good whiskey. Single malt, the peatier the better. Why don't we go inside and check out the selection they have here? Perhaps we'll find one for him."

"And you can drop off your business card with the store manager and let him know about the wine auction," Tess said, catching on.

With a quick wink for Tess, Quinn grabbed the door handle and ushered her friends inside.

As Tess passed, she whispered, "Way to go, Quinn."

"Oh my Lord, we're going to have to jump our guys and try your calorie-burning secret the second we get home," Mia said as they finished the last bites of a dessert platter that had included tiramisu, torrone semifreddo, and rose-infused panna cotta, along with chocolate and pistachio biscotti to go with their espressos.

Tess laughed. "As Anna would say, 'And where's the problem?'"

Mia grinned, her smile and eyes sparkling from the second bottle of champagne they'd shared. "I am so glad you and Anna have come into my life."

"Man, way to make me feel like chopped liver,"

Quinn teased as she handed Mia her shopping bags, one heavy with a very fine bottle of Scotch whiskey.

"Nah, you're my BFF, Quinn. Consider yourself a deluxe brownie."

"Much better." She grabbed Tess's and her own bags from under the table and followed her friends through the now empty restaurant—they'd outlasted the lunch hour crowd—to where the coat check attendant waited. Able to guess what the man, who looked about her age, earned as an hourly wage, she gave him a liberal tip and shrugged into her black wool coat, holding on to Tess's while she hugged Rupert, Paradiso's chef, and told him that he'd outdone himself.

Ward was leaning against their father's SUV waiting for them. A smile spread over his face as his gaze locked on Tess.

"Have fun?" he asked, not waiting for a reply before leaning in to kiss Tess. The kiss lasted long enough for Tess to wrap her arms about Ward's neck and for Quinn and Mia to exchange an eye roll and snicker.

"The best," Tess replied when at last they parted.

Tess's expression had Ward's head lowering once again.

Convinced they might be stuck on Fillmore for the rest of the afternoon if the two lovebirds kept this up, Quinn cleared her throat loudly.

Ward released Tess's lips to frown at Quinn.

"Home, James, if you please." She grinned at her brother as she opened the rear door. "Believe me, you want to get back to Silver Creek ASAP so Tess can tell you all about her special exercise regimen."

"Does it involve interesting yoga-inspired positions? Pole dancing?"

"Seriously, Ward? Your fiancée is far more creative than that."

Settling into the backseat, Quinn watched the city

streets slip by as Ward drove toward the Golden Gate Bridge. Mia, Tess, and Ward carried most of the conversation, with Quinn offering an occasional comment. For the most part she was happy to let the small talk and the music from the playlist Ward had selected—a mix of Johnny Cash, Elvis Costello, Emmylou Harris, and zydeco—wash over her.

The outing with Tess and Mia had been wonderful and exactly what she needed after the intensity of the previous night with Ethan. Starting with his nightmare and then ending with their lovemaking, she'd experienced the hurt of rejection, an aching sympathy for his terrible pain and guilt, and then a shattering joy when they came together. Each emotion only made it clearer how deeply she'd fallen in love with him.

Being apart today was probably the best thing that could have happened. It kept Quinn from hovering or, worse, giving into temptation and pursuing the topic of Ethan's supposed role in the deaths of those soldiers and that little boy.

Sitting here in her dad's tricked-out SUV, she realized that she could talk until she was blue in the face and she still wouldn't convince him he wasn't to blame. The Taliban or Al Qaeda was responsible. Not Ethan, who was only doing his job, just as the soldiers were in providing him escort. It was the insurgents' barbarous act that had taken the life of one of their own countrymen— an innocent young boy, not even a man.

She hoped whoever had rigged that roadside bomb rotted in hell, starting sooner rather than later.

Had she remained at the ranch today she most likely would have lost sight of the fact that Ethan needed to be *shown*, not argued with, if he was ever going to see the truth or acknowledge that the pictures he'd taken for his documentary project were important. Essential, even.

She had yet to figure out a way to demonstrate this to him, but she knew it had to be done. The guilt would eat him alive otherwise. And loving him as much as she did, it would end up hurting her, too. She wouldn't be able to bear watching him continue to punish himself.

To think that mere weeks ago she'd been convinced that she wanted nothing to do with emotional entanglements. How little she'd known about herself or about love.

Chapter
TWENTY-FIVE

TWO DAYS BEFORE Christmas, the idea of how to get Ethan to regard his photographs in the way Quinn knew the rest of the world would and not through a filter of self-reproach, came to her in a ringtone. U2's "One," to be exact.

The eureka moment was provided by Mia. She'd chosen the ringtone for Reid, who called Mia when she and Quinn had just come in from a trail ride and were tending to their mounts. Mia let Glory eat the rest of the carrot she'd been feeding him as an after-ride treat and answered on the third note, her voice low with pleasure. "Hey. What's up? Yeah, I'd love a latte."

Quinn waved, catching Mia's attention. "And a triple-shot espresso for Quinn would be much appreciated. No, I don't think she'll tell you what she bought you in exchange—"

That was all Quinn needed to hear to know what Reid was up to: fishing for what kind of presents he was getting. For as long as she could remember, he'd been a total sneak at Christmastime, peeking in bags, poking around in closets, shaking wrapped boxes, playing twenty questions. A good thing Mia knew exactly what a charmer Reid could be.

Besides, she had more important things to think

about than her brother's bad habits. The few bars of U2's song had jogged her memory. Suddenly she recalled the heavy-hitting "Ride of the Valkyries" Ethan had assigned to his editor, Erin Miller, as a ringtone.

Ethan often left his phone lying around. For instance, he never took it with him in the morning when he went to milk the goats because Hennie had developed such a serious crush on him. In addition to following him around, she'd taken to stealing anything in his pockets. For her, an iPhone would be like munching a saltine.

What if Quinn were to take Ethan's phone, scroll through his contact list, and call his editor? Better yet, what if she were to call the gallery owner—if only she could remember her name.

It was ironic that she couldn't, since she'd definitely spent time thinking about the woman after Ethan had let drop that they'd been lovers. She must have subconsciously blocked the name out of jealousy. Would she remember it if she spotted it among his contacts?

The light sweat Domino had worked up on the trail ride had dried. She picked up a hand towel from her carryall and vigorously rubbed down his speckled coat—as if somehow she might also wipe her conscience clean in the process. No such luck. Going behind Ethan's back and using his phone to gather the information she needed was lousy, plain and simple. She knew she would hate anyone snooping around in her phone, and she wasn't doing everything she could to hide away from the world as Ethan was.

It was possible she could justify her underhanded tactics by arguing that it was for a good cause. She was helping a man overcome his grief and also giving the dead soldiers' families a chance to see images of their loved ones in the final months of their lives.

But Quinn had been raised to know right from wrong. There was no pretending that taking names and numbers off Ethan's phone without his knowledge or permission could be right.

So if she followed through with this idea, it would be with the certain knowledge that she was going against her own moral code. Knowing, too, that Ethan would likely be furious with her.

He might even be more than that.

Jim and Carlos had helped untack the other trail horses, so she and Mia lent them a hand stuffing hay into the feeders positioned around the paddock. Since Tucker's colic, rubber mats had been placed underneath and around the feeders to prevent the horses from lipping up dirt along with any stray bits of hay. It seemed to be working.

Reid showed up, balancing two coffees in one hand and with a leash wrapped around his other. Mia's rescue dog, Bruno, was clipped to the other end of it. Mia received a kiss with her latte from both man and dog.

"Not bad service," Quinn observed, plucking her espresso from Reid's hand. "Did Mom make you take a hospitality refresher course?" she asked as she bent down and gave Bruno a vigorous pat.

"Ha. You're the one who rolls her eyes when the guests linger over their breakfast."

"I just don't want them to miss all the other great stuff to do around here."

"Right. So where's Ethan?" Reid asked.

"Why should I know?" she asked.

He gave her a pitying look, which she pretended to ignore. The secret of her and Ethan was out in the open. Amazingly, neither Ward nor Reid had teased her outright about having someone in her life, though Ethan did dryly report that the two had cornered him in the goat pen to inform him that if he messed things up with her they would chop off his balls and let the goats play soccer with them.

As if. She could tell how much they liked Ethan—and, contrary to general assumptions, they didn't like everyone.

Sighing loudly, she gave her brother what he wanted. "Ethan and Josh are putting away the tack from the trail ride they led. They took the advanced group. I led the mellow fellows."

Mia grinned. "Thank you for not labeling us rank beginners."

"You're welcome. Besides, you're improving with every ride. And you can bet what I think your New Year's resolution should be. It starts with an *l* and ends with an *e*."

"Love?" Mia asked innocently. "But I've already told you I love Glory. He's such a great horse."

"Lope, not *love*," Quinn replied through gritted teeth.

"Oh, well," Mia said with an eloquent shrug. "Not sure a lope on Glory is going to make my New Year's resolution list."

Quinn shook her head. Mia was getting as bad as Tess. She'd expected to win this battle with getting them to move out of a trot much sooner.

"Here's Ethan now," Mia said pointing.

She watched him approach their group. A quiver of excitement raced through her, its destination the area just below her navel. The man got better looking every day.

In deference to the wind, he'd donned a jean jacket. His hair was covered by the black Stetson that Ward and Reid had presented him with the day after Thanksgiving, his "prize" for having beaten her in the holiday races.

She loved the hat, a symbol of the good-humored affection and acceptance her brothers felt for Ethan, but she'd have liked to see his eyes. With the wind blowing from the north, the trail ride had been cold. Leading the beginners at a walk alternated with short periods of trotting, she hadn't had a chance to get her blood pumping with an extended lope. But Ethan's gaze could start a fire inside her.

Bowie was heeling at Ethan's side. When he spied Bruno, his ears cocked forward and his tail rose. A tap of Ethan's left hand on his thigh kept him from bolting.

Bruno was more exuberant, wriggling with excitement as Bowie neared. The wriggling turned ecstatic as the dogs touched snouts and began to sniff each other.

Reid spoke. "I was wondering whether these two could let off some steam together. That is, Bowie could let off steam and this guy could galumph after him."

"I'd love to see them play together. Reid told me it's hilarious watching Bruno try to keep up," Mia said, stroking Bruno's blocky head. The rest of him was just as large—Quinn guessed he weighed a good ninety pounds. He resembled a Bernese Mountain dog with a half dozen other breeds thrown into the mix. He was a great furry love, but hardly built for speed.

"Sounds good. I get the impression Bowie sometimes gets demoralized playing with Sooner," Ethan said.

Reid nodded. "I could see that. Sooner's one intense dude."

"He takes his job as top sheepdog seriously, is all," Quinn said.

Ethan's lips twitched. "You done here? Or are you going to work with Tucker?" he asked.

The signs were both big and small and revealed themselves to Quinn in countless ways. Ethan had entered her world thoroughly. He understood what she was about and recognized what she valued. His presence enriched every day at Silver Creek. How would he react when she entered his world, uninvited, a trespasser?

Afraid she might betray herself, she pushed the

thought away. "I'll be walking Tucker," she answered. "It's the best time for him."

"We'll run the dogs in the pasture, away from where you'll be. You'll head back to your place after you're done?" Ethan asked.

"Yeah. Lots of wrapping still to do, my Secret Santa present included." Tonight was the annual holiday party for the staff. Her parents always organized a Secret Santa and passed out presents along with the year-end bonuses.

"Who'd you pick, Quinn?"

"None of your business, Reid."

"I'll swing by the goat pen and give the does some pine branches," Ethan said.

"Thanks." She smiled. "They do love their treats."

"Don't we all." He nudged the brim of his hat, and suddenly she could see the silver gray of his eyes. A smile tugged his lips. There it was, a heat that penetrated deep as she recalled the wet slide of his mouth moving over the landscape of her body and all the "treats" he'd given her, her cries of pleasure his thanks.

Conscious of Reid and Mia's attention, she swallowed and said, "So, see you guys later."

By tacit agreement, Reid and Mia moved off with only Bruno looking over at Quinn, Ethan, and Bowie.

"Don't take too long. I've missed you," Ethan said. Angling his head, he swooped in for a kiss that seared for all its brevity.

Overwhelmed by a rush of love that was simultaneously weighted by worry and lightened by hope, her answering smile was tremulous.

Frank and Mel were sweeping the barn aisle when Quinn entered. The swish of their brooms melded with the munching of hay. The stalls in the barn were reserved for injured horses; the two broodmares, Cleo and Bianca, who were in foal; and six of their retired horses, whose old bones needed extra warmth and a deep straw bed at night. Outside each stall hung a red felt stocking. Tomorrow she'd be stuffing them with the treats that she'd picked up at Horse & Rider, the tack shop outside of Hopland—which was also where she'd found Ethan's Christmas present.

The shopping portion of the San Francisco outing had been a bust where Ethan was concerned. Nothing called to her when she made a sweep of the stores in Acacia, either. She'd begun to fear she would have to do some crazed Christmas Eve shopping down in Napa when she'd happened to spot an antiqued silver belt buckle in the glass display case by the register of the tack shop. The center of the buckle was beautifully worked in a swirling design, with a twisted rope trim around its oval circumference. It screamed "cowboy," and no matter what his past or his future held, Ethan was the cowboy of her heart.

Clint Stiles, the tack shop's owner, had an excellent collection of Western wear. She easily found a hand tooled belt strap in a rich dark brown that complemented the buckle and asked Clint to put them in a box for her.

It was a strange sensation, shopping for a man she loved who wasn't family, or a buddy like Jim, or one of her coworkers for Secret Santa. Though she'd tried to keep the present fairly casual, she hoped he'd smile when he opened it, and understand how much she wanted him to be part of her world.

Tucker held his head high as she led him out of the barn. His hooves rang in a quick beat that spoke of pent-up energy after so many days stall-bound. When he stepped into the courtyard, he stopped and reared. She let the lead rope slide through her hand, but when his forelegs returned to the ground, she gave a quick tug and resumed walking before he could try any more shenanigans.

"Just a few more days until Gary Cooney comes to check you out and perhaps give the green light for you to hang out with your buddies in the pasture. Don't pull something stupid now." Her tone was conversational, as easy as when she was grooming him, but she walked forward with purpose, checking him with another quick tug when he tried to break into a run.

He was a handful, but she loved his spirit all the more since someone had tried to beat it out of him. It didn't bother her that Tucker had probably taken a good ten steps backward in terms of his training. If he didn't colic again, they'd get to where they needed to be eventually.

She hand-walked Tucker for a half hour, and by the time she'd put him back in his box stall, stuffed his hay into a hanging net, and kissed him good night on his blaze, the sky was pitch black. "Sleep tight, big guy," she said as she closed his stall door.

"Still talking to your animals?"

She jumped. "Oh, hey, Josh."

"Sorry, didn't mean to startle you. You going to the staff holiday party?"

"Wouldn't miss it."

"And Ethan?"

"Yup."

"So, you two are together, right?"

She crossed her arms in front of her chest. "Yeah."

"That's good. Real good. I felt kind of bad about Thanksgiving."

The image of Josh and Maebeth pretzel-locked in a hot embrace flashed before her. How weird. She was so wrapped up in Ethan, she hadn't thought about that awkward moment once.

"How are things going with you and Maebeth?"

"Super. She's a real sweet gal. I'm picking her up in a few—Pete said it'd be fine if I brought her as my date."

"Of course."

"It seems like we both ended up with the right person, don't it? I knew Ethan was into you even when he said he wasn't, talking about how he babysat you and all. I figured it out when Tucker came down with colic." Her confusion must have shown, for he added, "I mentioned to Ethan that I didn't think it was a good idea to spend all that money on the operation for Tucker. Ethan told me I shouldn't repeat that to you if I wanted a chance with you. I could tell it was killing him to give me advice like that. So I'm glad it worked out for you guys—and it's great Tucker's doing well, though I still would have tried to argue you out of that decision if you'd been my girl."

"You could have tried. You wouldn't have succeeded. Whenever I adopt or rescue an abandoned or mistreated animal, it's with the knowledge that I'll do everything I possibly can for it."

He gave a slight nod that was more like a thrust of his squared chin. "Like I said, it seems like we're with the right people."

"True." Her smile contained all the relief she felt at having been spared the colossal mistake of not seeing Josh clearly. Sure, he'd praised and admired Domino. Who wouldn't like her striking Appaloosa, whose gaits and transitions were smooth as cream? Who wouldn't appreciate a cutting horse that could turn on a dime and had speed and stamina to spare? But it struck her only now that he'd never asked after Tucker post-operation, and never once stroked her nanny goats' noses or attempted to tell them apart. None of this meant that Josh was a bad guy; he simply was someone who would never understand her. Or want to.

She wondered at Ethan's comment to him but then remembered that earlier on the night Tucker came down with colic, he'd seen Josh and her kissing. Later, while walking Tucker in the barnyard, he'd quizzed her about

Josh, and she'd hid any ambivalence she was feeling. Perhaps she'd done a good enough job that he'd believed she wanted Josh. In advising Josh to keep his opinion about Tucker to himself, he'd done what he could to give her what she wanted.

He was a good man, she thought. Even if Ethan couldn't find it in himself to forgive her when he discovered what she'd done, at least she'd given her heart wisely.

Quinn opened the door to her house to the blare of elephants trumpeting. Ethan must be entertaining the animals with the National Geographic Channel. Even so, Sooner was there to greet her as she shrugged off her jacket and quilted vest. Bowie arrived in time to sniff at her socks as she toed off her cowboy boots. She'd all but given up entering by the back door and using the mudroom to shuck off her outerwear and boots. The only recent rain to fall was a few frustratingly brief showers. Not enough to fill a teacup. As Mia had said to her the other day, Mother Nature could be generous and bountiful. She could also be a teasing bitch.

The sofa was empty, but there were clanking noises coming from the kitchen. "Ethan?" she called, moving toward the sound and for the moment ignoring the screeches that erupted from Alfie in the study.

"In here. I'm making the dogs' dinner."

She stepped into the kitchen to find him pouring kibble from a measuring cup into a stainless steel dish. A second one was already full. He'd taken off his sweater and was barefoot. "How domestic." She grinned.

"Necessary," he corrected. "Bowie was drooling on my shirtsleeve."

"He must've worked up an appetite running circles around Bruno."

"Or he's figured out that your brand of dog food is as good as caviar." He told both waiting dogs to sit, deposited their bowls a couple of feet apart, and then gave them the hand signal to release them. For once Bowie beat Sooner.

"He's a hungry boy," Quinn said.

"He's not alone." A husky note entered his voice. "Come here, Quinn," he said, crooking his index finger.

She approached, trying and doubtless failing to keep a goofy smile off her face. She loved so much about him. "That right? You're hungry, too?" she said, stopping inches away.

He reached out and put his hands around her waist, lifting her onto the counter and then stepping between her legs. "Yeah. Definitely in need of a little something." His hands settled on her hips and she felt the strength and heat in them through her jeans.

Wanting more, she crossed her ankles around his legs, drawing him closer.

For a second his lips hovered inches from hers as his gaze traveled over her face. Afraid of what his too-perceptive eyes might see and wonder at the turbulent mix buffeting her, she leaned in and caught his lower lip between her teeth and tugged, releasing it only at his low growl of arousal.

"Now that's what I'm talking about," he whispered as he closed the sliver of distance between them and kissed her, his tongue thrusting inside to slowly rub against hers. His hands slipped beneath the layers of her wool sweater and long-sleeved Henley, and her stomach muscles jumped in response. Reaching her breasts, he cupped them, squeezing lightly as his thumbs played with her puckered nipples. With a gasp, she arched into him, asking for more.

His head dipped so his mouth could trace the path from her jaw to the base of her neck, where he'd unerringly find every nerve to set her shivering and trembling in his arms. Aware that within minutes he could have her jeans off and her body and heart exploding from pleasure, she reluctantly pushed at the shoulders she'd been grasping. "I wish we could continue this but I have to wrap my Secret Santa present and give Alfie some TLC before we head up to the lodge. I need a shower, too," she explained.

His fingers made another sweep over her breasts. "How about we meet in the shower then?"

"And engage in some multitasking?"

"Never a task with you, Quinn." He lowered his hands and eased her off the counter in a slow slide against his hard body. "Never," he repeated huskily.

Quinn hesitated a few seconds, tormented by the sound of the shower on full blast and the sight of Ethan's cell phone sitting on the nightstand by the side of the bed. She had to act fast and she had to act now if she hoped to set her plan in motion to coincide with their trip to New York. But taking this step, picking up a phone that didn't belong to her and copying down strangers' numbers, wasn't only repugnant, it was also jeopardizing her chance at love. Then she forced herself to remember the terror of his nightmare, the anguish in his voice when he'd told her about the soldiers' deaths. To do nothing would allow his guilt to fester like a cancer. And knowing that she wasn't brave enough to confront him would eventually destroy their relationship. If it was doomed either way, she preferred to live with having tried to help him.

Grabbing a pen and a scrap of paper that was lying next to the lamp, she picked up the phone and turned it on. As she suspected, it was unlocked. Going into his contacts, she thought, *I'm so sorry, Ethan.*

"Merry Christmas, sleepyhead," Ethan whispered before he pressed a kiss to Quinn's lips.

Her mouth answered him, her soft lips opening, moving beneath his. He released them and watched her lashes flutter and then open. She blinked and then smiled as she stretched in a move that shoved her arms under the pillows and arched her back. It was a beautiful sight.

He had a moment to appreciate the mounds of her breasts beneath her navy tank top that had whiskey and yoga emblazoned across the front before she settled back against the mattress.

"Merry Christmas," she replied in a husky, pre-coffee voice, adding, "FYI, my internal clock is telling me it's nowhere near time to wake up. It's infallible."

"Got a couple presents to give you before we head over to your parents' place."

"Wait a second. We took them over to my parents' place yesterday so that Reid could do some one-stop snooping."

The Knowleses were having a family celebration this morning before Tess and Ward took off to the airport for New York, where they'd celebrate with Tess's parents and visit her brother Christopher, who lived in a facility that cared for adults afflicted with severe autism.

"Yeah, well, I held a few in reserve."

"Did you, now?"

"Yeah. I'm feeling indulgent, moved by the holiday spirit and all that." "All that" being the way his heart seemed to expand whenever he looked at Quinn, or thought about her.

"Well, then, bring 'em on, bud."

"Scoot yourself up first. Here," he said, grabbing the pillows he'd slept on and placing them behind her back. Once she was upright, he leaned over and picked up the wooden tray. Setting it across her lap, he plucked off the dish towel, revealing a freshly brewed extra-strong espresso in her favorite mug, which had two goats butting heads on it, and a sticky bun that he'd reheated according to Roo Rodgers's instructions.

"Oh man, I thought I'd just dreamed the scent of coffee and sugar—two of my favorite smells."

"Nope. Christmas breakfast in bed." He grabbed his own cup and sat beside her on the bed.

"Wow. This is great. Thank you." She took the time to look at her tray in appreciation. Then she lifted her cup and, cradling it between her hands, inhaled deeply. "You know, I've never been given breakfast in bed—not since I was, like, twelve or something. I think I had the flu. Mom brought me up some buttered toast with grape jam and a big glass of orange juice."

"Funny thing to have missed out on, considering you live at a high-end guest ranch," he said with studied casualness. Once more a fierce possessiveness had seized him. There were countless things he wanted to be the first at when it came to Quinn. *Her first and only*, he added silently.

She took a sip of her coffee. "Mmm, strong, sweet,

and hot. Exactly how I like it. And I get a sticky bun, too?"

He grinned. "Only the finest for you."

Her glance slid sideways then lowered to the tray. "Not sure I deserve it."

"Been a naughty girl, huh?"

Instead of answering, she raised her cup and swallowed the remaining coffee. "That was delicious," she said quietly. "Thank you. This is a perfect present and a really nice way to start Christmas."

He'd expected a snappy response. She was so good at them. He wondered at her somber tone, too. She seemed subdued. Sad, even. Maybe the holiday was making her emotional. Some extra sugar might help.

"Have some of the bun," he suggested. "I followed Roo's reheating instructions to the letter."

She picked it up, tore a piece off, and made a sexy sound of pleasure as she chewed. "So what have you been up to—other than making excellent espresso and reheating exquisitely gooey sticky buns?"

Deciding he'd been imagining her melancholy mood, he clasped his hands behind his head and leaned back against the headboard. "Oh, the usual. Let the dogs out, fed them and Pirate. Alfie's still dozing under his blanket, no need to rouse the feathered devil yet. Called my parents."

She stilled. "You did? I bet they were really happy to hear from you."

An understatement. Both his mom and dad had gotten on the line, and he'd heard his mother sniff back tears at the news that he'd be seeing them at the wedding in New York. The only Christmas present a mother could want, she'd answered shakily. He swallowed a hard lump in his throat when he thought about all the soldiers who wouldn't be seeing their families or loved ones this Christmas.

Clearing his throat he said, "Yeah. When I told them I was coming to Tess and Ward's wedding, my mother got pretty emotional."

"I can imagine. Another excellent Christmas present, then. You're batting a thousand. Here, have a bite."

Lowering his arms he leaned forward to meet her fingers and opened his mouth for her to feed him. "Oh, yeah, that is good." When she made to lower her hand, he caught her wrist and held it. "This is even better," he said. Slowly he sucked her fingers, cleaning them of every trace of brown sugar.

Her breath hitched and her eyes widened in a brilliant blue flare before her lids, heavy with arousal, lowered.

"Know what? I believe it's time for your next present, Quinn. Are you ready for it?"

Her smile teased and seduced. "I can't imagine what could top a sticky bun."

"I'll do my best to rise to the challenge."

"Aren't you a cocky one?"

"Thanks to you, definitely." He grinned. "Shall I show you?"

The pulse beneath his fingers jumped and then began pounding. He could feel his own blood pumping as desire rode him hard. But he ignored his rising need. He wanted to go slow and savor every moment with her.

He removed the tray from her lap, set it on the floor, and then rolled onto his side, facing her.

"You're beautiful," he said. "Effortlessly, marvelously beautiful. Inside and out."

She opened her mouth to protest, but he wouldn't let her, not when he knew he spoke the truth. He kissed her and tasted coffee and cinnamon and sugar. Most potent of all was the unique flavor of the woman who'd come to mean so much to him. It was a taste he'd never get enough of.

Soft and deliciously tender, her mouth moved beneath

his, her tongue matching his probing cadence as their breathing grew heavy. His hands gathered up her tank top, fingers drifting over the silky skin of her stomach. Raising his head only to pull the garment over her tangled head of hair, he lowered his mouth again, this time tasting the sleep-warmed skin of her collarbone.

He'd come to know her well. Understood the things that made her smile, gasp, shudder, and clasp him with feverish strength. He loved her responsiveness and how confident she'd grown in her sexuality. Her pleasure mattered to him, more than it had ever mattered with anyone else. And while he'd learned the secret places on her body that if he licked or grazed with his teeth or caressed with an open palm or teasing fingers would make her arch and sigh, he'd come to recognize that he would never tire of searching them out or discovering new ones.

It was love that changed everything. And trust, too. After the night when he'd shared what happened in Afghanistan, he'd expected her to recoil from him; she'd seen the darkness that shadowed his soul. Yet she accepted him, told him she loved him, and welcomed him into her body. Amazing. He didn't deserve someone as good and generous as Quinn, but damned if he was going to let her go.

His mouth and hands traveled, taking time to indulge in the taste and feel of her, to breathe in her scent, to admire her sleek, athletic shape. Happiness filled him as she writhed and arched beneath him.

His hand slid beneath her panties, smoothing her nest of curls. His fingers parted her folds. She was wet for him. His cock grew harder, straining against his zipper. Ignoring his aching erection, he focused on rolling the silk scraps off her hips and down her thighs. She helped by wriggling out of them, a splendid move that caused her breasts to jiggle and her hips to rock into his fingers so they glided down her cleft to dip into her tight core.

A line of sweat trickled its way down his spine. He was surprised it didn't sizzle.

He slid two fingers inside her, loving the hot squeeze of her flesh. He watched her face as he moved in and out while his thumb played with her clit, making her pant and moan, "Yes, there . . . Oh God, more, Ethan, harder . . ." Sweet, crazed commands he was only too willing to obey.

He brought his mouth to her as his fingers moved faster and deeper, bringing her ever higher. Her inner muscles clenched him fiercely. Pressing his mouth against her, he sucked and then lightly grazed her sensitive flesh with his teeth. She came with a shattering scream, bucking wildly against him.

Christmas was off to a good start.

He eased the rhythm of his fingers while she rode the waves of her climax. Kissing her softly on her inner thighs and then on her mound and hipbones, he rested the side of his face in the cradle of her hips, his breath as harsh as hers.

Jesus, what her orgasms did to him. His heart felt close to bursting. His cock was painfully sensitized.

Her fingers dug into his shoulders, grabbed at his T-shirt. He looked up.

"I need you," she whispered. "Come inside me, please."

That hadn't been part of his plan; the orgasm had been for her alone. But he couldn't say no. He needed her just as much.

He whipped his clothes off, grabbed a condom, and, gritting his teeth, smoothed the latex over himself. He was so close already. It was possible he'd come as soon as he was inside her, and he wanted to prolong the pleasure. Give her more, give her everything he had.

Determined to take it slow and build the intensity between them, he positioned himself and sank into her slowly, inch by inch, his eyes locked on hers until he was embedded.

He held himself there, his arms trembling, his heart racing as he throbbed and her muscles clamped around him like a velvet fist.

"Ethan." She breathed his name as she wrapped her legs about his hips, bringing him even deeper.

"Jesus, Quinn, you feel so good. So incredibly good." Bracing himself on either side of her shoulders, he rocked against her, withdrew, then drove back to where he most wanted to be. She met him thrust for thrust.

It was unbelievable, their joining, a pleasure so sharp and so exquisite, a happiness so profound and complete. It pierced him, freeing the words he'd held in his heart. "I love you, Quinn."

Her eyes went wide with surprise.

For a split second he wondered how she would react to his words. He'd changed their relationship, no longer willing to pretend that this was all about bringing Quinn up to speed sexually. She deserved to know that his heart was involved, too. A heart that squeezed tight when she blinked and tears escaped from her eyes.

"Don't stop, Ethan. Please don't ever stop."

Linking their fingers, he answered her whispered plea with a promise. "Never."

UNLIKE HER FEELINGS for Thanksgiving, Quinn whole-heartedly loved Christmas. She adored the gleeful rush of furtive shopping, decorating the halls and trees, stringing lights, consuming platefuls of decadent treats, and listening to the glorious music hailing the blessed birth.

This year she appreciated even more the joyful chaos that accompanied her parents' Christmas. In the midst of the laughter that accompanied unwrapping some of the silly gifts they'd found one another—a set of animal wine stoppers for Mia; bride and groom toothbrushes for Tess and Ward; for her, a flask of caffeinated maple syrup for those days when she needed to be extra wired, Ward teased; a model tractor for her dad; a roping skills book for Reid; soap in the shape of goats for Ethan; and for her mother, a signed head shot of Neil Sedaka. In the midst of all the laughter, teasing banter, and expressions of thanks, no one, Ethan included, noticed her comparative quiet.

Guilt sure could do a number on a person.

Ethan had said he loved her. Would it be enough?

The thought drummed in her head as they finished their Christmas breakfast and then, leaving the dishes for later since Tess and Ward needed to stick to a schedule in order to make their evening flight to New York, they moved on to the presents piled beneath the Christmas tree.

"I think I remember some of these ornaments," Ethan said. "That one of Rudolph, definitely."

"One of Quinn's," her mom replied. "It's great, isn't it?"

The decoration dated from when she was four, a fertile artistic period. Rudolph's nose was almost as big as his head and her pre-k teacher had allowed her to use so much glitter, the red blob still sparkled mightily twenty years later. The rest of the ten-foot tree was decorated with many other of her handmade ornaments, as well as Ward and Reid's efforts—cowboy Santas and snowmen. The others, such as the blown and painted eggs suspended from thin velvet ribbons, were gifts from family friends. The tree shone with love and generosity.

As if following her train of thought, her mother pointed to the delicate glass icicles hanging from the tips of branches. "Your parents gave us these, Ethan. Cheryl brought them back from a trip they took to Prague."

"That must have been about ten years ago."

Her mother nodded. "I think of them both every year when I hang the icicles. I can't wait to see them in New York. Cheryl called earlier. Your surprise news about coming to the wedding made her Christmas—she sounded as happy as the day she called to tell us you'd sold your first photograph." Her comment was delivered in a light, casual tone, though Quinn knew it was anything but. Her parents were aware of Ethan's talent. They weren't the sort who'd be willing to see him waste it. Even if Ethan ended up staying and working as a ranch hand, they would make sure his work at Silver Creek posed no obstacle to his returning to his photography. They would accommodate his need to pursue his passion just as they did with Reid, who currently divided his time between his duties at the guest ranch and helping Mia with the vineyard.

Quinn was careful not to look at Ethan, but she could picture his guarded expression. He'd have shut down his emotions the way he always did when his art was mentioned—except for when the terror of his nightmares broke down the barriers.

In true diplomatic fashion, her father saved Ethan from replying to her mother's comment by saying, "Let's sit down and get these presents opened." He picked up the tray laden with coffee mugs and passed it around as her mother settled into her favorite chair by the window. They all followed suit, Tess and Ward sitting close enough on the sofa to hold hands, Reid and Mia choosing the two matching leather poufs by the crackling fire, and Quinn and Ethan taking two armchairs at the end of the sofa.

The unwrapping began.

She smiled as her mom and dad thanked her for the tickets she'd bought them to the San Francisco Opera. The performance was Bizet's *Carmen,* one of her mom's favorites.

She chuckled at the T-shirt Reid gave her, which read, IF HISTORY REPEATS ITSELF, I'M SO GETTING A DINO-SAUR.

Holding the shirt so everyone could see it, she asked, "How'd you guess my next move? I was thinking I'd like to have a microraptor so that Alfie could have a buddy. Thanks, Reid. I love it."

Mia and Quinn had bought Tess a navy blue garter belt that had a satin ribbon threaded through it, its color an exact match of her wedding gown. Embroidered on the ribbon were the initials *T & W* and the date of their wedding.

"We realized you needed something blue to wear on your wedding day," Mia said.

"You guys, thank you so much. No, Ward, you cannot see this. On our wedding night, yes," Tess said, holding the small box off to the side so he couldn't steal a peek.

After she'd closed the lid and set the box on the coffee table, Ward leaned over and whispered something in Tess's ear that had her laughing and blushing furiously and then leaning in for a kiss.

When her brother's hand slipped beneath the dark curtain of Tess's hair, Quinn cleared her throat. Loudly. "Save it for the plane trip, Ward," she said. "We still have loads of presents to unwrap." Her present for Ethan was lying directly under a big hand-painted ball ornament that she'd made in fourth grade. It had Santa on one side and Frosty on the other. She went to reach for the present, but Ethan moved first. He dropped to his knees and chose a small, flat box tied with baling twine. He'd even tied a little bow. And there was an envelope attached to it.

He handed the box to her. "Not that I have anything against dinosaurs, but here's something else to consider. Merry Christmas, Quinn." His voice was easy, his tone the one he used when speaking to Tess or Mia. Quinn doubted it fooled anyone gathered in her parents' spacious living room.

She stared at the package, her heart hammering against her ribs as if the box she held were square and velvet and its interior satin lined to protect a gem-studded ring.

How much more could he give her today when he'd already whispered his love? How much more could her heart take when it alternately felt close to bursting and ready to break?

She opened the box. Coiled in a nest of tissue paper

lay a braided bracelet, its strands black, white, and flame-red chestnut. A sterling silver clasp connected the ends. She looked up.

"It's from Domino and Tucker's manes?"

"Yeah." Ethan nodded. "I had it made by the lady who owns the jewelry store on West Street."

"Maeve Gowan? She makes wonderful pieces," her mother said when Quinn lifted the bracelet for her family to see.

"Good gift, Ethan," Reid said. "Exactly the sort of thing Quinn will wear."

"Maeve said she could expand the bracelet, adding new manes whenever you want, which brings me to your next gift. It's in the envelope," he said to her.

"Now you've got me curious. I love the bracelet. Thank you."

She tore open the envelope. Inside was a gift certificate from the equine rescue center where she'd adopted Glory and Tucker.

"Ward gave me the center's name. I thought that now that Tucker's doing better, you might be ready to adopt another horse."

Her heart squeezed tight. Her "Thank you, Ethan," came out in a choked whisper as she blinked away a fresh round of tears.

"You're welcome," he replied huskily.

She continued to stare at the certificate through a film of tears, managing to pull herself together—and even snort with laughter—only when Ward drawled, "Hey, Quinn, think we can move on? Tess and I have a plane to catch this evening."

She straightened and met her brother's grin, saw it matched everyone else's, and sniffed audibly. "They're good presents, okay?"

"They are indeed. Well done, Ethan. So who's next?" her dad asked.

"I have something for Ethan," she said quickly before anyone else could offer up a gift. She went to the present lying below Santa's grinning face and brought it to him.

"Here you go. Merry Christmas." As she spoke, she felt a blush crawl over her cheeks.

Seeing her color, Ethan crooked his lips in a half grin. She knew that had they been alone, he'd have grabbed her around the waist and hauled her close for a very thorough kiss.

"What'd she get you?" Reid asked.

"Still working on untying the bow for Adele's collection . . ."

Her mother reused bows and wrapping whenever possible.

"There," Ethan said. "I've got it." He removed the lid. He lifted the silver belt buckle and cradled it in his hands.

She watched his thumbs move over the chased design. He looked up. "It's beautiful, Quinn." His eyes said much more.

She swallowed. "Merry Christmas."

"Let's see it, Ethan," her mother said.

He stood and brought it over to her.

"It's lovely. The tooled leather belt is, too. Quinn must have guessed what Daniel and I intended to give you. Daniel," she said, angling her head, "do you want to do the honors?"

Quinn's father stood and picked up an oblong box nestled by the base of the tree. He handed it to Ethan. "Merry Christmas, son."

"Thank you, Daniel and Adele," Ethan said, and proceeded to open it. Slowly he lifted a steel-gray barn coat with a black corduroy collar.

Quinn recognized it immediately. It was the jacket given to all the ranch hands, and yes, embroidered beneath the stitched Silver Creek Ranch logo was Ethan's name.

"We hope you'll join the ranch crew, Ethan," her dad said.

"Come calving and lambing season, we're always in need of good, steady men," Ward said, rising from the sofa to shake his hand.

"And the salary comes with good benefits. Even a 401(k). Of course the downside is, now Quinn will really be able to boss you around," Reid joked.

Ethan arched a brow. "Worse things in life."

"True. Then again, you're not a man who scares easily." Reid looked over at their father. "Dad, you should give him a signing bonus."

"I'm way ahead of you, Reid. It's in the contract I've drawn up for you, Ethan, though it's not your typical bonus. We'll go fifty-fifty with you on the cost of a stock horse. Reid has a lot of contacts in the area."

"We'll find a beaut for you, Ethan," said Reid.

"And in the meantime, I'd be grateful if you rode Rio for these next few days and then while Tess and I are away on our honeymoon. I don't want him getting fat and lazy."

Listening to the men launch into a discussion of some of the horses currently on the market and whether Ethan might also want to look at some of the ones at equine rescue centers, Quinn wondered what they would say if they knew of her plans, plans being set in motion even as they spoke. Their enthusiastic embrace of Ethan into the fold made what Quinn aimed to do even harder, and yet she drank in this moment, so happy to see Ethan accepted by those she loved most in the world.

* * *

When Ward and Tess left to finish packing, Reid and Mia gathered up their presents as well so that they could spring Bruno and call Mia's uncle before the hour got too late in France. Her father announced a desire to get some fresh air in his lungs before spending several hours behind the wheel when he and Adele drove Ward and Tess to the airport.

"I'm going to stay and set the house to rights," Quinn's mom said.

"I'll help you, Mom."

"Thank you, darling." Her mother smiled and then turned to Ethan. "Go ride Forester for me so I won't feel guilty about not giving him a Christmas Day run. And don't let Kane beat you if Daniel challenges you to a race."

Her dad picked up the tray of coffee mugs and her mom followed him into the kitchen, leaving Ethan and her alone.

Ethan moved closer. Reaching out, he tucked a strand of hair behind her ear. "Everything good?"

"Yeah. I just want to spend some time with my mom and then take care of the animals."

"And you're okay about your parents giving me a job? You were kind of quiet."

Of course he'd noticed. The habits of years devoted to looking through a camera lens and bringing his subject into sharp focus stayed with a body.

For a second she stalled, unwilling to answer him when 95 percent of her wanted nothing more than a future with him here at Silver Creek. But it was the 5 percent that she needed to heed.

"I guess I was wondering whether you really want to work as a ranch hand. Will it be enough? Will it satisfy you?" she asked, turning the tables on him.

"Why not?" He shrugged. "There are worse ways to spend one's days. Besides, Silver Creek is where you are." He cupped his hand about the nape of her neck and kissed her. "You're good for me, Quinn."

She wasn't the only one being squirrelly and avoiding a direct answer. And he wasn't playing fair, damn it. He must know how she longed to hear him say that.

"What if I'm not enough?"

The lines in his face tightened. "Don't sell yourself short, Quinn."

That wasn't the issue—and he knew it. He was turning his back on something that needed finishing—his photo documentary. Quinn was a Knowles through and through. She'd been taught to never leave a job unfinished. She was about to press him again when her father returned.

"You ready to ride, Ethan?"

He gave a short nod. "Yes, sir." To Quinn, he said, "We'll talk later."

"Yes, and you won't listen," Quinn whispered sadly to the empty room.

Her mother had on her yellow rubber gloves and a sink full of sudsy water to scrub the pans. "You can put the dishes in the dishwasher," she said when Quinn carried in a tray laden with plates, glasses, and cutlery.

"Will do."

She was placing the glasses in the upper rack when her mother said, "It's so nice to see things are going well with you and Ethan, darling. Dad and I couldn't be happier for you."

"Yeah?" She straightened. "I had the distinct impression that you were eager to have me get up close and friendly with Josh."

"Friendly with Josh? Of course. 'Up close,' as you put it? Heavens, no. He's adorable, for sure, but I don't think you two would work in the long run. Unless he gets Campbell or Patricia Watt to cast him in a role, I doubt he'll remain in California too long. Unlike you, Maebeth'll fit right in down in Texas. I also have the distinct feeling that if you and Josh were a couple, he'd very quickly be trying to talk you into eating a porterhouse."

"Oh my God, you're right. He probably would." She and her mother exchanged a grin.

"And did you know he was born on August third? Mia and I were discussing how it would be nice if Maebeth could find someone—she really hasn't had much luck with the local men—and Mia mentioned that an astrologer predicted that Maebeth's soul mate would be a Leo. Well, I knew Josh's birthday from his job application. I decided it might be helpful if I dropped that tidbit of information one day when I was picking up the mail and Maebeth was on break."

"How'd you manage to simply slip that into a conversation?"

"Honestly? I can't remember. But I think I could have gone into the luncheonette with a T-shirt announcing his birthday and she wouldn't have questioned my motives. Her face simply lit up. It's nice that things are working out between them. Maebeth deserves a big ol' Texan to love, don't you agree?"

"I do. I really do. Excellent work, Mom. I stand in awe. And here I thought I was doing good work when I told Maebeth about the recipe for mac and cheese." Quinn shook her head. "Clearly I'm a rank amateur compared to you."

"Give it time, but thank you for the compliment, darling."

So her mom hadn't been trying to set her up with Josh, Quinn thought as she began to load the plates and cutlery in the dishwasher. All that fretting on her part had been unnecessary. But what about Ethan? Had her

mom been doing some behind-the-scenes maneuver-
ing with him and Quinn? "Hey, Mom, remember that
meeting when Dad announced that Ethan was coming
to stay? Why were you so reluctant about having him
here?"

Immersed in the sudsy water, her mother's hands
slowed. "Was I?" she said with an annoying vagueness.

"Yeah, you were. I remember thinking it was weird
since Cheryl and Tony Saunders are such good friends."

"Oh, well, I might have been worried."

Quinn didn't buy her bright smile. "About what? His
injuries?"

"Obviously."

"Mom."

She sighed. "Very well. I was concerned about you."

"Me?"

"Quinn, you're a rescuer by nature. You always have
been, ever since the day you found that baby bunny and
brought it home. From Tony and Cheryl's descriptions
of Ethan's injuries—not just his physical ones but also
his emotional state—I worried that he might be too
broken to heal. But he seems to be doing better, much
better. That's thanks to you. You've helped him."

"Maybe I have, but it's not enough. He's not really
healed, Mom," she said quietly so that her voice wouldn't
break.

"Oh, Quinn." Her mother wrapped her yellow-gloved
arms about her and hugged her close.

ETHAN WASN'T SURPRISED to learn that Quinn was the sort of person who preferred to celebrate New Year's Day by watching the sun rise on January 1 rather than staying up late drinking champagne on New Year's Eve and waking up to a sore head. In light of all that needed to be organized before they left for New York, with every one of them putting in extra hours to ensure the guest ranch would run smoothly in the Knowleses' absence, he was surprised Quinn made it to ten o'clock. The early bedtime had been fine with him. Lying with Quinn in his arms was a hell of a nice way to greet the New Year.

And watching the sun illuminate her face easily beat the wildest, craziest of parties.

He only wished she would relax. The faint lines of tension didn't detract from her beauty; the photographer in him recognized the allure of mystery. They worried him, however.

The only time he didn't sense her brain whirring as if it were fueled by a gallon of her strongest espresso was when they made love. Then he was able to see her eyes go wide with passion rather than narrow in preoccupation.

Even Lorelei remarked upon Quinn's unusual state

when she dropped by on New Year's Day for extra-strong coffee, brewed by Quinn, and a tomato, spinach, and mozzarella frittata, which was Lorelei's contribution.

No sooner had they sat down at the kitchen table that did double duty as Quinn's dining room than Quinn launched into a recital of the special treats Lorelei could give Alfie and Pirate should they act stressed. The list was substantial.

"And there are Kongs filled with peanut butter in the freezer for Sooner and Bowie. Bully sticks are in the cabinet to the left of the dog food," she added.

"Listen, Quinn, Francesco and I are going to take good care of these guys. And remember, you'll only be gone for five days. The world won't end."

Quinn gave her a funny look. "No, I guess it won't." She dredged up something that resembled a smile. "I suppose I'm freaking out."

"Yeah, kind of."

Ethan wisely remained silent.

"New York is so far from California," Quinn said.

"Nothing's going to happen." When Quinn looked far from convinced, Lorelei patiently persisted. "All your animals are healthy. Tucker's back in the pasture and giving free tetherball lessons to anyone who wanders over. If, God forbid, something should go wrong with any creature, furred or feathered, I have both Cat Lundquist and Gary Cooney on speed dial. Mel does, too. Okay?"

Quinn had asked Mel to care for Tucker and the nanny goats in her absence.

"Okay. Thanks, Lorelei. It just seems like so much could go wrong, you know?"

"Nope. I don't. This ranch has amazing people working here, wranglers who care about the stock as much as your family does. As for the wedding, I'm sure it's going to be beautiful and fun."

"Why can't people just elope?"

"And here I thought I could count on you as a bridesmaid."

"Oh Lorelei, of course! I'd be honored. Did Francesco propose?"

"Last night. At the stroke of midnight." Beaming, Lorelei held up her hand. The diamond on her ring finger caught the light and winked at them. "I've been waving this around waiting for you to notice."

"Sorry. Super, super distracted. It's beautiful."

For a few minutes the two friends bent their heads over Lorelei's ring while Ethan took another slice of frittata and wondered what kind of engagement ring would put a dazzling smile of happiness on Quinn's face. A sapphire to match her eyes? A ruby to symbolize her heart? A diamond as magnificent and bright as her spirit? It wasn't too early to plan, though now wasn't the time to propose. Better to wait until she was less crazed by everything going on.

He'd give her time and show her that he was fine working as a ranch hand, dispelling the doubt he'd read in her expression and silencing the nagging voice in his head.

Quinn and Lorelei straightened.

He took the opportunity to compliment Lorelei on the egg dish.

"Thanks. I'm concentrating on eating well today, since I have a feeling Quinn will leave us with way too many brownies. So how about you, Ethan? Are you looking forward to visiting New York?"

He swallowed his mouthful of frittata. "Yeah, I haven't been there in a while." His last trip there had been just a few days before his departure for Afghanistan. It included meeting Dara for a drink, the decision to end things between them perfectly amicable; taking the time to see the stunning and sobering exhibit of Mathew Brady's Civil War photographs at the Metropolitan; and sharing a lunch with Erin Miller, during which she'd told him again how excited she was about the project. Her words had made him feel as if his photographs had the potential to play as important a role as Brady's had in portraying men in battle. Buoyed by his meeting with Erin, he'd flown to Washington to say goodbye to his parents and then had left for the army base where the military liaison had arranged for him to hitch a ride on a military plane to Kandahar.

"Maybe you guys can sneak away and do something fun on your own," Lorelei said.

He shook off the memories of those first surreal days at Camp Nathan Smith, the motor of his camera whirring, his eyes burning from the strain of trying to take everything in. "Yeah, that would be good. How about it, Quinn? Want to plan on ditching the wedding festivities for an hour or two with me?"

She straightened in her chair, his question seeming to pierce her previous abstraction. "Yeah, all right." She nodded, at last enthusiastic about something related to the trip. "But I get to choose the destination."

Lorelei took a sip of her coffee. With a wince she set the cup back down and poured cream into it until it was a pale caramel color. "What do you want to bet Quinn takes you to visit the NYPD's new stables? Though I've heard they're really nice."

"I'll have to pass on the bet, Lorelei. Luckily, I have no problem with Quinn taking me anyplace she wants to go. Whatever makes you happy," he said to Quinn with a smile. It was true. He wanted to see her as happy as she'd been before the combined rush of the holidays and the frenzy of the travel preparations dimmed the light in her eyes.

* * *

Quinn fought the guilt, knowing it would suffocate her otherwise. As her mom had said on Christmas morning after hearing her confess her worry about Ethan, "If you love him, and I can see you do, darling, you have to do what's best for him. And then it's up to him, isn't it?"

True. But holding up the mirror of truth was a lousy and sure-to-be-thankless job.

And now Lorelei had provided the perfect cover for her plan, the final moment when Ethan would have to take a good hard look at what kind of man he really was and decide whether he had the courage to stop hiding away at Silver Creek. Quinn had been obsessing about how to fabricate a plausible reason for him to go off with her and not arouse his suspicion. Thanks to his offer to go wherever she wished, she could present the destination as a surprise. He'd be game, she knew.

Her stomach tightened at the depth of the trust he had in her.

"Do you need help choosing what dresses to bring?"

She started, then glanced over her shoulder at Ethan. He was lying on the bed, legs stretched out, bare feet crossed, hands folded behind his head, a smile playing across his lips.

"What?"

"Nothing." Ethan gave an amused shake of his head. "Only you've been staring into your closet for the past five minutes and haven't moved a muscle. Don't you already have the dress for the wedding?"

Thank God he thought she was worried about her wardrobe. Deciding to run with it, she gave a wave of her hand. "Pfft," she said. "The wedding's nothing. First of all, we'll be in New York City. There'll be dinners, lunches, cocktails, and who knows what in between. And the forecast is for cold, cold, and more cold.

Of course I'm stumped about what to pack." She sighed loudly.

"Quinn, anything you choose to wear, you're going to look beautiful in. Right now, dressed in your jeans and tee, you're the most gorgeous woman I've ever seen."

Lord, he turned her insides to mush so easily. With their departure a mere eighteen hours away, his kindness was making her feel like the slimiest of traitors. How did other people manage deceit with a loved one? Did they possess some ability to compartmentalize, block out their guilt, or rationalize away the wrong they were inflicting?

A part of her almost wished for the callousness that would involve, because it hurt so much to be with him, kiss him, succumb to the enchantment of his hands and body while knowing that in a matter of days she might lose him.

"I'm pretty sure Mom will kill me if I show up in my jeans to any of those events."

"Well, then, I vote for the skirt you wore on Thanksgiving. A particular favorite of mine."

She fought for a grin. "How about you? Are you packed yet?"

"Yup. Took about five minutes."

"Rub it in, why don't you?"

His smile spread. "Granted, I'll have to make a speedy shopping expedition and pick up a couple of suits and some other items when I get to the city. My time at the army base didn't exactly call for wedding attire." And with that his smile was gone.

She made a show of selecting the knit burgundy skirt, a fitted cream silk top, and a pair of cigarette-leg black trousers and carried them to the foot of the bed, depositing them next to her open suitcase. "What about your cameras and equipment?" she asked casually with a glance over her shoulder.

"What about them?"

"Are you leaving them here?"

He hesitated a moment too long. "Sure. Why would I bring them with me?"

Even if Quinn hadn't noticed his hesitation, she certainly would have heard the forced note in his reply.

As if nothing were amiss, she returned to her closet, where she fingered a black cocktail dress she'd worn maybe twice and pulled it out. Already she'd chosen more black than she wore in a year. You'd think she was going to a funeral rather than a wedding to celebrate the love of two fantastic people. On the other hand, the color suited her mood perfectly. A mood that grew bleaker when she forced herself to say, "Why don't you stow the cases here, where they'll be extra safe?"

"I'll bring 'em over today." The alacrity of his response revealed much.

"You can put them in the study closet. Alfie will watch them like a parrot."

When he laughed, the skin at the corners of his eyes crinkling appealingly, she realized it had been way too long since she'd attempted a joke. It made this one, lame as a horse with navicular, seem a freakin' laugh riot.

But not even Ethan's mirth could hide the fact that the prospect of being separated from his photography equipment for even five days left him as unhappy as she was at the prospect of leaving her animals. His photography tools and her animals were a vital part of their identities. While Ethan was denying his identity with everything he had, it didn't make leaving his cameras behind less painful.

At the thought, Quinn's guilt eased a fraction . . . only to resettle heavily over her heart as she began figuring out how to get the equipment cases to New York quickly and safely, with Ethan none the wiser.

Her transgressions were mounting, and they hadn't even reached New York.

Chapter
TWENTY-NINE

THE WALDORF-ASTORIA WAS big—big on marble, big on gold trim, big on mirrors. The grand hotel exuded an air of refined luxury. While Quinn preferred the warmer tones and textures of river stone and timber, along with vistas of rolling pastures and spruce-covered mountains, it was kind of amazing to walk into the soaring, cathedral-like lobby and be greeted by liveried staff and a concierge who offered them flutes of impeccably chilled champagne and congratulated her parents on their son's upcoming wedding before being whisked up to one of the suites and enveloped by gilded softness. And, as her dad remarked, it was a pleasant and welcome change to be in a hotel where, should the pipes in any of the glorious bathrooms clog, it would be someone else's headache.

Quinn's parents had chosen to stay at the Waldorf not only for its comfort but also for its location. They didn't want to waste time stuck in crosstown traffic when driving to Queens, where Tess's parents lived and where the church in which the wedding ceremony would be held was located. Brooklyn and Anna Vecchio's restaurant was also within easy reach from the midtown hotel. With so many friends congregating and events and outings planned, they hit the ground running. Ward's best friend, Brian Nash, and his wife, Carrie—also a good friend—had already arrived. They all met up at the City Winery, a SoHo winery and music club. Reid had bought the tickets for the evening's concert and must have tipped the manager a small fortune because they were taken directly to a reserved table large enough for the eight of them. The R&B band was great and the wine Mia ordered for them went down easily.

Luckily Ethan had figured out that Quinn's musical tastes were a little broader than Olivia Newton-John and Lionel Richie. It didn't stop him from teasing that he knew of a bar where they only played seventies hits that she might prefer.

On the second night, they had dinner with the Casaris and Anna Vecchio's family as well. Mrs. Casari—Maria—had insisted on inviting all the Knowleses, Mia and Ethan included, to their home. It had been an uncomplicated way for the families to meet before the more formal occasions took place. With the addition of Anna, her boyfriend Lucas, and Anna's parents, the modest brick house was filled to bursting with bodies and, in very little time, with laughter. And the food prepared by Mrs. Casari and Mrs. Vecchio . . . well, there'd been enough of it to feed four times as many people.

It was why Quinn had spoken up, asking the livery driver to pull over when they crossed back into Manhattan.

To her parents she said, "Do you mind? I'd like to walk off some of the zillion calories I consumed."

"Of course not, Quinn honey. You'll go with her, Ethan?"

"Yes, sir."

"I think a walk would do Mia and me good, too, Dad," Reid said. "You mind if we tag along, sis?"

"The more the merrier."

The four of them clambered out of the black Escalade while her dad and mom continued on to the hotel. Ward and Tess, who were staying in the Towers portion of the Waldorf for the extra privacy and VIP treatment showered on wedding couples, had remained at the Casaris' to help clean up. A nightcap with Anna and Lucas was planned.

The night air was biting, in the low thirties, and their breath came out in puffy clouds as they made their way to Park Avenue. Mia and Reid walked ahead of them, their heads almost touching.

When Ethan's hand found hers, she felt her heart lift. How remarkable to think that she was walking down a New York City street with the man she loved.

"Man, Italians sure can eat," she said.

"And cook," Ethan said. "That was the best pasta all'amatriciana I've had outside of Italy."

"Did you try the spaghetti with pesto, green beans, and potatoes? Incredible. I'll grow all the beans, basil, and potatoes Jeff wants if he'll make that dish for me back home."

"Now that we've seen how well the *madri* cook, I'm pretty sure the wedding dinner Anna serves at her trattoria will be extraordinary. I liked her. She's a spitfire."

"Yeah, Anna's great. I love that she's pulling out all the stops for Tess."

"They're funny with their stories of their school days," Ethan agreed. "I can't imagine Tess's childhood was easy."

She knew he was referring to the sorrow that must have cast a shadow over the Casaris' home on account of Christopher's severe autism. When his reactions became impossible to control, Tess's parents were forced to find a facility that could address his needs.

"It can't have been easy for any of them. But I guess

there's comfort in knowing Christopher's in a place where he's safe and well cared for."

She looked at Reid, walking a few paces in front of them. Her brother had wrapped his arm around Mia's waist, drawing her even closer. Their strides matched. Mia had already experienced heartache—losing her mother when she was little more than a toddler, never knowing her father. But should more misfortune or tragedy befall her, Reid would be there for her. Their love, like Ward and Tess's, like her parents', would weather life's storms.

She wanted the same with Ethan.

If only . . .

"So have you decided where you want to sneak off to—provided we have a free moment?" he asked, interrupting her thoughts.

She'd finalized the details with Dara Brendel and then called Erin Miller while Ethan was out, picking out his suits and buying accessories. It was Dara who'd suggested she bring Ethan to the gallery the evening of Ward and Tess's wedding, after the toasts were made, the wedding cake cut, and the dancing grown champagne-silly. The late hour would allow Dara the necessary time to set things up. Quinn had agreed because it gave her the chance to hoard every second she had with Ethan.

She forced a laugh to cover the nervousness. "Never fear, crazy schedule notwithstanding, I'm going to whisk you away when you least expect it. Just be prepared to stop whatever it is you're doing and come with me."

He raised her hand and kissed the inside of her wrist where her glove ended. "Your wish is my command. So tell me again, what's on tomorrow's agenda?"

"Mia, Carrie, Anna, and I are taking Tess out for some pampering. Pretty much an all-day event. Then we're taking her to dinner and a show. You're going to meet up with Ward, Brian, and Reid when the basketball game is over, right?"

Reid had bought courtside seats to see the Lakers play the Knicks.

"Yeah, I'll have dinner with my parents and then meet the guys at a bar."

"One of many, no doubt. Reid and Brian are taking their roles of best man and groomsman very seriously."

"A bar crawl. Haven't done that in a while."

"Just make sure Ward gets back in time to make it to the rehearsal or the priest may not let him marry Tess."

"We'll carry him if necessary," Ethan said.

"That's the spirit. Once the rehearsal's over, we're in the homestretch prep-wise."

"Maybe you and I could steal away then."

"No—no." She cleared her throat. "Because then we have the rehearsal dinner with the Casaris, the priest, Anna, Lucas, and Carrie and Brian. Mom and Dad are giving it. They've reserved a private room at Per Se. No ducking out of that."

"At least it'll be delicious—almost as good as what we had tonight."

"True, but much more of this eating with no riding or playing tag with Gertrude and the does to work it off and I'll be busting the seams of my bridesmaid dress."

He squeezed her hand. "I'll keep my eyes peeled."

She snorted. "Cheap thrills."

"The chance to see any part of your body? An exquisite thrill."

"You must be on a sugar high after that tiramisu. Dear Lord, I can't believe I went near a dessert. It would be awful if I popped a seam or if anything went wrong on Tess's big day." And that was another reason to postpone taking Ethan to Dara Brendel's Tribeca gallery until after Tess and Ward had cut the cake and perhaps even slipped away from the reception to celebrate in privacy. She didn't want anything to spoil their special day. "It's a good thing I love Tess, because I really hate weddings."

"So what kind of wedding would you want that wouldn't be an ordeal? Whoa!" he said with a laugh, gripping her hand more tightly and pulling back on it to prevent Quinn from doing a face-plant into the sidewalk. "Careful there."

"I swear that crack in the sidewalk appeared out of nowhere. What kind of a wedding would I want?" she repeated breathlessly, her mind scrambling. "I don't think I've ever really thought about it."

She could picture it, though, clear as day.

"Go on, then. Give it a shot."

"Well, I'd probably choose a field in the summer and just have my closest friends and family as guests," she said. And there, in front of the small gathering and the minister, she would pledge her love to Ethan. Her heart squeezed with painful yearning. *Keep it light. Keep it easy*, she told herself. "And I'd have a kick-ass band and everyone would dance. And that would be it."

"Sounds right. Sounds like you," he said. Coming to a halt, he gave a gentle tug, reeling her into his arms, and covered her mouth, which had opened in an "Oh!" of surprise.

Their lips were January-cold at first. Quickly the heat of the kiss, as intense as the pounding of their hearts and the straining of their bodies as they pressed closer, burned red-hot.

Pulling back at last, their breaths mingling in a moist cloud, he whispered to her, "In case I haven't said this, you're the best thing that's ever happened to me, Quinn. I like the way you make me feel—any time of day, anyplace we are."

She felt her eyes widen, and the glitter of the city lights on Park Avenue and Forty-Ninth Street grew even brighter. "Oh, Ethan." She swallowed the lump in her throat and then kissed him again, a frantic mashing of lips that made him laugh even as he responded with a matching desperation.

"Come up to the room with me," he whispered. "Let me show you how happy you make me."

No matter how often Quinn professed her dislike of weddings and the surrounding hoopla, not once did Ethan observe her exhibiting anything but grace and humor—albeit her own inimitable brand—in setting after setting, social event after social event, as the days leading to Ward and Tess's big day unfolded.

She hadn't exaggerated the whirlwind pace that the schedule demanded. Even he, standing at the periphery, was caught up. It put to rest any schemes he entertained to take matters into his own hands and steal Quinn away for a few hours, perhaps take her ice skating at Rockefeller Center or to the top of the Empire State Building to view the city spread like a sparkling silver blanket beneath them.

He doubted that even Quinn, as determined and clever as she was, would succeed in orchestrating a way to duck out of these functions. But he was rooting for her . . . for them.

Not that he wasn't enjoying himself. The Knowleses were hoteliers, Tess an obviously talented events planner. They knew how to have a good time. And the dinner with his parents offered an opportunity to erase some of the worry lines on their faces. In Bethesda, they'd been etched deep.

His mother reached out and laid her hand on his arm again, giving it a squeeze. "You look so well, darling. I can't wait to see Adele and Daniel so I can thank them for all they've done. We were so afraid . . ." Her voice faltered.

His father spoke to give Ethan's mother a moment to recover her equilibrium. "So what are your plans? Will you look for a place in Washington or stay here in New York?"

"Neither. I'm going back to Acacia. I'm taking a job at Silver Creek as a ranch hand."

It was a testament to their previous concern that his father and mother didn't immediately exclaim, *But what about your project?*

"Oh," his mother said. "We thought, we hoped . . ."

"That since you're in New York, you'd be seeing your editor," his father inserted.

"Erin seemed to believe so, at least," his mother finished.

He frowned. "You've been in touch with her?"

"Of course, Ethan. So many people care about you. Erin called on Christmas, hoping for word of how you were doing." His mother's voice was gentle, softening the reproach.

Quashing the guilt that rose inside him, he exhaled and then nodded. "I won't have time to see Erin—we're taking a noon flight back the day after the wedding. But I'll send her an email, bring her up to date." He'd avoid a telephone call, though. It would open the door for exactly this type of exchange, where he was reminded of what he'd been, what he was supposed to be doing. "I like being at Silver Creek."

"Of course you do. It's wonderful there. You always loved it as a boy."

"I'm also involved with Quinn Knowles."

From the happiness that lit their faces, he realized he should have announced that he and Quinn were an item the second they sat down. It would have spared them even a second of awkward dancing around the nontopic of his photography project.

"Quinn? Little Quinn?" his mother said breathlessly.

He intended to tease Quinn with that nickname later tonight. "She's grown-up now." *In all the right ways,* he added silently. He then proceeded to tell them stories about Quinn's goats, Bowie and Sooner, her adoption of Tucker—he even found a few kind words to say about Alfie.

"Well, this is terrific. Just terrific," his dad repeated. "Of course you should be at Silver Creek. Everything will fall into place eventually."

He smiled, choosing to ignore the implication that he'd return to his photography. He'd found his peace. It was with Quinn at Silver Creek Ranch. Nothing was going to change his mind.

It was midmorning, the day of the wedding. Ethan and Quinn had indulged in a delicious breakfast in bed, feeding each other bites of flaky croissant and cups of intensely strong espresso—the Waldorf's kitchen had quickly learned her preferences—and cuddling beneath the cloud-white covers. Then, while he lounged beneath the sheets and eavesdropped shamelessly, she'd called Lorelei and Mel for her daily update.

The animals were all fine, but that didn't stop Quinn from quizzing both friends like a nervous mother apart from her newborn for the first time. It was adorable.

"So, they're all good?" he asked after she'd said goodbye to Lorelei.

"Yup. Gertrude stole Lorelei's mitten and ate it. Man, I miss them."

"Yeah, I can see that. Come here and let's see whether I can put a smile on your face," he suggested, crooking his finger.

She gave him a look and then, with a laugh, launched herself in a flying tackle. One of her hands landed on his shoulder and he winced involuntarily.

"Oh my God, did I hurt you?" she asked, pulling down the sheet to inspect him.

"No, I'm good." He rolled the joint in its socket, then winced again exaggeratedly. "On second thought, why don't you kiss it better?"

Later they showered, and then Quinn insisted on packing so she wouldn't be rushed and frantic tomorrow morning before they left for the airport.

"You want me to check us in? I'm sure the concierge can print out the boarding passes."

"No, I'll do all that when I go downstairs to wait for the limo. I've got to stop by the front desk and thank the staff for the exceptional service anyway."

That was Quinn through and through. For all her laid-back quirkiness, she was thoughtful and 100 percent professional.

"Okay, if you insist."

"Mmm. I like to do these things myself." Keeping her gaze fixed on the silk shirt she was folding, she laid it in the suitcase. "There," she said, giving the folded pile of clothes a pat. "That's everything except my toiletries and what I'm wearing home tomorrow."

"And your bridesmaid's dress. You sure I can't have a preview?"

His question earned a quick smile. "No way, buster."

Quinn was being endearingly coy. She hadn't let him see the dress, keeping it stowed in a garment bag. He decided that it was a waste of breath to tell her again that the wow factor whenever he looked at her had yet to dissipate, that it never would. She simply couldn't fathom what she did to him.

"Okay, then." She turned to kiss him on the lips. "Ciao. Off to make Tess the most beautiful bride ever."

He caught her by the wrist and drew her to him for another, deeper kiss. "See you at the church. Will I even recognize you?"

"You'd better. I'd hate for you to kiss another woman like that."

He was still grinning when he finished dressing in a black suit, a snow-white shirt, and a slate-gray textured silk tie. He took a moment to inspect his image. His teeth were brushed. His hair was neatly trimmed, his cheeks freshly shaved. And his black oxfords had been polished to a soft gleam. He'd do.

At the Catholic church where Tess had been baptized and confirmed and would now be wed by the very same priest, he and Lucas, Anna's boyfriend, would usher the guests to their seats and then stand at the ready should the aide who was with Tess's older brother, Christopher, require help assisting Chris out of the church.

It was Adele who'd drafted Ethan into serving as an usher. He was happy to oblige her. Like Quinn, Adele was smart, independent, and competent. Yet that didn't stop a man from wanting to please either woman.

With Quinn, he wanted even more. He'd do anything to make her happy.

Whistling, he took the elevator to the lobby to catch a ride with Lucas to Queens.

The church was filled with the quiet, expectant murmur of voices and the rustle of paper as the seated guests, sleekly coiffed and garbed, chatted amongst themselves and studied the printed wedding program. Ethan stood by the large entryway, the carved wooden doors thrown open in anticipation of the bride.

The limo had arrived.

At the altar, Ward stood tall in his tuxedo. Reid and Brian Nash, similarly dashing, flanked him. All three men's attention fixed on the open doorway.

The opening strains of Handel's *Water Music Suite No.1: Air,* which Tess had chosen for the processional, sounded, and into the space walked Tess Casari, lightly grasping her father's arm.

She was a vision in ivory and lace. A light veil floated over her face, and her gown's train pooled behind her. A collective sigh of happiness, of pleased admiration, wafted into the air as Tess approached the altar and the man waiting for her there.

Something like a sigh escaped Ethan's lips, too, but his stunned sound of appreciation had been for the blonde walking three paces ahead of the bride. In a rose-gold dress that skimmed her body like a worshipful lover's hands, Quinn was heart-stoppingly beautiful. Her long hair had been twisted and pinned into a loose chignon that highlighted the elegant bones of her face and the length of her slender neck. The makeup artist hadn't needed to do much to enhance her features, and yet her eyes sparkled bluer than ever and her lips were a soft, lush pink that made him hunger for their sweetness. She glowed. Her beauty shone almost painfully bright.

He imagined that Ward, watching Tess close the distance separating them, shared the same thought as he. What had he done to deserve this woman in his life?

THE WEDDING WAS over. It had been flawless and deeply moving. After the Mass, the exchange of vows, and the tender kiss Ward and Tess had shared, Tess had broken with ceremony in the most wonderful way: she and Ward had gone directly to Tess's brother, and Christopher, his aide, the rest of the Casari family, and the newlyweds had walked together out into the late-winter afternoon. There hadn't been a dry eye in the church.

As predicted, Anna and her staff at the trattoria had pulled out all the stops. The tables were decorated in a symphony of white hydrangeas, roses, peonies, and calla lilies. Ropes of ivy were woven among them. Candles in glass holders and in sconces attached to the walls cast a warm glow. The dinner itself was a feast for the senses, with bowls of sorbetto to cleanse the palate between courses. Wine had flowed freely. The dinner's triumphant conclusion was the wedding cake, a sponge cake soaked in liqueur, its layers filled with whipped cream and raspberry jam, each slice served with a tulle pouch containing candied almonds to symbolize the bitter and the sweet in life.

After the flutes had been filled with prosecco, Reid stood and gave his speech as best man.

Quinn knew her brother had worked hard on his speech, but the best part was when he veered away from his prepared words to talk about what had moved him most at the wedding—not the last few minutes of the ceremony, when Tess and Ward exchanged their first kiss as man and wife, but rather the moment when Tess had chosen to walk out of the church holding on to both her older brother's and Ward's hands.

"It was beautiful, because that's exactly what Tess is: beautiful inside and out." With a smile Reid raised his glass to her. *"Evviva gli sposi!"*

Around the rustic interior, cries of *"Evviva gli sposi!"* echoed Reid's. Laughter and applause erupted as Tess rose and kissed Reid, and Ward and he embraced heartily.

When the music began and Tess and Ward took to the floor, Ethan found Quinn. "Hey, how are you?"

She swallowed. "Honestly? A little teary and a lot choked up. It was wonderful, wasn't it? Every moment, beginning to end. And Reid's and Anna's speeches rocked."

"So, a good wedding."

"Yes. It feels strange to admit it," she said with a shaky laugh. "But this was a very, very good wedding. Tess was radiant."

"She was." His fingers clasped hers and squeezed gently. "Have I mentioned that when I saw you enter the church, you took my breath away?"

Oh God, Ethan was tearing her heart to pieces with his tenderness. A part of her wanted to run to the table where she'd left her beaded clutch, dig out her phone, and start making frantic calls, canceling the plans she'd set in place. Ethan was everything she wanted. What if she lost him?

He raised his hand and rubbed her trembling lower lip with the pad of his thumb. "Come dance with me."

For a second she stared up at him, drinking him in. She hadn't had a chance to comment on how suave and cosmopolitan he looked in his perfectly cut suit, crisp white shirt, and tie that matched his eyes. With her heart and mind in turmoil, words were difficult.

"Hey, why the sad face, sweetheart?"

She gave a slight shake of her head and pinned a smile to her lips. "Too many emotions, that's all."

With her smile in place, she stepped into the circle of his arms, hating that she knew exactly how much time was left before they would have to leave. Hating, too, that Ethan would follow her with that sexy gleam in his eyes she loved so well. They would walk out of the restaurant with his hand resting protectively, possessively, on her lower back.

Of course the song the DJ played next was an Italian one.

She caught the words *ti amo,* and even with her limited Italian, Quinn understood their meaning.

Their gazes held for a second before he pulled her close, her head resting against his chest, the silk of her dress brushing his trouser legs. As one, they began to sway to the beat. His scent—clean notes of soap, citrus, and wood—filled her, so familiar and yet so potent, just like Ethan himself. She closed her eyes and forgot everything but the sweetness of being in his arms, stealing these last few moments for herself.

The song was nearing its end when Ethan's feet came to an abrupt halt. Opening her eyes, she looked up. Tony Saunders was standing beside Ethan.

"May I cut in and claim a dance with this beautiful woman?" he asked with a smile.

Ethan raised a brow. "Only with the greatest reluctance, and because I happen to know you're a happily married man." Angling his head, he whispered in Quinn's ear, "To be continued, sweetheart," before releasing her and stepping back.

It was another slow dance, the DJ doubtless intending to please the older guests before the night grew wilder. Just as well—Quinn wasn't up to busting a move on the rented dance floor. And she sensed that Ethan's father's request to dance stemmed from a desire to talk privately rather than boogie down.

Ethan had inherited his father's lean build and coloring. While Tony's eyes were a paler shade of gray, they shared the same piercing intelligence.

"How are you, Tony? It's so good to see you and Cheryl. Too many years have passed."

"Yes, it's definitely been too long, but I would have recognized that smile of yours anywhere, even now that you have all your teeth." His laughter joined hers and there was still a thread of it in his voice when he continued. "Right now I'm happier than I have been in many months. Ethan has healed better than I could have hoped."

She didn't miss his meaning. "So you see it, too."

"Since he landed his first photography assignment, Ethan's traveled the world and seen so much. But I think being embedded with these soldiers changed him. He was with them for such a long and intense period that they stopped being simply the subjects of his documentary. The friendships he made, the camaraderie they enjoyed, those things touched him. To have lost those very same friends in the IED attack when he was spared . . . well, you've glimpsed the scars he carries."

"Yes, I have. Both inside and out."

For a moment neither spoke as they followed the music's notes.

"You know what else I would have recognized any-

where, Quinn? Your generous spirit. You may not remember this, and for that matter Ethan might not,
either, but you were always rooting for him when he
was learning how to rope cattle. There's a memory I
have of listening to you talk to him as he was leading
you on that pony. You told him that the next time he
roped a steer, he'd be as fast as your dad. Ethan came
awfully close. I like to think it was because you believed
in him that he did so well." He paused a beat. "I've
heard from Erin Miller a little of your plan."

She raised her head to look into his kind eyes.

"I doubt my saying that Ethan's a man who follows
his own path is news to you, Quinn. He can be stubborn as a mule. But I think that of all the people who
love him, he's least likely to ignore you."

"I'm afraid he won't forgive me."

"It may be that first he needs to forgive himself."

Ethan was holding three flutes of prosecco when Quinn
and his dad stepped off the dance floor. After they'd
clinked glasses and toasted again to Ward and Tess's
happiness, Ethan said, "You haven't lost your moves,
Dad."

"Your mom likes to have date nights at the Jam Cellar. Speaking of which, it's time Cheryl and I do a little
showing off." Taking Quinn's hand, he raised it to his
lips in a courtly gesture. "A pleasure, Quinn. Let's keep
in touch."

"He's smitten," Ethan observed as his father moved
off.

"He's charming."

"Many people say I take after him."

She could see it. Especially when Tony and Cheryl
took to the dance floor. It was there in his athletic grace,

the way he angled his head to gaze into his wife's eyes, the way he smiled.

She made a show of squinting. "You sure you weren't adopted?"

He laughed. "From my mother's labor stories, I think not. At the risk of spreading more doubt in your mind, now that you've seen my dad twirl my mom around, do you care to dance?"

Not enough time left. The car service would be arriving in fifteen minutes. "Actually, I need to use the ladies' room. And then I was thinking that maybe you and I could slip away."

"Your duties are over?" When she nodded, he said, "By all means. I've been waiting to get you to myself."

She found Anna talking to one of her waiters. The man smiled at Quinn and then with a nod slipped through the kitchen's swinging door, leaving them alone.

"Anna, do you have anything I can use as a blindfold? It's to surprise Ethan."

Amazingly, Anna didn't question the request. "Lucky devil. He's totally got my stamp of approval, by the way. Hang on, I've got just the right thing."

Quinn waited by an abandoned table—the dance floor was getting crowded—and made sure to avoid eye contact with any of the guests so that no one would approach.

Anna returned a couple of minutes later. "Here you go." She smiled as she pressed a folded silk square into Quinn's hand.

The black and white pattern was distinctive. Given its history, it was unforgettable. Quinn stared at it warily. "Anna, wait. Isn't this your grandmother's scarf?"

"Good for you for recognizing it. I brought it with me

today in case Tess needed to 'borrow' something, but your mom had already lent her those gorgeous pearl earrings."

"Really, all I need is a dish towel or—"

"Nope." Shaking her head, Anna backed up a step. "What we have here is a clear case of karma. Have fun, Quinn. He's a keeper."

The clock was ticking down and Quinn's feet were dragging as if made of lead. When she went to collect her clutch and slip the scarf inside, she spotted Tess and Ward leaving the dance floor, hand in hand.

She wound her way past the tables to intercept them. After giving them each a hug, she asked, "Are you off?" Their flight to the Turks and Caicos left early in the morning.

"Soon, after we make the rounds."

"Well, I get to say it first, then. Have a wonderful time, Mr. and Mrs. Knowles." She hugged Tess again. "I'm going to miss you. This tall dude, not so much."

A hand slipped about Quinn's waist, and her breath caught in her throat as her heart flip-flopped. Unable to resist, she leaned against Ethan.

Ward nodded to him and stuck out a hand for Ethan to shake. "Take care of my little sister while I'm away. Take even better care of my horse."

Quinn stuck her nose in the air. "Definitely will not miss you," she said, but then spoiled the effect by launching herself at her brother and squeezing tight. "So happy for you, Ward," she whispered.

"Love you, sis."

Exchanging yet another hug and kiss with Tess, she let the newlyweds move off to speak to Tess's uncle Frederico, who was talking to Mr. and Mrs. Vecchio.

"They've got it, I know they do," she murmured to Ethan.

"Got it?"

"The kind of love and commitment to see it through—both the bitter and the sweet that life will yield."

His mouth brushed her temple. "I agree. Ready to blow this joint?"

She drew a breath. "Yes."

"I THINK WE can now say with authority that Italians not only know how to eat, they also know how to party," Ethan said.

"Big-time," Quinn managed to say with hardly a tremor.

They were seated in the back of the town car that Quinn had reserved. He was holding her hand as they talked, his thumb doing a slow sweep like an erotic metronome across the inside of her palm. She was only grateful that he'd chosen to caress that spot and not the inside of her wrist, where he wouldn't have been able to miss the hammering of her pulse.

She felt nauseous with nerves.

They'd reached the Brooklyn Bridge, and both fell silent, he presumably admiring the lights illuminating the bridge's suspension cables and the view of lower Manhattan, the newly completed Freedom Tower soaring above the other buildings. She beheld the same stunning view but could only think, with a growing despair, *I have to do it now, so he won't see where we're headed.*

She withdrew her hand from his and opened her clutch. Her cold fingers touched silk. Pulling the folded square out, she spread it open on her lap and refolded it along the diagonal so the strip would fit around his head.

"What's that you've got?" he asked.

"A blindfold for you." How could her voice be so even when her heart was jumping inside her chest like a jack-rabbit?

"Are you kidding?" Laughter mingled with confusion in his question.

"I don't want you to see where I'm taking you until we're there. Please, Ethan?"

His gaze searched her face in the shadowed interior. She kept her teasing smile in place. Finally he shrugged. "Sure. Okay." He turned his head so she could wrap the silk strip over his eyes. "Damn it, Quinn, I hope you're not taking me to a sex club. I don't intend to share you with anyone."

The door to the Brendel Gallery was locked, but when the livery car pulled up to the address, Quinn saw a figure of a woman framed in the pale light of the first-floor window, watching, waiting.

Ethan was by her side. From his alert stance she knew he was listening to the street sounds to determine where they were.

She wanted the scarf off his head as much as he.

She wanted this over with.

The door swung open while her finger was still pressed to the buzzer. With a nod for the tall woman with raven-black hair and dramatic eyes, she guided Ethan inside.

"Are we here? Can I take this damned thing off now?" he asked, clearly striving to retain his good humor—for her.

How quickly would her patience have evaporated had

someone pulled this stunt on her? Even with him, the bitch in her would have emerged.

"Just a second," she told him. "We're almost there."

The reception area was empty, the lights dimmed. Dara Brendel pointed toward the room beyond and motioned to follow her.

Quinn's hand was on Ethan's elbow. "This way," she said, guiding him into the white-walled space lined with photographs. Bringing him into the center of the room, she lowered her hand, and saw him stiffen with anticipation. Silently she moved behind him, unknotted the scarf, and stepped back, her eyes on him.

His reaction came quickly, even as he was turning, taking in and recognizing his work—Quinn knew there were at least fifty of his photographs displayed on the walls. "What the hell?" His head jerked in surprise when he saw Dara. "Dara? What's going on here?"

In answer, she rushed over to him and kissed his cheeks. "Oh, Ethan, it's so good to see you. I've been a mess, so freaked out about your injuries. So horrible—"

"The pictures, Dara."

"Your friend Quinn's idea. Of course I agreed." She stepped back and cast Quinn a quick smile before hurrying from the room. For a moment, the tap of her heels against the poured-cement floor sounded. Then the gallery was silent.

"Are you going to explain what this is about, Quinn? Why are you showing me my photographs?"

She heard the tension in his voice. He was holding on to his temper but barely, and only because he hadn't yet fully grasped her motive for bringing him here.

"I'm not merely showing you your photographs. I'm showing you *you*, Ethan. You can't deprive the world of your vision, of the things, beautiful and terrible, that you've seen. You have important, necessary work to do. You owe it to all the soldiers you knew in Afghanistan, and to the families and loved ones of those who died there. Your photographs and the book you make out of them will give every one of those people something no one else can, Ethan."

While she spoke, his expression had shuttered, a default defense tactic. "I thought you understood why I can't finish the project, why I can't look at those photographs. I fucking helped get men *killed*."

"No, you didn't. You were doing your job, just as they were doing theirs. Now you need to finish your job."

"Sorry." His tone was flat. "I have another one in California. Your parents gave me a contract. I signed it."

She'd dreaded that it might come to this. "Consider yourself fired."

"What?" The word came out with the force of someone on the receiving end of a blow.

"I'm one of your bosses. I'm firing you," she said through numb lips. "Once you've finished your project, I'd of course be willing to rehire you."

"So generous of you." His sarcasm lashed her. "You may have overlooked one minor fact. Even if I intended to do as you ask, my equipment is—"

"Upstairs, in Dara's apartment. I brought the boxes over myself when you were out getting your suits. Your luggage is up there, too. The concierge packed the rest of your things. You can stay with Dara or Erin. She should be here in a few minutes."

His expression had grown stone cold. She'd watched it turn hard and remote as he listened to her and began to understand the scope of what she'd done—all the calculations, planning, and deceptions that had brought them to this moment.

The words came out, escaping her in a doomed rush. "I love you."

He looked at her. "God damn you, Quinn."

Chapter
THIRTY-THREE

ONE MONTH PASSED and then a second. By the third, Quinn had discovered the many stages of grief. They were labyrinthine, sometimes doubling back on each other, sometimes leading her to a dark and dismal place so far from where she wanted to be.

The first stage: shock, an icy cold blast that withered the small, foolish, and too fragile hope residing in a corner of her heart. The wish that Ethan, upon seeing the images he'd captured, the beauty and honesty that shone in them, would have spoken before she had to utter a word.

The reaction she'd dreamed of? A simple one. Perhaps a slow but heavy exhale signaling his epiphany. Surrounded by his extraordinary pictures, he'd realize how important it was to overcome his guilt and self-doubts. The power of the work he'd already created would give him the strength required to finish the military documentary. She'd even believed that he would recognize that the endeavor, painful as it surely would be, would ultimately provide the catharsis and healing he needed.

In that Disneyesque script, love never dimmed from his eyes. He even accepted the necessity of her going through his phone and contacting his former girlfriend and his editor behind his back, arranging for all his gear and his equipment to be express-shipped to New York, and having his clothes packed and delivered to Dara's apartment. It was a stretch, but somehow she sort of, kind of, hoped that he'd accept her motive for not simply banishing him from the ranch but also kicking him out of their hotel suite.

As that incredible fantasy went, he'd then summon that half smile she adored and shake his head in rueful admiration at how carefully she'd orchestrated the details of her strategy while bluebirds sang and Thumper thumped.

How pathetic that when he'd acted as her rational self had predicted, it had crushed her. Like a sledgehammer smashing ice into fragments.

The worst moment came the second before he cursed her, when neither his face nor his expressive eyes reacted to her anguished declaration. He remained chillingly distant. Untouchable.

Her love hadn't mattered to him.

On the heels of shock came agony, the next stage of grief to torment her. As she returned to her life at the ranch, mechanically going about her daily chores and activities, how many times did she torture herself, replaying those minutes in the gallery space? How many sleepless nights did she pass, tossing and then turning, as she composed alternative speeches, ones in which she'd coax and sweet-talk him into agreeing to open up his equipment cases, take out the rolls of film and memory cards, and begin the job of selecting the images that best represented the soldiers' lives in Afghanistan?

The answer? Dozens upon dozens, until her brain was feverish, her stomach knotted.

But would any of those approaches have worked?

Of course not. It wasn't in her nature to cajole; it wasn't in Ethan's to tolerate flattery. But if she'd even remotely believed that wheedling would sway him, she'd have dropped to her knees and pleaded until her voice was gone.

Could she have played the diplomat and reasoned with him? He had a father in the State Department who'd failed. He had an editor who was persistent and likely excellent at her job—Ethan wouldn't have signed on to work with anyone less than top-notch on a project like this—and she, too, had failed to convince him to return to the project.

The only option remaining was to throw down the gauntlet and challenge him. And while she'd dreaded it, she also knew she might have to withdraw the offer her parents had made him: a job, but even more, a refuge.

Would that drastic step have been necessary if she'd been cleverer in her approach? Well, crap, she hadn't been. And up until that evening she'd never felt less than an equal in matching wits with Ethan. Remembering some of their conversations, how they'd laughed together, how they'd *gotten* each other, made her heart bleed a little more.

Those memories most likely triggered the next stage: anger. Damn it, why couldn't he text her if he couldn't bring himself to speak to her? She only wanted to know that he was all right. Wherever he was, whatever he was doing.

Had nothing they shared and given each other— passion, tenderness, laughter—mattered? Had her betrayal erased all the positive?

Did he truly have no idea of how deeply she'd fallen in love? He must have. She'd gone from a man-awkward virgin to an enthusiastic sex partner in zero to sixty, Ferrari fast. No other man could have made her lose her inhibitions and give herself over to him so completely.

Did he really not know how much it hurt to be separated from him, not to turn and see his face and feel her heart leap?

He was too smart and sensitive a man to be unaware of the pain she was suffering, so her only recourse was either to bawl her eyes out or stretch her vocabulary, amassing new curses and insults to whisper as she mucked out the goat pen, hiss as she turned the earth in the vegetable garden, and mutter as she patted freshly tilled and composted earth around tiny seedlings.

She managed to resist venting too much around the animals, aware they would sense her emotions and grow agitated. Bowie was on edge as it was, often running to the window and looking out, scanning the world for a glimpse of that human who'd thrown the ball so well. But every once in a while Quinn succumbed to her fury. Shutting the study door, she would recite the curses du jour to Alfie. His head cocked, his eye beady, he picked them up with the ease of a polyglot.

She hardly noticed when her anger faded, replaced by a weird numbness, as if her body had received a massive dose of anesthesia. Smiling still felt foreign, but at least it didn't resemble a rictus of pain. It meant, too, that she could hang out with her brothers and her friends without exhausting herself trying to pretend that she didn't have a gaping hole in the center of her chest.

Numbness was a blessed relief. It provided her a kind of floaty, above-the-scene distance as well. The vantage point allowed her to remember a previously glimpsed truth. At Christmas, her mother had said that Quinn had a deep-seated need to rescue and heal broken creatures. But Quinn had understood what she was really saying. That with respect to Ethan, Quinn *couldn't* let him become the human equivalent of Tucker or Una, two creatures forever handicapped by the suffering they had endured. Ethan had a chance to become close to whole again and live his live fully.

So she'd forced him to confront his obligation to the soldiers and their families—and perhaps even the world—to show these pictures of men at war. She'd done so knowing that if he finished the project, if he healed as she hoped he would, he'd in all likelihood return to his former existence, traveling the world, capturing its beauty, mystery, and ugliness. It was a life she couldn't share. Her ties were here at Silver Creek and the animals in her care.

Forcing him to go was the hardest thing she'd ever done. It was also the most selfless and loving.

Sacrifice wasn't something with which she was overly familiar. It might not have hurt quite so much if there had been one conversation between them where they wished each other well. But no closure was in the offing. Ethan didn't want to talk. It was as simple as that. After what she'd done, Quinn couldn't bring herself to initiate a conversation. Also simple. Heartbreakingly so.

Early April came and the world was filled with signs of renewal. Flowers bloomed, lambs bleated and gamboled, calves suckled and dozed in the sunshine, and two new foals, Flora and Zeus, raced each other in the pasture in short bursts before returning to their dams' sides. In the goat pen, five gray and white kids tottered around and nosed everything in sight. Only Gertrude, who always did things according to her own schedule, had yet to kid. But her hindquarters had softened and she'd been pawing the dirt; she'd birth anytime now.

Growth and change were all around her. Impossible to remain in this benumbed state, no matter how much protection it afforded her. The moment had come to accept that what she and Ethan had was over.

It was time to focus on the positive. She knew that she would survive the heartache. She had work she loved. She had friends and a family who had been treating her as if she were made of spun glass these past few months, and it was time to put their worry to rest. They deserved it. So did she.

This was the moment to start filling her heart with new things. While she would never experience a love like the one she'd known with Ethan, she refused to feel bitter or resentful any longer, not when there was so much life to be lived.

A sense of peace settled over her.

She knelt on the goat pen's stomped-on dirt and let the kids' tiny noses butt her sides and their cloven hooves press into her thighs as they scrambled over her, already determined to scale heights. And while she couldn't prevent the pang of loss when she thought of how much Ethan would have enjoyed the sight of the baby goats, she believed a day would come when her memories of him would summon a smile of affection and gratitude.

A larger head butted hers, and she reached up to scratch Gertrude's ears just the way she liked.

"Oh, Gertrude, I really need to get to that place, I do," she whispered. "I'm better, honestly I am. But there are these moments when I'm so scared I'll never feel as happy again as when I was with Ethan."

"Gertrude doing okay, Quinn?" Reid asked from the other side of the enclosure.

Better than I am, she thought. Surreptitiously she wiped her eyes and then straightened, making sure she smiled. "I'm pretty sure she's close to kidding. Her bag's tight and her ligaments and rump have softened. She's been pawing as well."

"You need help getting her into the kidding pen?"

"I'd appreciate it. I didn't want to do it alone in case Maybelle's buckling tries to escape. Ten days old and he's already a little devil. The lead's hanging by the gate."

After they'd led a swollen-bellied Gertrude into the

straw-lined pen on the other side of the small barn, Quinn filled the water bucket and put some fresh hay in a feeder for her to nibble on. The nanny didn't like being separated from her tribe. Fortunately, she was growing increasingly distracted by what was going on inside her body.

"It won't be long now, sweetie," Quinn told her.

"You want me to bring you something? Coffee? A sandwich?"

Her brother was so solicitous these days. Perhaps he remembered how awful he'd felt during the period when Mia had broken things off with him. Quinn would have been a lot nicer to him if she'd had the tiniest inkling of what he was going through. In Reid's case, with Mia as their neighbor, he had to contemplate the prospect of running into her and pretending he wasn't bleeding inside.

Yeah, she should have been a lot, lot nicer.

"No thanks, I'm good," she said. "Jim brought me a cup of joe and a donut while you all were at the meeting. How was it? What did I miss while I was hanging with my girls?"

"Roo had us sample some chocolate tacos she's planning for Cinco de Mayo. Messy but damn good. Don't worry, yours is waiting in the kitchen. She also gave us a taste of the lemon lavender polenta cake and chocolate pomegranate truffles she's going to serve at the wine auction next week. Jeff presented the menu he and Anna have planned."

"Anna's arriving the day before the auction, right? You need me to pick her up at the airport?"

"No!"

Quinn looked up in surprise at the force with which he'd rejected her offer.

Reid coughed and resettled his cowboy hat, pulling the brim down a little lower. "No," he repeated in a more normal tone. "Tess wants to go—so she and Anna can catch up and all."

That made sense. "Okay." She shrugged and returned her attention to Gertrude, who'd been walking in circles and then stopping abruptly to nose her belly. Yes, an alien body was in there, Quinn felt like telling her. But that might only freak Gertrude out. Instead she asked Reid, "Did Dad mention anything about a new hire?"

"Mom and Grant are still going through the list of applicants."

"At least Josh is willing to wait until we find a replacement. Mom called it, by the way."

"Called it?" Reid must have noticed the mucusy discharge leaking from Gertrude's posterior, for he put the kidding kit next to her, its items including rolled sheets of brown paper she'd begged from Harry Whiting, their local fishmonger.

"Thanks. And could you hand me those folded towels, too? Yeah," she continued. "Mom said she thought Josh would want to return home to Texas."

"And take Maebeth with him?"

"Yeah, that too."

"Have you ever considered that Mom might be a witch?"

"Yeah, but since she uses her magic for good we don't have to burn her." It felt lousy knowing she was her mother's sole matchmaking failure to date. "Nancy's going to miss Maebeth something fierce."

"I heard that Estelle's cousin is going to take her place."

"Oh, good." Usually she was the one who caught all the scuttlebutt and news around the ranch and town. She really had to get her head together. "Don't know if she has Maebeth's personality."

"Few people do. She's raring to take Texas on."

"The state won't know what hit it. That's right, take a load off," she told Gertrude as she dropped to her knees. "So, we'll soon be getting a new wrangler who doesn't long for the sight of bluebells, and the food at Mia's auction is going to be so good the bids for the wine will go through the roof and she and her uncle Thomas will be able to relax."

"From your lips to God's ears, sis."

"We do have a good relationship, He and I. I'll see what I can do," she quipped, making him grin and making her feel so good. "Anything else go down at the staff meeting, or did you just gorge yourselves?"

"Reservations are up. All the spring touch-ups to the cabins are complete, and we're going to wait to shear the sheep until two days after the auction so our hands are steady on the clippers."

"Excellent plan."

Gertrude's ribs were rising and falling. Between pants she would bleat, lock her thin legs, and strain.

"So what else can I tell you? Oh, yeah. Dad took a pass on Joe Trullo's piece of land."

With her attention on the laboring doe, Reid's comment took a minute to register. She looked up with a frown. "What? Last time he mentioned it, he'd decided to make an offer so the property didn't end up in someone else's hands."

"Must've changed his mind."

"And Ward didn't try to change it back? After all, Dad could buy it and then lease it, or at least sell it to a business we approved of. Do we know who the buyer is?"

"Um—oh hey, look!" He pointed at the ground. "Her water broke."

Discussion forgotten, Quinn knelt and cleared away the wet straw by Gertrude's rump, replacing it with a fresh armful. Lifting the doe's short tail, she spied another sac. Inside it, she made out a nose and a tiny hoof. "Almost there, sweetie," she encouraged softly, and then sat back to avoid interfering with Gertrude's labor.

The kidding didn't take long after that. Healthy and young, Gertrude needed no assistance from Quinn or Reid, who were both adept at reaching inside and straightening out a lamb, kid, calf, or foal that was attempting a cockeyed exit from the womb.

When the kid's head and shoulders emerged, Quinn laid several sheets of the brown paper on the straw. A few strong heaves later, Gertrude pushed a tiny body out into the world. The baby goat slid onto the paper square. Carefully Quinn cleared the mucus away from its nostrils with a soft towel and then moved the paper close to Gertrude's head so she could tend to the newborn herself.

She sat back against the pen's railing with a smile on her face. "This never gets old, does it?"

"No. We're damn lucky. And when we forget, these are the moments that remind us."

"Yes." So the pity fest and grief—in all its tedious stages—were at an end. She was going to see to it.

The kid, freshly licked and nuzzled by its dam, was already trying to work its legs. There were a few comic failures and then all of sudden, it was standing on splayed legs.

"Looks like you've got another healthy one. Congrats." Reid patted her shoulder. "I'll let Mom and Dad know. Hey, Mia and I were going to The Drop tonight to unwind before we get caught up in the auction prep craziness. Want to join us?"

The Drop. She hadn't been in months, and she and Ethan had never made it there, so no memories to haunt her. "Sure," she began, only to hesitate when she remembered that it was at The Drop that she'd fleshed out her plan to adopt a dog for Ethan. Silently she used one of the new curses she'd added to her vocabulary and then repeated, "Sure, I'd love to go."

And she was going to enjoy herself.

BETWEEN TESS'S UNFLAGGING energy, Silver Creek Ranch's staff, and Leo and Johnny, Mia's devoted pair of cellar rats—assistants to her winemaking genius—preparations for the auction at the Bodell Family Winery were proceeding without a hitch. Quinn had been assigned the task of greeter and director for the entertainment and extra help they'd hired.

"You can send the band to set up at the far end of the tent," her mother told her. "Make sure the florist—we're using Samantha Nicholls from Seaside Lilies—puts one of the big arrangements in the tasting room and two more on the long tables near the podium. The smaller arrangements—"

"Are to be placed on the round dining tables. In the center."

"Very good, dear," her mother said without skipping a beat. "And the photographer, well, I expect he'll know what to do."

"He? I thought Tess had hired Liz Reading to photograph the event."

"Oh, didn't you hear? Liz got hired away from us. Bribed by some obscenely wealthy tech mogul to photograph a sweet sixteen party for his daughter."

"Really? She threw us over? That's not very professional."

"No, but she's probably paid her mortgage off. At least Liz gave us time to find a replacement, so eventually I'll forgive her. I better go off and check that Anna and Jeff have everything they need. Enjoy yourself," her mother said with an easy smile, leaving Quinn standing at the top of Mia's long drive.

Samantha Nicholls and a van full of flowers, check. Four scruffily bearded musicians in another van, this one in considerably less good shape, check. Once the photographer arrived, she could leave her post, go find Mia's dog, Bruno, and sneak him some peanut butter treats.

At first she thought she was dreaming, a fantasy born of the word *photographer,* as if there could be no other one but him.

It couldn't be, she thought, staring as the apparition shut the car door and approached in a long-legged stride. But his features didn't morph into someone else's. They only sharpened. Those unforgettable gray eyes fixed on her as he closed the distance between them.

He was dressed in a light gray linen jacket, a white shirt, and jeans. The webbed strap of a tan camera bag was slung over his shoulder. "Hi, Quinn."

"You're the photographer?"

The corner of his mouth lifted. "I have been known to take a few pictures."

As she stared at Ethan, Quinn became aware of a noise filling her ears. As the sound reverberated, it took her a moment to identify it. It was her heart beating, pounding with love.

The feeling was not without pain.

"You can go up to the winery." With a wave she indicated the stone building behind her.

"I was hoping we could talk. The auction doesn't start for another hour and a half."

Her mother was going to pay for this. Truly. Quinn had a long memory. "I'm busy."

He looked around, taking in the scene. Inside the tent and the winery's tasting room and cellar, things were doubtless bustling. Outside, the only things moving were the sparrows sweeping across the afternoon sky.

"Yeah, I can see that." He paused. "You look good, Quinn." His voice was low. She could feel its effect like a caress on her skin.

She sniffed. And she would have crossed her arms to underscore her complete indifference to his comment except that she'd become absurdly vain in the past two minutes and didn't want to crease the silk knit top she'd paired with her long georgette skirt and cowboy boots.

"Quinn, I'd like to tell you what I've been doing these past—"

"Four months," she finished for him. "You didn't call. Not once." Her emotions got the better of her, and she whispered, "I thought you hated me."

He took a step forward, close enough to stroke her face in a gentle caress. "Never. But I was pretty angry with you . . . because I knew you were right and I was being a chickenshit."

"I don't think I used those words."

"You could have. And a whole lot more besides."

Their gazes met, searching. Afraid that he'd see the painful longing in hers, she looked away first.

He was silent, and she knew he was studying her. "The reason I didn't call, Quinn, was that I sort of wanted to sweep you off your feet, but I felt I had to earn the right to first."

"Earn the right?" When all she'd longed for was to hear his voice? To know he was okay?

"Yeah, pretty much. I kept thinking of something at

Tess and Ward's wedding. It was the moment you
walked into the church. You looked so beautiful it hurt.
But what made you beautiful to me was that I knew
you. What you were like on the inside, Quinn. That you
were smart, funny, and giving. Someone who truly
cared. I remember asking myself, what have I done to
deserve a woman like you in my life?

"I knew the answer even then. I hadn't. I've been trying to change that, Quinn. It hasn't been easy, but I
hope you'll be pleased with the results."

She looked out over Mia's vineyard with its neat rows.
The grapes growing on the trellises had bright leaves
just beginning to unfurl. The hope in her heart felt like
that: bright and fragile, but growing.

"Fine. Yes, please tell me what you've been doing."
Her voice sounded strange. Clogged with so much that
she was leaving unsaid. Like how much she'd missed
him. Every minute of the day.

"The first month was hard," he began. "When I finally pulled my head out of my ass, I got down to work
developing my rolls of film and uploading the digital
images onto my computer. For three weeks I shut myself
in a room in Erin Miller's apartment—she'd insisted I
stay with her. I think she was scared I was going to take
off again. But I was done with running away.

"When I'd gone through all the images—there were
hundreds upon hundreds of them—I called Roger
Snowe, my agent, and he and I had a meeting with Erin
and Dara where I showed them the work. Erin and
Roger negotiated the terms for a new book deal. And
Dara's offered me a one-man show later this winter."

"Wow. That's great, Ethan. I'm really happy for you."
How inadequate a phrase to describe all she was feeling
for him.

It struck her then that he looked different. The obvious change was that his hair was longer. He obviously

hadn't had time to cut it. Her fingers ached to run through the brown and silver strands. His face was different, too. The angles in it were as dramatic as ever, his eyes the same compelling gray—magnetic and intense. But the lines around his mouth had eased. He looked relaxed.

Still, there was more. It took her a moment to make out what it was. She was used to looking at animals like Tucker, who were hyperalert, ready to bolt. Ethan's body language had been different before, his stance more defensive. Now he held himself with confidence and assurance.

"Yeah, getting the book deal renegotiated felt good," Ethan said. "But there was more I had to do before I could think about coming back here—to you. I had to face what scared me most: meeting the families of Casey Logar, Archie Donovan, and Aaron Smith, the soldiers assigned to escort me into Kandahar and to the university.

"I knocked on their doors, fully expecting to be vilified and spat upon as soon as the families saw who was standing there. It didn't happen, Quinn.

"These people welcomed me into their homes. They sat and cried with me as I shared my photographs with them and told them as much as I could about the lives these men had lived at Camp Nathan Smith. How hard it was, how boring and terrifying it was. How damn funny they and all the men stationed there could be. And I told them how proud I was to have known such brave and dedicated soldiers. When I was done, they thanked me. Quinn, they hugged me."

The wonder in his voice made her ache with the need to hold him. But he was still talking, the awe in his tone unabated.

"You see, the guys had written and talked to their families about me and the project. They were excited to be a part of it because they saw it as a testament to their service, a service they were fiercely proud of.

"In the wake of the bomb attack and the guilt I carried, I'd lost sight of the fact that these men weren't me, Quinn. They were soldiers. They took the oath that they made when they enlisted to heart and wore their uniforms with pride."

"My first visit was with Aaron Smith's family. He came from Detroit. His mother looked so much like him, I got this idea. I asked whether I could photograph her and Aaron's dad and their home. I photographed his childhood bedroom. Then I did the same with Casey's and Archie's families. I photographed Casey's newborn boy, Casey, Jr. The final chapter of the book will be devoted to the people who won't get to see their soldiers return home. Dara's going to create a room at the end of the gallery for those images when we hang the show."

"I can already imagine how powerful that will be," she said quietly.

"I hope so. The soldiers deserve it. Speaking of soldiers, here—this is for you." From the pocket of his jeans he withdrew a piece of paper and handed it to her.

She unfolded it to find an email address. "Who's Randy Lytton?"

"Bowie's owner. I tracked him down. I've written and told him how Bowie's doing and that he'll be here waiting for him—Randy's tour of duty is up next year. He seems like a good guy, and he loved knowing Bowie was learning to herd sheep. I thought we could make a video of Bowie, to show Randy all the new skills he's learning, and email it to him."

She willed herself not to cry because it hurt so much to see him and to be falling back in love as deeply as ever without knowing if he felt the same.

Nodding tightly, she said, "Sure, I'd like that. How long are you staying?"

His laugh was a short huff. "I guess that depends," he said with a crooked smile. "I have something I need to show you."

Stuck on what he could mean by "that depends" and what else he could possibly need to show her—except his love—she saw him shove his hand into the side pocket of his jacket. When he drew forth a distinctive white and black scarf, she blinked in disbelief.

"That's Anna's scarf."

"I thought you'd recognize it." Already his long fingers were working, opening the scarf and rapidly folding it into a blindfold.

She looked at it as she would a rattler. Her heart began pounding harder than ever. "Where'd you get it?"

He was holding the wide band by its ends. "From Anna."

"When?"

"Ten days ago, after your mom contacted me about taking photographs for the auction. Anna called me, inviting me to the restaurant, where, instead of feeding me, she interrogated me. Then she gave me this and told me not to blow it. She wasn't friendly about it, either. We came on the same flight. She gave me the evil eye for most of it. I have a whole new respect for Lucas."

Ethan's arrival yesterday with Anna explained Reid's weird reaction when she'd volunteered to pick Anna up at the airport. At least some things were becoming clearer.

"Where'd you stay last night?"

"In Ukiah, actually. I had some business to attend to this morning before I came here. Come on, Quinn." Ethan made the scarf dance between his fingers. "Turnabout is fair play."

She sighed, and shrugged in resignation.

He stepped behind her, and warm silk covered her eyelids.

"I can't believe this is necessary."

"Have faith."

The light touch of his fingers on her elbow had her jumping, her awareness of him acute.

"This way," he instructed, the timbre of his voice lower, huskier. They began walking, he leading her God only knew where.

They'd gone about fifty steps when he stopped. "Just a sec."

She heard an electronic click and felt him reach forward. A car door opened.

"Here, watch your head." His hands shifted, guiding her down, and cupping the back of her head as she slid into the seat.

She sat still, not daring to breathe, while his hands continued to move, brushing her middle, brushing the slope of her breast as he drew the seatbelt across her body and fastened it. Everything inside her tightened as her fingers dug deep into the leather seat.

He pulled away and shut the door. A second later, a door on the other side opened and from behind she heard a soft thump. *His camera bag,* she thought as that door slammed and then another opened. She heard him settle behind the wheel. Could feel the heat from his body. A second later, the engine roared to life.

It was pointless to ask where they were going, and she was too keyed up to speak coherently. She'd caught his scent as he leaned over her. It had left her dizzy with need. Now she inhaled deeply, hoping to catch it again. Hoping and yearning.

She knew Mia's road well, sensed when they turned onto Bartlett Road, counted the seconds in her head as they drew closer to Silver Creek Road, which led to the guest ranch, and passed it. So that wasn't their destination.

As if he read her thoughts, he said, "It won't be long now."

They'd come to the end of Bartlett Road. He turned right, in the direction of town. A minute or so passed and then the car slowed and Ethan pulled off the road. She frowned in confusion as the wheels bounced over what felt like a plowed field.

The jostling came to a stop, and Ethan turned off the engine.

He helped her out of the car. Taking her hand this time, he guided her a few steps away from the car before he came to a halt. Her skin prickled with awareness, and she knew his gaze was traveling over her.

"Quinn." She'd heard that low rumble in his voice before, when he was deep inside her, their bodies joined, his gaze locked with hers as her core began to clench about him, pleasure streaking as bright as fireworks through her.

Her lips trembled.

"Quinn," he repeated as if he couldn't say her name enough. "Sweetheart, you're killing me." Then his mouth was on hers.

The kiss was achingly tender, his lips moving just as she remembered. Coaxing and then sweetly commanding. Tears slipped from her eyes and down her cheeks.

His hands framed her face. "No, love," he whispered. "Don't cry." Reaching up, he pushed the scarf up off her eyes and then off her head. Stuffing it back into his pocket, he swept the tears from her cheeks with his thumbs. "Here, take a look."

She sniffed, and then blinked to clear her eyes. "This is Joe Trullo's property."

"Yeah. I bought it. It's for you."

"For me?" she said blankly.

"For you," he repeated. "The advance from my book deal came in handy. You can open your sanctuary now. Only, I had this idea, Quinn."

"Yeah?" she asked, dazed. He'd bought this land? For her?

"About the sanctuary. I was wondering whether you'd consider expanding it to help not only animals but military vets, too. The ones in need. It'd be something along the lines of what you did with me and Bowie."

"What do you mean, you and Bowie?"

"You thought I didn't catch on, huh?" He smiled. "Of course it wasn't just me and Bowie you paired up. You gave me Maybelle and the other nannies, and then the horses once I was strong enough. You knew being with the animals would help me. Physically and emotionally. And you were right. Some of the soldiers coming home, they need that kind of therapy, too. Desperately."

"I know. I've read about shelters reaching out to vets, matching them with rescue animals. I just never thought . . ." Her mind was awhirl as ideas came rushing in.

"I've done some research. California has a number of these organizations, but there's a definite need for one in this area, Quinn. We could give both the vets and the animals a chance to help each other. It'll take time and planning—"

"And training. It'll be tons of work, but yes—yes!" she repeated excitedly. "I want to do it."

He smiled, a smile that lit his eyes, making them sparkle like polished silver. "I knew I could count on that generous spirit of yours. I have something else for you, too."

He stepped forward and kissed her again with a fierce tenderness that left her clinging to him. When at last their lips parted, he whispered, "Here, Quinn."

She looked at the small velvet box he'd pressed into

her hand. With trembling fingers, she opened it. A heart-shaped diamond winked at her. "Ethan—" She swallowed and tried again. "Ethan, it's so beautiful."

"I love you, Quinn. Will you marry me? When I left Walter Reed, I was lost. I didn't have a reason to live, let alone love. You changed that. You changed everything. Now I want it all. I want to build something important with you. I want to raise a family with you. I want babies—little girls with blond pigtails who grow up wanting to protect every animal they see."

"Oh, Ethan, I love you." Throwing her arms about him, she whispered "Yes" in his ear before raining kisses over his face.

With a laugh, he caught her hand. "Here, I need to do this." Taking the ring out of the box, he slipped it onto her finger and then kissed her again. "Good. Now you're mine, Quinn. Forever."

"I always was. Consider me swept off my feet."

He grinned and found the spot behind her ear that never failed to make her shiver with pleasure. "What caused this miracle?" he asked. "My hunting down Randy? Finding the guts to finish my project? Buying Joe Trullo's land? The ring? My eloquent proposal? I rehearsed it on the flight from New York."

"Can I check D, 'all of the above'?"

"Ah, Quinn, that was just the warm-up. Wait until I get you home."

Home. Her heart felt close to bursting. "Wait. What about little boys who can ride every breed of horse under the sun?"

He grinned. "Anything for you. Although I know already they'll do their best to make every hair on my head turn gray."

"Nothing wrong with that, since you'll only look more like a wolf."

He laughed.

They began walking, and Quinn told him about the bucklings and doelings that had been born.

"I can't wait to see them. Bowie's good?"

"He's missed you." Her hand tightened around his. "Like all of us."

"I've missed you all, too, Quinn. More than I can say. I've even missed Alfie. He as colorful as ever?"

She bit the inside of her cheek. "More so."

"I guess it was too much to hope that he'd taken a vow of silence."

"Pretty much."

"I love you, Quinn."

"Yeah." She smiled. "I believe you do."

EPILOGUE

Six months later . . .

THE OCTOBER SUN was warm on Quinn's back as she filled the feeder with fresh fir branches, a treat from Ethan, who'd been clearing brush over at the sanctuary in preparation for the horses that would soon be living there. She shrugged out of her jean jacket and slung it over the top rail. The nanny goats were too busy enjoying the freshly cut spruce to destroy the jacket.

Gertrude ambled over, a branch sticking out of her mouth, looking a bit like a crazy old lady enjoying a stogie. She rubbed her creamy gray head against Quinn's thigh in a not-so-subtle demand for a good scratching.

She checked her watch. Gertrude butted her again.

"All right, I hear you." She hoisted herself up on the top rail and leaned forward to scratch the side of Gertrude's face. "Luckily I'm ahead of schedule, and believe you me, that's a rarity these days. And with Mia and Reid's wedding, the next week is going to be even crazier, but I don't mind. It's gonna be great. I'm so excited for them—"

Gertrude swished the branch, slapping her knee.

"Yeah, I know. My chronic allergy to weddings seems to have disappeared. Good thing, huh, considering Ethan and I will be walking down the aisle—make that a freshly mown path—next July." Even she heard the giddy happiness in her voice.

"I like how some things never change. Whenever I come down here I find you talking to your goats."

"That's because we never run out of things to say to each other." Her fingers continued to rub the bony lines of Gertrude's jaw as she returned Josh's smile. "You and Maebeth all packed up?"

"Yeah. We'll set out after lunch, get in a good five hours on the road, and then break for the night. I don't want to tire Maebeth out."

Maebeth was five months pregnant and glowing, but her first trimester had been a little rocky. A concerned Josh had postponed their departure until he was sure Maebeth could make the drive back to Texas comfortably. In Quinn's mind, such consideration earned him major brownie points.

"Ethan around? I was hoping to say goodbye."

Quinn gave Gertrude a pat and jumped down. "He's at the sanctuary. I was about to head over."

"Can I give you a ride?"

"Sure. Thanks. We'll take Ethan's car to our class this afternoon. It's cleaner."

"How's that course going?"

"Fantastic. We're learning a ton." She and Ethan had enrolled in an animal-training class. They were also working with psychologists from the local VA to understand the range of needs the veterans had so that the best match could be made for human and animal alike.

"And here I thought you knew everything about four-legged critters."

She laughed. "Not hardly."

Josh and she chatted easily on the short drive. As they neared the sanctuary, Quinn's gaze took in the newly erected wood and wire fences running along the front of the property and bordering the asphalt drive Josh turned into. These were the future pastures for the larger rescue animals. Two buildings under various stages of construction came into sight. One was a barn to house the larger animals, and the second would serve as a kennel for cats and dogs. The space in between was destined for the staff office and visiting areas.

The ringing of hammers and the buzz of electric saws filled the air as she jumped out of Josh's truck. She spotted Francesco, Lorelei's fiancé, first. He was up on the roof, laying cedar shingles. When Francesco heard about the sanctuary, he had volunteered his and his crew's services. Lorelei and Marsha were playing an equally important role, working with Ethan and Quinn to help identify which dogs that came to their shelter might be suitable companion dogs for the veterans.

Her eyes scanned the construction site, passing over one blue-jeaned form after another. Then she found him, and her breath caught, as it invariably did, while her heart squeezed tight in joyful recognition.

Shirtless, his tee tucked into the back pocket of his jeans, he hammered nails into the barn's siding with smooth efficiency. He looked good slinging a hammer. Ethan looked good, period. Healthy and strong. The scars crisscrossing his shoulder were no longer an angry red, but now a few shades lighter than his tan.

She cupped her hands around her mouth. "Ethan!"

He turned, his smile a flash of white as his gaze focused on her. She broke into a run, her own smile spreading. Reaching him, she threw her arms about his neck. He caught her by the waist and captured her mouth in a kiss that was salty with sweat and sweet with love.

Josh had tactfully kept his pace to an amble, allowing them to finish their embrace before he reached them. "Hey, Ethan," he said, by way of greeting. "Things are really coming along here. Seems like only a few weeks back the barns were just wood frames."

"Yeah." There was no mistaking the ring of pride in Ethan's voice. "Quinn and I are hoping to open the sanctuary on January first. With so many people chipping in, I think we're going to make it."

"I've been meaning to say that I think what the two of you are doing here is great. For the animals and the vets." He extended his hand with unaccustomed formality.

Ethan shook it, keeping his other arm wrapped about her waist. "Thanks, Josh."

Quinn, too, shook Josh's hand. "I'm sorry you and Maebeth won't be here for Reid and Mia's wedding, but tell Maebeth we'll be expecting you and the little one next July to celebrate ours."

Josh grinned. "We'll be there. Count on it. I'll be keen to see the sanctuary up and running." He gave the site a final sweeping glance and adjusted his hat. "Well, 'bout time I hit the road."

"Safe travels, Josh."

"Yes, and good luck to you and Maebeth with everything. I know you'll be happy together," Quinn said.

Josh's still adorable dimple returned as he smiled and tipped his head. "Like I said, you and I, we found the right people."

"That we did."

Ethan's hand squeezed the side of her waist.

Together they watched Josh depart. "I never thought I'd say this, but I may actually end up missing Josh," Ethan said.

"Me too. He's changed. I think Maebeth and the baby have been good for him."

Josh hadn't been the only one to evolve in the last year. Ethan often told her how she'd helped him heal. Quinn liked to think it was so. What she knew for certain, however, was how much he'd given *her,* how much he'd helped her grow as a person. Unlike Ethan, she hadn't been broken in body and wounded in spirit. She'd simply been afraid and filled with self-doubt. Yet those had been sufficient to stifle her.

Opening her heart to Ethan and seeing his courage in overcoming his darkest fears fueled her own determination to be better, to be braver . . . to be more.

"So were you nailing those shingles in happiness or frustration?" she asked. "What did Erin say to your idea for your next project?"

"She was all over it. She thinks photographing the veterans with the animals will be a really good and compelling way to show the public faces that are too often ignored or invisible."

"I knew she was a smart woman."

"Yeah. I can't wait to get the sanctuary up and running." Ethan's hand shifted to the small of her back. "That reminds me. I've got something to show you. A surprise."

Her gaze slid to his. "Yeah? A good one?"

"I think so. Come with me." He took her hand, lacing their fingers together, and led her to the row of parked dusty cars and trucks. They stopped in front of a black one and she realized it was her dad's SUV.

"You borrowed the monster?"

"Had to pick something up. A big something. The monster was required." He walked with her to the rear of the truck. "Since Anna retrieved her scarf to spread love in the Big Apple, you're going to have to promise not to look until I tell you. No peeking, Quinn."

Impossible anyway, since the windows of her dad's truck were tinted like some super VIP ride, something she loved to tease him about.

"Fine, I won't peek." She harrumphed just to make him smile. Crossing her arms, she squeezed her eyes shut and strained her ears.

She heard the click of the rear hatch being opened, then a heavy rustle—was he dragging something?—followed by a grunt and a thud and a whoosh.

"Okay, open your eyes, sweetheart."

"Oh Ethan! It's the sign," she cried. She stepped forward. "Oh my God—"

"You like it?"

"It's beautiful. They did such a fantastic job with Madlon's design." Her gaze pored over the carved and painted wooden sign. Under the words COBBLE FARM SANCTUARY was a kneeling soldier in fatigues with an arm draped across the shoulders of a dog—a dog that bore a striking resemblance to Bowie. "It's Bowie."

"Yeah. I thought you'd like that."

"Did you tell Randy that Bowie's going to be the canine face of Cobble Farm Sanctuary?"

"He's stoked. His exact words," Ethan said with a grin.

She blinked rapidly and sniffed. "Oh, Ethan."

"Ah, babe, are you crying? Come here." He pulled her gently into his embrace and she sniffed again, pressing her nose against the warmth of his chest. "So I thought maybe you and I could set the sign up together."

"Now?" She tilted her head back to meet his gaze.

"Class doesn't start until five o'clock. More than enough time to dig some holes and mix and pour some cement, don't you think?"

"I do." She beamed. She turned her head so her cheek lay over his heart and looked at the painted design. "The sign. It makes it all the more real."

He closed his hand over hers and brought it to his lips before placing it over his heart. "Yeah. As real as my love for you. Now let's find some shovels," he said with an eager grin.

"Bet I can dig my hole faster than you," she said.

"You're on, Knowles. And I already know what I'll

claim as my prize." His smile alone was enough to send hot shivers through her.

Quinn didn't know whom to thank first—the higher powers, her mother's matchmaking prowess, the magical properties of the scarf Anna Vecchio had inherited from her beloved nonna, or the wisdom of her own heart. But some force, maybe a combination of all of them, had allowed her to find the man of her dreams.

A friend, a lover, and a partner.

ACKNOWLEDGMENTS

I WROTE THIS book, but it was made immeasurably better with the help of Marilyn Brant, Maureen O'Neill Downey, and Anne Woodall—my very first beta reader. Thank you, my friends, for your careful reading and invaluable comments. I consider myself a very lucky writer, to be cared for by the amazing publishers, editors, and directors at Penguin Random House. I would walk a country mile in high heels for Linda Marrow, Gina Wachtel, and Junessa Villoria. To Lynn Andreozzi, art director, my endless admiration for the sublimely sexy covers you designed for the Silver Creek series. My gratitude to production editor Janet Wygal for correcting all those pesky mistakes. To my friend Lorelei Buzzetta of Lorelei's Lit Lair, for letting me borrow her name. To Michelle Prima, website designer and all-around lifesaver, I don't know what I'd do without you. Finally, to my agent, Emily Sylvan Kim, I think this is the beginning of a beautiful friendship. . . .

As ever, without the loving support of my family, this book would never have been written.